E. CHRIS AMBROSE

THE NAZI SKULL

A BONE GUARD ADVENTURE

ROCINANTE

CONTENTS

CHAPTER ONE

T rashing the cultural center had been going alright until the old man walked in, shouting, "You put that down."

Adam Lones swung about, a fistful of tribal flag in each hand as a light came around the corner. The old man squinted at him. "Do I know you?"

Fuck. Frank Manuel. What was he doing here? Adam lunged, and the old man stumbled back, quicker than he looked, his black hair flailing around his lined, frowning face. Not quick enough. Adam brought his hands together on the flagpole he had in his right. He slammed it forward, catching the old man in the ribs. Something cracked and the man staggered, but his face barely registered the blow. Maybe his lips compressed, that was it, but his eyes locked to Adam's. Then he raised his flashlight. Heavy, silver thing —like the silver at his wrists—but no way he could reach Adam at the end of his pole. Adam laughed and twisted further out of reach, shoving the pole harder against the old man's side.

But the old man didn't lash out with the light. Instead he shone the beam into Adam's face, blinding him. The pressure against the pole abruptly ceased and Adam lost his balance. The wooden pole cracked as it slammed into the wall. "Fucker!" Adam shouted.

"Maybe once." A flat voice echoed around him. Echo. Had to be in that big room. Now he listened, he could hear the soft wheeze of the old man's breath. That big room, for sure, and he was heading for the baskets.

Gripping the broken flagpole Adam launched into motion. Glass from the trophy cases crunched under his boots. He skidded on the torn papers and kicked something out of the way—one of those brass-painted running pygmies from the top of a trophy, most likely. He slid around the corner into the assembly room. Motion-sensor lights came on. Wrong way, then. If the old guy came this way, the lights would already be on.

The flashlight slammed into Adam's shoulder just short of his neck. Adam roared. He put on the face of hatred, the face of the devil incarnate, and lashed out with his weapon. It struck something and the old man let out a grunt of pain.

"I've seen the case. You got it already."

Indeed he had, tucked in at the back of his pants. Adam held his tongue, rushing toward his assailant. Wooden benches lined the walls with display cases in between, cases emptied of things he had torn or stomped or crushed. "Why'd you do all this, if you already have the basket?" The old man gestured with his flashlight at the ruin around him.

He'd been recognized, no doubt. How had the old man seen through tonight's get-up to the Adam underneath? Well, that was how he had been served for his attempt to do this nicely. He didn't have to be nice. He was Good Cop and Bad Cop all in one. He'd offered the old man a carrot last time, a little incentive to cooperate. Now all he had left was the stick.

Adam howled. That one got them every time. The old man's black eyes widened as Adam bounded toward him like an unholy angel, coat flapping, stick held high. That's right, Injun, time to get scared. The old man turned to run. He tripped over some piece of crap artifact and nearly lost it right then. The flashlight tumbled away, its beam illuminating a long wedge of the room, catching on splinters of glass, tufts of reeds and weeds and feathers and shards of wood. Adam kept howling. The old man nearly made it to the door, then he paused to kick over a bench. Even then, he hesitated, unable to commit to the destruction Adam had begun. The pause was enough.

Adam vaulted the bench. He knocked the old man off his feet, the both of them careening against the wall and down, the old man leaving a smear of blood from the back of his head. His eyes rolled back in the topography of his face as the breath left him.

Immediately silent, Adam stepped back. He listened hard and heard nothing. Vandalism, that's all this was supposed to be. He hefted the broken flagpole in his hand, aiming the jagged end down to where the old man lay. Could be he was already dead.

Calculations flashed through Adam's mind, decision trees. Old man already dead: Adam unrecognized, his true crime never revealed. Adam identified by some small detail, some overlooked bit of evidence in the chain, Adam arrested for murder, committed during the execution of a felony. Bad. If he were already dead, Adam could not help him. If he were not, Adam could use his influence to be certain there would be no prosecution.

He ran a mental inventory of his clothing: cloth bandanna; heavy overcoat, black, well-worn; cell phone, wallet, keys in the inside pockets where they could not be stolen; "Occupy Tucson" T-shirt that was the precise reason he'd chosen his target; slouchy jeans, though they had been tight on the other man, containing two business cards, half a cigarette, and a lighter; motorcycle boots with decorative chain, also large; black leather gloves, incongruously a bit snug. He carried only one thing that belonged to him—the rest, and all the trace evidence that adhered to it—belonged to someone else.

Adam stepped over the body and strode quickly from the room, down the hall, pivot left, out the side entrance where he had come in. He bestrode the other man's bike and let it glide down the slope silent until forced to turn it on. It spit and snarled to life.

Back to the cheap hotel. He methodically stripped down from his borrowed clothing, setting aside the item he had claimed for himself, and the other man's cell phone. He dressed the other man, rolling his snoring body this way and that as he hauled limp arms and legs into their rightful places. That done, he removed his own clothes from their plastic bag and returned it to the trash can. He dressed himself much more carefully. With the other man's finger, Adam prodded the phone's "emergency" button.

"Please state the nature of the emergency."

Adam stared at the other man, recalling the voice, the manner, and putting it on before he spoke, deep and boozy. "Break in at the cultural center, that native place. Didn't mean to hurt anybody," Adam slurred into

3

the phone. "Shit. M so drunk. Sorry." He let the phone slide off the bed and clatter underneath it.

Pity for him and the old man both. As of now, they no longer had a place in Adam's problem matrix. Adam picked up his treasure and let himself out into the night.

CHAPTER TWO

Grant Casey stood with his back to a stele, the creaking and squealing of jungle insects almost overwhelming. In deference to the heat, he wore his Kevlar vest over light-weight dark clothes but he kept the helmet, in spite of the sweat that oozed along the rim. No sense losing his head. He held his gun down low, barely breathing. There, again, the louder scrape of metal on stone. To his right, a single red light glowed, and winked out. Nick had seen the perp. Grant turned left and tapped his own signal light twice. He flicked his night-vision monocle into place and scanned the site around him. The black bulk of ancient buildings came into dim focus, spanned by an overgrowth of trees and dangling vines. A bright green image shifted briefly into view, then out again, behind the pyramid. Another, just a flash. Two at least. Grant sank down and hurried forward, letting the ridge of a ruined wall shield him from view.

Nick was on high, making up for his limited mobility with a less obstructed view. He got to climb the pyramid and Grant didn't. Not tonight, anyhow.

At the end of the wall, a big, metal bin stored the researcher's tools and equipment. Grant dropped to a knee when he reached it and peered around the edge, pressing himself close to the bin to merge his silhouette with its bulk. Yes: two green human forms bent over the base of the pyramid, prodding at it with a crowbar. Where was D.A.? She must have seen his signal. There—between the trees, flickering like copper salt tossed into a fire, another human form, compact and fast. She needed a few more minutes to get into place, or the looters could just—

Something at his thigh vibrated, and the bin, pressed tight against him, resonated with the vibration, letting out a metallic thrum. Shit. He jerked away from the bin and slapped at his thigh pocket where the emergency phone vibrated. The perps froze in Grant's vision, their indistinct heads swiveling in his direction, then they took off running— straight toward where D. A. should've been.

"Alto! Alto!" Nick shouted from above.

Grant shoved away his night vision as Nick cued the giant array of lights that transformed midnight into noon. "Stop or I'll shoot!" Nick's voice thundered from a megaphone in Spanish and English. Grant broke cover, pounding after the looters. He leapt the trench, gaining on them. The two men panted and cursed. One of them flung a crowbar over his shoulder, and Grant dodged aside, stumbling over a root.

D.A. leapt into view, gun leveled. "Alto, assholes," she said.

One of them swung toward her, hands half raised. The second man shoved his partner, pushing him into D.A.'s stance then launching himself past them both. Grant skirted the fallen man as D.A. rolled him, already taking control. The second man ran harder. Grant could take him down that way, like a cheetah, but Nick had delivered the warning, up to Grant to make it good. He brought up his weapon, rounded a giant tree and pivoted, taking aim. Heartbeat. Squeeze. Heartbeat. The guy spun as he fell, shouting and grabbing his butt.

Breathing a little harder, Grant strolled over and held his gun at the ready. The guy sobbed, blood streaming between his fingers. Keeping him covered, Grant pulled the offending cell phone from his pocket left-handed. "Susan."

"Yes, Chief." Her voice came on immediately, in a flood of nervous words. "I'm so sorry. I thought—"

"Susan." He let the tone of his voice carry through her words, and she fell silent.

"Yes, Chief." This time, she remained silent, waiting.

"Get the federales. And an ambulance."

"On the way, Chief."

"Good work. That part, anyhow."

"What the Hell was with that phone call?" D.A. demanded, coming up beside him, pushing her prisoner in front of her. "I should've been on comms, Chief, you know that." She shoved her perp to the ground beside his friend. "Let me talk to her."

"We'll never train her up if we don't let her do the work." Grant handed her the cell and slipped his weapon back into the holster. He took a knee beside the wounded man. "How's the damage?"

"You shot my ass off, you fucking Americano!"

"Only half." Grant pinned the guy's shoulder to stop him thrashing while he inspected the wound.

Behind him, D.A. said, "What the Hell was with that phone call, Susan? We're on ops—you can't let calls through!"

"Emergencies only, you said. If something is very wrong, then I put it through. Isn't that right?"

Torn jeans framed an angry wound to the guy's lower buttock, bullet probably lodged in there, at least, no sign of an exit wound. Already the jungle sounds crept back from the silence of the single gunshot, but he could hear the growing roar of the jeep engines as the police approached. "What's the emergency?"

Nick emerged from the klieg-lit ruin. "That's what I want to know. Man, Chief, for a minute there I thought the whole op was screwed by a spammer."

D.A. turned the phone to face them. "Well, Susan? What kind of emergency warrants sending a call through when you know we've got incoming."

"The Bone Guard line rang a few minutes ago from Arizona. The Chief's grandfather is in the hospital. Somebody beat him half to death." She paused. "That seemed like an emergency—I thought he'd want to know."

D.A. blinked and Nick gave a soft whistle, both of them staring at Grant. He kept deliberately still, though his pulse raced as if he were charging through the jungle, gun in hand. His grandfather in the hospital, beaten half to death. Wasn't that long ago, he'd wanted to clobber the old man himself. But he would've finished the job.

CHAPTER THREE

S heriff Jamie Li Rizzo tapped her pencil on her notebook. "That's all you know?"

The native woman shrugged her shoulders, looking at the old man in the hospital bed. "I don't know anything until he wakes up."

If he woke up. He looked waxy beneath the bruises and bandages. "Well, I'm the acting investigator, until the feds send their man, so when he wakes up—"she gave the word a little emphasis and slight smile as the woman's dark eyes met hers—"You give me a call, okay? We've got the perpetrator. It looks like he was freaked out on something. Probably a random crime, maybe looking for drug money, something like that."

The woman, Cecile Jessup, regarded her with those flat black eyes. "I don't think so. Grampie wouldn't be there at night. There was a tribal council that night about the wall. No way he wanted to miss that."

Except that clearly he had. "Right, I've got that in my notes." She tapped the page a little more pointedly. Her phone sang a few notes of Beethoven, signaling an incoming call. "If you'll excuse me?"

"Sure." Jessup turned away, patting the old man's hand.

Jamie stepped into the hall and pulled out the phone. Her dad's face in a frozen smile showed on the screen. New Year's fireworks sparked around him, and a ruffled lion dancer wagged in the background. She slid the icon. "Hi, Dad."

"Ni hao," he answered. "You really ought to practice the language—

you'll lose it if you don't use it!"

Reaching an alcove with chairs and windows overlooking the highway, Jamie settled into a chair. "Dad, you've been using it for what, forty years? You still sound like a white guy."

"A man will do crazy things for the woman he loves, Jamie. Someday, you'll see." He swallowed audibly on the other end of the line.

"I dunno, Dad, your love is pretty special." Oh, Hell, today was their anniversary and she hadn't said anything. Another anniversary without her mom. "You called China didn't you. Did they let you talk to her?"

He sighed heavily, and she could picture him running a hand through his thinning hair. "Maybe for the right price, they would. She never should've gone back there! She knew they'd arrest her."

Jamie listened. The same lament, every time, but it grew more hoarse, more resigned. Every time. After almost three years, she wasn't sure if it was a good sign that he didn't call there so much, or if his resignation should be a warning to her. "I know, Dad. But this is what the Lord asked of her, right? I mean, she was quoting Daniel and the lion's den when she got on the plane."

"Sometimes I don't care what the Lord wants, I just want my wife to come home!" He drew a ragged breath. Must've been a tough week. "Sorry, I'm sorry. I don't mean to lose faith, either with God or with your mother. Grace... Has a calling. That's one of the things I've always loved about her."

"I know, Dad," she said again. "Some days I wish I could feel that strongly about something."

"I think my letters are getting through, but I never really know what to say. Wish you were here?" He gave a snort. "Or would that get the censors' attention? I don't suppose, I mean, you know a lot of government folks. My contacts haven't panned out, and our senator didn't do shit—sorry. Is there anything you could do?"

"I've done everything I can, Dad, seriously," she said, then immediately felt guilty about it. Was that even true? He sounded desperate. Jamie tapped a nail against her teeth. The right price. She knew some deep pockets locally, people who might be willing to spend for a good cause. In mostly-white, mostly conservative southern Arizona, having an immigrant relative complicated her candidacy. She didn't advertise the fact that her mother had been imprisoned, but word leaked out—probably thanks to that same deep-pockets cabal—that her mother was a Persecuted Christian Minority, regardless of her actual nationality, and that whisper had brought a lot of people around to supporting her. One side voted for her because she wasn't just white, the other side because of her mother's religion, which they presumed to be her own. Still, backing a candidate was a world away from giving money to bribe corrupt officials. Jamie pinched the bridge of her nose, furious that she was even having these thoughts. Her mother's detainment should not be exploited for political gain. Not on either side of the aisle.

"Never mind. I guess I'm just missing her more today. How are you doing? Any interesting cases?"

"Are you asking as a journalist, or as my dad?"

"The second one."

"You must've heard about the break-in at the cultural center. Trashed the place, beat up one of the tribal elders. The perpetrator's the one who called it in, though, so we got him, too."

"Open and shut."

"Pretty much, as long as it doesn't turn out to be a hate crime." Her phone vibrated against her ear and she registered an incoming text. "I've got another message, Dad."

"A woman's work is never done, right, Jamie?"

"I'm glad you called. Hang in there, okay? We'll find a way to get her home."

He rang off, and she stared at the phone a long moment. She wanted to be optimistic, but they'd already exhausted most of the usual means—their congressman was a little busy; the lawyer they hired in China couldn't get any headway; the president wasn't interested, or maybe was downright hostile, given relations with China. What was she supposed to do next? Her job. Mom would want her to keep moving forward, both of them. She'd been so proud when Jamie won the election, viewing it as a breakthrough for Chinese Americans, even though Jamie suspected her opponent's recent infidelities, both financial and physical, had more to do with it. Her job. Jamie tapped the message button.

Dr. Lindsey, down at the morgue. Now what could he want? She wanted to go check on her other vegetable, the nameless wetback brought in earlier this morning. Which one of them would wake up first? Jamie put her money on the wet—he looked skinny, but strong, probably worked landscaping. The old guy had that wiry frame, and, if his niece were any guide, tenacity might well run in the family. The other vegetable could wait. Even if he woke up, it would just be to face an extradition proceeding. Jamie strolled to the stairs, bypassing the bank of elevators with a sigh of regret. She needed to lose a few pounds and tone up. Use the stairs. She used them on the way down, anyhow. It felt like a good compromise. Still, her knees throbbed by the time she made it to the basement. She pushed through the doors and found the morgue, as much by the smell as from memory. With a rap on the door, she opened up. "What you got, Doc?"

Lindsey started, and gave a chuckle. "Didn't expect you so quickly." His teeth flashed against his tanned skin. "Border patrol brought in this wetback—not for me, not actually dead yet, but pretty close. Beaten half to death, I guess." The coroner chuckled. "Strange, that. Usually if a coyote wants to take out a client, it's gun or knife. We've got some crazy coyotes out there, at least four wets shot that we've found, over a period of months, a level of violence—"

"I know," she interrupted before he could start properly ranting. "The strangulation is unusual—they sent me the same report. What else?" The wet, presumed Mexican, about fifty years old. The tribal track team had been running in the desert practicing for their next big meet when they found the guy or he'd've been Dr. Lindsey's patient from the start.

Lindsey frowned, but moved on like a professional. He picked up a tray with an object rolling inside. "They pumped his stomach, in case he had swallowed some balloons, but what they found was this. The nurse brought it down to me, along with his personal effects, to see what I made of it. He knows I'm into artifacts and that."

"Not drugs?" She reached out for the tray, used to the sight of little balloon full of contraband. Instead, she found a small, gray rock, oblong and knobbed at one end. "What's that? Some kind of gizzard stone?"

The coroner chuckled again. "I doubt it." He plucked the object between rubber-gloved fingers and held it up to the light. Its surface looked pitted, but smooth at the knobbed end as he turned it carefully. "What does it look like to you?"

Broad and stumpy, but still a knuckle bone, clear as day, with a reddish patina rubbed into the hairline cracks. Why would a wetback sneaking across the border swallow a knuckle bone? Nobody smuggled dead things. She flipped to an earlier page where she'd made note of the case's particulars and added this detail. "Weird. Is it human?"

Lindsey dropped it back into the tray, though he continued to stare at it. "Hard to say. It's clearly old. Maybe it's some kind of lucky charm? A family heirloom?" He shrugged and set the tray aside. "No clues to his identity, though."

"Figures. That doesn't give me much to go on."

"Be serious, Jamie, how hard were you really going to investigate anyhow? Aside from the beating, and now this, he's just another wetback. Fought with his coyote, or maybe with another migrant, and now he's like to die in a hospital bed before he gets shipped off home."

"Hey, if you think I'm not doing my job, take it up at the polls next fall."

"I'm sure you do it just as well as anyone." He surveyed the room with its stainless steel tables and long, narrow drawers. "I'll bag this up for you,."

"Right. Thanks. Looks like you've got a slow day."

"We haven't had as many corpses since talk of the wall. Half my work used to come in from the desert."

Jamie managed a smile. "Guess it's already working, then."

"Somebody's still trafficking through the desert, or else we wouldn't need the wall. Then there's the bodies with the bullets—some of those people are armed and dangerous." Lindsey dropped the loose bone into a small baggie, zipped it shut and made a note on it. "I, for one, wouldn't mind a few less Jose Does around here. You want?" He held out the baggie.

"Sure." She tucked the baggie into her pocket, followed by the notebook. "Can I take his clothes, too?"

He hefted a larger sealed bag. "You having a rummage sale to support your campaign?"

"No, but I've got a dog who can sniff out where this guy came from."

"Suit yourself. Hardly seems worth the trouble."

Jamie smiled. "It'll get me outside, doing some exercise. Maybe put off the day you see me on one of these tables."

"In that case, Sheriff, carry on." He waved her away with her evidence.

Probably a waste of time, as Lindsey said. She carried the bag down to the elevators and punched the button to ascend. But something about that loose bone stuck in her craw, so to speak, just as it must've stuck in the wetback's. In her experience, there was always a reason. You might swallow drugs and hope to poop them out later, or swallow evidence to a crime, and hope nobody suspects. Why else would a man eat a bone? Jamie didn't know, and she was just curious enough to see if she couldn't find out.

CHAPTER FOUR

A dam adjusted the usb camera attached to his computer. The screen showed a pair of steepled hands, as lined and pale as old linen—all he had ever seen of the person known only as the Warden—and the speakers played the sound of soft, patient breathing, slightly raspy. A smaller inset showed the view from his own office, the scene changing as he tweaked the angle to focus on the basket. About the size of a large dinner plate, it occupied a large corner of the dark leather blotter. Dark grasses and white ones bound thicker groups of weeds into a coil, and formed a pattern over the surface, a swastika framed by little v's. The spiral formation of the basket made it look as if the image spun like a galaxy. For primitive work, the piece had a certain appeal, an ancient symbol of Aryan culture worked in black and red over the dull green of the grass. "Is the message inside the coils? How do we read it?"

On screen, the fingers of the hands tapped together, then separated, and one of them reached off to the left for the book, a pocket-sized worn leather journal. The breathing altered, then the Warden sighed. "That is not the right basket."

"What do you mean? This has to be it—this was the only Rosemary Manuel basket in the case, and it's got a swastika in the center." He tapped it, then his finger froze. He couldn't have gotten the name wrong, could he? Adam scrolled back through his memory log to the moment he had seen and recorded the name. No, it was correct. *Rosemary Manuel.* Certainty: one hundred percent.

"I can see why this target might appear to be correct, however, the book made no mention of such specific patterning. It states—" a pause while the hands on screen opened the book midway and turned a few more pages right— "'she formed a basket with her clever fingers and I marveled at how quickly the work was done'." The voice spoke more slowly, and occasionally muttered in German before supplying the correct translation. "'How will this help?' I asked of Rosemary, and she tells me this is only one step, the basket. That the pattern she makes will show the way.' Later he says, 'The basket will hold the key.'" The voice fell silent. Sometimes, he convinced himself the voice was male. Other times, he thought it sounded more feminine. Years of cigarettes, most likely.

Adam waited as well, and finally, as he always did, broke the silence himself. "It doesn't say the basket has no clear pattern, though, only that it will show the way." He nudged the basket on his desk, prodding it in a little half-circle so the swastika rotated. A spiral galaxy, or a circular blade. "What more is there?"

"He describes the size of it, and gives the colors—white, black, pale green, red, as you see in the basket you have there."

"How can you be certain this isn't the one?"

"I believe he would have mentioned if it showed a pattern, especially one of personal significance."

"If you would send me the book, or make some copies, I could—"

The hands thumped flat to either side of the book. "You have yet to establish your credentials with sufficient care, Mr. Lones. In fact, your seizure of the basket was rather crude. It is hard to know if I can trust you with the details of this operation."

It stung, so Adam went low and precise. "All of the information I had at my disposal established that the place should be empty and I dealt with the old man as efficiently as possible. You need me, and I will see this task to its conclusion."

"We are looking for the greatest treasure the Nazis ever lost, Mr. Lones. It is not merely a task."

That, they agreed on, although the Warden had not been specific about the nature of the treasure in question. This was the opening move of an extended assault, a single tactic in his long-term strategy. But he was nothing if not versatile.

CHAPTER FIVE

People said there were only two stories in the world: someone leaves home, and a stranger comes to town. Returning to Arizona, Grant embodied them both. Was he the stranger come to town, or was this meant to be home? Who knew. Duffel bag slung over his shoulder, Grant paid off the taxi and stood outside the hospital in the desert heat, half-way missing the muggy Mexican jungle. The dry wind seared his nose and throat. The expanses of sand and rugged hills he'd flown over looked like Afghanistan. He took long, deliberate breaths, easing the tension from his spine. He was thousands of miles from war—and about to head into a completely different kind of minefield. Truth be told, he'd only gotten on the plane because Susan had already bought the ticket, and D.A.'s dark stare promised he'd regret it if he stayed, though whether that meant he'd regret not seeing the old man again, or she'd make him regret staying there, he couldn't be sure.

A blue pick-up, fifty years old and well-preserved in the manner of desert vehicles, pulled up and rocked to a stop in a nearby parking place. Grant shifted his bag and stepped toward the hospital door. Nothing good ever came of waiting. He could master a thousand resources to save an ancient ruin or identify a stolen artifact, but this...wasn't like any intel could help him navigate his own past. The door swished open at his approach.

"Grant! That you?"

He pivoted hard, feeling jumpier than he had during his first tour. A woman jumped down from the pick-up and slammed the door. You had to slam it, or it'd just bounce right open again. How had he not recognized the truck, or his cousin Cecile in the driver's seat? Long time since he'd seen either one.

Cecile ran the first few steps toward him, her arms raising as if she planned to embrace him, then they lowered as she slowed down, the joy ebbing from her round face. "She said you were in Mexico or something, that girl, but she sounded Asian."

Joy. Seeing him? Hadn't expected that, but he'd been hum-int way too long to mistake that expression. "She's American, actually. She bought me the ticket. Good to see you, Cece."

She took the last step up to join him on the sidewalk, a head shorter, dark hair like his. "She your girlfriend, or just your secretary?" Cecile swayed a little side to side, rolling her feet like she'd been doing since she was eight.

"New hire. Haven't decided if she's going to work out." Considering Susan had tried to kill him the first time they met, it was working so far.

Cecile's smile returned, almost shy, then she giggled. "I used to have such a crush on you. Look at you! How long's it been?"

"Fifteen years, seven months, eight days. Give or take." The tall facade of the building rose before him. "Is he still unconscious?"

"Just woke up—that's why I'm here. Come on. He'll be so surprised to see you." Her glance flicked over him and away again.

Surprised probably wasn't the right word. "Sounds like he'll pull through."

Her smile evaporated. "That's right. You've got another chance not to turn your back on your family."

One ally, and he'd already offended her. Grant set aside his own mixed emotions, and imagined the situation as Susan and Cecile did: a prodigal son, a dying old man, a family breach, a chance to reconcile rather than live with regret. He imagined opening the dossier on a mission. Infiltrate the hospital, disguised as a loving family member; greet a man he hadn't spoken to for fifteen years; put on a display of piety; book the next flight back to the jungle operation. Instead, he had Operation: Small Talk. Grant sighed and rolled his shoulders back. "Sorry, Cece. It's not just the years, it's everything." He tried a brief smile, and earned a longer one in exchange. "I'll do my best."

"That's all we ask." She slipped her arm through his, patting his chest. "Besides, you gotta tell me what you've been doing. Dropped out to join the army—I know that much. Did you see combat?"

"A little." Every night, in his dreams. They walked through the doors together, his arm the only part of him that felt relaxed and natural, and only because he intended it to. "What about you? I heard you got your degree?"

"Took a while." She led him toward the elevator as she chuckled. "Pulled a lot of all-nighters while I was waitressing."

"Must've been good practice for Kitt Peak."

She hesitated a half-step and glanced at him sidelong. "You know I'm at the observatory? That was Grammy's doing, always talking to me about the stars, like I could reach right out and touch them."

"I remember." He brought her arm a little closer against his side. "You were my favorite cousin, too. It's not because of you I didn't come home."

Cece poked the elevator button, her averted face almost hiding a softer smile. "Times I thought it was. Because you figured out I had a crush, and you didn't want to break my heart."

Hadn't stopped him, though, had it. He remembered his role—she didn't have to know what he was, who he had become. "What else is going on? What's the word around the rez?"

At the ding, they stepped inside the car, and she spent the ride telling him about the challenges of astronomical funding, and the community meetings recently turned rancorous over the proposed border wall and the new casino. As they stepped off on a different floor, she told him, "I wasn't crazy about the casino before, but now we'll have to re-build the cultural center. You heard about the vandalism? The creep who got Grampie ruined so many things. It's awful. Grammy's basket and some of the others got shredded. All those trophies broken. Bunch of 'em yours." Cecile gave a shudder. "Here we are." They stopped in front of a shared room, though the other bed lay empty. She knocked softly. "Grampie, it's me, Cecile?" She tugged Grant through the door. "Look who I've brought."

Grant stopped in the doorway. No amount of impersonation could get him through that door. On the stand by the bed, a pair of silver cuff-bracelets the old man never took off. A potted cactus with an unrelated flower glued to the top. A handful of cards arrayed to view from the bed. In the bed, the old man lay swaddled in bandages, his left arm bound to his chest, his lean, familiar face creased with age and blotched with bruises. Years ago, Grant had imagined seeing him just this way, and himself the one who'd done it.

Cecile approached the bed, leaned down and gave the old man a kiss on the cheek, just as he'd done for her so many times. She stroked back his gunmetal gray hair. "Hey, Grampie."

"Cece," the old man breathed. "You bring your husband?"

"Nope, he's on a long haul, won't be home 'til next week." She tipped her head, looking back at Grant. "Brought you somebody else, somebody you didn't think would come, I bet." She pulled over the guest chair, and sat down, clearing the old man's view toward the door. "Somebody we haven't seen for a real long time." She swallowed, and her eyes now glinted with tears.

No. This was not a tear-filled reunion. That wasn't the mission, that wasn't his scene.

The old man snorted. "I've seen everybody worth seeing. The rest of your cousins been hanging 'round, haven't they? I could hear 'em talking. Wasn't even out the whole time, just waiting for a bit of peace and quiet." His gaze moved from her, down the bed, down the floor, up toward the window. A mirror hung on the same wall. Grant's reflection stood there, caught between worlds, tattoos coloring his neck above his shirt, wrapping his arm where the short-sleeve ended, his fist knotted around the handles of his bag, deliberately carrying it right-handed so he wouldn't be reaching for his gun. He wore one of the Bone Guard embroidered shirts Nick had gotten all excited about, displaying the skull and shovel logo, like some kind of gravedigger—he could almost see the old man thinking it.

"Only one I haven't seen," the old man continued after a moment, and faced Cecile again, gripping her hand, "and he's got better things to do than hang around here." The old man's face went solemn as if he were speaking of the ancestors. "You see Casey's boy, you tell him I don't need him around here. Take a run, Casey. That's what you tell him."

Grant survived fourteen years in the special forces, and in fourteen seconds his own grandfather cut him dead. He turned on his heel and stalked from the room.

CHAPTER SIX

In a tall, well-lit laboratory, Professor of Anthropology Nicola Tran bent over her microscope. Jamie leaned on the counter nearby, prodding a group of bone fragments with a fingertip. The bones represented a cross-section, if she could use that term, of human history and pre-history, each carefully labeled as to age and provenance.

"It's hard to say if the stomach acids have done any damage, though I don't believe it was in there that long," Tran said, her voice low, as if she might disturb the dead. "I would definitely put my money on human, and on very, very old." She leaned back and picked up a scalpel and a small, lidded plastic container. "You don't mind if I take a chip? A section would be better, but a chip is a good start."

Jamie nodded and watched as the professor took her sample. "You gonna do DNA testing?"

Tran blinked at her, then said, "Given the age of the specimen, I don't believe there would be any recoverable DNA. No, I was intending a radiometric approach—like carbon-dating."

"I thought that was for fossils."

The professor carefully placed the lid on the container, and a few strands of black hair slid from behind her ear. "Just what do you think you have here, Sheriff Rizzo?"

The professor's tone grated against her, just like the tools against the bone. "It's not a gizzard stone, I know that. I already figured human from the shape of it, though it could be an ape, given the overall thickness to length ratio. Somebody strong, manual laborer, probably."

Tran's eyebrows notched up. "Sorry, Sheriff. Given that your office is political, I wasn't sure of your credentials."

"I guess that's a compliment," Jamie said, with a tip of her head. "Given the politics, my hope is that this isn't going to bring a demand for repatriation before we can even work out what the evidence means."

"I am certainly curious about the crime this bone presents evidence of —if it's a murder victim, then it's a very cold case indeed."

"Clearly, it's a lot older than I thought. How old—ballpark estimate, though I'd like an idea of how long it'll take to get the results of your carbon-dating?" Probably about as long as any kind of dating.

Tran moved the tray with the bone in it, and rolled it speculatively across her palm. "The morphology tells me it's earlier than Cro Magnon, but not Neanderthal. It resembles the Australopithecus, to my eye, but my specialization is much more recent than that, and much more local. America wasn't even settled until perhaps fifteen thousand years ago, at least in this area. I don't believe you have any repatriation concerns with this specimen."

Sinking onto a lab stool, Jamie said, "You're talking, what, hundreds of thousands of years? Maybe a million? Where the hell did this thing come from?"

The question came out rhetorical—Jamie was already cataloging museums or collections locally where such a sample might be found—but Tran dragged a heavy book across the counter toward her, and turned a few thick, glossy pages before tapping the spread. "The matrix, that is to say, the soil or stone in which the bone originally lay embedded, was a distinctive red color. It would be possible for it to acquire the coloration through later exposure, but not so deeply into the crevices." She used the scalpel to indicate where she had carved off a little of the bone earlier. "That leads me to believe the coloration is original. Given the age and morphology of the piece, the red matrix..." She gave a slight shrug. "Asia. China, most likely." Then her eyes brightened, and she tucked the escaped strand of hair back behind her ear. "Maybe you stumbled on the last resting place of Peking Man."

Jamie laughed aloud. "I heard about that one—went missing after World War II, maybe it went down in the South China Sea, maybe the crates got chucked on a railroad track. Most likely it was ground up and used for medicine. That was decades ago, and thousands of miles away." She spread her hands. "You can't be serious."

Tran gazed at her steadily. "Sheriff. Perhaps you are not familiar with Arizona's own history from the 1940's. Thousands of prisoners of war, Italians, Germans, Japanese, all were shipped over here. They spent their time picking cotton and planning escapes. Some of them even made it. Look up the Great Papago Escape, if you're curious. We're landlocked and dry, that's true, but not so distant from the war after all." She pointed to the bone. "Could your bone be from that particular skeleton? Superficially, at least, it meets all the criteria." Tran leaned forward, elbows on knees. "Now will you tell me where you found it?"

"I'd rather not say." Jamie waffled her hat up and down. "How long for the test results?"

With a sour expression, Tran said, "If I get some graduate students excited about it, maybe a few days." She took a deep breath and straightened. "To be frank, I would very much like to participate in this process. As you must know, women, and Asians, face particular difficulties in either of our careers. A discovery of any magnitude could mean a lot to me. If it's an important case, well..."

"You get me those test results, Professor, I will let you in on anything I can. I can tell you I didn't find this in situ, but I don't know the circumstances yet of the guy who did." Jamie stood up and put out her hand. The other woman eagerly took it. Then Jamie slid her mystery bone into its baggie and tucked, almost reverently, back into her pocket as the professor showed her out.

A joke, sure, Peking Man. But a joke that fit the evidence so far. Imagine if it might be true. It wasn't just careers on the line here. Bones from ancient China? It could mean more than a headline, it could mean her mother's life.

CHAPTER SEVEN

Adam stepped out of the car and adjusted his hat so the wide brim properly shadowed his face. Other organizations, including, of course, the father of them all, employed the symbolism of their ancient homelands, claiming the hammers and claws of long-dead religions. The Sons of A New America preferred a more localized tradition. They weren't going back to Europe, certainly, not without expelling the socialists. Not without an army. He settled a string tie over his immaculately pressed shirt. Maybe someday. His driver, a man known as Remington, got out on the other side and pulled a Stetson of his own from the back seat, turning the brim in his hands a few times.

"Something you'd like to say?" Adam prompted. He put on the face of authority, the voice of command.

Remington swallowed audibly. "Well, sir—the Central Finance Committee was expecting your report, and maybe a timeline? For when the second payout would occur? There's a property coming up for auction soon, and we'd—"

"We'd all like that, wouldn't we. Isn't that precisely the plan." Adam turned on his heel, finding the other man standing right behind him. Fury welled behind his breastbone and he stifled it with a will. Much as he disliked working down here among mud people, at least they typically knew their place. He cocked his head and donned an expression of curiosity. "Remind me. Do I report to them, or do they report to me?"

Remington stepped back a little. "You are the Grand Master, of course, but they are appointed to—"

"To enact the will of the organization, yes? To carry forth our kinship into a new era. Under my leadership." He wanted to howl and watch the man scurry across the desert like the rat he was. He failed to live up to his name, but then, Adam hadn't named him.

The man nodded so hard the loose skin under his chin wobbled. "Yes, sir. Just—if you could, when you get the time, send a report?"

"Of course." Adam offered his tight smile and slid a .45 into his waistband, then tugged his jacket back into place. "Did you have anything else to request, or may I proceed with the interview?"

"No, sir." Remington straightened and finally put on the hat. He did wear it well, at least, his identical .45 worn likewise. He was new, yet, perhaps he would find his place in the organization. If not, Adam could conduct an exit interview. Taking up the gun case, Adam led the way into the wilderness.

As they walked through the gloom, the other man stumbling in his wake, Adam ran the numbers. The CFC occupied a prime position in the heart of the organization and apparently they were making this person their flunky. Adam's reputation as a man of action sometimes worried such people. Office workers. Bureaucrats. They would be needed for the new republic, but prior to the revolution, they simply got in the way. For now, at least, he was the power, and the flunky had best remember that. The Warden came to him, not to anyone else, not to some larger, better known organization. The Warden preferred... He paused at the turning. Perhaps the Warden, too, was local. He had presumed the Warden lived far away, perhaps as far as the Fatherland, and there discovered the legacy that was to lead them to their promised reward. The Warden didn't trust him yet. Perhaps there was some other way to win that trust and get hold of the diary for himself.

"Problem, sir?"

Without response, Adam pushed ahead. Among the crags ahead, a flicker of light shone from a handful of torches. The patrol schedule of the border agents would keep them far away tonight. Eight men already stood in the hollow around those torches. They straightened and squared their shoulders as he entered. Each man wore a matching hat, Western-style jacket, and blue jeans. From each waistband peeked the butt of a matching gun—all save one. They looked good, and for a moment, Adam considered if he should take the organization more public, joining in protests and parades. Surely their polished and genial appearance could further the cause better than some group of boys in brown uniforms who were so proud of their razored heads and tattooed faces.

"Welcome, Grand Master, to the ring of the faithful," a tall, broad-shouldered man announced. Miller. An excellent recruit.

"Thank you, Friend." Adam touched the brim of his hat in acknowledgment. "Let our candidate step forward."

The man without the gun, who stood a little apart, and looked a little fidgety, strode up at that. "Here, sir."

"Do you believe in the cause of liberty for the American people?"

"Yes, sir." Strong answer. Adam liked that.

"Will you fight for a homeland where true Americans can be free?"

The flash of a grin. "Yes, sir."

"Are you prepared to prove your faith with these friends of our cause?"

"Tell me what to do, sir."

A variation on the response, but in a positive direction. Adam permitted himself an expression of encouragement. The Sons could use a few more men willing to improvise on its behalf. He raised his hand, and two more men emerged from the shadows. Between them, they hauled a third man, his hands bound and head hooded. "Welcome to America," said one of the guards, a paunchy man with a heavy mustache. He pulled the hood from their prisoner's head and pushed the man to kneel before them.

The man's eyes flicked over the group. "More money?" He smiled uncertainly, more of a grimace than an expression of pleasure, an attempt to appease the men around him, probably more than he was expecting to see. Definitely more white than he was expecting. "No hay mucho dinero." He held up his hands, indicating that he should be freed. "Ho pago." Maybe he had paid, but not enough, not yet.

"This criminal was apprehended while invading our country from the south, sir."

Adam turned to the candidate. "Does America welcome criminals?"

The man gave a derisive snort. "Too many of 'em."

"But we don't. Not here. That's why we are the new America." Adam lifted the case and opened it on his other palm, revealing a .45, not fancy, not flashy, but solid American workmanship. "We have the right to bear arms in defense of our state. And around here, we're not afraid to use them."

"Yes, sir."

The criminal twisted, looking up toward his captors, then tried to scramble to his feet. "Puedo tener mas dinero! Puedo, yo—ah, money, si? More money?" One of them pushed him down again, gripping his shoulder as he squirmed in the sand. Pathetic. Where would vermin like this get more money? By stealing. By robbing houses or selling drugs.

The candidate reached into the case and hefted the gun, weighing it in his hand.

"Senores!" the criminal yelped, looking from one to another around the circle. "Hay familia, tres hijos, por favor!" He wrung his hands as if praying for their mercy.

So the mudman had already spawned, but couldn't afford the brood. If the man would've just stayed where he belonged, none of this would be necessary. Turning, the candidate drew a bead on the criminal. The man thrashed violently and broke away, scrambling up and staggering from the circle of torches. The candidate lunged forward and grabbed the criminal's hair with his other hand, jamming the gun against the back of his neck as he pulled the trigger. Jerking and twitching, the criminal's body collapsed into the dirt. The nearest of the faithful stepped away from the blood, but it wouldn't spread far in this dry soil. The gunshot echoed through the desert night, just another rancher, taking care of vermin. The smell of a freshly fired weapon lingered in the air over the tang of blood. Adam breathed deeply. Another shot fired in the secret revolution. One of the guards squatted near the carrion and tugged free the restraint on the hands, letting them flop back into the dirt.

The candidate stepped back, gun resting against his shoulder, his breathing a little uneven. He wet his lips and glanced swiftly back at Adam, then the others, uncertain. Had he really done that? Had these men all witnessed? Oh, yes, he was one of them now. No going back.

"Congratulations," Adam told him. "And welcome to the faithful." He put out his hand. After a moment, the candidate took it, and shook firmly despite the sweat in his palm. The first one was always the most exciting. "I charge you, never let another person handle your weapon. It is your sacred weapon and the symbol of our common cause. You will be known as Hammer." He smiled. "And you are among friends."

Whoops and back-slapping echoed among the stones as the faithful welcomed their new friend.

CHAPTER EIGHT

The truck bounced along, first down paved county roads, then down the private tribal roads, Cecile in the driver's seat, Grant taking shotgun, watching the desert: mountains in the distance getting a bit closer, scrub and cactus, the occasional mesquite tree, vultures. "I can stay at the Motel 6 in town, Cece, it's really no problem."

"No problem here, either. In spite of what he said, I think Grampie would want you at his place." She held her hands close together on the wheel, gripping at the top and squinting against the long afternoon. "Everybody at the hospital's been so nice to him—hard to see that he'd even want to come home!"

His place. Grant shifted and the ancient vinyl seat squeaked. Nothing around here ever changed, did it. They passed a few settlements, clustered houses with paddocks of horses or sheep, pick-up trucks that looked like clones of the one he was riding in. Cece turned abruptly and Grant flicked her a glance. "Road moved. Up ahead, there's part of the wall. Straight through our people's land. Joe Clark, remember him? Has to drive four miles for water now because his well's on the wrong side."

"If the wall's a done deal around here, why the meeting?"

She frowned. "The wall we have here isn't really working for much except making it hard on us. They want to make it bigger and harder to cross, all that. The route is supposed to go straight across Cache Mound."

"No wonder the old man was pissed."

The frown deepened, carving grooves between her eyebrows. "It's your heritage, too."

Half of it, anyhow. They pulled up outside another cluster of houses, dust settling as the truck rocked to a halt. The low rectangular buildings with their pre-fab roofs did nothing to dispel his memories of Afghanistan, or even Mongolia, as if all the deserts of the world had the same architecture. Made sense, a long while back. The residents confronted similar problems of heat by day and cold by night. Grant climbed out on his side, duffel over his shoulder once more. The place looked just like he remembered, with its neat row of cacti, and a pattern painted on the house wall behind, checks and lines like a basket, underneath the small windows, broad sills carved into the thick walls. Something twitched and shifted in the slanting light and Grant moved closer. A bit of cloth, a few threads, clung to the spines of the cactus nearest the left-hand window.

"What did you say happened at the cultural center?" Grant leaned in, studying the fibers. His leg itched a little, as if the skin remembered encountering those same spines twenty years before.

"The break-in?" Cecile stood on the threshold, the door already open. A shadow cut between the buildings toward them, long and broad in the shoulder.

Grant tensed, but kept his breath even, shifting his grip in case his duffel bag became his weapon. "What was Frank doing there?"

"I wish I knew. Sheriff says it was just random, a junkie or a migrant looking for something to sell."

"The perp knew everyone would be at the council meeting to talk about the wall." Grant straightened as a familiar figure came around the corner. "It wasn't random."

"Fuck it wasn't." Randy Manuel folded his arms, his eyes just as narrow as they'd ever been. "Frank probably went over there for the maps and surveys, to bring to the meeting. You don't have to show up here and start putting ideas in people's heads, showing off some big-city skills. Ain't no mystery, just business as usual. Matter of fact, you don't have to show up here at all." Randy turned his head and managed a smile. "Hey, Cece. How's Frank? Happy to see his favorite runaway?"

Cecile stared at her brother. "Don't make this any harder, Randy."

"No, seriously, what'd he say? Was it all 'kill the fatted calf?'"

Grant considered swinging his duffel wide, with lots of warning, so when Randy moved out of the way, Grant's foot caught him in the kidney, folding him in half as if he were taking a bow. Come down hard on the back of Randy's neck with a high probability of breaking it. Big city skills indeed.

"Grampie told him to take a hike, after he came all this way," Cecile called back as she walked through the door into the cool interior. "Get in here and let's have a lemonade. Maybe you boys can have a pissing contest later."

"The lemonade would help with that." Grant inclined his head toward the door. "After you, Randy."

Randy snorted. "Take a hike. Good advice. It's a little late to start playing at the good grandson all of a sudden."

His grandfather, alone of all the tribe, and already angry about the wall, would never have missed that meeting. He would have approached it the same way he'd broken a horse, and tried to break a grandson: cold and methodical. And recently, someone had gone in through the same window Grant used to use sneaking out. The door around the corner and the other windows could be seen from Randy's place. *Take a run*, his grandfather had said. Not "take a hike." Completely different thing. After the rituals of polite company, Grant had every intention of taking that advice.

The kitchen hadn't changed: Formica table with metal edging, the surface clustered with round burn marks from holding too many hot pots because the counters weren't big enough, faded yellow curtain separating the living room, a short hallway leading to the bedrooms and the bathroom—and the window.

"Same room?" he asked, and Cece nodded. "Back in a minute." Grant walked the hallway and dropped his bag on the bed. He swept a glance over the room with its narrow bed and faded quilt. Most evidence of his youth long-gone, except for a few model horses, that model submarine that belonged to his grandmother, and a shelf of books that used to be hers, too: history, anthropology, geography. The collection he pretended to despise, only to devour them whenever he spent time in his room, in the echoes after a slamming door. A few gaps showed on the shelf, a few titles missing, and he felt a momentary sense of loss. The books weren't his, they never had been.

Grant turned away. Avoiding the memories, the familiar sage and coffee grounds smell of the place already getting to him. He stepped back to the bathroom instead, shutting the door, then dropping down to examine the windowsill and toilet seat. Paranoia was one of the symptoms—that's what he and his team always said. Was it just paranoia that linked the attack on Frank to a few strands of fiber on the cactus outside? When he had a chance, he'd check out the fibers, too, but no need to signal his concerns to Randy. Seemed like Cece already thought something was up. The scraped paint of the sill could've been from his own escapades years earlier, but the dirt scattered underneath had to be recent. Grant stood up and flushed the toilet, then ran a little water and pushed the door open. "Has Frank had any other visitors lately?"

Randy, his hips resting against the stove, gave a shrug and took a long swallow of lemonade. "Some white guy, probably campaigning. Had that look about him. Somebody asking about mineral rights, you know how they do. Couple of wets looking for water. Covers the last month, I guess."

Setting down her own glass, Cece frowned and ran her gaze over the counters. "The politician left a card, didn't he? Thought I saw something like that."

"Haven't voted for years. Don't plan to start now." Randy took another swallow. "Army, though. You're prob'ly all about civics and shit, am I right?" He aimed the rim of his glass at Grant. "What's with the shirt? You working landscaping now?" He leaned closer, then gave a snort of laughter. "Looks more like burying bodies."

"It's a private security firm," Grant said, but Cece added, "He owns it." She flicked him a smile. "You're not the only one with Google."

"Wow, big time now!"

Grant reached deliberately between them to retrieve his own glass from the counter and take a sip, sweet and tangy. Randy's eyes jittered and his breathing looked off. He could be on something. Sheriff thought the break-in was drug related, and Grant allowed himself the petty luxury of imagining that Randy had been involved and he'd be justified in working him over, but that fantasy didn't last. This time it wouldn't be Grant breaking Cece's heart. "Teo still around?"

"Someplace. Haven't seen him lately." Randy's arm tremored and he took a drink so fast he splashed a little on his cheek. Just the drugs, or something else? Randy glared back at Grant, as if daring him to say something with Cece standing right there.

"He still does a lot of things around here. I think sometimes, he's waiting to see if Grampie's gonna need him, the way Grammy did at the end." Again, she glanced around. "I would've thought he'd come over when he saw the truck. Still has no phone, but he'll want to know Grampie woke up." She walked out the door and across the yard to the little house where she knocked on the door, the sound echoing across the yard.

Grant set down his glass and straightened. "Randy—"

"Look, I gotta tour this afternoon. VIP thing, after hours, all that. It's been nice catching up with you. I have to do it again some time." Abandoning his drink, Randy hustled out the door, giving Cece a quick hug before making his escape complete. Grant met her in the doorway.

"No answer, but Teo was helping out with repairs on the church, too. Prob'ly he's over there. You'll see him tonight."

"Randy said something about a tour?"

She nodded and her expression cleared. "He's working over at Davis. More like your kind of thing, I thought. Were you really trying to get left behind that time?"

"Not hard enough. What fourteen year old could resist getting locked in at the airplane boneyard and having to sleep in a B-29?"

She shuddered. "Sounds creepy to me. All those planes, in the dark? They're like giant skeletons, hanging over you. How could you get any sleep?"

"Says the woman whose job is to stay up all night."

They shared a laugh, and, just for a moment, Grant thought maybe he missed having family.

CHAPTER NINE

Buster was a rangy, big-boned hound, as eager to run the trail as his father had been, and the sight of his tail held high as he moved through the scrub warmed Jamie's heart as much as the fading sunlight warmed her back. A cowboy hat shaded her eyes, and she imagined herself for the tourists, the very image of a Western rancher, checking on a fence, or riding the range after cattle, jogging along on a painted horse, with a hound to go before. This hound, though, was all business, nose to the ground, big, floppy ears bouncing as he moved right along. Nice to be outside again. Maybe her doctor had the right of it, and some more exercise would do her good. She should've brought along a photographer and used this in her next campaign, presenting the image of Western tradition regardless of gender; they didn't need to know the horse's name was Princess. Voiceover could talk about the many years she'd lived in the state and her commitment to law and order, get kind of a Reagan vibe. Maybe add some shots of her interacting with Border Patrol, with the wall in the background. No need to mention the immigrant problem—that context would be clear. Arizona needed someone who could take a balanced approach, weighing the state's needs for security and labor. And her campaign slogan at the bottom: *Justice for All*. Which was a great slogan because either side could assume it meant what they believed. She reached for her cellphone to record some notes and froze as Buster stiffened, staring straight ahead. Princess, too, perked her ears in that direction.

Jamie slid the cellphone back into its holster, and reached for the holster just behind, flicking off the snaps and easing the grip of her sidearm into her palm where it settled like an old friend. She debated dismounting, and decided to keep the height and speed advantage for now. Who knew what she'd meet over the next rise. She nudged Princess a little faster and they cantered up the slope. They crested a low ridge of broken stone and tufted grass. Beyond, the mound continued, but it dipped before her into a rocky depression spotted with prickly pear cactus. Digging marked the center of this, a tumble of stone and earth with a square wooden box in the middle, like half a coffin. A water bottle stood to one side on a rock, probably left by a migrant when it turned up empty. Nothing to explain—

Buster gave a low growl, his long nose aimed a little to the west.

"Ho." Jamie gave a gentle tug on the reins and Princess stopped short. A single thick saguaro about ten feet tall loomed over its shadow in that direction, and the leaves of the mesquite brush trembled just a little. "You behind the cactus!" she called, drawing her weapon in full. "Come on out and keep your hands where I can see 'em!"

A breath of hesitation, then a man stepped into view, a neat pivot, his hands held at about the level of his head, the sun casting his own shadow long across the ground. "Yes, ma'am," he said. No discernible accent.

"Get over here where I can see your face." She waved the gun toward the bowl of sandy ground in front of her, and he walked over, efficiently, but not in a hurry. Tall, dark, and handsome, her mother would say, with that sidelong glance to be sure Jamie was paying attention. Hard to miss this particular specimen, given he was probably a narco or a coyote in spite of how he was dressed. Wearing running shorts and sneakers, his bare torso showed the ripple of working muscle, not workout. Also an intriguing collection of scars and tattoos that moved from his wrist all the way up that arm and encircled his neck. His skin, a light reddish-brown, glistened with sweat, and his fingertips showed flecks of mica. The damn stuff clung even when you tried to wipe off the dirt. Looked like this was some sort of cache, maybe a dead drop for a Mexican cartel.

Rizzo let the moment stretch, but the guy showed no sign of impatience or nerves. Finally she said, "Who are you, and what are you doing here?"

The guy's direct gaze tracked over her face, as if the gun were the least important thing about her. "You've got the advantage on me, ma'am," he said. "Several, I think. This is my homeland, and I was out for a run." He pointed toward the water bottle, moving just his hand. No sudden moves, no attempt to distract. Not the first time he'd been held at gunpoint, but the tattoos didn't look like prison work, or like any gangland stuff she'd ever seen. If anything, they looked mythological, but not like the Chinese stuff everybody seemed to be doing these days, tattoos of isolated characters that made her mother chuckle, saying only that they didn't mean what the wearers thought they did. Maybe her dad was right, and she should practice the language. Meantime, there was this guy. Nothing about him said Native, or local, or trustworthy.

"Mind if I get my bottle?" His lips quirked into a smile. "It's a little warm out here in the sun."

Several advantages over him? Yeah, right. She had the feeling he'd already sized her up, and that explained his total comfort with what should be a nervy situation. "So you're O'odham? That's your claim?"

"Half. What brings you out here?" His glance dropped to the dog who paced a little nearer. "Hey, big guy, what's your name?" His voice took on a dog-soothing lilt.

"Buster, target."

At the sound of her command, the dog, took a few long sniffs around the suspect, then she said, "Find it." His head dropped and he started circling, trotting around the cactus, over to the hole, a light "whuff" at the water bottle with a wag of his tail, then past it, moving along one of the thousand paths among the scant vegetation. A runner from the rez might have come from that direction, sure, and Buster didn't identify any other stashes—no gun, no drugs under the bushes. The guy clearly wasn't carrying. No place to hide anything in that outfit. Still, his well-muscled physique and general attitude gave her the uncomfortable feeling he didn't need to be carrying. She whistled, and Buster circled back toward her, plopping on his haunches not far away.

"What are you tracking? Not me, anyhow." He tipped his chin up, a gesture that let some of his dark hair slide across his brow. Doing his best to look harmless.

"Maybe. That's what I need to determine. I'm guessing you don't have any ID. What's your name?"

"Grant Casey. I grew up around here, until I left for college. You sound local, but I don't remember you."

"We might've been moving in different circles. How about you back into the shade over there and make yourself comfortable."

"Hands down?" he asked, with a little shrug.

"I still want 'em where I can see 'em."

He almost smirked as he sauntered into the shade of the giant cactus and sank down to his haunches, hands hanging over his knees. Dropping the reins, trusting Princess not to move a hoof, Jamie plucked the radio from her hip. "Rizzo to base, you copy?"

After a moment, a crackly voice returned, "Got you, Riz. Whadya need?"

"Guy called Grant Casey. Claims he grew up around here, on the rez? Ten or fifteen years ago?" she said, directing this toward the man, who gave a nod. "Can you confirm? Anybody over there who'd vouch for you?"

The guy paused, then said, "Cecile Jessup, my cousin, but she's—" He cocked his head to look at the sky— "on her way to work right now."

"Night shift," she said. He flashed a grin, as if they shared a private joke, and goddamn it, she was starting to like him. Jessup... That name. "What's your relationship to Frank Manuel?"

The grin vanished and his finely honed muscles went taut in an instant.

"Stand down. I'm the sheriff. I'm investigating the attack on your grandfather until the feds get their guy in. Dunno what the holdup is." Speaking of. She met his gaze, both of them appraising, then slipped the gun away, though she did not yet secure the holster. She pulled her leg over the saddle and dropped to the ground on the far side of the horse, not liking its bulk between them, but preferring that to putting her back to him.

"And that investigation brings you out here."

By the time she rounded the horse, Casey was on his feet. She shook her head slowly, not sure how much to let him in on. Sure, he was involved, and maybe not just as a family member. "I'm not really at liberty to answer a lot of questions, Mr. Casey." The radio buzzed, and she pressed the button. "What you got?"

"Positive on the ID. There was a Grant Casey in high school here, track star, rodeo Indian, that kind of thing. He's all over the archives for a few years, won some trophies and stuff."

"Rodeo? Like he was a pow wow dancer?" She frowned, trying to picture the guy in front of her wearing a traditional headdress and leggings.

"No, ma'am," the voice crackled. "Like cowboys and Indians, not the tribal rodeo, the real thing."

She raised her eyebrows, and Casey scanned the horizon. "Not my finest hour," he murmured.

"Trophies and archives say otherwise, unless you've got a lot more accomplishments since then?" She dangled the question, hoping to lure out some more information, hoping, at the same time, that she'd pegged her man right, and he wouldn't say a thing.

"I don't know if this is the same guy, boss, but I've got a hit on the name from a few months ago, that thing with Genghis Khan's tomb? There's no pictures of him, though, just of the Mongolian team, and that researcher who found the songs."

"You were part of the team that found Genghis Khan's tomb," she said slowly, on behalf of her Chinese ancestors, not sure how to feel about that. On the other hand, she had a certain ancient artifact in her possession, and she might need a little help tracking down where it really belonged. "Was that your finest hour?"

Casey's lips quirked up. "Might've been. You haven't spoken to Frank since he woke up. What scent were you tracking to get here?" He took a step out of the shade.

To the radio she said, "Rizzo out," and put it away. Called his grandfather by his first name. Interesting. "You first. What does this place have to do with Frank Manuel?"

"That was my family's sacred cache. Somebody broke it open and cleaned it out, and it sure as hell wasn't Frank."

CHAPTER TEN

The sheriff looked from him to the broken crate, and her mouth scrunched, as if she were deciding how much to tell him. For an elected law officer, she was smarter than she looked, and more cagey than her job required. She presented as white, but her eyes, nose and cheek bones, hinted at Asian ancestry. Could be a great ally if she decided in his favor, and he could use someone on the inside of the investigation, someone who might agree the break-in wasn't just about money. Not after finding this. The broken cache lay open before him, like a tomb already plundered. Even he didn't know what had been in there, but Frank had suspected something would be wrong. Was that some kind of spiritual BS? What else did the old man suspect? No two ways around it, he'd have to talk to him. Later.

Grant took another step out of the shade, then paced over to his water bottle. The dog, the woman, the horse, all watched him go. That was a damn fine horse, still standing exactly where the sheriff left it. Dog must be pretty good, too, everything on command, a tracker, not a guardian. If only the dog could tell him what they'd been tracking.

Taking a sip from the bottle, Grant regarded the sheriff. "I flew out here when I got the call from Cece—Cecile Jessup, the cousin I mentioned. I arrived at the hospital around the time Frank woke up, and he told me to take a run. He knew I'd come here. No offense, but he never would've told you about this place." She didn't need to know those were the first words his grandfather had spoken to him in fifteen years. He aimed the bottle at the dog. "Buster brought you here, based on some other evidence. Someone else who's been to the cache, maybe the person who stole my family's legacy."

She chewed on that for a little while. "Could be," she said at last. "We found a migrant, half-dead in the desert. Tracked him back here. He didn't have any artifacts on him, though." She swallowed, and her eyes shifted down. A tell? He didn't know her well enough. "Good chance he bartered whatever he found for food or water—"

"Before he collapsed in the desert."

Her jaw knotted. "We have reason to think he wasn't alone. His companion likely took your relics when they parted ways. I would appreciate a description of the contents, but I think it's unlikely we'll find the items again. There's a strong market for native goods, as I'm sure you're aware. I'm sorry, Mr. Casey."

She spoke in a case closed manner, as if this place explained everything: two migrants found the cache, stole the items, one of them went on alone and hawked his family's regalia. She pulled out a large cellphone and a stylus. "Can you tell me what the cache contained?"

"My family's sacred items, Sheriff Rizzo. I can't really be more specific than that." Even if he did know, it wouldn't be appropriate to tell her—even a lousy Indian like him knew that much.

Tapping the stylus against the side of her phone, she said, "How about bones? Any bones likely to be in there?"

That caught him by surprise. "No. It's not a grave, or a reliquary. It's for ceremonial gear." Grant dropped to one knee to examine the broken cache. Someone had scraped all the rocks and dirt out of the way, then pried up the lid, not even noticing the slots that allowed it to slide open. Someone in a hurry—but why rush in a place like this? Only members of the nation would know that a cache existed, and only a handful of people related to Frank would know where theirs could be found. The sheriff must've been around here long enough to know a thing or two. Did she ask out of ignorance, or was she gathering intel, like he was? "What makes you ask about bones?"

"We found one on the migrant. It's probably nothing."

Target acquired. He rose and faced her. "But you don't think so. Nobody follows up on migrants found in the desert. Was it his injuries that made you suspicious, or the bone?"

"Both. Who are you really? Not your name, Mr. Casey, but whatever you really are?" She waved a hand toward him, using her stylus to indicate the full sleeve tattoos, the scars on his chest. "Some kind of adventurer, or an international treasure hunter?"

"I'm the bone guard. I make it my business to protect cultural heritage sites from damage like this."

She blew out a breath. "It's gotta burn that now it's your own culture being wrecked. Not just your culture, your family."

She offered him a role, and he stepped into it with a slow, dangerous nod. "You better believe it. My grandfather's been attacked, my family cache stolen, my tribal center vandalized. I don't believe this is random. The migrant whose trail you followed to get here. Was there any chance he was involved in the break-in?"

"No evidence links him with the perpetrator, and we got the perp on camera, at least part of the time. Just the one guy, and he's already in custody." She put away the phone and stylus, reaching into her saddlebag for a crumpled mass of fabric. "I offered Buster his shirt to—"

Teo. Grant swiped the shirt out of her hand and unfurled it as she protested. Worn and frayed, the western-style shirt had a fancy yoke, aged and marked with sweat, the sleeves cut off above the elbow. Because the elbows tended to wear out when the original owner had been riding hard. He balled it in his fist. A minute ago, he exaggerated his personal stake in the case, hoping she would drop her guard, but the surge of anger through him now was nothing feigned. "Your man is Teodor Betancourt. He's worked for Frank for twenty years at least. Those silver bracelets Frank always wears? They're a gift from Teo."

"What are you, Sherlock Holmes? You figured all that from a shirt?"

"Yeah—it used to be mine. He's in the hospital?"

"Somebody beat him, strangled him and left him for dead, about half a mile from here." She hitched a thumb in the direction she'd come. "Dehydration would've gotten him if the track team hadn't gotten there first.

Do you know what his immigration status is?"

Their eyes met, a standoff just as sharp as the one with the gun. Finally, Grant said, "I need to know everything you have on both cases."

"It's pretty clear, Mr. Casey, this isn't two cases, it's one. I can't share everything, you understand, but I'm open to a dialog. You have a car?"

Open to a dialog, yes, she was a politician. "Cece gave me a ride from the hospital. I'm staying at Frank's place near Cowlic."

"Let me get Princess here back to the paddock and I'll pick you up. I have a little time before my dinner tonight. We can head down to the station and talk about what you know, and what I know." She almost smiled as her glance slid over him. "But you're gonna need some clothes."

CHAPTER ELEVEN

Adam drove slowly through Tucson, glaring at the tourist shops with their windows full of fake baskets. He'd already been taken in by one fake, and the Manuel house hadn't yielded anything more useful. The guy's own wife made the thing, hadn't he kept any of her work at all? Nothing of hers? He re-played what the Warden had read to him about Rosemary Manuel, working the cotton fields alongside prisoners of war, Nazi prisoners, held on American soil. It sounded crazy, but he'd been doing the research and the story checked out. When twenty-four of the POW's escaped on Christmas night, 1944, it was only natural that they look for help from those who had accepted them, maybe even been kind to them. He asked if the native woman and the escaped Nazi had been lovers, but the Warden declined to state. Maybe the diary didn't say. What did he have now? Where else would the damn basket be stashed—and why couldn't they have just made a map? Adam smacked the steering wheel.

Secrecy would have been critical lest the camp guards knew what they'd been up to during their brief escape. Not escaping, not really, just planting the trail so they could recover their treasure at a later date, when the war had blown over. Ironic, to think of German soldiers on American soil, trying to flee across the very same border where Mexicans now crowded into the desert to do the same damn thing: pick cotton and sponge off the American government. Of course, the Germans had no choice in their dependency. They'd've given anything to get back to Germany and back to the war.

The sheriff's office occupied a nondescript tan brick building with an oversized parking lot near a few laughable environmental "projects." He wondered if they meant the term in the same way that the benighted citizens of Chicago and New York thought of the slum "projects" where the human refuse dwelt. It was after hours, but Rizzo's vehicle sat in the parking lot, nearly alone. Her beleaguered assistant Rachel looked up when he entered. "Oh, Mr. Lones!" she practically yelped. "She's with a visitor, but I'll—"

"That's alright. I'll just wait." He flashed his big spender smile and gave a little wave as he continued past her desk to the trio of chairs outside the sheriff's office. He plucked the phone from his pocket and slid his thumb around the screen as if reviewing his messages. The Bluetooth earpiece he always wore let him know it was connected. Rachel settled back into her seat and turned away toward her own screen. Adam lowered his hand and pressed his phone against the wall behind him.

"—hospital and give them his name, if you're positive about the ID." Sheriff Rizzo.

"He kept every one of my rodeo shirts. I can't see him giving them up now. If he's awake, I'll want to get over there." A man's voice.

"As would I, Mr. Casey. Meantime, I can't show you everything from the break-in, of course, but there's some photos—" Papers shuffled. "We got the perp on the exterior cameras."

Adam smiled faintly, his leg crossed over his knee, toe tapping the air.

"You ID'd him from his clothes? It looks like he's wearing gloves and his face isn't visible. Unless you have better images than these."

Adam's foot stilled.

"He called the police from his cellphone to confess," Rizzo answered. "And those clothes contained a lot of trace evidence from the crime scene. That's pretty damning."

The man made a sound that could have been assent or doubt. Who was he? Why would Rizzo be sharing even that much information about the case? Adam had high hopes for her, but not if she couldn't hold her tongue. She had an instigator, apparently, and one brighter and more suspicious than she was. He'd have to put a stop to that. Could this be the FBI contact she was waiting for? Adam thought he had already deflected that with a steak dinner and a healthy bitch session about local law enforcement needing to carry their own weight.

"Hello, yes. It's Sheriff Rizzo." A long pause. "That migrant, the one found by the tribal runners? Yeah. I have an ID on him. Teodor Betancourt." She spelled the name out, then muttered, "You'll ID Betancourt based on his shirt, Mr. Casey, but you can't accept— yes, that's the one. Has he woken up?" Pause. "Babbling?"

Papers shuffled on the desk. The man's voice. "What is he saying?"

Adam amused himself by calculating the number of bricks in the wall in front of him while he waited for them to get back to the case that mattered.

"Yes, if you could, thanks. The nurse is going to pick up the phone in the patient's room so we can hear. He said it's the same sounds over and over, some kind of rhyme, maybe you can make sense of it."

After a moment, a rough whisper, "Huesos peligrosos huesos peligrosos,"

"I can't make it out. Something dangerous?" Rizzo said. "Is that it, just that?"

A new voice, brusque and male, "Yes, Sheriff, that's it so far. He seems agitated, and the doctor recommended we might give him an additional sedative so he can fully recover. Even this level of vocalization is likely painful and potentially damaging given the injuries to his throat."

"Alright, do what you have to. What room is he in, so I can check in later?" The sound of pen on paper. "Thanks." The soft blip of a severed connection. "Osos peligrosos? Dangerous eggs?" the sheriff mused.

"Not eggs. Bones." The man's voice, unequivocal. "You asked me about bones, Sheriff, back in the desert, because you found one on the victim, Teo."

"Well, shit on a shingle." The squeal of an office chair, then footsteps and the riffling of clothing. Adam braced to apply his cheerful persona, but the door didn't open. "I brought it over to the university for testing—hey, that's not open to view."

"Your perp—did you test him for Rohypnol?" Papers being pushed around, the visitor apparently snooping where he didn't belong. Maybe not an ally for Rizzo after all. In which case, she needed back-up, and maybe a push back in the right direction.

"Gimme a break. Nobody assaulted this guy."

"His symptoms suggest drug use, as you noted, but that doesn't explain these other hairs—"

Too close. Adam stuffed the phone in his pocket and stood up to rap on the door.

"Rachel, I'm busy!"

Adam chuckled, and answered. "Sorry, Sheriff. Just thought I'd—"

The door popped open and Sheriff Rizzo stood there, a little red in the face. Her visitor sat in the second guest chair, the one with its back to a corner. He made no move to rise, but closed the folder he was holding and slid it back onto the desk. Lean, his skin-tone somewhere between tanned and Mexican, the guy wore a khaki polo shirt with some kind of logo, matching pants, low hiking boots. Okay, the effect was of some kind of uniform, but nothing law enforcement. Plainclothes? But then she'd be open about sharing everything.

"Mr. Lones. I am so sorry. I thought our dinner wasn't until later."

"No, no, no." He waved away her concern. "I'm interrupting. I just thought maybe you'd be ready early, but it's no problem, really. Don't let me keep you." He flashed his teeth toward the visitor. "Adam Lones. I'm helping out with Sheriff Rizzo's re-election campaign. I hope we can count on your vote?" He leaned out, offering his hand.

The stranger offered a shrug in return, and a vague smile. "Sorry, I'm not from around here. But she seems like a shoo-in. Very competent."

"Thank you, Mr. Casey," Rizzo said, though her furrowed brow suggested anything but gratitude. She gestured toward the visitor. "You may have seen the coverage of the break-in over at the tribal center? Grant Casey is the grandson of the man who was injured."

"Oh, well." Adam absorbed this, rocking back on his heels. "I was so sorry to hear about that. Tribal elder, isn't he? Thank goodness the miscreant is already behind bars. It's awful what drugs will make some people do. You must've known some people who just..." He shook his head, his spread hands inviting confidences.

Casey's head tilted just a little and he regarded Adam with hazel eyes. "Most of the users I've known turn against themselves."

"Mmm. Overdose or suicide?"

"Mostly the latter." Casey leaned back and let his gaze drop to one side.

"See, that's the kind of thing we're hoping to combat, isn't that right, Sheriff Rizzo? But we need to get health organizations and education on our side. Law enforcement should be the last defense."

She grunted. "Addiction's a big problem, no doubt. I just try to hold up my end."

Adam turned back to her, hands open, and clasped one her hands in both of his. "Have you ever thought—" his phone shivered inside his pocket, and he broke off, smiling at her. "Phone call coming in—I am so sorry again for interrupting. Are we still on for dinner, though?"

She glanced at Casey. "Seven o'clock at L'Rose, right? I can wrap this up by then. I apologize if I seem distracted. It's not that I don't appreciate all that you do."

"It's no trouble, really. I am a proud supporter." The phone agitated in his pocket. Could be nothing, save that he hardly ever gave out that number. Continue with his distraction, or trust that he'd been disruptive enough. He let go of her hand and waved a little. "A pleasure to meet you, Mr. Casey. I certainly wish your grandfather all the best." He slid back out the door and tapped his earpiece to answer as he left the office.

"Adam Lones? I heard, that is, you were out on the reservation, right? Looking for artifacts."

A man's voice he didn't recognize. Adam slowed his walk and stood in the shadow of the building, the gleam of a reddening sunset spanning the sky in front of him as his mind raced. "I have some interest in such things, certainly. Baskets, in particular."

"Right, right. And you're willing to pay?"

What would he say? He became a collector, fingering his wallet and imagining himself one of those big-hearted, liberal spiritual types. "That's true, but it's important to me to honor the creators. I'm afraid I can't purchase anything that may have been stolen or looted. My preference is to buy direct from the maker, or at least, to be able to validate the authenticity of the work by knowing the maker's name. May I ask your connection to the reservation?"

"The stuff I've got," the guy blurted, "It's good, super authentic. Dates from the forties."

"That's good, it's a good start," Adam said encouragingly. "But without knowing the artist, well, I'm sure you understand."

"Rosemary Manuel. She was one of the greats. They've got her stuff at that national museum, y'know? In Washington." A little cough, then, "Frank, her husband, he said you were interested. He don't sell her stuff, of course, but it's not like he controls everything. You in the Tucson area? I'm in town tonight if you want to see it."

And just like that, he was back in business. "Yes, of course. I'm busy this evening, but I have an associate I can send over to see the basket. He's fully authorized to negotiate on my behalf. His name is Hammer."

CHAPTER TWELVE

The operator left, his departure as abrupt as his arrival had been, and Grant stood up. "I overstepped my bounds, Sheriff. Please accept my apologies. And get a hair test if you can. If the perp was drugged, it might still be detectable."

She raised her eyebrows. "Aside from this business with your family cache, Mr. Casey, there is honestly no reason to think he didn't do it. Maybe it really is just some crazy coincidence. For you, it's personal, but if you look at it from my angle," she shrugged. "Yeah, I'll keep an eye on things, at least until the case gets transferred to the FBI. If you want to open a case about the cache, we should get that taken care of."

Another investigation, more people tromping around the cache site, which was meant to be secret. Grant sighed. "I'm not sure that's what my grandfather would want. He prefers to keep this kind of thing in the tribe."

"I understand. I'm sure the tribal police can handle it."

"Thank you for giving me so much of your time." He shook her hand briefly. "I should head over to the hospital."

"Do you need—?"

"I'll just grab an Uber. Thanks." With a nod to the secretary, he showed himself out. In perfect time to see Adam Lones across the parking lot, moving toward a BMW the color of gilded parchment. Lones's interruption in the sheriff's office felt timed, his conversation scripted, and his attempts to lure Grant into dialog a little too forced. He was up to something. Grant stopped in the shade, pulling out his phone as cover.

"The airplane graveyard?" Lones said, and Grant almost forgot his fake texting. "Well, I'll be sorry to miss it," Lones went on, "but my associate Mr. Hammer will be on his way to inspect the basket," he was saying as he stepped inside.

Now here he was talking baskets, which he hadn't mentioned at all in the context of the vandalism at the tribal center. And talking about the airplane graveyard. That was at least one coincidence too many. Lones made the break-in about a crazed drug addict with no reference to the artifacts the guy destroyed. Shifting the narrative, but it shouldn't be his narrative to shift. None of this should have anything to do with him Grant hung by the doorway in the shadows until Lones's car reached the street, then he bolted for the bike rack where a few bicycles leaned as if they'd been there a while. The mountain bike on the end had full tires and wasn't chained. No time to jack a car, and probably not smart in a place he barely knew. His intel instinct told him to follow Lones, but he knew where he'd find the man at 7 o'clock. Instead, Grant jumped on and took off, following a sweeping route to the east, wrapping a big installation.

Long strips of cracked concrete stretched behind a wire-topped fence that surrounded the Air Force base. A tingling unease built in Grant's chest and he fought the urge to peddle faster. He was close. Lones's associate, Hammer, couldn't be much closer, and he'd have no reason to be watchful. Still, out here, there was nothing to camouflage Grant's tail, and he didn't even have his go-bag with its stash of easy costume changes. Head down, hope for the best. Road signs, pointing toward the Air and Space Museum, and Airplane Boneyard. That twisting feeling hardened into a knot of anger. There were no coincidences, not in his line of work. Didn't mean he had to like where this particular arrow was pointing, though he felt a certain satisfaction that his mistrust had not been ill-placed. He took a turn, and through the fence to his right marched row upon row of airplanes, antique fighters lined up like a child's models, then hundreds of jetliners, ranks of deteriorating wings, skeletal cockpits, rubber tires subsiding into the graveled paths. Some of the planes lay collapsed upon the ground, being carved into pieces for reclamation. Miles of gray metal fuselages, so many they began to seem bizarre, like hulking creatures of a bygone era. They stretched out as far as he could see in orderly rows. Somewhere among them stood squadrons of B-52's and a few B-29 Superfortresses, the reason the base had been developed out here during the war.

A tour bus trundled along inside the fence and pulled to a stop just on the other side of a large parking lot. A stocky figure in an imitation flight suit hustled over to meet the bus. Randy. He grinned, shook hands, thanked people for coming as they unloaded from the bus. When he spoke with Cece, he made it sound as if he were giving the tours, when, in fact, he was just the doorman. Grant peddled past. Leaving the bike next to the building, Grant moseyed along the side as if he were meeting someone from the tour. The VIP's trickled out of the bus. For a long time, they stood there talking with great animation, not that much different from Grant's schoolmates when they came here years ago. Most of the tour members wore baseball caps, and Grant considered swiping one as an attempt at concealment, but as he drew closer, he noted the similarity in the caps. Each cap had insignia and embroidery identifying their service units. The veterans emerged talking with their hands, their eyes and voices bright as if visiting the ghostly aircraft had brought them back to their glory days. A few needed walkers or canes, working their way toward the back door of what was otherwise a secure facility.

A pale sedan pulled into the parking lot and pulled into a vacant space. Not a Beemer, like Lones's, but still a high-end automobile. A man stepped out, broad-shouldered, short-haired, wearing a faded denim shirt and nice cowboy boots, a projection of Western pride. The man hesitated, then pulled something from under his seat, fumbled in the car for a moment, and pulled on a sports jacket that hung a little awkwardly toward the left. As if he'd just put something heavy in the pocket. The guy looked around, but with the unfocused glance of someone unused to performing a surveillance sweep. Slamming the car door, he strode closer to the fence, watching more intently through the open links.

Randy noticed and gave a slight wave. "Mr. Hammer?"

The newcomer nodded. "Are you Randy Manuel?"

Randy opened a gate in the fence and the veterans began to file through. He beckoned Hammer to step inside and walk toward the bus. Once their backs were to the exit, Grant straightened up and jogged over, adopting an air of military focus. He held the gate open, standing ramrod straight, eyes forward, his off-hand in a stiff salute. "Thank you for your service, sir," he said as the next man passed through, moving slow. The guy gave him a nod and said, "You, too, son."

The bus driver emerged, carrying a bundle of crushed water bottles, and shaded his eyes as he squinted toward Grant. He gave a thumbs up and hollered, "Lock up, would you?"

"Yes, sir!" Grant hollered back. In his peripheral vision, he saw Randy and Hammer climb into a golf cart at the front of the bus and start down one of the roads, a plume of dust rising in their wake. Shouldn't be too hard to follow, but he hoped they weren't going far. When the last of the veterans had made their way outside, Grant stepped through and swung the gate shut, pulling the chain around to the inside and hanging the padlock off of it. Never paid to close your known escape route. He walked purposefully across the road behind the bus, maintaining his military air in case anyone was paying attention. From the far side, he scanned the array of airplanes laid out before him in tidy rows of industrial decay. Close-to, they loomed over him, their shadows cast in jagged darkness over the streets and over each other. Down one row ran a tell-tale streamer of dust.

Grant darted toward the nearest plane in the right direction, placing himself behind the landing gear. Then he ran to the next and the next, the planes washing over him, like waves of an air assault. He remembered Cece's shudder when she thought of spending the night here. Yeah, he would've loved it. But he hoped he wouldn't end up staying tonight. Up ahead, the golf cart bounced along another road and came to a halt. Randy killed the engine. Grant ducked along the grounded fuselage of an F-4 in the process of disassembly. At the tail section, he peered around the corner. Two planes down the road stood a partially disassembled B-29, not one of the ones proudly displayed for the public, but a parts plane, being slowly cannibalized to keep a few of the antique planes in flying condition.

"You're into history, like Mr. Lones, right Mr. Hammer? Old stuff. You gotta check this out." Randy led the way toward the stairs at the belly of the

B-29.

"Not really."

Randy deflated. "Oh. You mentioned Papago Park, so I figured."

"POW stories, sure, but not this stuff." Hammer waved his hand around at the airplanes. "Mr. Lones sent me over here to look at baskets, not airplanes."

"Right, yeah, sorry. This bird's like my private office, y'know? I got the artifacts stashed over here." Randy bobbed his head toward the airplane.

Hammer cast a dubious glance over the plane and shifted his weight, the lump in his left-hand pocket looking so conspicuous to Grant that even an idiot like Randy would have to notice. No sign that he did. "Let's go," Hammer said.

As Randy mounted a narrow ladder into the belly of the plane, Hammer looked around again, squirrelly as hell, and climbed up after him. Grant sprinted into the shadow of the big, old plane and hunkered down against the under-wing landing gear where he'd be hard to spot from the inside. The big, bald tire smelled of warm rubber. Doors removed, the open bomb bay revealed the gutted belly. Just in front, the belly gunner's turret was missing allowing a partial view of the crew cabin. Randy sat in the radio officer's chair, his lower body visible. "Pretty cool, huh? They take parts from here for the planes that are still flying."

"Anybody else know about this office of yours?" Hammer asked.

Randy chuckled. "I told you it was private. Can I just get behind you there? There's this tunnel where the crew could get to the gunning positions at the back. It's a great place to stash things."

"Yeah, I can see that it would be." The metal plane echoed as the two men traded places.

"My grandmother knew some of the guys from Papago Park, y'know. Used to talk about working with them when they got out on work details." Randy's voice came more clear as he reached over the door and pulled down a bundle wrapped in a blanket. An old, hand-woven blanket that Grant had seen only a few times before, on ceremonial occasions. With an effort, he relaxed his hands. Fucking Randy had broken into a sacred cache for what— to sell his family heritage for money? Then came the thought that clenched his fists all over again, Sheriff Rizzo's voice echoing inside his head, *"His companion likely took your relics... Somebody beat him, strangled him and left him for dead."*

Randy. If Hammer didn't pull the trigger on him, Grant just might.

CHAPTER THIRTEEN

J amie checked her workout watch. 7,360 steps today, and she still had forty-five minutes before she met up with Lones to talk campaign finance. Maybe if he was feeling generous—maybe after a few glasses of wine—she could broach the subject of her mother's detainment. Jesus. How was she supposed to do that? Now she had this Casey person messing around with her investigation, suggesting that the man they had in prison, the man who had confessed, for God's sake (sorry, Mom), had been drugged while somebody borrowed his clothes. Crazy talk. And the minute she turned her back, he was into her files. Then he just left like there was nothing else to talk about, without even looking at the bone. Asshat. Sliding the pages back into their folder, she popped it in a drawer and locked it for safe keeping. She grabbed her jacket off the hook and pushed out of her office.

Rachel looked up. "Anything you need?"

"Nope, all done for tonight. Have a good weekend."

"You, too, Sheriff. Enjoy your dinner with Mr. Lones." Rachel smiled broadly as Jamie stalked out the door. Her assistant almost winked, as if she thought Lones and Jamie were having an affair.

Or was she just getting paranoid, thanks to Casey's insinuations. What if it wasn't that he was done with her, but that he was following Lones? Asshat. Paranoid, sneaky, asshat. Still, unless there'd been a sudden boom in the Tohono O'odham artifacts market—but the cultural center hadn't been robbed, it had been trashed. That was the opposite of antiquities collecting. Of course, given the state of the place, would they even know if something were missing? And yeah, there'd been a few stray hairs on the guy's clothes, the kind of thing anybody might have picked up from their spouse or roommate. Except that Anderson lived alone. Shit. She stomped over to her truck and heaved herself inside, slamming the door. Driving to the lock-up like she had a mission from God, as bad as her mother flying back to China, except Jamie's own people weren't planning to arrest her.

The officer at the desk looked up, startled, from some game of shooting castles on his cellphone. "I want to see Chris Anderson."

"I don't have—"

"It doesn't have to be formal." She pulled her gun and left it on the desk. "Just want to see if he's remembered anything."

"Uh, okay, Sheriff." He pushed the register toward her, and she signed in, watching as he counter-signed for her gun, then placed it in a small safe. "You can go on back. Jerry'll let you in." He pushed a button and she passed through the metal detectors to enter the jail proper.

Jerry wafted his hand through the air to draw her forward. "Evening, Sheriff. He's down here waiting for transport." His brow furrowed and he chewed his mustache for a moment. "Still haven't heard from the fibbies?"

"Not a thing." If she really were getting paranoid, she'd think the lack of response was deliberate, when, chances were, it just had to do with federal priorities not being on the reservation at the moment. Which might, maybe, have to do with the tribal protest against the wall. Or was that just a different manifestation of paranoia? She came around the corner and found Anderson slumped on the cot in his cell, wearing a prison jumpsuit because all of his clothes had been taken into evidence, leaning his head back against the wall.

"Mr. Anderson?"

He bolted upright, then swayed on his feet. Sure moved like an addict —unsteady. "Sheriff! When can I get out of here?" He walked over and set his hands on the bars, then, as if his burst of energy faded, he winced and his body sagged. Medium height, body-builder, hair that brushed his shoulders, five o'clock shadow, but if that was his usual look, or just the effects of being in jail, she couldn't be sure. Twenty-eight, according to his file, not bad looking, once he was stripped of his biker gear. Young and wary.

"I'm sorry, Mr. Anderson. The court-appointed lawyer still need to work with the feds on that, but we'll be transporting you over to county pretty soon, and that should be more comfortable."

"County? That means prison" He swallowed hard, hands wrapped around against the bars. "God's honest truth, Sheriff, I wouldn't have done something like that. Not mess up the cultural center, and certainly not attack one of the elders."

"You don't have to talk with me until we get a lawyer in for you, you know that."

"I know it, but I am not guilty. I didn't do that." He stared into her face, eyes flicking anxiously. "Look, Sheriff, I know the call was made from my phone, but it wasn't made by me, swear to God. Yeah, okay, I had some drinks, but that's not even my voice on the call. Please—" He broke off.

"We went down to that bar you mentioned, but nobody remembers seeing you there."

His face reddened. "Maybe it was a different one."

"You don't remember."

"I went to a few. I was...hoping for a hook-up."

"Which is why you got the hotel room."

"I don't remember getting the room!" He slapped his palm against the bars.

"The hotel clerk remembers it, and so does your credit card. The clerk said you seemed excited." Giddy, was the word the guy used, actually. "So unless you've remembered anything else, anything helpful, I don't see how you're getting off for this."

"I'm gay," Anderson blurted.

Jamie cocked her head. "Excuse me? I mean, I heard you, but I don't see how that's relevant."

"I'm gay, I went to a few bars, looking for a hook-up—as I said. Maybe nobody's admitting they saw me because they'd have to admit they're queer. If I looked happy maybe that was because it worked, right? Maybe I found somebody, and he was waiting outside, and that's why I went in to the clerk, right?" He poked his finger against the bar with each point. "If that's what happened, why would I go off and wreck the cultural center? Think it through, Sheriff! I'm a first time offender, no history of anything. Even if I went on a bender, how the Hell would I end up there, wrecking the museum?"

Jamie's conviction about paranoia settled into concrete. If he hung out at bars, looking to pick up strangers, that could well account for the stray hairs on the evidence report whether or not he'd gotten a date that night. "That's a whole lot of if's all piled up. Nobody saw you leave with anybody, the clerk didn't see you come in with anybody, and we have no evidence that anybody else was in the room." She sighed and pushed back. "Transport should be here soon."

"Sheriff." He looked pale and strained as a bowl of pasta. "I can't go to prison! Jesus, you've gotta know how guys like me fare in those places—I've heard stories." As she started to walk away, Anderson practically lunged against the bars, moving fast enough to startle her, maybe explaining how he'd gotten the jump on Frank Manuel at the cultural center. "Okay, so I had a few drinks, I never said I didn't, but this guy, my hook-up, he was on my bike, I'm sure of it! We must've hugged, made out, something."

"You don't even remember which bars you went to, and now you remember that you had some guy on your bike? Gimme a break, Anderson." She kept walking.

"No, no, no!" he hollered after her. "I woke up in the room, right? You and the deputy knocking on the door, that's what woke me up. But I was lying there for a minute, and I could remember the smell! Of him!" He sagged. "Oh, shit. I sound like an idiot. Seriously, this is how I am. I'm masc, y'know? Leather, motorcycle, all that." He stood back for a moment and squared his shoulders, offering a roguish grin that made him look younger. "But...I'm attracted to how guys smell." He spread his hands in a shrug. "That's what I cling to. When I woke up, I could still smell him, something tangy, almost woodsy. Like a hunter."

She drew a deep breath, ready to get royally pissed, then she looked at his face, his expression bleak, like some kind of hopeless romantic. Oh, Hell. It didn't have to mean she believed he was innocent, if she believed he'd be a goner once he got to prison. "Look, I'll order in pizza for the crew, and tell them to get the transport tomorrow instead. I'll light a fire under the public defender's office." His face lit up, and she growled, "I'm not saying I believe you, because it's still a load of horseshit." She jabbed a finger at him.

"Got it, Sheriff. Thanks."

Shaking her head, she walked away. She paused to issue some instructions to the guards, who readily agreed to share pizza with their prisoner and hang onto him until the next day. Walking in the door at L'Rose, where Adam Lones stood up to grip her hand, she felt like that woodsy smell Anderson described still lingered in her memory as well.

CHAPTER FOURTEEN

I got a couple of dance masks here, a pipe—collectors dig pipes, right?"
Randy lay the bundle where Grant couldn't' see it, abut he could hear
the rattle and thump of the package being unwrapped. "There's the
basket, and there's—"

"The basket is what he's interested in, that's it. How much do you
want for it?"

"That's it?" Randy said, almost yelping as if the reply scalded him.

"Yep. Can we make a deal?"

"But the pipe is a real beauty," Randy offered, in a tone that made
Grant want to jump up there and smack him, but he held back. Hammer
wanted the basket—Lones wanted the basket—and nothing else, but why? If
he could just conduct a proper intel mission...

Grant stood up, and rounded toward the bomb bay, where the ladder
stood. "Randy? You up there?"

"Who's that?" Hammer's voice, hard as his name.

"Hey, Randy, sorry I'm late." Grant climbed up the ladder, and let
surprise wash over him as he came into view of the crew area to find a
stranger looking back at him, with a hand in his pocket. Bingo. "Oh, hey,
sorry to interrupt. Mr. Hammer, right?" He put out his hand, and Hammer
slowly withdrew his own from his pocket, the social conventions and Grant's
utter normalcy overcoming his suspicion. They shook hands, firmly, and
Grant finished his climb, forcing the guy back into the cramped space.

"Guess it's a good thing they pulled the gun turret or no way we'd all fit." He flashed a grin at Randy, who plonked into the engineer's seat, blinking at him across the open forward hatch. To Hammer's left, on the navigator's chart table lay their family's sacred dance masks, a soapstone pipe, a ceremonial knife with a carved hilt, a few other items obscured by the basket. "I didn't think you were gonna just sell it all to the first person who answered. That's good stuff—you could do an auction, go online."

Hammer cleared his throat. "All we want is the basket." He nodded toward it. "It's a Rosemary Manuel, right?"

"Yes, sir." Grant reached over and picked it up, letting his smile linger fondly over his grandmother's workmanship. Coiled from bear grass and wound with split strands of yucca, it spanned both of his hands, bigger than a soup bowl, smaller than a platter. Darker bands of devil's claw pod fibers worked the pattern, a variation on the classic Tohono O'odham "man and the maze" design. The maze usually wound five or six times around toward the center of the basket, but this one made only two wraps, with a few dead ends, and a single strand of red contained within one of the box canyons. He thought of the labyrinth at Chartres, or the hedge maze of Longleat. Even the Greeks worked mazes into the mosaics of their great houses. What made this one so valuable? Slipping out his cell phone, he snapped photos front and back and put the phone away. "It's a beauty, isn't it? Some of her finest work. Museum-quality, I'd think." He turned it carefully, examining the back and edges. A paper tag stuck to the back with a few letters on it, an archival tag as if it had been in the tribal center until recently. The pattern looked familiar, though he couldn't have seen it for decades.

Randy bleated, "Yeah, yes, I think it's at least as good as the one in New York." His glance flicked from Grant to the buyer and back again. Grant almost felt sorry for him. Almost.

Grant nodded slowly. "What were you thinking of asking for it?"

"Look," said Hammer, but Grant kept his attention on Randy.

His cousin wet his lips and said, "Ah. Like, three grand?"

Grant recoiled. "That's pretty low. I know a few museums back east that would be interested. Why don't we just hold off a bit, and put together that auction, okay?"

"Look," Hammer repeated, adding a jab of his finger to Grant's bicep. Hammer's face displayed a flash of reaction at that, as if he hadn't expected the newcomer to be the iron to Randy's obvious deficiency. Hammer swallowed. "Look, Randy contacted us first. I'm already here. Don't mess with a sure thing because you think you can get more money. Ain't gonna happen."

"Money in hand, right? He just wants the basket, so maybe later we could do an auction? For the other stuff?" Randy's brows knit as he prepared this little speech, and a few beads of sweat slipped down his cheeks. He obviously had no idea what Grant was up to—he just didn't want him to screw up the deal. He was about to be pretty upset.

Grant rubbed a hand over his jaw. "Sounds like you're willing to spring for the three grand? I hate to disappoint you, but I just don't think we can let it go for that."

Hammer's ice-blue eyes narrowed. "What price did you have in mind?"

Bringing the basket close to his chest, Grant said, "Honestly, sir. It's a family heirloom. And especially with our grandfather in the hospital right now, I just don't think we're ready to sell."

"We are ready! I'm ready. Jesus, Grant, what are you doing?" Randy stood up.

"Who are you?" Hammer demanded leaning toward him, maybe trying to take advantage of a few inches and a few dozen pounds.

"He's—" Randy started, but Grant cut him off. "I'm the asshole who screwed up your deal. I think we can all agree on that."

"Damn straight," Hammer replied, and Randy giggled.

"Why don't you head for home," Grant suggested, "and we'll be in touch after we've had a chance to work this through. If we decide to go to auction, I'll make sure you get an invitation."

With a low rumble, Hammer said, "I have to make a call." He passed Grant to the ladder and practically slid down it, fireman style.

"What the Hell are you doing?" Randy hissed, leaning over the hatch. "What are you even doing here? Why are you—"

"Selling off our family heritage? Gee, Randy, I'm glad you asked."

Beyond the curved and divided windshield, Hammer paced, cellphone to his ear.

Randy thrust to his feet. "So now you care? You ran from here years ago, you've got no right—"

"Don't talk to me about rights, Randy, these things don't belong to you. If you don't see my right, then what about Frank's? What about Cece's? You don't think maybe her kids deserve to dance in their grandfathers' masks?"

Outside, Hammer shifted the phone to his left ear, brought up his left hand to take it, his right hand reaching.

Randy snapped, "You got no idea what's been happening around here, you fucking self-righteous—"

Too bad Randy didn't get to finish as the first shot shattered the antique glass, cracks flaring behind him like a silver halo.

CHAPTER FIFTEEN

A dam poured Rizzo a fresh glass of wine. Her third. And the entrees weren't out yet. All around them rose the subdued hum of conversation over fine dining, intimate tables for two and business dinners hosted by expansive men with excellent taste in suits and wine and women. "Now that we've gotten the pleasantries out of the way, Jamie, I hope you don't mind my saying you look a little tired." He smiled solicitously, focused on her. At times, he perceived a sense of yearning from her, as if she'd developed a crush on him in the two years they'd been working together. Anything to smooth his way.

"Weird afternoon, that's all. Most of my job's routine, y'know? Even this vandalism case should be open and shut. We have the perp, we have his confession." She shrugged, then took a sip of her wine.

"And yet, you hesitate. Last time we spoke about it, I don't recall any hesitation." He raised an eyebrow at her. Then his phone chirped. The distinctive tone he had chosen for Sons business. He let his eyes shut and shook his head, then glanced up at her. "I am so sorry. Duty calls. I'll try to make this brief—maybe it's about the gala dinner." Flashing a grin, Adam rose from his chair and moved away, down the short hallway toward the restrooms.

"Hello, friend," he said into the receiver.

"It's Hammer. The deal is off. Some other guy showed up, disrupted the whole thing. How do you want me to proceed?"

"If you get our contact alone, do you think you could close it?"

Hammer gave a growl. "Not with this asshole in the way. He's a stronger personality than your contact."

"Who was it? Did our contact bring him in?"

"I don't think so. If anything, he seemed pretty put out about it. He knows him, though. Called the guy Grant."

Grant. As in Casey. He had known something was off about Casey. "Do what you have to, neatly, if you can. We need that basket."

Hammer rang off without another word. Yes, Adam had a fine recruit in that one. Much as he liked to be hands-on, he'd have to delegate if he wanted his enterprise to be successful. Replacing his pleasant demeanor, he resumed his place at the table, pleased to see Rizzo's glass down by a few swallows. "Sorry about that, Jamie. Where were we? Oh, right you were expressing some misgivings about the case against that addict."

"If he is an addict. I don't see much evidence of regular use, not in his apartment, either. If he's addicted to anything, it's the secret lives of famous people—that's all he's got on his shelves."

"That could be worse, though, am I right? If he's not habituated..." Adam trailed off, turning his own glass in little speculative circles.

Rizzo steepled her hands on the table. "I know that look. What are you thinking?"

He shrugged and shifted position as if he were uncomfortable with his own thoughts. "What if the man had some other reason? Your drug explanation makes a lot of sense, of course, but perhaps... He might have been put up to it, or talked into it. Maybe someone who had a grudge, someone connected to the tribe." With a chuckle he waved away this speculation. "Oh, don't mind me. Too many cop shows, I imagine."

Rizzo gave a slow shake of her head. "Your theory's not completely off base. He insists that someone was with him, but that he doesn't remember the guy."

Adam felt a chill and any number of calculations he considered finished were suddenly running through the back of his head. He transformed all of that into an appropriate expression of surprise. "Really? Sounds like he's been more forthcoming lately."

"He's remembered a few things. Nothing important." She shrugged and leaned back as the waiter appeared to place a steaming plate in front of her, the creamy scent of carbonara sauce wafting up around them. "Mmm. That looks good."

"Well, the feds will be taking over the case soon, right? Shouldn't he already be in federal custody?" He tucked in his napkin as his own dinner, a slab of pristine almond-crusted sole arrived in front of him.

"I put off the transfer, just until tomorrow. I feel like I want another chat with him." She wound a forkful of pasta as he carved a few bites off of his fish.

"Speaking of chats, that visitor you had, another relative of the elder who got injured, wasn't he?" He blew gently on the fish, then placed it on his tongue and let it seem to melt away. Purity incarnate. Exquisite.

"Mmm." She finished her mouthful and took a sip of wine.

"I hope his presence isn't what set you off tonight. It's already a complex case without interference from people like that. Was he really snooping in your desk?" Having planted a few notions, Adam helped himself to another bite, building a little cabin of suspicions in the good sheriff's mind, setting up Casey as suspicious in the extreme. Exactly the person likely to wind up dead on federal property. After killing his cousin, perhaps. Or vice versa. Adam didn't need to know the details.

"Snooping? I—"she frowned, and Adam knew he'd hit on something. What was Casey really up to? Just a nosy relative, or something more? Jamie continued, "He's just understandably concerned about the case, besides —"she broke off again.

"Anyone would be, of course, his grandfather is in the hospital, after all. But you still look concerned."

Rizzo glanced away. "I shouldn't be burdening you with all of this. We should be talking about the campaign, next steps, all of that." She waved her fork to encompass the next phase of her political career.

"You know, Jamie, this is one of the reasons I so admire you. Most people, involved in a difficult case, having to deal with the relatives and with the federal government delaying everything, they'd be pretty upset by now. Not you." He aimed his fork at her, his gaze sighting along it, as if he had her in his crosshairs. "Your commitment to justice is unshakeable."

"No, no, be serious. Besides, that's not even the case that's bugging me." She idly started curling more noodles.

"Really? There's something more interesting going on? Do tell." He maintained his conspiratorial tone even as he soured on the conversation. The druggie was remembering things—he had to stop that—and now this Casey person had inserted himself into Adam's business, though he had been dealt with by now—and Rizzo was wandering off on a tangent.

"An immigrant who may have violated tribal law, then ended up in the hospital. Mr. Casey ID'd the victim, or the perpetrator, it's hard to tell. Sounds like he stole some things, but Casey won't or can't say what."

"Casey again. Certainly seems as if he knows more than he's sharing. I won't tell you how to do your job, just sounds like this guy has earned some closer scrutiny."

"I'll take that under advisement." She reached for her wine glass, then pulled back, with a deep intake of breath. "Tell you what's really going on, Adam? It was my parents' anniversary this week. Forty-two years together. Or rather, forty years together, and now two years apart. My dad thinks if we could just come up with enough money, we could bribe our way through the system and get her out of prison." She rubbed her eyes. "At the same time he's telling me this, I'm thinking about how well the story will play with my constituents."

"Christian missionary imprisoned? Absolutely. I know you don't want to exploit your family's grief, but say the word if you want to run with it." He pasted on sympathy and reached across the table to grip her arm. "I know how much that must be hurting you. Let me set you up with the congressional delegation while they're on break. There's got to be something else they could do."

"Thanks." She offered a weak smile as he withdrew his hand. "You must still miss your own parents. A crime like that, unsolved for so long."

"I think of them every day," he told her. Every time he drove by where their bodies had been dumped, and saw the bougainvillea that grew so lush over what was meant to be their grave. As he skewered another bite he told himself, next time, dig deeper.

CHAPTER SIXTEEN

Dropping the basket back onto the table, Grant latched onto a grab bar with his left hand. He grabbed Randy around the chest with his right and hauled him across the open hatch, both of them sprawling onto the floor as another bullet whizzed overhead and sparked off the metal.

"Is he shooting at us?" Randy rolled frantically, trying to scramble to his feet.

Grant hauled him back down again, then propelled him into the radio operator's corner. "Yes."

He pivoted and popped up so he could scan the chart table where the sacred cache lay spread for the world to see. He tossed the basket across to Randy. "Hang onto that." Underneath it, the only weapon readily to hand, a ceremonial knife with a wrapped handle and a beaded sheath. Was it even sharp? He slipped it out and found the old steel glistening with an oiled sheen and a keen edge. He slid it into his waist at his back, a hard assurance.

"Shit!" Randy yelped as if the sight of Grant with a knife was somehow more frightening than the stranger with the gun. Footsteps ran across the gravel. Grant snatched the steel ribs overhead, sliding his heel through a gap and pulled himself tight to the ceiling inside the crew compartment. Randy pressed himself in where the radio gear had been. Grant's shoulder ached; the wound he had earned in Mongolia letting him know. For a moment, nothing. Everyone listening. Randy clutched the basket against him like a shield.

Then the shuffle of feet below, the tink of something against the rung of the ladder—the assailant's wedding ring, his hand just visible from Grant's skewed vantage. "Turn over the basket and nobody gets hurt."

Randy's eye's flared, and he started to move.

Hammer launched himself up the ladder, head and shoulders popping through the hatch as he aimed in the direction of the sound. Grant swung down, kicking hard. The bullet cracked into the arch above Randy's hiding place. Hammer slammed against the rim of the hatch, grunting, his hand flying free of the ladder. He flailed for a grip, then collapsed through the hatch where he'd emerged, the gun still clenched in his hand. Damn.

Before Hammer could rise, Grant dropped down on top of him, feeling a rib crack. Hammer's breath rushed out, but he was already rolling, tumbling them both, bringing up the gun, the knife now pinned underneath. Grant caught his wrist, twisting away, the fingers of his left hand aiming for Hammer's eyes.

Hammer reared back, making space between them. Grant brought up his knees and rammed his feet upward, knocking Hammer off of him—but not letting go of his wrist. Hammer howled, twisting his body, trying to avoid breaking his arm. The gun shook free.

Grant was on top again in an instant, knife in hand against Hammer's throat. "What do you want with the basket?"

"No idea," Hammer wheezed. He pushed upward, slamming his forehead into Grant's, letting the knife slice him, but not deep enough, not by far. They rolled, rocking hard against the ladder. Hammer grabbed on and used the leverage to pull away. He jumped down immediately, slid his hand into his pocket, and pulled another gun.

Grant dodged and rolled as a bullet spat dust over his face. Finding his feet, he propelled himself behind the huge tires. The first gun lay maybe five feet away.

"Who the hell are you?" Hammer roared.

Tuck and roll, hand out, come up with the gun in a shooter's crouch. Eyes locked to Hammer's furious, blood-streaked face.

"Take it!" Randy bleated, and the basket soared like a frisbee out the shattered front windshield. Hammer bolted toward the flying basket.

Grant squeezed off a shot that struck the golf cart. Jumped up, running.

Hammer spun about and peppered the area with rapid fire, his new weapon much more powerful than the one he'd dropped. Grant slid like a baseball player with the golf cart as his home plate.

A squeal from behind, and Randy's voice. "I'm hit! Jesus! I'm bleeding!"

Hammer took off. Grant leaned from behind the golf cart as Hammer snatched up the basket and kept running, dodging into the next row of planes.

"Jesus, Grant, don't you even fucking care?"

Randy talked a lot for a dying man. Turning, rising up, Grant crossed the scarred ground between, the sandy gravel now smeared with blood. Mostly from Hammer's superficial neck injury. Knife in one hand, gun in the other. Grant's pulse lowered, his senses supernaturally alert to the fading sound of their assailant escaping with exactly what he'd come for. Grant knew the guy's car, knew where it was parked, and briefly regretted leaving the gate unlocked. Hammer was a body-builder, no doubt a powerful guy, but Grant could've outpaced him to the gate with minutes to spare.

He paused to wipe off the bloody blade, and tuck the gun at his back. "Where are you hit?" He called up.

"My chest."

Grant sprang into motion, one-handed up the stairs, knife joining the gun as he took a knee next to his cousin. Randy sat, his back against the bulkhead that separated the crew from the bomb bay. He fingered a tear in his shirt, edged with blood. Grant tore the opening wider, and found a shallow furrow, maybe as long as one finger, where the bullet had glanced along Randy's ribcage, blood oozing. Some chest wound. Randy's eyes glinted and his breath hitched. "Am I gonna die?"

Grant bit back his response. He cradled Randy's head, and slid him to the floor. "Lie down—that'll make it easier to breathe." Glanced around the cabin and spotted the green metal box with a distinctive red cross on its lid. He tugged it from its perch and popped the latches. Antique bottles of iodine and alcohol, and a few yellowed rolls of bandage and sterile dressings. That would do. He pressed a pad to the injury and wrapped it on, securing the ends. "You have a car here?"

Randy nodded. "I don't think I can drive. Should we call an ambulance?"

"It doesn't look bad, Randy. You'll be just fine."

"How the hell do you know?" Randy shot back.

For a moment, flashes of gunfire sparked in Grant's memory. Grenades popped and IED's blew a few Humvees into bits, along with the men inside. You can't tourniquet a gut wound. You can't replace a man's brain when a sniper smears it across the wall. Blood streaked the air around him as Nick absorbed the explosion that should have taken him. Tension flared through Grant's neck and shoulders. With a will, he set all of that aside. "Don't ask me that. Not now."

Something must have shown on his face because Randy went a little more pale. This has been Randy's first firefight. Even someone like him deserved the grace of a few moments of shock.

"Keys?" Grant asked, but the distinctive jagged lump in Randy's pocket revealed them. He helped Randy to his feet and sent him down the ladder where he stumbled and perched heavily in the golf cart. Grant took the knife's sheath and slid it onto his belt, securing the blade where it belonged, with thanks to whatever ancestor had provided it. He wrapped the rest of the items in the blanket and tucked it under his arm as he descended.

"Don't you think we should hurry?" Randy said as Grant climbed in beside him.

He started the motor. "Same parking lot?" At Randy's shaky nod, they turned and moved at top speed of maybe twenty miles an hour, back to the gate. It stood wide open, Hammer's car gone, a few spatters of blood marking his trail. Taking the basket with him. Leaving the golf cart inside the fence and locking after them, they climbed into Randy's Chevy, the sacred bundle secured in the trunk with a jumble of old bags and work boots.

"You'll want to turn—" Randy's hand pointed left.

Grant turned right.

"There's an urgent care," Randy said.

"I'm taking you to the hospital," Grant told him.

"Oh. Right. Thanks." Randy settled back a little, but stiffly, giving Grant the side-eye all the way to the hospital. Instead of pulling up to Emergency, Grant parked in a visitor slot. He took a moment to tuck the gun underneath the seat. He stepped out, sliding the keys into his own pocket, taking Randy by the arm as his cousin got out, already aiming toward Emergency. Grant steered him through the front door.

"What—I thought you said—"

Grant tightened his grip. "There's someone we need to see." They were a little grubby, but with Randy's injured side placed between them, no worse than the average laborer.

A receptionist glanced up, and Grant gave a little smile and a wave. "We know the way," he told her, "thanks."

"I don't think we should bother Grampie right now, besides I—"

They rode the elevator in silence, Randy leaning slightly away, wary. The elevator gave a ding, and they stepped out. Grant walked with a purpose, towing Randy along to a shared room with three beds, one empty, one occupied by a large black man with a bored expression as he stared up at the television news. In the second, a thin man lay under the sheets, his strong arms resting on top, one of them with an IV dripping fluids. Teo's skin looked gray, bruises standing out brightly on his cheek and throat, his face, usually so animated, lay slack.

Randy stumbled as they entered, his feet resisting as Grant drew him closer. "Oh, shit. Is that Teo? He looks awful! I wonder what—"

Grant's banked fury burst into flame. He spun Randy against the wall between the beds and pinned him there, as much with his eyes as with the palm against Randy's wild heartbeat. The guy in the next bed jerked and turned away from the television as Grant said, "You beat him, strangled him, and left him for dead, and you have ten seconds to tell me why."

CHAPTER SEVENTEEN

O kay, okay, but can we—not here, okay?" Randy's glance darted toward
Teo and away.

"Should I call somebody?" the other patient asked, a nurse call button
in his grip, thumb poised.

"What do you say, Randy? Do you want security to hear your story?"

"No!"

Grant looked at the patient. "Thanks, but I think we can handle this."
A tattoo of pilot's wings peeked out from the inadequate sleeve of the
patient's johnnie. "Air Force?"

The guy nodded. "Instructor, now. Stationed on base in town. You?"

"Army. Retired."

His eyebrows rose, then his gaze flicked to Grant's own tattoos around
his throat, down his arm. "But not regular army."

Grant smiled. "No, sir."

The patient settled back in his bed, a faint smile quirking his lips.
"Carry on, soldier."

Grant backed off, letting Randy slump against the wall.

"I'd like a minute with Teo. Wait right there." He took a knee at Teo's
bedside, assessing his color (poor), breathing (steady), heartbeat (also steady,
if a little more faint than he'd like—probably that was the meds). Teo's right
hand rested on the sheet, slightly cupped. No sign of defensive injuries.
Would he have fought back against Randy, of all people? Grant looked

closer. Flecks of white and gold edged his nails. Paint, embedded from regular work. Cece mentioned he'd been working with the team restoring the church. Grant examined him again, then said, "Randy, where's his cross?"

"Oh, shit," Randy mumbled.

Grant turned his head, very slow, with the focused energy of the raptor about to strike. Randy stuffed his hand in his pocket and thrust out his fist toward Grant, letting a thin chain of gold tumble into his palm, the small cross still attached. For a moment, Grant held it tight, letting the corners dig into his palm, then he leaned close over his old friend and slipped the chain around his bruised throat, letting the cross rest against his chest. Did he breathe a little more easily or was that just Grant indulging his imagination? Not what he was known for, for sure. "What's next, Randy, Frank's bracelets?"

"Damn. You stole that guy's crucifix?" The air force instructor said.

"Jesus, Grant," said Randy, with no apparent irony, "Can we get out of here?"

"If I was you, soldier, your buddy there would be staying right here—as a patient."

Randy blanched, and Grant gave a chuckle. "I don't know, Randy. I'm beginning to like it here."

Jerking into motion, Randy lurched away from the wall and past Grant toward the hallway, pausing there with the slumped attitude of a man who knows he's got nowhere to run. Grant flicked the air force man a brief salute, earning one in return as he stepped outside.

"Where should we go?" Randy asked, swaying first one direction, then the other.

A cleaner stood across the hall, fiddling with a bucket, but in a way that convinced Grant she'd been listening and watching just a moment ago. Cece mentioned the hospital staff being awfully attentive to their grandfather—apparently they were paying attention to everyone.

"We'll talk in the car. You need to drive, though, I have a phone call to make." He led the way back to the car, waving to the receptionist on the way out. Randy trailed, accepting the keys and wincing a little as he got into the driver's seat.

"Not just army, that guy said. What'd he mean by that?" The engine turned over with a growl. "You like a green beret or something? I mean, those moves you did back at the B-29, that was impressive." Randy gave a forced chuckle, a hostage trying to get on the good side of his interrogator.

"You're on a need-to-know basis, Randy. Trust me on this, you do not need to know."

Randy laughed louder. "Is this like, if you tell me, you'd have to kill me?"

Grant reached toward his pocket and Randy gave a yelp, then sagged as Grant brought out his cell phone. He aimed it at his cousin. "All honesty here, Randy? Don't push your luck. We're heading for Mission San Xavier."

"The church? We playing tourist now?" Randy started driving. "But seriously, Grant, it stings like Hell. You sure I'm okay?"

"Should probably clean it with some alcohol and change the dressing. Do you have a first aid kit in here?" When Randy shook his head, looking a little mystified, Grant opted to tune him out. He tapped a contact and brought the phone to his ear. Two rings. Hang up. Tap again. On the third ring, responding to the urgent request he signaled, D.A.'s cheerful voice answered the phone. "Hey, Chief? Anybody dead yet?"

"Could be soon. I've got a situation. I need some intel on Adam Lones. He's some kind of real estate magnate, into local politics in Tucson. He's got at least one bad actor associate, a guy called 'Hammer'." He told her the license number of Hammer's vehicle.

"Right, Chief." All business in an instant. "You need the works?"

"Everything—things his mother never knew. This guy was behind the attack on my grandfather, and Hammer just tried to kill me and my cousin."

The car jerked as Randy shot him a look. "Grampie? That's not the same thing. They got that guy already. Besides, you're the one who fucked up my deal. Hammer was gonna give me the money until you showed up. Even then, he said if we gave him the basket, nobody would get hurt."

Was his own cousin really that blind? "Hang on, D. A." Grant covered the phone briefly. "He said that to get you to reveal your position so he could shoot at you. Which he did. The only thing I fucked up on was handing you the basket." Grant walked a narrow line between intimidating Randy so he could get the intel he needed, and dropping into an abyss of fury he had thought he had erased with decades of discipline. He got back on with D.A. "It's got something to do with my grandmother's baskets—Rosemary Manuel —and maybe some ancient bones. I don't have much else to go on right now. I'm working in the dark here, D A., and I need you to shed some light."

"Do my best, Chief."

"Papago Park," Randy blurted. He blinked a few times, gripping the wheel a little too tight. "That guy, Adam Lones, when he came by to Grampie's place, he was asking about Papago Park and the Nazis."

"You got that, D.A.? Randy, what else did you overhear?"

"Guy seemed concerned about the wall, y'know? And he was all up on local history, seemed like they were hitting it off. Said he'd heard Grammie worked with some of the POW's. Then he asked about baskets, and Grampie shut him down pretty quick after that."

Grant held the phone so D.A. could hear what was being said, though he felt a little tempted to bash it into his cousin's temple. "And it never occurred to you this might have anything to do with the break-in at the tribal center?"

"It was a few days earlier, besides," Randy swallowed, "I wasn't exactly in the room, y'know? You think Lones had something to do with the vandalism? That doesn't make any sense—he wanted to buy stuff, not wreck stuff."

"Your buddy there sounds like a real winner," D.A. said.

"Who is that on the phone?"

"Somebody else who wants to kick your ass." Grant put the phone back to his ear. "I need the intel ASAP."

D.A. snorted. "Of course you do. You do know we're busy cleaning up at the job site without you, right?"

"If I don't solve this thing, you might have to do without me indefinitely."

"Right. Stay safe out there, Chief." She hung up, and Grant put the phone away.

"Your turn, Randy."

"So this guy, Lones, you think he sent one of his flunkies, maybe Hammer, to wreck the cultural center?"

"Working that out is my job, and D.A.'s helping. Your job is to tell me why you violated our family's cache and tried to murder Teo."

"Jesus, that's pretty harsh."

Grant slid toward him across the bench seat, grabbed the wheel and turned hard right at the same time that he stomped on Randy's brake foot, mashing the pedal down. The car screeched onto the gravel shoulder and Grant leaned into Randy's personal space, the smell of his sweat infusing the air between them. "You put your hands around his throat, Randy. That's no fucking accident."

He drew back, controlling his breathing. Released Randy's hand, eased up the pressure on his foot. Too far. He shouldn't be on this case at all, should be leaving it to the locals or at least, to his team. Not if he couldn't keep himself in check. At the same time, a hard truth settled at the back of his skull. The sheriff was in bed with Lones, figuratively, if not literally. Local fibbies hadn't shown up, and until he got there, Teo could've died without a name while Randy sold off everything their grandfather cared about. Grant didn't. Wasn't supposed to. His anger bound him here tighter than love, closer than family, and Hammer had seen his face. He shouldn't be on it, but it was far too late to back down.

Randy killed the engine and sat there for a moment, head bowed, both hands still on the wheel. "Cece's gonna kill me," he breathed. "Assuming you don't."

"Drugs?"

Randy shook his head, stringy hair flapping. "Gambling. I play poker. I'm good at it, y'know? I was up pretty high, then I wasn't. I was just—if I could get that big score. So I heard about a game, high-stakes, private. Guy I knew through the circuit invited me in, but I needed a big buy-in." He finally took a ragged breath, winced, and dropped a hand to his side.

"Three grand wouldn't be enough, would it."

Randy shook his head again. "My friend knew a guy who would stand me the money, if I had some collateral, like some property, like that. My car's a piece of crap, y'know?" Swallowed hard. "I gave him the deed to Grampie's house. The whole property, the whole thing. Teo's place, the trailer. I don't have a deed just for my place. It's all like, family. All tied together. It's a mess."

Big time. "You played the game, and it was really close, but you lost at the last minute, last hand, just when you thought you'd pull it off, big money on the table." Grant leaned back in his seat.

"How'd you guess?"

"It wasn't a game, it was a scam. You were the target, real estate was the goal. On the rez, just short of the border. Your buddy set you up with coyotes or narcos, looking for a safe house, and a mark who'd be too freaked out to go to the police."

"It's not like that." Randy jabbed the keychain, watching it swing. "I've got some time to buy it back. They'll let me make installments, even, but I gotta get them the first part by Sunday."

"What were you planning to do if you lost? Never mind—you're good at this, you weren't going to lose."

Randy's head lowered, but Grant heard him mutter, "Fucking self-righteous son of a bitch."

"Damn straight. What does Teo have to do with this?"

Randy's shoulders hunched. For a long time, they just sat there, Grant letting the silence carry the weight of the question. Finally, Randy said, "I told him we should check on the cache, after the break-in, y'know? To make sure it was safe. The minute I said it, it was like I had—anyway, he was super-worried, so we headed out there right away."

Glossing over the fact that Teo knew where it was, but Randy, an actual family member, didn't. Good thinking, Frank. The old man knew who he could trust. "But it hadn't been disturbed," Grant prompted.

"I started digging, Teo got upset, but I needed that stuff, something, anything. And it's my family, too! I should have some say in it, right?" He flashed a look at Grant, then hurried on as if he knew he didn't want the answer to that question. "So I start taking the stuff out, wrapping the blanket around it, and he's still objecting, but not loud. A few little things fell out of the bundle. He darts his hand down and grabs something, and just—takes off! With our family legacy! I don't even know what he got, but something small, and had to be valuable, right? Like a coin or something, right? Or why bother? I take off after him, and I grab him. Show me your hands, I say, but he doesn't have anything. I start searching his pockets. It's not his family, I don't care how long he's been hanging around, sponging off our grandparents. He's not even a tribal member. But I can't find it, and I knew he took something, I knew it. It's like he swallowed it or something, like a drug mule, right? Isn't that how he got across the border in the first place? I started shaking him, trying to make him cough it up." His hands gripped each other over the steering wheel, as if playing out the scene, and Grant could picture Teo there, trying to protect something, some small part of the Manuel legacy, but unwilling to hurt a member of the family to do it.

"I was just so mad about him taking our things, y'know? It was like—" Randy's eyes brightened and he turned on Grant. "It was like them building the wall, right down the middle of the rez, cutting off half of our land, or like the whites coming here in the first place—taking things that don't belong to them!"

"Because they're so desperate for land or money that they can't keep their hands to themselves."

"Yeah! Yes, exactly." Randy slapped the steering wheel, grinning as if he'd won something. Grant stared at him, seeing a lot of their grandmother in his face, watching his grin become fixed, become a grimace, until his gaze dropped, and his own hands clenched the wheel again.

"Sounds like you've got some praying to do. Let's go."

Not looking at him, Randy went through the motions: checking the mirror, using his ticker, staring at the road. He eased the car back into traffic and kept driving, until Grant said, "Pull in here."

"The church is a little further." Randy pointed.

"There's a pharmacy. We need to get that wound cleaned up and get a fresh bandage on. Maybe something manufactured this century. It's not bad, but we don't want it to get worse." They stopped in the parking lot and Grant reached for his door.

"What about stitches?"

"Negative. The damage is mostly epidermal and subcutaneous, but shallow. Can't be bridged with sutures. You'll have to wait it out."

Randy grunted. "And you know that 'cause you've seen it. Or you've had it happen to you. Or both." He stared straight ahead toward the ornate tower of the mission church just down the block. "Okay if I wait here? It stings like a—" he didn't finish the sentence.

When Grant returned in six minutes and seventeen seconds, first aid supplies in hand, the parking lot stood empty.

CHAPTER EIGHTEEN

Securing the final stitch in Hammer's wounded throat, Adam snipped the suture thread and stepped back. "You're certain our contact called him, 'Grant?'"

"Yes, sir, one hundred percent. Clearly they knew each other, and were familiar with the artifacts." Hammer wrapped a bandage around his throat, glowering at his reflection in the bathroom mirror. "Casey has experience. Some kind of military. Too quick, too smart. That's no excuse. I should've been smarter, sir. I could have taken them out, then gone for the basket."

"The basket was the critical thing, though this incident does leave us with a few potential issues." Not least of which was the problem of Casey. Not just an interfering family member. How had he shown up just then, moments after Adam got the call? It made Adam feel twitchy.

Hammer's jaw clenched, perhaps to conceal a wince as he swallowed past the cut. "Sir, I apologize for my failure to take care of it right away. I hate to have failed you on my first mission."

Yes, he had failed. On the other hand, when Casey had held a knife to his throat, Hammer hadn't rolled over, he had fought back. Was it time for an exit interview? Adam performed a quick calculation of the possible scenarios: discard Hammer as a failed candidate? Or embed him even deeper? He gripped Hammer's shoulder, meeting his eye in the mirror. "We'll take care of the loose ends. I've already set some things in motion."

During his dinner with the sheriff, his intention had been merely to discredit the dead, but any suspicions he'd planted then would now serve them well. Would the cousins call in law enforcement of their own, that was the question. The more extreme his own actions, the more credible Casey would look. Yet if he failed to act, the witnesses would mount against him. It seemed clear to Adam that Casey had followed him outside, and overheard the phone call. No other hypothesis fit. Was there any chance that Casey had other information? That he had some idea what he had stumbled into? If Adam could just get them in the desert, the probabilities would all collapse into alignment with his own plans.

In the other room, his computer chimed. Adam pulled away, wiping his hands on a towel. "Stay silent."

"Yes, sir." Hammer followed him back into the office, but sat to one side, well away from the screen.

Adam keyed the program open and sat down in front of the screen. Once the connection spiraled into being, he also triggered another program, something simple, subtle. The Finance Committee wanted their money, as did he. He was done playing the Warden's games. It was time to play a few of his own.

"Warden. Thank you for responding so promptly to my message."

"It is my pleasure." As ever, he saw only his informant's hands, the small book off to one side. "You say that you have found it?"

Reaching to one side, he retrieved the basket and held it in front of the camera.

"Yes," the Warden breathed.

"I don't know if you can make this out, but these threads here form the outline of a Gila monster." He tilted the basket, his finger tracing a series of wrappings laid slightly off from the rest. A small label hung at the back, as if it had been a museum display at some point.

"So it is meant to resemble the tribal pattern, but it has been altered to suit the purposes of concealment. Ingenious. How do you plan to proceed?"

"The prisoner camp lies close to the Gila River in Phoenix. I think that's our starting point. Does the diary mention what we're looking for next?"

The ancient hands leafed through a few pages. "The writer worked with Rosemary, but he wasn't one of the principals unfortunately. Still, one can narrow down the possibilities. Any landmarks would have to be things in existence during the 1940's, places the prisoners would have seen or known about. Their movements were limited—the routes to and from their work details, primarily, though they were frequently able to slip away."

"And after the escape, Commander Wattenberg eluded capture for a month—he had plenty of time to reconnoiter the area."

The hands came together. "Indeed."

Adam turned his camera to face the map of the county spread on his wall, and indicated the area between Phoenix and the border, from the prison camp to the promised land of Mexico, where the escaped Nazi's believed they would make their way to the ports and return to the fight in Europe. From this aerial perspective, he could almost trace the pattern of the basket's darker threads. "Through here? I and my team are familiar with the area, Warden. I'm confident we can identify the location." Lifting the camera, Adam placed himself in the center of the map, holding up the basket to one side. "Now that we have acquired the basket, when should we expect the next payment? My organization is eager to move forward with our plans."

"Naturally. But I think we must first confirm that the map does, indeed, continue. It is entirely possible that the destination has been obscured, or even obliterated in the intervening decades."

At the other side of the room, Hammer sat immobile, or nearly so. His chin tucked as if he were withdrawing from the scene. Mistake, letting him sit in. Adam's smile felt forced. "You seemed quite confident in our prior conversations."

"Follow where the basket leads, Mr. Lones. Show me what you find there, and I shall be assured of the course we are taking. Good evening." The window went blank, and a small red symbol flashed to indicate the closed connection.

Adam dropped his smile. He slid back into his chair and replaced the camera.

"That sounded—"

Adam put up his hand, and Hammer stopped speaking immediately. Tapping keys and opening tabs, Adam brought up another window, an error message stamped across it. He hit "refresh," leaning in as if he could will the program to work. The window cleared, showing a low-angle view of a desktop, a broad expanse of old leather, an edge of oak, a chair. Beyond that, a wall at an angle to the view, and a painting of a man in a full, black military uniform. Adam zoomed, widening the window, eagerly searching the uniform for any sign of insignia, but the view grew hazy. The camera he had connected to had limited power. It could be an SS uniform. It could just as well be Salvation Army. He'd been hoping for a window, anything he could use to identify the Warden's location, at least, much less their identity. No matter, he was in: his back-door to the Warden's camera clearly transmitting. He slid the window to the back of his desktop and straightened.

"We have some work to do in the morning, Hammer. Will you be ready?"

"Sir, I am aware I didn't handle the basket retrieval up to your standards—I need the chance to redeem myself."

"Excellent. I need you to pick up some things, so we can take care of one of those loose ends."

CHAPTER NINETEEN

Even the next morning, Jamie's head pulsed with the after effects of the wine, not to mention the interruption of her evening. Looking forward to getting home and crashing into bed, she had walked in the door to a ringing phone. Given her job, it could be anything and anyone, and she couldn't afford to miss it. Tossing her keys into the bowl on the hall table, she grabbed the receiver. "You've reached Jamie Li Rizzo, what can I do for you?"

"Sheriff Rizzo, Grant Casey. I trust you had a good meal."

So much for the pleasantries. Adam's concerns echoed in the back of her mind. He'd questioned Casey's true role, now here was the man himself, bothering her at her home number. "Is this something we can handle during office hours?"

"Just a quick question. Maybe two. The wreckage from the burglary at the tribal center. Did the torn baskets include one with a lot of red fibers?"

"How should I know? I didn't memorize them."

A beat, then he said, "Understood. When you have the opportunity, I'd appreciate it if you can scan over the images and see. A basket about the size of your hand, with lots of red and black fibers. Red is uncommon. You'll know it if you see it."

"Right. Is that all?"

"Adam Lones. How well do you know him?"

"Absolutely not your business. Now are we through?" In his crate by the kitchen, Buster gave a quiet whine, reflecting his master's anxiety.

"One more, Ma'am. You asked about bones. We didn't get to talk about that back at the office. You found one in Teo's stomach, am I right? It did come from the cache, but I don't know yet what it means. Anything more you can tell me about it?"

Dangerous bones. Casey's translation of the victim's muttering. "It's being analyzed by someone at the Uni. They haven't gotten back to me."

"Thank you, Ma'am. The individual responsible for the assault on Teo is Randy Manuel. Unfortunately, I don't know his current whereabouts. I don't believe he was related to the burglary. Sorry to bother you." He rang off before she had a chance to ask about Manuel. His cousin, presumably, whom he had now accused of assault, possibly attempted murder. No wonder he was so popular with the family. On the other hand, he'd given her more information than he got—an interesting exchange.

Rizzo tried to set aside his questions, but she still didn't get to sleep until she'd scrolled through the digital images from the crime scene. No red fibers in the shredded baskets. What the Hell. He referred to it as a "burglary," now he pointed toward something missing. She had pulled up some photos from the center's renovation grand re-opening a few years back, squinting over the shoulders of proud tribal members to see into the cases they posed near. Sure enough, down low in a glass case full of baskets, along with a number of version of that man-with-the-maze thing, and lots of striking abstract patterns, she spotted the red and black basket. Low, as if they were trying to hide it. No doubt, the piece came accompanied by some words about how the symbol had been co-opted by the Nazi's. Working the pattern in black made sense, fit in with their culture and all, but outlining the piece in red? You couldn't pass that off as coincidence. Why display it at all? Still, if somebody were going to wreck the place and steal one thing, that would be it. Fine, burglary. Still didn't make it anything but an act of fury.

She had let Buster into the yard for a bit, then gone to bed, pulling a sleep mask over her eyes, her head rustling into a buckwheat pillow. No sleep. Chris Anderson didn't strike her as a Nazi, not neo-, not old-school. He read up on secrets of the rich-and-famous, maybe he thought he could join them by selling the piece. If he had taken the basket, he'd gotten rid of it before he got back to the hotel. Have another chat with Anderson, or take a closer look around his apartment, maybe both. If Adam were right, and Casey was behind the break-in, presumably he already had the basket, and that's why he knew it had been missing, rather than destroyed. Now Casey tried to cast doubt on someone else in his family. What kind of person turned in his own cousin? Either somebody super honest, or super guilty. One way and another, there was nothing to be done until the morning.

CHAPTER TWENTY

G rant woke as dawn stretched across the bed where he lay. Teo's house, sure to be empty, unlikely to be a target of any follow-up from yesterday's attack—only he and Randy knew the place was empty. Cece would be done at the observatory by now, and had probably gotten his message, brief, and not too informative. Teo hospitalized, Randy upset, hopefully not going off either suicidal or murderous. More likely, he was holed up accessing E-bay to auction off what remained of the sacred cache. So far as Grant's surveillance of the premises revealed, Randy's place was empty, too. What would he say to Cece when she arrived? He felt reticent to expose Randy's stupidity, but no amount of panic or money would be worth what he'd done to Teo.

Half of the long, narrow converted storehouse now provided Teo with a kitchen/living room, and a bedroom. The other half, from his recollection, contained storage and workshop space. On the wall between hung a crucifix and a Bible quote: Matthew 25:35 *I was hungry, and you gave me meat; I was thirsty, and you gave me drink; I was a stranger, and you took me in.* Words that Teo might take readily to heart. He had been crossing the desert forty years ago, hoping for a better life, hoping to escape the increasing drug-fueled violence of his home land of Columbia. When he staggered over the border, Rosemary found him and brought him home. Never knew how Frank felt about that, but as Teo recovered and made himself useful around the fields and the horses, he gradually became part of the family. During

Rosemary's decline, he tended her just as once she had tended him. While Frank tried to raise an increasingly fractious grandson and preside over everything else.

Grant found himself oatmeal and instant coffee for breakfast, then began a methodical search of Teo's small home. Kitchen built into a corner, with a small stove, and everything for a bachelor life. In the years Grant had known him, Teo never brought home a woman. No telephone—he used Frank's when he had to—on the bedside table, a few books from the library: thriller, romance—whatever was new, apparently. And alongside those, a few larger books with familiar titles: *The Story of Peking Man, Arizona During the Second World War*, a couple of books about submarines, all from the shelf in Grant's old room. The popular fiction, sure, but Teo could've read the history books any time. Apparently, Randy wasn't the only one who'd been hearing about Papago Park, where the crew of several captured U-boats were imprisoned during the war, and from which, a number of men had escaped, digging a tunnel over a period of weeks, to slip into the surrounding desert on Christmas Eve. Most of them had been picked up soon enough, but a couple of the so-called Super Nazis remained in hiding for more than a month. Frank, barely out of high school himself then, had been one of the trackers hunting them down. Just the kind of thing to get a kid interested in history.

His phone rang twice. Stopped, rang again, and he answered. "Casey."

"Chief, it's D.A. You won't believe what we got on this guy Lones. I'm dropping a dossier in your box. You got a way to receive it?"

Grant turned back to the kitchen. A tower computer sat on the floor beside a wobbly table covered with its peripherals. "Affirmative." He walked over and poked the power button. No log-in screen. This far in the middle of nowhere, folks didn't worry so much about security. Over the computer, a faded poster of Lynda Carter as Wonder Woman. The only time he and Randy got along was when they were invited to join Teo's personal ritual: *Wonder Woman* re-runs.

"His surface material's squeaky clean, or should I say, just messy enough that it won't raise alarms. Parents murdered when he was in high school, made a good recovery, went to college on the pity money. Now he's in real estate, mostly. Diversified portfolio. He's been in negotiations for a huge parcel of land coming on the market up in Washington state. A lot of properties in the same area have been sold in the last few years, and if you dig deep enough, you see he's been involved in a lot of them. Shell corporations, that kind of thing."

"That's what he does, right? Maybe on behalf of clients who'd rather not be named. Washington seems a little out of the way, though." Grant slid into the seat at the computer desk and started navigating to the file retrieval system D.A. had created for the Bone Guard. DSL on the rez. Very nice.

"All of his Pacific Northwest deals lead back to a group that calls itself the Sons of a New America."

Her edgy tone caught his attention. Grant's fingers hesitated over the keyboard. "What did you find?"

"Their whole website is coded white supremacist bullshit, Chief. The whole thing is a freakin' dog whistle to trolls and assholes. I don't know what they're up to, but I don't think they're building a baseball diamond. His Arizona gig seems to be all about the wall, shutting out immigrants, political activism. You need help taking this guy down, you let me know, okay?"

"First point: nothing you've said indicates a crime. There's some separatist groups who want to set up self-governance in that region. They're obnoxious, but not criminal. Second point: I might need help, but—no offense, D.A.,—I'm not sure sending a Jewish woman into a neo-Nazi organization would produce actionable intel."

She let out a snort of laughter. "Got that right, Chief. I'd rather produce some busted heads. What else can I do?"

"I need you to set up some searches, looking for a new cache of Tohono O'Odham artifacts coming on the market. E-bay, maybe, maybe some kind of back-room offers. I let the seller believe the stuff is pretty valuable, so he might be approaching museums."

"This the guy you were driving with yesterday? Want me to set up as a buyer, see what comes of it? We still have that gallery website we set up for the sting in San Francisco."

"Sure, go ahead."

"So, Chief, awkward questions... Is this a case? Are you the client?"

He lifted the edge of the kitchen curtain, his grandfather's house across the yard in the growing sunlight. "Looks like it."

"What's that thing Nick says? It's supposed to be details, not ops. Especially not ops where you're personally involved. Maybe this is one to turn over to local law enforcement."

"The lead investigative officer hired Lones as her campaign finance manager."

"Yikes. K, then, do what you have to." The phone beeped into silence.

Grant started decrypting the files she had set up, and stalked back to the other room, the phone still in his hand, weighing heavy. Finally, he lifted it and tapped another contact.

"Detective Gonsalves, talk to me."

"Gooney. Do you have any vacation time coming up?"

"What the fuck, Casey! My life's just about back to normal, and you pop up again. My last so-called vacation with you resulted in a broken arm and the mother of all suntans."

Same old Gooney. "It's your tan I wanted to talk to you about."

"I don't have one, Casey. Unlike the rest of you, I've gotta work at it."

"Perfect. I need a white guy."

Gooney hooted with laughter on the other end of the phone. "Oh, Jesus, do I even want to know what this is about?"

Just asking the question told Grant he was already hooked. "I need an experienced operative to infiltrate a white separatist organization and figure out whether they or their leadership is up to anything illegal. They have a cell down here in Arizona—go to the Bone Guard server and you can get D.A.'s files."

"You want somebody to go play Nazi. What makes you think I'm the man for the job?"

"I need somebody who can operate unsupervised, without contact."

Silence for a long moment, then Gooney's voice, more serious. "Sounds like a high-risk potential."

"They've only tried to kill me once so far."

"Shit." Muttering and clicking echoed softly from Gooney's office back in Boston. Finally, he returned. "You better get me on payroll and insurance for this one—I've got an ex to support."

Payroll and insurance. An implicit statement that he was sending Gooney behind enemy lines, to a place from which he might never return. "Absolutely. I'd hate for your ex to run out of champagne."

"In that case, next time I see you, I'll pretend I don't know who you are. Bye, Casey."

A shelf running around the top of the room held curiosities: strangely shaped pieces of wood, a few fossils, black and white photos from reservation history, and some more recent; a dozen of the little hand-made shrines Teo had loved. Grant brought in one of the heavy wooden chairs from the kitchen and climbed on top, studying the photographs. Too many in black and white. Teo hadn't come to the country until around 1980, long after the advent of color photography, and Grant wasn't aware that he'd brought a photo album along with him.

Now that he saw the photos more closely, he recognized a number of them, shots of Rosemary and Frank, shots that used to hang in the corners over at Frank's house. Grant came home from school the first day he had gone back after her death only to find all the photos of her vanished. Another brick in the wall between him and Frank. Teo rescued them from the trash and added them to his own collection of shrines. These mingled with more contemporary shots—Grant's mother looking painfully young, Cece's dad at her side, and his uncle Matt, still in short pants; Grant himself on Thunder at a barrel-racing competition, focused on victory. Maybe the very day Thunder went down with a broken leg. The day Frank, without a word, handed him a gun to shoot the only living thing he loved.

He had to focus now, tuning out the newer photos. Whatever was going on had something to do with his grandmother's history, and the Nazis she had known. Gooney's involvement made the stakes clear.

A few minutes into his perusal, his phone pinged with an incoming text from D.A.: *Gooney says to set him up on payroll. SRSLY?*

Senior status, full access, company insurance active immediately, esp. Death and dismemberment. The most expensive damn policy they had, given their line of work. The policy he hoped they'd never have to pay out.

Wishful thinking?

He chuckled. In spite of their rocky relationship, Gooney came through in Mongolia, big time. *Need him to infiltrate.*

Hiel Gooney!

You got it.

Slipping the phone away, he got back to work. A few photos showed Rosemary at various occupations, teaching basket-making, picking cotton during the war years. In one shot, a half-dozen young men and a few women posed with their harvest, white bolls of cotton poking from baskets. Rosemary smiled from the front row. The guy next to her had the distinctive "PW" painted on his pantlegs, marking him as a prisoner of war. Pay dirt. Grant took the image down, thick paper with blunted corners, yellowing tape peeled off the edges. Thicker than it should be, the back glossy. Turning it over, Grant found a very different image, another photo taped to the back, a sea-scape with an edge of a railing crossing in front of the waves. An arm and hand thrust into the image at a strange angle, clearly the photographer's; and in the hand, as if it smiled for a selfie, a patch-work skull.

If it had been a human skull, Grant might have dismissed the image as a grizzly war memento, but the receding forehead and protruding jaw signaled something else entirely. He sank down into the chair, holding the photo in the light of the small window. Partially white, partially reddish-brown, the skull stared back at him with gaping eye-sockets, resisting any attempt to make sense of it. The photo, associated as it was with the POW's on the front, seemed likely to have come from one of them. Papago Park, the prison camp everyone was talking about, contained the crews of captured or sunken German submarines. The picture, taken on the deck of a ship, didn't contain enough detail to work out what kind of ship it might be—it could as well be the top deck of a submarine as anything else. That skull...something seized from a museum? Submariners weren't like other soldiers, they didn't do sorties or occupy towns, they didn't loot museums, and might never even see their enemy. U-boats existed only to sink other ships, and they didn't have a lot of room to pick up souvenirs. Slowly, Grant turned back to the nightstand with its incongruous pile of books. U-boats, Arizona During the Second World War... Peking Man. *Dangerous bones.*

CHAPTER TWENTY-ONE

Adam waited around the corner from a nondescript, low apartment building, checking his watch. He had a map to trace, but this, too, was important. He wore casual clothes a little tight, his hair brushed up, his shoes down-market. Every possibility his clients wouldn't recognize him; it was a guise he had worn only once before. A dark sedan drove past and parked opposite. Two men emerged, one of them pin-sharp and professional, the other looking disheveled in borrowed clothing, off-size. Tall and sandy-haired, scruffy with a few days' growth of his beard. Time to pretend he was attractive.

As the pair approached the front of the building. Adam prepared himself—or rather, his persona, lurking at an angle where they were unlikely to notice him.

"I can't begin to thank you, Mr. Remington. You're sure you don't need my statement?" Chris Anderson didn't sound nearly as cocky as the first time they had met.

"We'll get to that, don't worry. For now, Chris, I really think you need to get some rest."

His brow furrowed. "I don't want to waste time that we need to work on my defense. Especially if word got out about my arrest—I need to prove my innocence."

"Of course you do. I'll start following up on what you remembered. But you'll be more helpful if you get a little break. Take a shower, and get into your own clothes."

Chris glanced down at his prison clothes. "They took my jacket into evidence?"

"I'm afraid so. But at least you got your shoelaces back, right?" Remington chuckled and clapped his "client" on the shoulder. "I'll give you a call later today to set up for the deposition. Word of warning: the police have searched your apartment, so a few things may be missing—that'll be in the inventory you signed for, but it's likely to feel strange. If you have a friend you can call, you might feel better with some company."

"Yeah, maybe I'll do that. Thanks, thank you." Chris shook his head, his entire body, really, as if casting off the last two days. He squared his shoulders and put his key to the lock. Remington gave a short, professional wave, and pivoted to walk back to his car.

As Chris stepped through the door, Adam slid from the alley. "Chris! Hey, wait—Chris—is that you?"

Chris jumped and spun about as Adam stepped into the foyer. Chris stood, shoulders hunched, pushed back against the glass wall into the stairwell, one hand braced against the rank of mailboxes. "Shit! Who are you?"

Adam let himself sag a little bit. "You don't remember me?" He sighed. "I guess we were both pretty drunk. I guess...sorry. I thought you might..." He held up his hands and started to back away, as if he were the man who'd been cornered.

Chris frowned, then stepped away from the wall. "Wait a minute, wait." He pointed at Adam, finger wagging a little. "You do look a little familiar."

Laughing, Adam said, "Well, I should hope so, after what we did! I mean, I know it wasn't my face you were focused on, but I hope at least parts of me were memorable."

His cheeks reddening, Chris looked down. He sidled a little further forward, head cocked, then took a little breath in through his nose, and his eyes widened. "You're the guy I picked up that night, on my bike. Did I take you to a hotel? The Desert Palms?" His whole demeanor charged with excitement. Bingo. Chris needed him. All Adam had to do was convince him of it.

Adam did put up his hands then. "Shh, shh. I told you, I need to be discreet." He glanced around.

Chris glanced around as well and looked a little more wary, the keys clutched in his hand. "How did you find me?"

"You really don't remember much, do you. You told me to call you? Gave me the address?" Adam bit his lip and let it go. "I heard about the—" He dropped his voice to a whisper—"the arrest. I knew you were a bad boy, but really." He flared his eyes like he found the whole thing exciting.

"Right." Chris straightened. "I'm innocent. I was totally passed out when it happened—that's why I need your help. Look, you mind if I call my lawyer? He can—"

"God, no! I can't, no way." Adam stumbled back.

"Hey, hey, it's okay." Chris practically pounced after him. "Don't go yet. Can you come up?" He gave a nervous chuckle. "I didn't mean that the way it sounded. I just need to talk."

Adam matched the nervous laugh, dropping his gaze, bringing it up again. "No, really, I should just go. I just—" He backed off again, as if in a dance, drawing Chris a little closer.

"No, wait—don't." Chris spread his hands in desperate plea. "If you remember anything from that night, Jesus, Man, I could really use your help." He fumbled the keys again, rushing with the inside lock. "I really need to talk with you. Please? I won't call the lawyer, just you and me."

Crossing his arms, biting his lip, a little worried he was playing it too strong, Adam hesitated. When the inside door stood open before him, Chris holding it open like a doorman, or like an expectant date, Adam wavered, and finally stepped inside, playing it cautious, letting himself be convinced. He followed Chris up a flight of concrete and metal steps to the door of an apartment. "I'm lucky you came by," Christ said.

"I've drive past a couple of times. I wasn't sure when you'd...get out." Adam followed him inside, the door clicking shut behind them. He glanced around, taking in the contemporary artworks on the walls, dove gray sofa, sleek furnishings, shelves of books.

Chris chuckled then, a little shyly. "I know, not what you were expecting right? I get that a lot. Not that I bring a lot of guys up here, I don't!" He hung the keys on a hook. "Hey, make yourself at home, okay?" He edged toward the short hallway—bathroom, bedroom, office could be seen through doors left open by the police. "I'll be right back, I'm just dying to get cleaned up." He kept looking back at Adam, as if afraid he would go. "There should be coffee, but I can't vouch for the milk." He pointed toward a single-cup coffee maker in the corner of the neat kitchen.

"Thanks, I take it black." Adam started walking that direction. "You don't mind my helping myself?"

"No, go ahead. The police have already been all over this place. I'm so glad you came. I was just talking to my lawyer about how we could find you." His gaze wandered again, then back to Adam, tracing his figure as if he were a dream come true. "Mugs are by the sink."

"Take your time."

Chris hesitated in the hallway. "It would've helped a lot if you'd come forward once you knew I'd been arrested."

"I'm sorry, I really am." Adam sagged against the counter, stuffing his hands under his arms so he wasn't tempted to touch anything. "It's my job, my family. I'm not like you—I'm not—confident about who I am."

"You're still in the closet."

Nodding weakly. "I'm not that brave."

Chris blew out a breath. "I get it, Man."

"But I want to help you. You shouldn't go down for something you didn't do. I mean, we just need to find a way to..." He shrugged.

"Discreet. I understand. Just—give me a few minutes."

Adam shooed him toward the hallway with a brave-face smile, then turned back toward the cabinets, reaching toward the coffeemaker, watching the blurred reflection in the black steel fridge as Chris stripped off his shirt and stepped into the bedroom. Adam pulled on a pair of rubber gloves, held his hands behind him as if he were shy. He turned on his heel and stalked down the hall, mustering a guilty schoolboy air. He stepped through the door, and Chris spun about, stumbling as he moved too quickly, and ended up sitting on the bed, shirtless, his pants around his ankles. Convenient positioning.

Adam feigned shock, then slowly smiled. "I need to stop freaking you out like that, I am so sorry."

Chris blinked back at him, breath racing. "I thought you were making coffee."

"I was just thinking, if you need to relax, I mean. I know a way." He winked and took another step forward. "Maybe two."

A single laugh. "That's a nice offer, seriously. But now's really not the time."

"Are you sure?" Adam stepped again, forcing Chris to lean back to gain a little space. "I mean, this whole thing...bad boy, wrongful arrest—I've never been anybody's alibi before, it's kind of hot, y'know?"

Too strong. Chris's wariness returned. "I'm really not in the mood. Look, maybe you should just leave me your number, and I can call you in a little while." He started to rise.

With a rush of strength, Adam grabbed his chin and shoved him back against the bed, pinning him there left-handed. His right hand came around with the syringe. He shoved it into Chris's nostril as the other man began to struggle. Adam pressed the plunger, filling Chris's skull with enough fentanyl to knock down a horse. Chris's eyes flew wide, his throat working though he could produce only strangled grunts of protest. His tangled feet kicked impotently. He slapped at Adam's hand, grappling with him. Then the drug hit hard, and his body rocked, spasming, those dark eyes rolling back. Adam pulled away. He grabbed Chris's hand and wrapped it around the syringe, letting both fall onto the bed. Satisfied, he stepped back from the thrashing form, taking a moment to tug Chris's pants the rest of the way off, leaving him naked and sprawled on the bed, just as he had done before. Different drug this time. Turning away, Adam let himself out, shutting the door gently behind him. He rolled off the rubber gloves once he reached the street, tidily bundling one into the other as he walked away.

CHAPTER TWENTY-TWO

J amie glowered at the dashboard as her phone rang through. She sat at an intersection, staring at the back of a construction vehicle as it lumbered along the line of cones. Finally, the desk officer picked up. "Hey, Sheriff."

"Martinez. Good morning. I'm on my way over there to talk to Chris Anderson. I've got a few more questions, but I'm stuck in traffic here. If the transport gets there before I do, can you let them know I'm coming?"

"Transport's been canceled."

"Perfect, no problem then."

"Actually, his attorney showed up and bailed him out."

That pushed her back in her seat. "His attorney? Last night, he didn't have an attorney."

"Yes, Ma'am. Just a minute."

She drummed her fingers on the wheel, and inched forward as the road-ripper moved aside.

"Here it is. Leroy Remington. Never heard of him, but the paperwork looks legit."

"Office address?"

"Sorry, the card he left just has a number. It's all properly executed though. I passed it over to the clerk for filing."

"Text me the number—or better yet, send me a shot of the card. And get a closer look at the paperwork. Find me an address for this guy." Remington. The name meant nothing to her, and she thought she knew all the guys who would take a case like this.

"Yes, Ma'am." Martinez rang off.

One speed bump after another. Fine. She'd head over to Anderson's place. She still had the spare keys, but his attorney might well have brought him over there to pick up some clothes. Chances are, Anderson wouldn't be too happy with whatever the jailors had found for him. Also, it would get her out of this damn traffic. Swerving out of the line, the cars around her too afraid of her official vehicle to honk, Jamie jolted into the other lane and made a hard turn at the next corner. The emergency light tempted her from its button on the dash, but she really had no justification for that. Being pissed at traffic made for a lousy excuse.

A few minutes later, she pulled up at the nondescript building, parked and considered leaving her duty belt, then decided to go for it. Stick with the regulations, especially in an election year. She strapped her belt on and strolled up to the door, hitting the buzzer for Anderson's apartment. No answer. The lawyer probably took him straight to the office for a deposition. Taking out the keys, she tried one, then the other of the larger keys. She let herself in and mounted the stairs, ringing the bell outside his door, and calling out, "It's Sheriff Rizzo. I'd like to have another look around." Still no answer, but she'd followed protocol. With a shrug, she opened the door. The place smelled like piss and she recoiled. Given how into body odor the guy seemed to be last night, she expected him to clean his bathroom more often than that. She didn't remember it smelling bad the first time they'd been inside, but some things did tend to ripen.

A shirt lay in the hallway between the bathroom and the bedroom, its door ajar. "Mr. Anderson?" The odor got stronger as she walked down the hall, her hand resting on the butt of her gun. She rounded the corner, spotting a pair of feet, still clad in white socks. Jamie kicked the door fully open and pounced into the room. Anderson lay sprawled half on the bed, arms flung wide, blood dribbling from one nostril, a syringe on the bed not far from his right hand. Shit—shit! She lunged for him, fingers pressed to the side of his throat. Something, anything! Was that a heartbeat, or was it the adrenaline streaking through her? His skin felt cold, his lips bluish. No visible rise and fall of the chest, though a soft gurgle issued from his throat.

Scooping one hand under his head, the other grabbing his upper arm, she hauled him onto the floor. She scraped her back against a half open drawer and stifled a curse. Flat, hard surface, prepping for CPR.

"Anderson!" she shouted, "Wake up!" as if dragging him onto the floor wouldn't be enough stimulation to wake him—if he were going to wake up. Ever.

From one of the bands on her duty belt, she yanked the sealed Narcan packet and tore it open. Inside rested a plastic tube with a nasal syringe. She pulled it open and applied it to the nostril that wasn't already leaking blood, then tossed it aside and began chest compressions, praying the drug was the miracle everybody claimed. Heel of her hand against his sternum, holding back the fingers with her other hand clasped over the top. Call for help. She needed to—he jerked under her hands. Anderson thrashed and coughed, flailing at her, slapping her hands, then punching as he came alert.

"Take it easy—It's Sheriff Rizzo. Hey, hey, take it easy."

He fought her, punching and scrambling backward. "Get off me! Get away from me!" His voice came out in a wheeze and he broke off, gasping for breath, one fist pressed against his chest. At the training they warned her that the addict might get angry when they came-to, or even fight off his rescuer. She shifted a little out of reach.

"Chris! It's the sheriff, for god's sake, calm down!" The Lord's name in vain. Her mother's disapproving face flashed before her eyes.

He slumped, gulping desperately, his other hand fumbling against the nightstand as if it searched for a weapon.

"Chris," she said, more gently now, on one knee before him, but keeping her distance. "It's me, Sheriff Rizzo. You're gonna be okay. You overdosed, but you're gonna be okay. Can you tell me what you took?"

"No!" he shouted, the power of his voice shocking her back. He shook violently, trembling all over, pulling his legs up, hunching away from her even as he fought for breath. His skin looked too pale, teeth chattering and lips still off-color.

She reached up and dragged the coverlet off the bed, coming close enough to toss it over his huddled knees. "Can you tell me who you are?"

"Chris, Anderson." He gulped again. "You know that." He snaked out an arm and wrapped the coverlet around him as best he could without rising, pulling it against his shoulders. He blinked a few times, his gaze growing more focused.

She nodded encouragingly. "Can you tell me where we are?"

He glanced around wildly. "My place. Scene of the fucking crime." After that long speech, he took a moment to recover.

"Okay," she muttered, more to herself than to him. Maybe whatever he took had mental as well as pulmonary effects. "Look, Chris. I'm going to call you an ambulance—"

He grabbed her hand as she brought up her radio, and his arm shook so badly that it rattled her, too. "Don't. Please. He, they, got me here, out of jail. Tried to kill me. He's—he'll know. Sheriff, please."

So. He knew who he was, he knew who she was, in spite of the fact that nothing else he said made any sense. He was pretty messed up, but medical care could probably wait a little while if the prospect of treatment was only going to make him worse. Carefully, she replaced the radio and settled herself, resting her hand over his where it clutched her wrist. "Okay, Chris. You say that someone tried to kill you. Can you tell me about that?"

"Record me." He tugged the blanket better into place around his shoulders. "With your phone. Something. So that if he gets me next time, you'll have the record."

"O—kay." Drugs could make a person get a little unhinged. Might as well humor him, at least until he calmed down enough to go nicely to the looney bin. If the drugs were addling his mind, that could explain why he didn't remember the break-in. And, as Adam implied, if he were an occasional user rather than habitual, it could exacerbate the effects. Jamie pushed the drawer closed and settled herself more comfortably. She pulled out her cell phone and brought up the camera, training it first on herself. She stated her name, the date, their location, then framed him in the camera's view. "Can you state your name, and confirm that I am filming at your request." Should make it legal enough.

"My name is Chris Anderson," he swallowed, and took a deeper breath. "I asked Sheriff Rizzo to make this recording in case I wind up dead." For a moment his eyes closed, then they reopened and he met her eyes for the first time as, in a shaky voice, he told her everything that led up to this moment from his elation at suddenly having a lawyer, to her saving his life. Partway through, her phone started to blink low battery, and she pulled a charging brick from another loop, plugging it in without interrupting. He went hoarse, trying to describe the man who had attacked him, and she paused to bring him a glass of water, biggest one she could find, then settled back into her spot, camera aimed at him. "...this horrible rush of—dread, darkness. I couldn't breathe, couldn't shout, I kept feeling his hand on my jaw, his body pressing me down."

He placed a shaky hand over his mouth, tears seeping from his eyes.

After a moment, she asked, softly, "Did he rape you?"

Chris shook his head, but with a shudder, an almost involuntary horror, and she guessed it still felt that way, his attacker bearing down on him, unable to escape as the darkness overwhelmed him. She clicked off and lowered the phone, glancing around the room with renewed interest. He sounded utterly credible, and his story, utterly bizarre. Chris hadn't seemed creative enough to spin a story like that off the top of his head. Smart enough to ask her to record him, though. "The man who attacked you. Did he touch anything?"

Chris blinked a few times, looked to the door, the bed, shoulders slumped. "I don't—he reached for the cabinet, as I was coming back here. Before that, he leaned against the counter, his hips. When he took his hands out, he was wearing gloves."

His beard concealed whatever bruising there might have been. The assailant was a pro, meticulous. Jesus, was she starting to believe him? He had been picked up at the jail half an hour ago, and the last people in the apartment before that had been her own team, searching for drugs: how had he even had time to acquire the drugs? "Look, you still need medical treatment—" She put up her hands to forestall the protest he was already beginning—"there's a clinic outside of town, they'll see you anonymously." She really should get him back to prison, but if he weren't making this up... "I'll pick you up there, and we'll go see a judge. If this lawyer, Remington, was in on it, then your release is illegal. I don't want you to get in more trouble, okay?"

He nodded miserably, wiping his face, then jerking as the sight of the blood. "I need to take a shower. Please." His voice sounded a little more steady.

"Yeah, okay. And you'll want to pack an overnight bag, couple of days maybe."

He swept the room with a glance. "No way in Hell I am coming back here." He tugged the coverlet around him as he swayed to his feet and shuffled past her toward the bathroom.

Using an evidence bag, she collected the syringe that had been lying by his hand, betting the only prints on it would be his. No evidence she could see, not even any trace, if his story were true. Nothing to confirm that it was. She stared at the syringe again. Nothing that could be seen by the human eye, maybe. "Hey Chris—how do you feel about dogs?"

CHAPTER TWENTY-THREE

B reakfast eaten, D.A.'s files digesting, Grant stepped out of Teo's little house into the growing day. Hammer and Lones had the basket, and presumably knew what they were looking for: the most famous missing person short of Amelia Earhart. Rizzo knew something, but she'd been asking him about bones, so apparently she wasn't in on the fact that her buddy was hunting the skeleton, or she didn't know enough to conceal their interest. Or she wasn't as close with Lones as Casey thought. File that away for later.

When he stopped in at Mission San Xavier, the caretaker told him Teo hadn't been there for a few days, but Teo's nailbeds showed flecks of paint. What else could Teo have been painting? In the brilliant Arizona sunlight, his grandfather's house practically glowed, tan stucco with a black decorative band. The pattern ran around the entire outside, the image Grant had seen so often he'd almost forgotten. Man-in-the-maze, a classic Tohono O'odham symbol, shown on the tribal border signs, among other places. Woven by his grandmother into a basket worth killing for.

Grant imagined the scene, Teo working on the house, maybe with Randy's help, while Frank sat inside, sharing a cup of iced tea with Adam Lones, talking about baskets. Teo getting worried, starting to add things up in his mind, and borrowing some books from Grant's old room. Later on, Randy convincing Teo to show him the cache, just to make sure everything was alright.

Approaching his boyhood home like a crime scene, Grant walked a slow circuit around the outside. The painted figure of the man stood near the door, maybe inviting, except for the two shallow marks where its face would be, as if its eyes were closed. One time, he made the mistake of asking why his grandfather had a painting of a dead man by the door. The old man swatted him for that, but his grandmother explained the man was just sleeping. To the north and east, the band of black paint showed a few squared-off bulges, to the south, the final rise and fall, the round mark of what would be the center. Nothing white, like the paint on Teo's hands. Huh. Nothing had disturbed the dirt around the base of the house, no rain, so it retained the scuff marks he'd noticed when he first arrived. Signs of a possible break-in? Or just signs of the work being done? Grant paused in his perusal. On the horizon, a plume of dust arose from an approaching vehicle, a glint of blue. Looked like the truck. Still... He stepped into the shade of the house, near what had originally made him pause: a pair of square indents in the dry earth. Ladder tracks. Pressing his hands into the sides of a window frame, Grant hoisted himself onto the sill, then grabbed the roof joists where the eaves stuck out to block the afternoon sun. He crept his feet up the wall, got one arm onto the roof, and pushed himself up over the edge. He kept low as the sound of the truck approached. Fingertips of one hand braced on the low-angled roof, he scanned the tarpaper. Black, flecked with white. It looked as if Teo had been painting something up here and carelessly dripped a few marks, but why? He snapped a photo of the spatters.

Cece pulled into the yard and killed the engine., Grant waited a moment longer, letting her climb out of the truck and call his name. Satisfied that she came alone, Grant stood up. "Cece. Up here." He walked to the front of the house. Shielding her eyes, she tipped her head back. He couldn't see her face.

"Grant? What's going on? Your message didn't make any sense—why might Randy want to kill himself?"

He squatted near the edge. "Have you spoken with him?"

"He called me after you did, telling me you were that angry at him, that he couldn't come home." She planted her other hand on her hip. "That true, Grant?"

He sighed. "Yes, ma'am. He broke into the sacred cache."

"That doesn't make any sense—I don't think he even knows where it is."

"He didn't. Teo did." Cece, the sacred cache. The paint marks. He glanced back at the roof. "Can you come up here? I think you should see this."

Her scowl deepened. "I know you and Randy never got along, but accusing him of something like that—I don't even know what to say. Fighting with Randy, climbing all over things—like some wild teenager. My lord, Grant, I'd've thought you'd grow out of all that."

Maybe he'd grown into it instead. "Cece. I'd rather that Randy told you his part himself, because it's not going to sound good coming from me." Or from Randy, for that matter, but at least she might believe it from her own brother.

"My own brother's afraid of you, Grant Casey. You get down here and tell me what's happening, and you tell me now."

He braced the fingers of one hand on the roof, then jumped down, landing lightly, knees bent, a few feet from her. She stepped back swiftly, coming against the cab of the truck. The glint of her eye stung more than he cared to notice. "Cece, Randy's been gambling. Maybe he started at the casino, I don't know. He got into a high-stakes, private game and put up the deed to this house as the surety for his bet. I believe they set him up as a mark to get the property. He broke into the cache—"

"What the hell? Grant, what are you even—" She broke off, shaking her head, her body shifted as if she'd retreat from him even further if she had the chance.

Grant spread his hands, low and open, demonstrating in the universal language that he meant no harm. "He broke into the cache to see if he could sell some family heirlooms and get the money men off his back."

"If any of that is true—" she sucked down a breath. "Teo. You told me he's in the hospital. The doc said somebody tried to kill him. You're saying that was Randy? That my own brother tried to kill a man who's been like a second father to us both?"

Grant let his hands fall, the barrage of words assaulting him. "He is a desperate man, Cece."

"No," she said, strongly, then ferociously, "No! Maybe he was a jerk to you when we were kids, but this has gone way too far. You need to go." She pointed toward him, then swept her arm toward the road. "Get out of here, out of my grandfather's house." She blinked rapidly, trying to clear her tears. Shadows ringed her eyes from nights at the observatory and days when she should have been resting, but had to worry over her family instead.

Grant retreated. "I'll get a room at the Motel 6. You'll know—"

"Why don't you just fly home? To whatever it is that passes for your home? Why'd you even have to come here, upsetting Grampie, taking up some stupid feud you should've left behind in high school."

Because his work there wasn't done. What did pass for his home?

"Let me get my things." He walked around the truck toward Teo's, where he had spent the night, and she turned, tracking his path.

"You broke into Teo's place? My God, Grant, I should have you arrested. Is that what you've been doing the last fifteen years? I told my kids you were some kind of hero. What the hell did I know?"

He walked efficiently across the yard, mentally armoring up. Civilians would have their own concerns, a long-past CO had told him. They'll take it out on you. They won't understand, and they'll pick the status quo every time. You stay calm, stay strong, stay focused on the mission. So much for being a civilian himself. Inside, he scooped up his bag, her words echoing after him

"I'm calling a car to take you to the airport!"

"I have a car parked up the street," he called back. Among a cluster of stones and an old trailer, where it wouldn't be noticed. A moment's hesitation, then he took the photo of the mysterious skull and slipped it into his pocket.

"To think I had a crush on you. That I was proud of you." She was sobbing by the time he emerged, shutting the door quietly behind him.

Stung like the sands of Afghanistan. "Cecile—"

"Don't you dare try and defend yourself now."

Across the yard, the Sleeping Indian painted by the doorway kept its eyes shut as if it couldn't bear to watch. Take a deep breath, let it out slow. Stay calm, stay strong. Focus on the mission. He regarded her levelly.

Defend himself? No need; she would learn this was no grudge, not of his, anyhow. What worried him was how that lesson would be delivered. Grant squared his shoulders and delivered his report. "This is what you need to hear. A man tried to kill us last night, Randy and I. The assailant got what he wanted, but this is not over. What happened to Frank is part of it. Don't stay at your own house, and don't meet up with Randy—they'll be on him. Send your kids to a friend's house. If there's a bunk for you at Kitt Peak, I would strongly advise you to use it." Then he modulated his voice and said, "I'm sorry."

She stared at him a moment longer. "I used to think Grampie was such an ass for the way he treated you, but I don't even know what you are." She fled into the truck, slamming and locking the door after her. The sound of that slam echoed through him. Hands gripping the wheel, Cecile started the engine, distant and burning as the stars she studied.

Grant turned away. He indicated the direction of his car, a beater he'd bought with emergency cash, choosing one old enough to be anonymous in a place where most folks drove something at least half as old as they were. She followed him up the street, and he resisted the urge to place his hands atop his head like a prisoner under escort. The sound of the engine behind him tightened every muscle. Change the narrative. Grant walked before his family like a minesweeper, checking for explosives that could take out his team. Come to that, it wasn't far from the truth. Except when a soldier walked in front of a troop transport, everybody knew that any step he took could be his last.

CHAPTER TWENTY-FOUR

Adam stalked the broken pavement back into the green paths of the park, a surreal falsehood planted here in the middle of Tucson. When they founded the new republic, it would be someplace green all the time, someplace that need not lie. At his side, Hammer held the basket, turning it slightly this way and that, frowning. They had combed the area for signs of the camp, and found cacti, low mounds of stone, the bend of the Gila River, like the Gila monster outlined on the basket in those faint markings. The pile of rocks called Barnes Butte, which the Germans compared to a sleeping giant, with a bedraggled mess of buildings creeping in all around. Most of this stuff hadn't even been here when the basket was made.

"Maybe this isn't even where to start," Hammer muttered.

"Where else would it be? Why else would she have placed a Gila monster there, south of the map?"

Hammer fell silent. Another reason he made an excellent addition to Adam's organization: he knew when to shut up. Nearly two hours to drive to Papago Park, for what? The basket contained the start, it had to, but the pattern didn't match the roads or the shape of the hills, not on the map, and not here, in person. The tag on the back of the basket had a few random letters on it—nothing meaningful. Of the original POW camp, little remained but a few sheds now re-used for other purposes. Part of the land had become a recreation area, part now held low-rent apartments full of migrants and illegals, squatting on the land where the submarine crews—

proud, strong men, had been imprisoned. Where they had escaped from...

"You have the map of the camp?" Adam let the glasses fall back to his chest and took the paper from Hammer, a hand-drawn diagram of rows of barracks, shower buildings, towers that provided only partial coverage of the camp's perimeter. They occupied the highest point they could find among the camp's remains, trying to envision the layout of those old streets and structures. Hammer could have a point, though. What if the start were more specific than that? Figure on the outside, at the start of a maze, red mark on the inside, not far from the river. Of course, it was an artifact of the indigenous, the indigent, really, living off of American money. There had to be more to it than this. If the camp itself weren't where to start, then what could be? He scanned the map again: entrance to the tunnel, exit from the tunnel, not far from the canal that joined up with the river. Three of the escaped Germans planned to use the river to escape, not realizing that most of the year, the river bed lay bone-dry. A figure worked in black. A Gila monster. A red mark. The whole damn thing made in imitation of the local symbol.

So from that perspective, it wasn't just a figure, but an Indian. He reached out and took the basket from Hammer. They'd been looking at it from the orientation of the figure with its feet on the ground—what if it wasn't? He rotated it ninety degrees, lying the figure down. Not a sleeping giant, the Sleeping Indian, that's what they called it.

"Let's go!" Adam bounded off in reckless jumps, utterly unlike him. Somewhere on that mound lay the key that would unlock a fortune for the Sons and secure his place in a new regime as orderly and proud as any submarine crew.

Hammer jerked in surprise and scrambled after him down the grassy slope to pile into the car. Adam explained as he fired up the engine. "Barnes Butte, according to my research, the Germans called it 'the Sleeping Indian'. They used to look at it past the fence and imagine they could just go up there and take a walk. Sometimes, they even got permission to go, or they'd skip out on a work detail. One guy who worked at a bakery used to let the prisoners ride in his truck sometimes. That mound of rocks was like freedom to them, as far away as the Fatherland."

They careered out of the park, cutting corners, aiming for the butte that rose up in a red mound before them. The road carved a square around it, past sports fields, and he pulled into a lot near a softball game, where the car wouldn't attract much notice. They scouted for a few minutes before locating a path up. A gated road led to a few round tanks, and Adam glared at them as he strode past, the ground rising steeply. At the back of his skull lingered some doubt that they were even seeking something real, but the Warden had come to him, and their money had been good so far—just not enough of it. A few paces behind, Hammer grunted and hissed softly to himself.

"Are you up to this?"

"Just a few ribs, sir, nothing I can't handle," he replied, though he sounded a little sharp. "I'll feel better when we can handle Casey and his cousin."

Adam smiled. "No more than I." Their path wound among outcrops of stone, kicking up red dust that settled over the scrubby plants. Too bad they weren't already in Washington, basking in the lush green of their private domain. "My guess is we're looking for a cave, maybe even the one where Wattenberg hid out." His gaze swept over the surrounding stones. Couldn't be too obvious, or it would have been found by now. Might even be deliberately hidden by stones. "I'll go over the top, you search these channels." He gestured toward a series of broad divisions in the stone. Hammer had done well to keep up so far, no need to push his companion too far.

Adam scrambled up the face of the stone, digging in his fingers, gritting his teeth. He was a strategy man, a thinker, yet he could not simply appoint another of the Sons to undertake missions like this, despite the fact that he'd get dirty. He wiped his hands on a bandanna when he reached the top of the rise. A series of lumps rose yet higher from his post, chipped with age and exposure. Nothing like a cave, or even a shallow dell where a man might hide out, much less for weeks. Something in the shade caught his eye and he moved closer. The surface of some of the stones showed darker red-brown, the patina chipped away by age and weather, and...the crude marks of human hands. Here and there among the jumbled rock pictographs emerged from the gloom. Scraped through to pale stone, they depicted spirals, handprints, weird figures he could barely discern. A few animals lurked among the more abstract designs: goats, snakes, a big fish with its skeleton revealed. And, toward the back, a cluster of man-shapes inscribed with markings of their own, including the familiar swastika.

Adam glared at it. Already, he'd been taken in once by this earlier version of the symbol, tricked into trashing the tribal center and injuring the old man whose feeble-minded ancestors created this "art." First in a series of mis-steps. Now this. He started working the probabilities, determining the likelihood that the Warden was just prodding him into a trap, a way to humiliate him in front of his organization when he came out with neither money nor treasure. He'd be a fool, stripped of status, probably shot in the desert to be stripped of more than that. At least one of the loose ends had been tied off this morning.

Hammer puffed up the trail from a different direction. "Anything?"

Adam waved his hand at the pictographs. "Doesn't look like much. You?"

Hammer shook his head. "Nothing like a cave. What about these?" He pointed toward the cluster of figures associated with the swastika.

"Proto-Nazis?" He made a harsh sound at the back of his throat. "Alas for us, our own ancestors were not the first to employ that shape."

Hammer squatted down, wincing, to examine the figures more closely. "This your basket-maker?"

Adam bent down beside him, peering under the rocky brow that protected the images. One of the figures, near the proto-Nazi, held a circle over its head, inscribe with a maze. He snapped a few pictures with his cellphone, five figures, overlapping, including the basket maker and the Nazi. Great, but what did it mean?

Hammer groaned and turned away, standing up in the shadows and bracing a hand on his side. The ribs must be bothering him. "Sir," he whispered, and Adam lifted his head. "Somebody's coming." He pointed toward the rocks near the base of the mound. For a moment, Adam saw nothing, then a lone figure slipped from one stone to the next, failing to reappear promptly. Both men held their breath a long moment, then the figure moved again, fast, toward another outcrop. If Adam hadn't been looking exactly there, he'd never have seen the man's dark head, visible for just an instant. Casey. Who else could it be?

Adam squeezed Hammer's shoulder and gestured up the ridge of stone that sheltered them. From a higher vantage, they'd be invisible—and maybe take care of a second loose end. Adam grinned. The day was looking up.

CHAPTER TWENTY-FIVE

Back to the stone, Grant breathed carefully, playing the odds. Two
sets of footsteps, clear in the red dust, preceded him along parts of
this trail. Up near the top of the Butte, he glimpsed movement, a
tall form that quickly melded into the shadows. He'd tried to come around
the backside, but the Arizona Military Museum, with its adjacent National
Guard HQ, backed up to the property, complete with a squadron of
helicopters, and all the fencing and armed patrolmen that implied. Secure
civilian facilities claimed the road, leaving broad swathes of open land—
access, but no cover—in between. What were the chances they'd already
seen him? Somewhere on the Sleeping Indian rested the next clue, the thing
that made his grandmother's baskets worth stealing, his grandfather worth
beating half to death. Teo painted spots on the roof of the house, and
maintained the pattern painted on the walls, a three-dimensional
representation of the basket's maze. That same history teacher who brought
them to the airplane graveyard had taken his class on a tour of the POW
camp that didn't even exist anymore, trying to make World War II come to
life for a busload of bored kids—and teenage Grant, who pictured himself
digging a tunnel with a spoon, or maybe tracking Nazis through the desert.
Hadn't pictured them hunting him.

He could wait for them to come down. If they had spotted him, if it
was Lones or his associates, they'd be laying an ambush right about now. So:
see who could wait the longest? give it a miss and head back to Tucson?
Odds were they didn't have a gun long enough to hit him from up there, and

he didn't think they were smooth enough to—

A scrape of stone on stone echoed from somewhere above. What the Hell? He tipped his head back, angling for a view toward the top. A glimpse of movement. Could be a squirrel. The sound came again, soft, but distinct. These men trashed the tribal center and had already tried to kill at least three of its members. Even Randy counted in that regard. What would they do? What wouldn't they?

Only one thing for it, then: call out the National Guard.

Grant crouched low, did a 180 and sprinted the way he'd come, circling down toward the chain link topped with barbed wire that surrounded the base. No gunshots from above, but he had more cover over here, a greater bulk of stone between him and their last known position. Two men on patrol, crossing and continuing in opposite directions, rifles on their shoulders. Grant palmed a small stone, shifted position, and waited. At the moment the guards turned, he popped up and took aim, rapping the stone over the fence to ding against a storage bin. The guards leapt into motion, both charging that direction.

Moving with reckless speed, Grant launched himself out of his position. He let off a wild cackle of laughter and sped into the rocks.

"Hey! Stop right there!"

"Catch me if you can!" he hollered back as he rounded a pillar. The stone, they might've passed over as mischief, but the taunt was unforgiveable. In seconds, a whistle blew down below, then the tramping of feet. At least two men, with a clatter of chains and a sliding gate.

Grant darted uphill. He paused to strip off the light jacket he'd been wearing and kick it under a stone, then up further to where his meandering course met the more direct trail the other men had used. Taking a sharp turn onto a stony outcrop, Grant lunged upward, hands to the stone, and scrambled up. He kept low, moving fast, but in the opposite direction.

From below, the muffled sounds of soldiers in communication, the grunts of running men, angry now that they'd bothered, but not wanting to lose face by giving up. Grant spidered his way across a steep slope, close to the highest point.

"What the Hell?" a mutter, closer than he'd like.

Grant froze.

"Soldiers, sir, two of them, should we—"

"No place to run to, eyes on me, Hammer."

"Yes, sir."

"You! Freeze!" A hoarse shout from below.

Someone shuffled on the stone maybe fifteen, twenty feet away. "Yes, officer! Don't shoot."

Grant used the cover of the confrontation to creep downward, to a narrow trail that edged the cliffside. He stripped off his shirt and flipped it around, winding it into a bandanna which he wrapped around his head, letting his hair puff around it.

"What are you two doing up here?"

"Out for a hike, officer—soldier? What should I call you?" Lones, definitely. He added a soft chuckle. "Are we trespassing? We sure didn't mean to. I heard about the rock art, and I wanted to come check it out. My friend here's from the coast—he's never seen anything like this."

"It's really amazing, what those Indians did," added another voice.

"You seen anyone else out here?"

"No, sir, just us. It's already getting a bit hot for hiking, isn't it? Whew. I'm glad I don't have to be up here with all that gear."

If Lones talked them down, Grant lost his cover, and with it, any chance to see whatever they'd found. He wet his lips, and gave a soft whistle, then called out, "Lucky!" He whistled again. "Oh, shit—Lucky!" louder this time, a man pissed on his own behalf. He edged around the stone, coming face to face with the scene: two civilians in fancy pseudo-military pants confronting two soldiers fully armed and helmeted. One of the men had his rifle in his hands, but down low, rising a bit as Grant came into view.

Lones startled and flashed a scowl, while his companion, Hammer hissed, "Jesus!" as Grant came up behind them.

"Officers! Thank God. Have you seen a little dog around here?" Putting on the faintest Hispanic accent, Grant indicated size with his hands. "Brown, chihuahua cross? There was this kid who practically ran me down, and Lucky took off after him—"

"A kid you say? What'd he look like?" The lead officer practically barked at him.

"Dark hoodie, pulled up, laughing like an idiot." Grant shook his head. "Probably on something." He wiped his forehead and glanced around, then whistled again. "Lucky!"

A long panel of pictographs fronted the ridge, mostly familiar shapes, telling all the old stories. At the near end, tucked low, a series of long scratches marred one of the groupings, obscuring their forms and obliterating any decoration beyond the knowledge they had been human. Bastards. Between this carnage and the rest of the panel, a long oval fish marked the darker surface of the stone. Grant's breath caught. A fish, near a dried up river, for a people who didn't eat fish. How many years had he lived in Arizona, this was the only fish he'd ever seen depicted on stone. "Wow! That's pretty awesome!" He whipped out a phone and squatted, back to the rocks, fingers up in a 'v' to take a selfie, tapping the phone into panoramic mode to be sure he got the whole thing.

The men stared down at him, Lones and Hammer clearly wishing they could whip out a gun just as quickly and take a more permanent shot.

"Is there anything else you can tell us about this kid?" The soldier asked. "We had a disturbance down by the base."

"You want me to show you where he went? Come on." Sticking the phone in his pocket, Grant straightened up. He gestured down the path and started walking. "Lucky's probably halfway home by now."

"You—" Hammer started.

The second soldier glanced at Hammer, then prodded back his helmet to squint at the sun. "Definitely time to head inside. Sorry to disrupt your hike." He gave them a nod.

With long strides, Grant led the way back toward the base, peeling off from the trail toward the stone slope he had used to cover his tracks. "Over this way. I was thinking of joining the guard, y'know? What's it like?"

The soldier eyed him skeptically, tracing his tattoos. "It's pretty regimented. Might not be for you."

"Y'think? 'Cause I'm pretty sick of working landscaping, y'know? And I want to do something for my country. Some kind of service."

The two soldiers shared a look, tolerating Grant's questions as he led them toward level ground. Once there, the three stopped, looking around. The soldiers studied the ground, scanning for footprints, while Grant peered into underbrush and shadows. "Lucky?" He whistled again. "Hey, sorry I couldn't be more help—I gotta find that dog or my girlfriend's gonna kill me. Lucky!" He wandered off toward the nearby suburb, cupping his hands around his mouth and calling out a name pulled from a hat, a name that felt pretty apropos. The bastards ruined a bunch of figures, sure, but he suspected they left the most important one: that strange fish with its pointed nose, and profile tail. It was no fish at all; it was a submarine.

CHAPTER TWENTY-SIX

After a busy morning back and forth from Chris's apartment, Jamie led Buster into the office. She'd already been out longer than 'traffic' would cover, and she didn't want to take the extra time to bring the dog back to her place.

Rachel looked up from her seat behind the counter. "Buster! How's my buddy?"

He ambled toward her with a sigh. The receptionist dropped down from her chair to scratch Buster's chin and ears, cooing at him as if he were a lap dog. Buster sat heavily and rolled his eyes back toward Rizzo as he endured the attention. She scooped her messages off the counter: her dad, unable to get through on her cellphone, called the office instead; Adam Lones about approving designs for a new logo—or maybe just calling to chat up Rachel, seemed like he had a thing for her; lock-up to say they were sending over the paperwork about Anderson's release; the smuggling taskforce on a notice about an artifact sale, sneaky enough to maybe be illegal; AP wanted to know how she felt about the proposed changes in immigration policy.

She waved the pile at Rachel. "Anything else I should know?"

Rachel let go of Buster's droopy face and stood up. "That was it. Captain Morales was able to reschedule from this morning to two o'clock, which is in—"an ostentatious look at the clock—"half an hour. I didn't see anything on your calendar, so I wrote him in. But..." She leaned on the counter. "He was pretty pissed! That meeting was on your calendar for like a month." She glance down at Buster, then back at Jamie. "It would've helped if I could tell him why I had to reschedule."

"Buster and I had some work to do." She sorted through the memos. "And there was a change with the prisoner transport."

"Right, that came through on email." Rachel glanced down at the dog again, then finally settled back into her seat.

"Speaking of—I'm gonna send over an image of the lawyer's card who got our suspect released. I need to know anything you find about him. Check the bar, the law review, all of that." She prodded her phone to life, removed her "Do not disturb" responder, and sent the shot over to Rachel.

Buster stood up and walked to the door, glancing back at her again. She sighed—should've taken him to the bushes before they came inside, but she didn't want to be even later getting in. "I'll start returning these while my partner does his business." They strolled back out again, and walked to the far corner of the building. Buster started nosing around, looking for exactly the right spot. The artifact thing she should pass along to tribal police, at least make sure they'd already heard about it; Adam could wait a bit longer—and hadn't she already told him all the designs looked fine? She jabbed her dad's number and held the phone to her ear, taking a few steps into the shade and fanning herself. A car pulled into the lot just as her dad's voice came on the line.

"Jamie? Oh, good. We got another call from one of those lawyers. Are you sure we shouldn't—?"

Adam got out of the car and gave her a cheerful wave. He looked a little red in the face, his hair damp as if he'd been sweating. Strange.

"Hang on just a sec, Dad."

Buster moseyed around the corner and squatted. Jamie turned away from him. He didn't like to be watched. "Adam—can I get back to you later on that logo?"

"Right, right, sure. I was just on my way back from lunch, so I thought I might stop by." He smiled broadly, but didn't walk away.

"Jamie," said her father's voice, "I have to be in court to cover a trial in about five minutes. I just want us to consider hiring somebody."

"Dad, there's no such thing as a Chinese human rights lawyer, okay?

The good ones are all in prison already. The ones they haven't arrested yet are just spies trying to make money off people like us."

Adam put on a sympathetic expression and gave a little shake of his head, then held up his hands as if he'd startled himself by listening in. The guy was a busybody, no doubt. Liked to know what everybody was up to so he could help out any way he could.

Buster trundled back around the corner, nose high as he drank in the breeze. He turned sharply, ears perked up, then walked straight toward Adam. He gave a light "whuff," a single wag of his tail, and sat down. Adam chuckled and bent down to pat the top of Buster's head in the awkward way that people do when they're not fond of dogs. Jamie lost track of what her father was saying, she gave a grunt of assent, not taking her eyes off the dog. "Look, Dad, honestly, I need to call you back. Gotta go."

"Late—after court closes."

Adam chuckled again, straightening away from the dog.

"Right." Jamie tapped the call off, gripped the phone for a moment, then slid it back into its holster on her belt.

"I think he likes me," Adam announced.

"Your scent is probably familiar—all those late night meetings." Jamie forced a smile. Familiar alright, but the last scent she asked Buster to track was on the syringe she found at Chris Anderson's apartment. Buster followed the invisible path where a stranger walked in the front door, into the kitchen, into the bedroom, pinned Chris to the bed and rammed that syringe into his nose then left him to die.

Her throat felt suddenly parched. Adam, whom she'd known for years, wanted her to distrust Casey, whom she'd barely met. Who had tattoos from wrist to throat, some of them clearly there to disguise his scars. Some kind of mercenary treasure-hunter, who called her up out of the goddamn blue to ask what she knew about Adam. "The second one," she blurted. "That's what you're here about, right? The logos? The second one's a little sharper."

Adam blinked and gave a shrug, sliding his hands back into his pockets. "Are you alright? You seem a little—" he shrugged again. "Sorry, it's not really my place."

Shit on a shingle, could she be any more obvious? "No, Adam, you're not wrong. I was delayed getting into the office, and now I got a boatload of stuff to catch up on. Had to take the dog to the vet, and ran out of time to take him home, then I made the mistake of calling my dad." She plucked off her hat and ran a hand over her hair. "Used to be a sleepy corner of the world, Pima County, and now, I dunno."

"Hmm." Adam's face rumpled into a sympathetic frown. "Well, that tribal center thing, the suspect's out of your hands now, right? So at least that's off your docket."

"Some lawyer came and picked him up." She nodded.

Was that a flicker of—what? Damn, she was getting paranoid. But he could have said anything else. A friend would've asked about her dad. A campaign manager would've taken her thoughts on the logo and gotten out of her way. Adam did neither of those: he wheedled for information about the one case he should know nothing about. Buster still sat by his feet, waiting for her praise, waiting for her to acknowledge that he'd found the right man.

"Good boy, Buster. We'll catch you later, okay, Adam?" She bit back a wince at her turn of phrase.

"Sure thing." He patted the dog's head again, and climbed into his car. By the time he'd pulled around the corner, she was back on the phone. She had to get Chris out of town, and fast: before his murderer tracked him down for another try.

CHAPTER TWENTY-SEVEN

Adam strangled the steering wheel all the way to his office. Damn dogs. And the first dog hadn't even been real: Casey invented it. How had he even gotten the National Guardsmen up the hill in the first place? No matter: Adam and Hammer already had their photos, many and detailed, and left the figures a ruin to cut off any pursuit. The difficulty was, he had no idea what they meant. Basket maker, Nazi—fine as far as it went. What about the others—and the spirals and markings that surrounded them? The situation felt dangerously out of control. Then Grant-fucking-Casey takes a stroll through the middle of everything, just as they think they might be able to take him down, and walks off with a selfie and the National-fucking-Guard as his escort.

Deliberately Adam uncurled his fingers from the wheel, returning to center as he waited for a light. Rizzo didn't reveal anything about Anderson, but in all probability, his body wouldn't be discovered until it started to rot, the corruption of the body revealing the corruption of the soul.

Could sending the rock art photos to the Warden shake loose the next part of the funding, or would he be required to reveal their meaning? What could they be pointing to? Adam had no fondness for puzzles, but he had never yet allowed one to get the better of him. Pulling into his reserved spot at Lones and Company Investing, Adam put on his high roller smile and the attitude that went along with it. Pressing the flesh, making the deal, always ready to help a client, Adam Lones stepped out of his Beemer, sliding the strap of a leather laptop case onto his shoulder. He listened to the click of the automatic car locks behind him. He swept into the elevator lobby and rode up to his floor, envisioning the Warden's pleasure, the millions that would arrive in a few different bank accounts, the green and shady compound up north that never let in any undesirables.

"Good Afternoon, Mr. Lones," said the group receptionist, a highly presentable Asian girl. "I hope you enjoyed your morning at the course. You have a visitor waiting." She held out a card. At least Asians knew their place.

"Thank you, Amanda." He smiled warmly, running a finger over the embossed law enforcement badge: Lt. Derek Montgomery, of the Storrs, Connecticut police department. Windows between the reception area and his own antechamber showed a large man studying the glossy photos of various Lones and Company development projects around the area. In spite of his slight paunch, he had the bearing and buzz-cut to match the business card. But then, Adam knew how easy it was to fake a card these days. Just ask the desk officers who let Remington leave with his new "client."

Walking in with a long, hips-forward stride, Adam put out his hand. "Lieutenant Montgomery. Adam Lones. A pleasure to meet you. Won't you come into my office. I hope you haven't been waiting long?"

"Your girl made me some coffee." Montgomery lifted his cup to display it, with a smile of his own. "Good stuff. Columbian?"

"Kona, actually." Adam swept into the inner sanctum, sliding the laptop case onto the immaculate desk. Lights came on automatically as they entered, illuminating a tasteful selection of Old Master-style paintings.

The other man gave a nod. "Buying American. Glad to hear it."

Interesting. Adam waved him to the client's chair while he settled into his own. Along with the gravelly voice of a habitual smoker, the man had full lips and a long nose, complexion slightly swarthy. Sharp green eyes. Eastern or southern European origins, perhaps. "What brings you to my office, all the way from Connecticut? Are you looking to invest in commercial real estate?"

Montgomery started to set down his cup, then glanced at the thick slab of glass that formed the desk, raised his eyebrows, and took a coaster from the little stack provided. Something about the way he arranged coaster and cup made Adam feel that, in his own life, he was not nearly so fastidious. "Actually, I'm on vacation. Keep hearing about the border, the crisis, all of that."

"It's certainly on the minds of many." Adam folded his hands and settled back. "I don't have any special interest in that area myself."

"No?" The man grunted. He, too, settled back, hands folded. "Then maybe I came to the wrong place."

"I don't follow." Adam's smile felt a bit tight. Perhaps he should actually go to the golf course one of these days.

"I heard from some people I met back home that not everyone out here was waiting for an official solution."

"I've heard the same." Adam tapped the card on his desk. "I'm sure you meet all sorts of people in your line of work."

"Damn straight." The man snorted again and shook his head. "Sorry. I'm used to streets, not fancy offices like this." He waved a hand around the room. "Streets where I come from, we gotta lotta drugs, lotta people who shouldn't be there. It's making my life difficult, if you see what I mean. And I already have a hard position, between the brass making nice with ACLU types, and the decent citizens counting on me to keep their families save. There's a number of fine people in prison now for doing what's right, trying to clean up the streets, maybe the whole country. I'm having a hard time pleasing everybody, and that doesn't please me." He leaned forward, placing his joined hands on the desk. "Mr. Lones. I'm looking to make a difference. Some folks take their holiday to build houses and clean up litter. I'd like to take out a bit of trash myself, if you see what I mean." He drew out the last words, his eyes locked to Adam's face.

"I'm not sure I do, quite frankly, but I gather you're not ready to be quite frank."

Montgomery straightened up, his broad shoulders straining the confines of his suit. "I don't know you, you don't know me. I heard about you, and your organization, from some of those fine folks I had to lock up, people who shouldn't be in prison for saying what we've all been thinking." He jabbed his finger at the card. "Look me up. If you think you can help me have a nice trip, you give me a call. If not, well, it was a great cup of coffee anyhow." He stood up, lifting the cup in salute—and knocking the coaster to the floor where the thick carpet muffled its fall. The guy shook his head.

"Damn. Sorry about that." Adam had risen as well, but the other man knelt down to retrieve his coaster and fumbled it back into the holder. "And that's why we can't have nice things. Just lucky I didn't spill on your carpet. It was a pleasure to meet you, hope I didn't waste either of our time." Gripping the cup around the middle, Montgomery shook Adam's hand again and let himself out.

A very strange interview indeed. The door snicked softly shut behind him, and Adam sat down again, his laptop coming on with the speed of fine technology. On the camera monitor in his left-hand drawer, Adam watched Montgomery bring the cup over to Amanda's desk. "Hey, thanks for this," he said, his voice emerging very softly from the speaker.

"Certainly, sir. Have a nice day."

"I'll do that—you too." He gave a little salute, a flick of his finger at his hairline. Ex-military? Not too surprising a background for a police officer.

Adam entered his name and city into a search engine, and almost immediately came up with a news article. Apparently, Lt. Montgomery's 'vacation' was an administrative leave—after shooting a suspect who may have been reaching for a gun, or may have just been getting away, depending on whose version of the story could be trusted. The incident took place at a protest near the UConn campus where a conservative speaker had been booed off the stage. Well, well. No wonder the officer wasn't too forthcoming about his visit. He might be just the sort of man Adam needed after all.

CHAPTER TWENTY-EIGHT

O nce the two guardsmen had tramped out of sight, muttering about their missing vandal, Grant doubled back to his car, parked in a lot next to an auto-body shop where it fit right in. Sliding off the blanket he used to deflect heat from the ripped vinyl seats, he pulled a new laptop from the floor and flicked it on, transferring the new images from his phone so he could study the submarine layout on a larger screen. That done, he swiped back through the last few images to the basket framed by the B-52, and forward again to the pictogram. Why use the basket to draw the searchers all the way to the top of the Sleeping Indian, just to present this? The graven image was enigmatic at best. He searched up a diagram of a type IX-C sub, like the ones the submariners had been rescued from. Skeletal markings on the image might correlate to the battery compartment in the belly of the sub, if he looked at it just right, and the thing that could be taken for a fish's eye would be somewhere in the forward torpedo room, maybe even a torpedo tube itself. The variation in internal structures would be more meaningful if he had the sub right in front of him, but it sank seventy years ago, depth charged by the British. The submariners had been lucky to escape with their lives: only two men had gone down with the ship.

He expanded the image of his grandmother's basket, the Sleeping Indian outside the familiar maze, the little red mark at its center. Lones had the basket itself, and it brought him here, while Grant made the leap from interpreting the x-eyed painting near his grandparents' door. That little red mark... Grant could've smacked himself. The Indian wasn't the center of the maze, it was the beginning—the figure lay on the *outside*. Stupid. He rotated the image until the figure lay on its back, at rest. The maze took shape as a pathway around the butte. He found an aerial view of the butte and superimposed the basket, imagining walking around the base of it, following roads long re-used for suburbs and businesses. This placed the red mark not far from the National Guard base and its adjacent Arizona Military Museum. What had that history teacher told them about the building? Google, which knew almost as much as D. A., informed him the place had begun as a WPA project in the thirties, then was converted during the War into a machine shop. It wasn't just a museum, but one of the few structures remaining from the Papago Park POW camp. Bingo.

From his go-bag, he pulled a sun-blocking shirt with long sleeves and a collar that would obscure his tattoos. He added a pair of wire-rimmed glasses and a camera bag. Baseball cap on his head—apparently he was rooting for the Chargers this year—Grant walked back toward the Military Museum. He casually kept an eye out for Lones and Hammer, but he suspected they were long gone, believing they had destroyed the clue he'd been looking for. Hopefully, they hadn't succeeded. He couldn't rule out the chance that the figures they damaged had been vital to understanding the diagram and a prize that made a basket worth killing for. Dangerous bones.

The low adobe building hulked near the fenced-in National Guard facility, and the alarm had been turned off. He spotted a few people in uniform inspecting the area around the helicopters, and an additional guardsman now stood by the butte-side of the fence, field glasses in hand, scanning the slope. No sign of Lones and Hammer up there. Grant stepped from the heat of mid-day into the cool interior, the thick wall blocking the fierce Arizona sun. Didn't miss that one bit. He gave a nod to the old man behind the counter, scanning to make sure his opponents hadn't preceded him.

"Sign the guest book?" The old man rose ponderously, a smile trembling to his face. "Where you in from?"

"San Diego," Grant told him as he scrawled illegibly in the book under a group of earlier visitors from Scottsdale. No sign that Lones had figured out the map. Good. "Is there a fee?"

"Nope, nope, just come on in and have a look around. Not many visitors today." He tipped back a cap of his own, with an army insignia and service designation Grant couldn't immediately place.

Gesturing toward the cap, he said, "You were in the war?"

"Not quite." The smile faded a little. "But I did serve here on the home front. Y'know this building was once utilized by Nazi submariners? Yessir." At Grant's expression, the smile returned. "Maybe you've heard of the Great Papago Escape?"

"I knew that was around here somewhere!" Grant pivoted, pointing vaguely outside. "I actually came in to learn more about it."

The old man pointed more firmly. "Right over there. This was the machine shop, general repairs, working on the jeeps and such. I signed on the moment I could, year after Pearl Harbor. I was pretty green, and they needed guards for all those prisoners coming over, so I was assigned here. My folks was just as glad I didn't end up seeing combat."

Grant let his excitement show, but the old man shook his head again. "I wasn't here for the escape, unfortunately, but I spent a lot of time around here. Come on." He flapped his hand, drawing Grant to follow him deeper into the museum, past glass cases with mannequins in uniform and decommissioned ordnance. They stopped in front of a table-top case occupied by a model of the camp, showing where all the buildings had been located, and the docent explained how the guard towers had a blind spot, allowing the prisoners to dig a tunnel underneath the canal through which two dozen of the men escaped. Grant scanned the layout and snapped a few photos, giving all the right cues of interest, wondering where the true mystery lay. The basket led here, but none of this stuff had been inside the building at the time. Good chance nothing remained from the 40's. His phone rang, but not in the right pattern to signal an urgent call, so he ignored it, turning to the man.

"Were you in this building when it was part of the camp?"

"Sure, lots of times on escort duty, like that." They turned their backs to the case as his hands and words sketched in what the place had been like back then. "That entry way used to be a big door for driving or hauling vehicles in, and over here..." He spoke of tools and tasks, saying, "Those boys might've been Nazi's but they sure loved their machines. I'd guess that's why they wound up in the Kriegsmarine. You needed to be pretty savvy for that." He tapped his own temple.

Unfortunately, nothing he described remained in the renovated space. Still, Grant nodded and murmured at the right places. "You've got a great memory—I'm glad I ran into you," Grant told him.

The old man chuckled and waved him off. "I'm glad of any audience these days, but I'm not gonna give you the rant about young people and history. Clear to me, you're not like that."

"I was a history major in college." One of the few things from his life before that still gave him a twinge of regret. Hard to imagine him as a history teacher or writing books about the stuff he now fought for.

"In that case..." The guy glanced around, back toward the door. "Come on—lemme show you something special." Shuffling through a door at the back, he waved Grant along with him into a cramped room full of file cabinets, boxes and unused displays, a mannequin stacked on top, its arms upraised as if it were reaching for help.

"This is the archive? Am I allowed to—"

"No, no, over here." He caught Grant's arm and tugged him deeper, to where the smell of old grease and motor oil still permeated the air. "Here." He pointed, then brought out a jangling key chain and flicked on a tiny flashlight hooked among the keys.

In the storage area, the walls remained free of frames and display cases to make more room for boxes. Braced with wooden beams, the adobe hadn't been painted in a long time. The old man's thin arm indicated a pillar that must be part of the original structure. The accumulated dust of decades had settled into the grain of the wood, and a series of markings carved into it. As he ran his light down the pillar it caught the shapes, illuminating a column of letters in groups of four. Grant's mouth went dry.

"Do you might if I take a picture?"

The old man grinned, bringing his light under his chin to make himself into a ghoul in the dim space. "You know what that is?"

"It's an Enigma code." Generated by the Nazi's famous encoding machine.

"Woo-hoo!" He crowed. "Yessir, it is, but one that nobody can ever solve. Go on, shoot it if you want to. Can't be solved without the key." He shook his own keys.

Grant pulled out his camera as the docent shone his light on the letters once more. "That's crazy," Grant murmured under his breath.

"What's that? Finding a code here? No, those Nazis were all about the codes All kinds of folks've tried to crack this one. Can't be done."

Crazy because you couldn't read it without the key—worse yet, you couldn't even make it without the machine. Choosing a letter on each of four rotors determined which letters would be substituted to transform a message into the code, but the rotors themselves were set through a complex system of random words and Roman numerals. A book of keys governed which key would be used on any given day, and even then, the actual sender chose part of the settings, using Morse Code to deliver that part to the recipient, who also had a copy of the book. A Polish mathematician worked on the code for years to understand part of the pattern, laying the groundwork for when the Allies captured an Enigma machine and its code books.

The old man was right: in spite of the clear nature of the letter groupings, here was a code they'd never break. Could be the whole thing was nonsense, a joke on their American captors, still antagonizing them all these years later. If not, then the man who carved it had brought this code with him, memorized or concealed, all the way from the submarine they left behind. What else had he taken along? Photographs at least, like the image of the skull he found at Teo's house—maybe still in the camera. Had he carried some other record: letters? A diary? Something his American captors allowed him to keep—and an openly recognized Enigma code wasn't likely to pass security. After sharing that moment of wonder in the store room, the docent tired out, moving more slowly to his perch at the front of the museum. "Anyway, that's the good stuff we've got here about Papago Park."

"I can't thank you enough, sir." Grant stuffed a donation in the provided box and let himself out, the rotors of his mind still turning.

CHAPTER TWENTY-NINE

I don't know what to do, where to go," Chris murmured, staring bleakly through the windshield. He clutched his overnight bag in his lap as if it could defend him.

"I'm working that out, okay?" Rizzo pulled up to the curb and killed the engine.

His eyes widened. "Why are we stopping?"

"Hey, hey." She put on the soothing voice she'd use with a child at the scene of an accident. "I'm just dropping off my dog. That's the kennel, okay? I want to make sure he's taken care of."

Chris's gaze flicked toward Buster, who lounged in the back seat. "You're taking care of everybody today, huh. I'm sorry. I don't want to be a burden." He drew a deep breath and expelled it. "What if I stayed at the rehab? They seemed nice."

"Nice. Not secure. We'll figure something out. You just—wait here." She glanced past him at the cars moving beyond, the broad streets of the suburbs. A hazy Arizona afternoon. Why did everything look so sinister? "Maybe you want to duck down in the seat. Make it look like my car's empty, okay?"

He sank down, like a man trapped in quicksand. "I'll make it brief," she told him as she got out, and summoned the dog out of his door. She tapped the locking mechanism as she walked away.

Buster's tail and ears lifted and he pulled forward a little, eager to head anyplace where they fed him too many treats and didn't make him work for it. Assured that he'd be fondled and spoiled, Rizzo left Buster in the hands of the staff and headed back to the car. If only she could turn Chris over to someone she could count on just as much. Before she got in, she found herself glancing around again, that uneasy feeling hovering around her beltline.

Once they were underway, Chris peering up at her, she waved him back into his seat. "I know a guy, maybe. Someone who's better with all this cloak and dagger stuff."

"You trust him?"

She shrugged. "I think he's trustworthy. He's not very forthcoming, always getting more out of you than you out of him, if you see what I mean."

Chris looked grim. "I'm not sure I'll like him."

Rizzo imagined Grant Casey as she'd first seen him: shirtless, tattoos rippling, a sheen of sweat over his well-defined torso. "You'll get on fine." Unfortunately, he wasn't answering his phone. Not knowing what to say, she left no message. Try again later. Meantime, she had a message of her own to follow up on. As they headed out of town toward the Uni, Chris started to relax, finally leaning back into the headrest. His eyes slid shut, only to flare open again the moment the car parked outside the university's small museum. His brow furrowed and he glanced over at her. "Kennel for people under surveillance?" He tried a crooked smile.

Jamie grinned back at him. "Almost: we're meeting the head of the anthropology department. With any luck, she'll confirm what this is all about." The grin ebbed. "Look: this is all confidential, you know that, right? Until I have you someplace secure, someplace those guys don't know about —" She still couldn't quite name Adam as the head of—what? A gang? A criminal underworld?—"I'm keeping you close, and that means you're likely to hear some stuff I don't want to have repeated."

"Yes, ma'am." He straightened up and raked his fingers through his hair, checking his beard in the mirror. "On any other day, I'd be all in for the mystery, like those books I read. The Kennedys, the Roosevelts: they always have skeletons in their closets." For a moment, his reflected glance shot toward her. "It would be kinda fun, if somebody hadn't tried to kill me."

She clapped him on the shoulder, giving a quick and gentle squeeze.

Ever since she saved his life, she couldn't quite see him as just the suspect, or even the victim. He depended on her, and the obligation weighed her down and made her walk taller at the same time. "Come on."

She flashed her badge to the door guards, and was shown into an inner sanctum with lights that came on as you walked by and low cabinets full of drawers, meticulously labeled. Chris trailed after her, mumbling, "Oh, wow," and, "Huh!" as they caught glimpses of the ancient tools, pots and weapons laid out for study.

In a lab at the back, Professor Tran bent over a large, brightly lit table covered with a jumble of bones. Tran straightened up, bracing a hand against her back, and frowning at Chris as they entered. "Don't touch anything."

"Right." He started to put his hands behind him, then crossed his arms in front instead, shoulders hunching. A guy whose life would never be the same.

"Who is this?" Tran pointed toward him.

"He's an associate. I'd rather not give out his name."

Tran pursed her lips, then said, "I guess it's your game."

"It's no game," Chris said sharply. "People are getting hurt."

"Spoken like someone who watches too many cop shows." Tran turned away from him, back to sorting bones on the table according to some criteria only she knew. "I don't know how your bone got here, and I know you're not going to tell me, but let's just say that speculation I made when you dropped it off?" She waited for Jamie's nod. "Confirmed. The substrate, the age range, everything matches except what it's doing here. Do you have any way of knowing if this thing is from the original discovery?"

Under Tran's rapid-fire speech, Jamie plopped back onto a stool, her mind reeling. Peking Man, the skeleton lost for decades, might well be a thing worth killing for. "No idea. It came from a Tohono O'odham sacred cache." She watched Chris's eyebrows notch upward, connecting her words with the crime he'd been held for.

"As long as we're not violating the Native Graves Repatriation Act by running the tests." Tran snorted. "I'd hate to be spending my radiometry lab budget on stuff I never get to publish." Then she briefly showed her teeth.

"The institute that performed the original dig for—" she didn't say the name, but continued, "they got funding from the Rockefeller Foundation back in the twenties and thirties. You don't suppose I can get in on that grant?"

"Thanks for your time, Professor. Send the report over—no, on second thought, let me know when you've got the results written up, and I'll collect the report from you." Rizzo stood up and offered her hand, then ushered Chris out of the lab and let the door shut behind them. The lights came on in eerie patches as they moved down the hall.

"Productive?" Chris asked.

"Confirmation via scientific evidence of something apparently impossible."

"'When you have eliminated the impossible, whatever remains, however improbable, must be the truth,' or something like that. Sherlock Holmes. You know what else the Rockefellers were into in the thirties? The Nazi eugenics program." Chris's hands grew animated again as they pushed out into the daylight. "Seriously. They sponsored the institute where Mengele got his start. The one-and-only Josef Mengele—funded by the fucking one percenters. Sorry, pardon my language. Some of my friends think I read that stuff because I want to be them, but really I want to be ready to recognize the crap they get up to with all that money and power." Chris walked a few steps further, then turned back when he saw she wasn't beside him.

She felt rooted to the spot. "You're not joking. About the Rockefellers."

He paced back toward her, head shaking. "I belong to an org that's been tracking this kind of thing, where the money comes from, where it goes." He shrugged. "The Rockefellers distanced themselves from eugenics pretty quick once the Holocaust came out, but yeah, they were paying the bills to prove the whole idea of superior races, probably because they think they are."

Jamie jolted into motion. "Come on."

"What? Was that important?"

"It could be. Let's go." She practically slid across her hood Dukes of Hazard style. She still didn't know how it all added up, but there was a link, a strand, however tenuous, connecting Peking Man to a desert full of Nazis.

CHAPTER THIRTY

When Grant drove past the Motel 6 parking lot, the first thing he noticed was Sheriff Rizzo lurking out front, her hat and hair pretty distinctive, in spite of the absence of an official vehicle. He'd missed two calls from the same Arizona number—one while he was at the museum, one while he was driving back from Phoenix, looking forward to connecting with D.A. about the Enigma code. He'd sent her the photos already, just in case she could work anything out even without the key, maybe track down which codebook the sub would've been carrying. On a hunch, Grant drove past and pulled into the strip mall a little way down, turning so he could watch the motel. He tapped the button to return the call, and saw Rizzo reach for her pocket after the first ring. He hung up and reversed course to drive around the back of the hotel and park next door.

He slung the laptop in an old satchel across his back. On foot, making it hard to connect the old Chevy with him, Grant came up beside her as she glared at her phone. "Sheriff."

She startled and blew out a breath, eyes narrowing. "You just called me?"

"You called me first. What can I do for you?"

With a quick glance around, she said, "Not out here. And I have someone with me." She beckoned to him, gesturing to the official vehicle tucked behind some overgrown landscaping. Not bad camo for an amateur. He'd spotted something back there, but hadn't pegged it for her car. Damn, this mission was eroding his skillset, just when he had to be on the top of his game.

He didn't move to follow. "Not sure we should be seen together."

"Shit on a shingle, Casey, I need to talk to you."

"Got it." He gave her a wave as if saying good-bye, flashing a card in his palm, then letting it fall to the ground when he lowered his hand. "See you in a bit." He kept walking, to the adjacent convenience store where he picked up some snacks. She was pretty bright, she'd pick up on it.

A few minutes later, sipping a bottled iced tea, Grant rounded the building to his room and let himself in. Setting down his laptop and goodie bag, he knocked on the adjoining door and said, "Trick or Treat," when Rizzo opened the one on her side.

"What the hell, Casey?" She waved the keycard he'd dropped in the parking lot.

"Always get two rooms. Keeps 'em guessing." Three, actually, but she didn't have to know everything. On the bed behind her sat a younger man, pale face, beard a little shaggy, eyes shadowed. The guy smothered a yawn, then he raised his eyes when Grant stepped through. The guy's cheeks went slightly pink, his lips parting in a little breath of appreciation. And Grant wasn't even trying at the moment. So, not her boyfriend. He looked familiar —then it clicked. "Chris Anderson? What brings you to my doorstep?"

The guy's expression shifted from attraction to concern, as if the use of his name triggered something. Anderson fumbled his way off the bed, bolting to his feet. "Don't."

Rizzo jumped between them, body tensed as if ready to fend him off, her right hand hovering near her duty belt. "Chris, it's okay. Swear to God."

Grant took a step back, holding up his palms in a gesture of peace. The guy had come through some kind of trauma since the drugged-out mug shot Rizzo had on her desk—and so had she, if she were prepared to mount a defense of a suspected perp. "Stand down, Sheriff. You came to me, and brought him along. Neither of you would be here if you thought I was the enemy."

Chris's glance flicked from the sheriff back to Grant, maybe calculating whether Grant was, in fact, the enemy. "You know my name, but I don't know you."

"Grant Casey." He squatted, resting his arms on his thighs, making himself look smaller. "I'm a registered member of the Tohono O'odham tribe, and my grandfather's the man you're accused of attacking."

Anderson retreated even further. "I didn't do that—I've never even been there."

"I know you're innocent," Grant told him, low and even.

Taken aback by this statement, Anderson deflated a little.

Rizzo added, "He's the guy who tried to convince me that you'd been drugged."

"He tried again," Anderson blurted. "Tried to kill me this time."

"So, we've got that in common; he tried to kill me, too." He nodded to Rizzo as he rose and retreated to his side of the divide. "You like sweet tea or lemonade?"

After a moment, Rizzo stalked after him. "Sweet tea." She caught the bottle he tossed her. "I think we know what we're looking for, what—he's looking for."

"Still can't say the name?" Grant took a swallow from his own bottle and sat at the table. He snagged the satchel and pulled it closer, taking out the laptop. "I don't blame you, but if you're ready to work together, clarity is the starting point. Adam Lones, your campaign finance manager, recently defaced a group of pictographs on Barnard's Butte. He found them by following a basket his sidekick stole from my cousin at gunpoint, after the one he took from the cultural center proved to be a bust. With me so far?"

He brought up his image file. Anderson came to stand in the doorway, wary, disappeared again, and emerged with a chair from the second room which he placed on the other side of Rizzo, and carefully sat down, eying Grant sidelong. Grant pushed the grocery bag toward him, and focused on Rizzo. "He's following a treasure map to...?"

"Cards on the table." She drank from her bottle and leaned forward. "You're not gonna believe this." Another breath, then she committed. "Peking Man." She blinked at him. "You're not surprised."

"You tested the bone?" At her nod, he pulled out the photo from Teo's house, the patchwork skull, and flipped it across to her. "What I can't figure is how the bones would get anywhere near here."

"I have an idea about that," Anderson said. He swallowed hard. "I have an interest in the one percenters, how they accumulate all this wealth and power through, like, decades. Concentrating everything for their own families. Anyway. The anthropologist mentioned that the dig in China was sponsored by the Rockefeller Foundation. They also sponsored the Nazi eugenics program. They had a lot invested in proving who was sub-human. It seems like that skeleton is just the kind of evidence the eugenicists would have wanted. Don't you think?" His hands grew more animated as he spoke.

"So when the bones went missing in China, maybe they were given to the Nazis." Grant's fingers flew on the keyboard, pulling up websites, finding the confirmation of Anderson's facts, if not his connection between them. "What else?"

Rizzo backtracked, talking about how she'd brought Buster to Anderson's apartment after whatever it was had happened—they might be trading information, but that was Anderson's story, and he wasn't sharing, not with Grant—not yet. Given how Lones focused on the idea that the perp was an addict, Grant could take a guess how the murder attempt went down.

"We need a work flow, a way to break this thing up and figure out what's going on before anybody else gets hurt."

"And maybe find the world's greatest missing person," Rizzo muttered.

The historian in him agreed. Keeping the bones out of the hands of a guy like Lones made for a strong incentive all by itself, but he knew it was already personal. Lones and Hammer would be pissed about the Butte. Grant had gotten too close to that end already. Better to lie low for a little while.

Rizzo's phone tweeted and she glanced at the message, then flicked back through a few more, growing more alert by the moment. "I think we have a line on your family artifacts. There's an auction, local deal it looks like, established buyers only. One of the tribal police caught wind of it, but they're not interacting, don't want to scare the guy off. So we have no clue where and when."

"Randy's gotta be a little jumpy by now. Send me the info—I have a gallery contact who can work it."

"For real?"

He smiled. "Real enough. Website, Google street views, all that. Based in Monterey."

"That's pretty far outside my jurisdiction." For a moment, she chewed on her thoughts, then sighed. "Yep, this is me, deciding not to ask."

As they spoke, Anderson unwound a little, reaching out to peek into the bag, hand hovering between a package of almonds, and one of Twinkies. Go for the comfort food. The Twinkies won. Every time. "I don't know if my people can get out here fast enough. If we set up the bona fides, can you get in there for the capture?"

"You want me to arrest your cousin?"

"If that's what it takes to keep him getting killed over this. He's in deep with some shady characters. Narcos or coyotes is my guess, looking for real estate on this side of the border, and far from people like you."

She brightened. "Gamblers? I know that gang—we haven't been able to get a mark to turn over on them yet. Oh, yeah, if your people can set it up, I am all over that." Her thumbs slid over the phone, and the message alert appeared in the corner of Grant's screen.

"Which is another reason we don't want the locals to know we're talking."

"I can't stay off the streets—the work's piling up as it is, even without setting up a sting in the next twenty-four hours." She cut her eyes over to Anderson, who had polished off the second Twinkie.

Grant tapped a quick note to D.A. and forwarded Rizzo's intel. "You can't stay off the streets, and he can't be on them."

"Jesus," Anderson whispered, crumpling the package in his fist.

"I was hoping...ah, Christ, Casey, I don't even know how to ask this—I don't even know if you're the person I should be asking." She sat up straighter, tipping her hat back. "I feel like I know what kind of man you are, but I don't know you from—" again, she couldn't say the name, even in a cliché.

His phone rang twice. Anderson and Rizzo stared at him as he made no move to pick it up. Silence. Another ring. Grant held up a finger to ask for their patience, and answered.

"Chief, you want me to turn over the op to this total stranger? Family stuff, right—you sure you want—"

"Two things. One, I'm establishing mutual trust with a new ally." He met Rizzo's dark gaze, and she didn't blink. "Two, I need you on sigint."

"Eyeballing Gooney's plant?" She snorted. "That's hardly taxing my energy, Chief."

"I need a code-breaker. We're talking old school. You've heard of the Enigma device?"

That one even shook Anderson a little out of his own head.

"Sure, Chief, took years and a roomful of geniuses and died out before we were born."

"That's the one. I'll send you the pictures."

"Holy shit, Chief, you're not kidding? You got the key? There's online simulators for that, all you have to do is plug it all in."

"No key, just code, that's where you come in."

"Did you not hear the 'years and a roomful of geniuses part?'"

"We can't afford more geniuses—how about a smaller room?"

D.A.'s laughter hooted down the line. "Sounds like a blast—send it over, but do me a favor: if you find any random sets of three Roman numerals followed by random letters, end 'em my way, okay?" She rang off.

Rizzo aimed the mouth of her bottle at him. "You found an enigma code? I feel like I stepped through a time warp."

"Total Dr. Who moment," Anderson murmured.

Rizzo tipped her head to study Grant. "Guess that makes you the new doctor?"

Anderson's lips hinted at a smile.

Hum Int was the ancient art of becoming someone else, gaining trust, and breaking confidences. Grant had never watched the show, but it was one of a million topics he knew just enough about to fake it. "You're trying to sign me on for a new companion." He closed the lid of the laptop and regarded Anderson. "She's afraid to place you in protective custody. This guy has a lot of support in law enforcement, if they got you out of lock-up once, they'll find a way to do it again. It's better they think you're dead, at least for a while." He shifted his attention to Rizzo. "I'm assuming this is where I come in. You want me to keep him alive."

Anderson's shoulders slumped. "Jesus," he said again, softer this time, closer to prayer than protest.

"Keep him safe, I would've said, but that's about the size of it. I don't know what else to do, who else to trust."

"I'm not a bodyguard, Sheriff—that's not my line, but I could use an extra pair of hands on this, and extra set of eyes on the evidence. If you're on my team, even temporarily, you live by my rules. You do what I say, you don't take risks, you don't blow my operation."

Anderson shifted in his seat. "I'm a little out of my depth here, Mr. Casey." Anderson delivered the line with a nervous chuckle, acknowledging it for the understatement it was.

"Agreed, but you didn't ask to be there. Somebody pitched you into the deep end and that is not right. I'm not sending you into the field. If anything, you'll be on lockdown right here, along with all the Twinkies you can eat." He put out his hand. "I stand by my team, Anderson. If it is in my power to keep you alive, I will do so."

Anderson's throat bobbed. He wet his lips, but when he reached out, his handshake was firm. "What is it you want me to do?"

"We need to figure out the link from China to the Nazis. In order to do that, I need an expert on U-boats. Are you willing?"

"Okay?" Chris managed a smile.

"Makes sense." Rizzo pushed back and stood up. "I've got an artifact sting to run. Where are you planning to start?"

"Another trip through time. Tracking the money of an American billionaire."

CHAPTER THIRTY-ONE

Thank you, Mrs. MacAllister. Sheriff Rizzo will be so pleased to hear of your support. I'll look for your check." Adam grinned at the mirror as he concluded his call, then the smile dropped away like the prop that it was. A smile helped him sound appropriately enthusiastic. It made him think again of that curious encounter with Rizzo before lunch. Her and that dog. Was it truly the stress that weighed on her face? Something more was going on, but if he pressed her any harder now, he risked alienating her entirely. Friendly, solicitous, but entirely professional, Adam Lones. Casey at the butte, then Rizzo and her dog. He did not appreciate being surrounded by cagey individuals.

Settling back in his office chair, Adam switched screens to the primitive scratchings he and Hammer had viewed that morning. Basket maker, Nazi, box of wavy lines. The natives made wavy lines all the time: snakes or rivers or who knew what. It could be possible some of these images predated the Great Escape, and had nothing to do with his quest. He glared at them, and zoomed in closer, trying to discern any detail that might help him determine their age. He'd already spent far too long researching petroglyphs to see what he could learn. Grant Fucking Casey probably knew. His grandfather probably did, too. What about Randy? No doubt he would blubber like a fool if he did know. Adam's hand hovered over his private line. Call Remington, tell him to reel in Randy instead of finishing him?

An alert flashed in the corner of his screen. Adam tapped his intercom. "No calls, no interruptions."

"Yes, sir."

He slid his finger down another panel, and the broad windows of his office opaqued as he switched to a new screen. Finally! The Warden's voice-over-internet software opened, and a pleasant, unfamiliar voice said, "You've reached the Rockefeller Foundation Archives, how may we help?"

"Hi, there. This is Professor Engel, from the anthropology lab at the Harvard Institute?" Another pleasant voice, male, confident, mid-range, and utterly familiar: Grant Casey. What the Hell scam was he pulling?

"Good afternoon, Professor, what can I do for you?" Whoever was speaking on the Warden's end didn't supply a name. Interesting, when Casey's intro clearly fished for one. Adam steepled his fingers, leaning closer. The zombie computer showed the same view it always did, including the hands and arms of the person in front of the screen. The Warden? Definitely a female voice. Her duplicity stuck in his stomach like bad Tex-mex.

"I'm following up on some notes regarding the Peking Man excavations, and I understand your institute participated in supporting that research. I hadn't realized your philanthropy stretched so far, both in time and space."

"The Foundation has always committed both financial and personnel resources to important research, the world over. I'm not familiar with the Harvard Institute, however—do you have any research the Foundation should consider funding?"

A college professor's wet dream. And an attempt to draw out the person on the other end of the line.

The fake professor chuckled. "That would be fantastic. I'll ask one of my grad students to write a brief about our current projects that I can send your way. But I know we're close to the end of business hours, and I'd hate to keep you too long. In tracking down Peking Man references, I came across this name, Terrance Cartier? He was at the Beijing Embassy, and may have received the two cases of specimens that later went missing—but I can't find any follow-up. Then he pops up as one of the officers of your Foundation's Asian branch. There's not much on the web, of course, but I found this number on a related article. Can you help me track him down?"

The Warden's fingers ticked over a keyboard through a long moment otherwise silent. "Professor Engel, I'm afraid your Mr. Cartier is rather far back in our records. Perhaps you'd like to come to the archive to conduct your research in person?"

Adam scowled at his screen. Each of them was trying to get the other one to commit, and neither of them was falling for the bait. Casey asked for a routine search of the archives, the Warden tried to con him into giving her more. If it weren't for the fact he recognized Casey's voice on the Warden's line, the whole conversation would be utterly meaningless. Could it be some sort of coincidence? Another investigation Casey was running at the same time? Far too much of a coincidence that Adam's own contact would be involved. He did some finger-tapping of his own, pulling up reams of speculation about the missing bones.

"I'm actually at a conference at the moment, just filling sometime between sessions. Maybe I can schedule a visit at a later time."

"The name does ring a bell. If you'd like to leave a contact number, I can check the files and perhaps get back to you?"

"Sounds great—I would very much appreciate anything you can tell me." He rattled off a number. "I'd be particularly interested to know if Mr. Cartier had any other international assignments for the Foundation."

"Certainly, Professor. Enjoy your conference." The chipper voice rang off.

Given their recent encounters, Adam didn't think Casey was the kind of man to idle when he was on the trail of something. How much did he know about the treasure at the center of this map? Adam had already used his Trojan Horse to rifle the Warden's files and found the computer nearly empty: clearly a machine she used only for communication purposes. While on the call with Casey, the Warden had searched on the name and institute Casey gave, finding that both were real, and the professor in question was even listed on a conference schedule. The phone call on her end could be completely legit. What had Adam really learned? That she worked for the Rockefeller Foundation? Maybe that's how she'd gotten hole of the diary that sparked the quest.

Peking Man. Adam's fingers pressed together. That couldn't really be what they were searching for. "The greatest treasure the Nazis ever lost?" From what he could tell, they'd never had it. But if it were...the Warden's perfidy grated. He had imagined a treasure worth even more than the quite healthy finders' fee the Warden was paying him. He had envisioned perhaps cutting her out of the bargain altogether, or ransoming her prize for an even greater sum. Adam worked a quick decision tree in his head, thinking through the costs and benefits of betraying his source. If he did find something as iconic as Peking Man, he could take a page from the unfortunate Randy's playbook and host an auction. The Warden would, of course, be welcome to bid.

For a time, mundane affairs captured his attention, then the alert came again, the Warden dialing out this time, the very same number Casey had just given her. "Professor Engel?"

"Speaking."

"I'm calling with the Rockefeller Foundation. I have some information you might be interested in."

"That's fantastic! I didn't expect to hear from you so quickly."

The warden's hands folded lightly together. "Given that you are currently on stage delivering your paper, Professor, I wasn't sure you'd pick up."

Casey took a breath, and the Warden continued, "No need to dissemble any further. I am impressed that you went so far as to choose an actual person at an actual conference. Pity you didn't know about the schedule change for Professor Engel's talk. Alas, the sponsoring organization is not prompt with their online updates. Would you care to tell me who you really are, and why you called?"

A chuckle of something like appreciation. "Quite frankly, I'd rather not—and I expect you'd say the same."

"You intrigue me, Mr. Anonymous. The line you called is hardly common knowledge, nor is it easy to locate."

"It's a trigger, isn't it. Just calling that number. Dang."

Casey didn't sound remotely upset. Now, the Warden chuckled, with a warmth that added to the growing snarl in Adam's gut. Once again, Casey was moving in, seducing Adam's own sources. How? Why? He clearly had information that Adam lacked. Just for a moment, he imagined that knowledge wasn't all that Casey had over him, a thought that constricted his vision and hardened his teeth.

"The number is a little lure, a way to winnow the casual treasure-hunter from those who might truly apply themselves."

"And yet," Casey continued, still agonizingly casual, "you don't know where the bones are, do you."

"Nor do you, or you would not have called. You were following a link that shouldn't exist, a thread across time and space. I've been pursuing that thread myself, for rather a long time. I don't suppose you'd like to follow it on my behalf? I could, of course, provide a handsome reward."

Adam's hands ground into fists and he forced them smooth, pressing his palms against the glass surface of his desk. She wouldn't dare to cut Adam out of this deal. Not for Casey, not if she didn't even know who he was. But if she did? The Bone Guard, the hotshot organization that found Genghis Khan's tomb. Adam never should've injured the old man, but that was a decision tree that couldn't bear fruit.

"Tempting. But as you say, the thread's pretty old, maybe it's broken. Maybe it's just in a tangle."

"You have followed it this far, which is more than I can say for any other seeker."

Adam stiffened as if she had just jabbed her accusing finger at his sternum.

"Let's be clear, you've got no idea how far along I am, or how much further I'll go. Aside from the money, what else could you contribute to untangle some of those knots?"

"Perhaps you can give me some idea of what you need?"

Another pause. Longer this time, as if Casey were constructing a tree of his own, then he said, "Roman numerals. Three of them."

"Oh, my!" She gave a peal of delighted laughter, a sound Adam had never heard before. He wanted to wrap his hands around her scrawny throat. "I see, Mr.—?"

"Sorry, still not that friendly."

"No matter. You've got a code. How marvelous. Yes, I might have something you'd find of use." Her hands reached aside, and drew forth the familiar soft leather book, caressing its surface. "You may call me 'the Warden.' I'll be in touch." The connection went dead.

Adam swept his arm across his desk, sending pens, mints, stapler, coasters flying across the room, and bolted to his feet. The imprint of his sweaty hands remained on the desktop. A code? What code did Casey find? How would Adam get hold of it? He closed his eyes and breathed through his nostrils, then picked up the phone, and put on his smile.

"Memorial Hospital, how may I help you?"

"My name's Randy Manuel," Adam said, "My grandfather, Frank, has been recovering from his injuries, but I know he'd really like to come home. Is there any chance he could be released?"

"Hold a moment, please." For a little while, tinny music played into his ear, then the voice came back on. "Yes, Mr. Manuel, I'm glad you called. The latest note from his team says he could return home, but they'll want to set him up for physical therapy when he's a little further down the road."

"That's great news." Adam's grin turned genuine. "I'd like to be there as soon as possible. When can you have him ready for pick up?"

CHAPTER THIRTY-TWO

J amie plodded up the slope diagonally, pausing every so often to listen. She'd heard a car over the rise a little while ago, but nothing since, not even the slamming of a door. Damn, but she wished she could've brought Princess out here and covered the ground in half the time. She came up behind a fence, split-rail with stones at the bottom, the wood weathered silver and splintery by the passage of time. A few rusty strands of barbed wire skewered the air around it, but the fence enclosed only tumbleweeds. The back of the first house came into view. What kind of a wise-ass held an exclusive auction at a ghost town? She hadn't met this Randy, but he was already pissing her off.

A bare handful of buildings remained in the little town of Ruby, some of them wooden structures left over from the Pre-Cambrian era, and a few buildings from a farm that had tried, and failed, to reclaim the ruin. Long twilight shadows stretched across the ground from the craggy old cottonwood trees and the legs of a windmill that had lost its head. Pity the place didn't have one of those saloons with the swinging doors, or for sure, Manuel would be doing his business inside of it, probably wearing a ten-gallon hat and a tooled leather holster. She smiled at the image and make sure her own gun slid easy in its holster before she moved closer. Dry grass swished against her legs. Boards covered the windows at the back, though the crumbling roof would hardly keep out weather or trespassers. Another car purred up beyond the building—she caught a glimpse of the pale, gleaming shape as it cruised along the street. It passed the next structure and stopped. As she stalked closer, she glimpsed the hood of a dark sedan then the whole shape of it, pulled in behind the crushed remnants of a barn. Jamie froze, staring in that direction. Her beige uniform provided good camouflage in this environment, so long as motion didn't give her away. The sun came from her right and behind the ridge she'd come over, leaving her in shadow as well. The glare on the windows of the hidden car made it hard to tell if anyone were waiting inside.

After a long breath, she sank down low and tapped out a text on her phone. "Gold car just pulled in."

This earned her a thumbs up from Deputy Johannsen in place on the south side of town.

She added: "Broken barn hides dark sedan. Nobody visible."

Her deputy sent a thumbs up. After a moment, their back-up, an additional pair of deputies waiting in an official vehicle outside of town, sent a thumbs-up of their own.

Great. She wanted communication, and got "likes." In an ideal world, she'd have a helicopter up there, giving her the overall view. Maybe a drone would be a good investment for the department. That'd look good for her campaign: investing in the latest crime-stopping technology. Better than those fools who bought Bearcats with federal funding. Of course, her campaign manager might be a thief who had attempted murder. Her shoulders itched in her uniform.

From the sleek new car, a door opened, then slammed, and a second door a bit later than the first. One person getting out, then getting something from a seat she guessed.

"Mr. Manuel?" A man's voice called out. "I'm here about the items you advertised?"

For a moment, nothing, then boots on a wooden floor at the front of the building. "Why, good evening, Mr. Remington. You're the first bidder to arrive."

Remington? Like the lawyer that picked up Chris? Jamie's hand felt slick on the butt of her gun.

"I'm not the only one?"

Manuel sounded pleased with himself when he replied, "The other bidder's on the way, just running a little late." One of Jamie's people, using the credentials of Casey's fake gallery in Monterey, but the bidder's damn car got stuck in the sand. "I hope you brought some extra cash. Why don't you come on up?"

"Are you sure that flooring is safe? It looks pretty old."

Jamie moved forward at a crouch, toward the back of the house, then along it toward where Remington had parked. Get between him and the vehicle, and maybe she could make sure he didn't get away. If this were the same bastard that set Chris up for assassination, they were gonna have words. Except he was supposed to think they had gotten away with it. Two more steps and she would emerge from the shadow of the hill that darkened half the house. Down the field, she caught movement out of the corner of her eye. The empty beams and rafters of the ruined barn stuck up like the skeleton of a cow picked half-bare then left to dry out in the desert heat. Just enough remained of the back wall to shelter the car and shade the man who leaned against one of those beams, hat pulled low, denim pants worn to gray. Probably one of the narcos, keeping an eye on their investment.

"You'll want to get a look at the merchandise," Randy said. "I can vouch for its authenticity—it's all been in my family for generations."

"Is that so? Are you sure you want to part with it?" Footfalls in the dirt as Remington approached.

"We gotta move on to the new world's what I say. Here—" Randy moved around, then he gave a hiss of breath.

"Are you alright? You look a little piqued."

"I got a cut. It's nothing."

Jamie retreated rather than work her way into the sun and leave herself exposed to the narco by the barn. The shady end of the house was closer anyhow. She inched around it, then, seeing nobody and nothing to hide anyone, she straightened, and walked tall, but careful.

"It looks like a fine collection, no doubt," Remington said. "No baskets or pottery, and you know, that's where the real money is."

"Sure, sure, but look here—"

Jamie's last step brought her to the edge of the porch, which stood about mid-thigh.

"Would you mind bringing that blanket down, out in the sun? I sure don't like the look of that porch."

Manuel cleared his throat, then said, "You did bring the money, right?"

"Oh, yeah. It's in my trunk. Once I'm sure I like what I see, you can help me carry this stuff over, and I'll give you the cash, nice and easy, say, twenty percent more than we agreed? There's no need to get into a bidding war."

Fabric rustled, Manuel grunted as he moved again—that cut he mentioned obviously hurting. Jamie pulled her cellphone, making sure the back camera was on, and held it just a little past the edge of the siding, getting a side-long view of the porch on the screen. A makeshift table occupied part of her view. A stocky Native man carried a blanket over his arm as he made his way down the ancient porch steps. Another man in a pale suit and a wide-brimmed hat watched his approach from the street. She couldn't make out much of his face aside from the smile that spread as Manuel came out into the sun.

"This good?" Manuel planted his feet with another soft grunt of pain, then he unfurled the blanket, holding it up by the corners, arms spread. "The pattern is pre-war, woven by my great grandmother."

"It's a fine example—definitely good to see it in the sun." The other man shuffled closer, making more noise than warranted to cover the sound as he drew a gun from the waistband of his pants.

Jamie snatched out her own weapon and lunged past the porch. "Manuel! Get down! Remington—drop your weapon! Hands in the air!"

Manuel pivoted, his eyes flaring in surprise. The blanket whipped up around him as a gunshot cracked the air. He tumbled to the dust like a character in a Western movie. Jamie got off a shot of her own, but Remington was already sprinting for his car. He staggered but kept running, blood spattering the leg of his fine suit and specking the sand. Screaming, Manuel flailed on the ground, the blanket over him.

"What the hell!"

Remington's shout snapped her attention away from Manuel. Remington stumbled short of his car. Two men in denim and low hats already stood there.

"Where's the money?" One of them said, in a low rumble that Jamie could feel from her shooting stance. Holy fucking shit. The narcos. She jammed the emergency button on her phone.

On the ground not far away, Randy Manuel writhed and wailed under the ruined blanket. Jamie sprang forward, diving low. She grabbed the blanket and Randy's shoulders underneath it. A boost of adrenaline and she rolled him onto the blanket, hauling it toward the back of the building as fast as she could.

"There is no money," Remington snarled back. He brought up his gun.

Jamie scrambled backwards as fast as she could. She sprawled on her backside, got up again and kept hauling as the shriek of her deputy's siren echoed down the street.

"County Sheriff! Everyone just cool down and hold it right there!" Deputy Johannsen called out from his place on the far side of the street. "We've got you covered!"

The narcos stopped short then ran for their car. Remington jerked open his passenger side door and launched himself inside.

"The car! Shoot the car!" Jamie hollered, then she was out of line-of-sight, shoving Randy onto his back as more shots echoed and a car roared to life, scattering gravel.

"Hey, it's okay—I've got you." Twice in one day. Jesus and Mary. Blood streamed from his lower ribs, right side where the bullet had caught him as he turned in response to her warning.

He gasped for breath, both hands clutching at the blanket. The squad car rushed by and rocked to a stop, disgorging Deputy Poirier, a first aid kit clutched in his hand.

"Remington, the guy in the gold car, shot him. Remington's injured, too."

Poirier nodded rapidly, pulling out a radio to call in a request for a Lifeflight, while the remaining deputy jammed the gas and the car took off.

Jamie yanked a bundle of gauze from the kit and pulled Randy's own belt. "Hold this in place." She grabbed one of Randy's flailing hands and pressed it to the bandage, then pulled on rubber gloves. "We've got a copter on the way. They'll get you to the hospital."

Randy's head bobbed in a desperate nod.

"Maybe you can share a room with your grandfather." Jamie pulled the belt tight, applying pressure to the wound and holding the bandage in place.

Poirier cocked his head. "Frank Manuel, you mean? We got word while we were waiting—he's been released to the custody of his grandson."

"Fucking...Casey," Randy muttered.

Casey was holed up with Anderson, tracking down history—the last thing he wanted was custody of his grandfather. Jamie took Randy's wrist to count his heartrate, watching blood seep at the corners of the gauze. Watching the gauze soak through.

"Not Casey—another Manuel." Poirier checked his phone. "Randy Manuel—wait." He frowned and his glance flicked to the wounded man. "Isn't that you?"

As far as Jamie knew, only God could be everywhere at once, and Randy was about as far as a man could get from God. Unless he was about to be a good deal closer.

CHAPTER THIRTY-THREE

Grant's computer gave the chime that indicated an incoming call. The Warden again? Could be—a couple hours had passed. D.A. reported that Lones had a tap on the Warden's computer, and he'd gotten so pissed after overhearing Grant's call that he'd knocked everything off his desk and disrupted the bug Gooney planted on his coaster. Rotten luck, just when it would have been most useful. He closed a few windows of research. The indicator showed an unknown contact, priority level: urgent. Grant's skin cooled. "Chris, back to your room—I need silence."

Anderson gave a nod. He scooped up his own laptop—thank you, one-hour office delivery—and retreated beyond the adjoining door as Grant answered the call. "You've reached me."

"Casey. We've got someone here who wants to talk with you." Hammer's voice, unless Grant missed his mark.

The sound of breathing on the other end of the line. Hammer again, not as close. "Come on, fucker. Say something." More breathing—then the slap of a hand against flesh. "You want me to kill you? That what you want, old man? Don't go all silent Injun on me." Another slap, harder.

The blow rocked him, but Grant went still. "You've got Frank."

"That's right, you son of a bitch. I have your grandfather, and unless you do exactly as I say, you'll never see him again."

"Hadn't seen him for fifteen years until this week."

Hammer growled into the phone, "That's how you wanna play this?"

It was the truth, but it didn't bear repeating.

"Oh, right. That pretty nurse told me a few other things, like about how my sister would be up at the observatory—"

How far would he go for his grandfather? How much would he risk? But Cece didn't deserve any of this. "What do you want?"

"Here's the coordinates. Just you. No law enforcement. No hero shit."

An IM flashed below the empty video box, with a stream of digits.

"You've got twenty minutes. Hope you're not still in Phoenix." The connection severed.

"Chris!" Grant was already on his feet. He plugged the numbers into a mapping program and saw the destination, a track in the wilderness. Barely that.

Anderson popped his head through the door. "Do you—what's the matter?"

Grant traced the route on-screen with his eyes, committing it to memory. "Abduction, death threats. The usual." Lones didn't want Frank, he wanted Grant. He started to slide his phone into his pocket—then stopped. It contained a wealth of intel and the last thing he wanted was to deliver it to enemy hands. Instead, he held it out to Anderson. "Okay, Lazarus. Call D.A. tell her they've got Frank. This thing is priority one. If she can reach Gooney she needs to—" What? Twenty minutes to rendezvous, half an hour to be a sack of meat by the side of the road. "Scratch that. Tell Rizzo—" He glanced at the clock. She'd still be out at Randy's meet. "When she calls in. Tell her where to look for the bodies."

"Yours or somebody else's?"

Grant flashed him a smile. "You learn fast." He stripped his pockets of anything that linked him to the hotel. Ditched his wallet. Took the car key. His hand hovered a moment over the ceremonial blade in its beaded sheath, then he tucked it at his waist.

"And you called me Lazarus." Anderson held the phone to his chest, probably an unconscious effort to ease a racing heart. "What are you walking into?"

"God only knows and I don't have time to ask him." No back-up, unless Frank could be counted on to listen and follow orders. Grant shook his head, eased back his shoulders and took a deep breath, letting it out slow.

Slow is smooth and smooth is fast.

"Don't die." Anderson blurted as Grant set his hand on the door.

"Do my best." He slipped out into the night. Two minutes found him behind the wheel. Sixteen minutes, and the last of the city lights died away in his rearview mirror, leaving him alone in the desert with the occasional cactus or distant home that quickly faded as well. Between the warden's call and now, Lones had orchestrated an abduction from the hospital and set a rendezvous, and those coordinates weren't random: the satellite showed a cluster of old vehicles around a rusted-out barn, a common feature anyplace land was cheap. They knew he was coming. They knew the territory and they'd have people in place. No time for plans or back-up, no time for a proper risk assessment. He turned off the reservation road into a dirt track, then another. He rolled the window down, listening. A few hills rose and fell around him. Nineteen minutes. His headlights glanced off of shattered glass in the windshield of a battered Ford. Cars lined up to the left, an old bus far right, wrecked barn straight ahead, the most likely hideout. If it were his op, he'd have someone in the bus, on or under it. Someone among the cars, someone on the roof. They got here in a vehicle, one that still ran. Two choices: camouflage with the wrecks, or put it in the barn. If he were right and it wasn't the first time Lones employed this site, either area could be prepped.

They were expecting him. Time to do something unexpected.

Grant gunned the engine, spinning sand out behind him in a swirling cloud as he drove straight for the barn. He smashed the remaining door off its hinge and heard a satisfying yelp from behind it. Back end of a van in the headlights. Odds were his grandfather was inside. Stomping the accelerator, Grant swung his car around, skidding sideways and stopping just short of the van.

"What the Hell!" Somebody dove out of his way, a gun winking briefly through his headlights.

Kill the lights, pop the door, slide across the old vinyl seat and drop out the other side. They didn't want him dead, not until they knew what he'd found, and that would buy him some time.

"Freeze, Casey!" Hammer, with a gun aimed through the empty car.

In two bounds, Grant vaulted over the hood and felled Hammer like deadwood.

Grab the gun, continue his roll as Hammer gasped for breath. Grant came up in shadows on one knee, gun in both hands trained back toward Hammer and the van beyond.

The sound of a trigger being cocked, and two figures standing by the door of the van, one with a gun to the chin of the other. Good choice. Gun at the temple, a prepared hostage could just duck away and clear the weapon long enough for his partner to squeeze off a round.

"If you want him dead, keep on fighting." Lones, cold, clear and serious.

A gunshot from his right, outside, shattered the back window of his car. When the echoes ebbed away, another round chambered.

Wheezing, Hammer dragged himself up and stuck his arm into the car. "Lights," he groaned, and turned them on, illuminating Lones with a grip on the nape of Frank's neck. The old man looked a little pale, combination of the harsh light, the hospital stay, the current circumstances. He wore a sling on his left arm, thick and probably concealing a cast. One of his silver bracelets decorated the other wrist, hanging loose. His black eyes stared straight ahead, and he might've been in a trance. He hadn't spoken to confirm his own life; maybe he hadn't even cared if Grant took the call.

Three hostiles in the barn, at least two of them even more hostile since Grant's entrance. At least one outside who had a range weapon. If that were a member of his team held hostage, the guy would've signaled the total number of hostiles, made some attempt at communication for coordinated action.

Blood marked the corner of the old man's mouth and his eyelid slouched on that side, showing the effects of the blows. Lones held Frank a little in front of himself, trying for more cover, while at the same time trying to look like he didn't need it. Plenty of his head remained exposed. Grant estimated the distance at fifteen yards, an easy shot. He nails Lones, the guy outside nails him. Do they abort the plan without Lones to lead them, or do they keep Frank alive, go for Cece, for Teo, for anyone who might help them acquire their target?

Grant released his grip. He dropped the weapon, then took out the knife as well, tossing it alongside. Did Frank's eyelids twitch at that?

"Push it away, then I want you face down, hands behind your back."

He followed orders, head slightly turned toward the action. Hay dust tickled his nose. He refused to sneeze. In this narrow view, Hammer climbed into the car and started it up. For a moment, he stayed behind the wheel, engine running, the hood pointed in Grant's direction. Left front tire ready to crush Grant's skull into the gravel. Or maybe he'd aim with the right tire, so he could do more damage to the corpse.

Lones cleared his throat, and Hammer backed the car up, letting it crunch into the far wall. Couldn't have made him as happy as crunching Grant would have. He emerged, holding himself erect, and walked stiffly over to claim the gun Grant had co-opted. "Fucking asshole." He sounded breathy, not yet recovered from his earlier grounding. He dropped down, planting a knee in Grant's back as he wrapped Grant's wrists together with cable ties. Three. That should do it. Grant's ribs ached from the pressure on his chest. Hammer eased off, then wrestled Grant's hiking shoes off, apparently checking for other weapons. He tossed them aside.

Hammer rose, a little unsteady still. He hauled Grant along with him by the elbow and steered him toward the van.

Frank's dark gaze remained distant, staring through the broken doors into the last of the dusk. Lones turned a little to watch his minion's progress, but kept his weapon at the ready, nestled beneath the old man's chin.

Just behind the side door, Hammer shoved Grant's back against the side of the van, then slammed a kick into his sternum. The breath rushed from Grant's lungs and his head rebounded from the metal. Pain exploded at the back of his skull and Grant slumped to his knees. His eyes watered as he gasped for breath. He could fight back. He could rise up, right now, land this guy and sprint into the desert. He could be gone in moments, and his grandfather could be dead. How many times as a teenager had he wished that very thing?

Stones ground into his knees and the old roof above showed a ragged hole. Clear desert night arched above him, decked with stars, home to the deities of a hundred nations, and he did not run.

CHAPTER THIRTY-FOUR

Adam let himself relax. Casey's vigilante Batmobile entrance had put him on edge, but his men handled themselves well, in spite of everything. Even Hammer, furious as he was, didn't give in to any wild urges. Excellent. Now, his opponent crouched near the van, struggling for breath and already bleeding. Casey blinked a little too much, his eyes slow to focus. And the Warden imagined Casey could find the treasure Adam sought.

"Find his phone."

"It's not here," Casey murmured, lifting his gaze toward Adam.

The old man still hadn't acknowledged Casey's presence, or much of anything else since he got outside and realized that Hammer was not anybody's friend from work, and that nobody he knew, or wanted to know, was bringing the car up to take him home.

"Bullshit. Find it." Lones punctuated this with another dig of the gun barrel into the soft flesh of Manuel's throat. The old man had recognized him right away. Maybe now that he'd met Casey, he wasn't too surprised. Two of a kind: cagey, quick and obstinate. And totally in Adam's power, now.

"Sir." Hammer dragged Casey to his feet again, pushing him face-first against the van this time and kicking his feet wider apart. He groped Casey roughly up and down. With a growl, Hammer swung Casey around and searched him again, rougher this time, in spite of the fact that the nondescript jeans and sun shirt wouldn't hide much. Adam thought of his morning's work, fooling that faggot into thinking he cared. Had it just been that morning? How time flew.

"Nothing, sir. Not even a penny." Hammer crossed to the car without being told and bent through the open door. Compartments opened and closed with increasing frustration. He emerged, hands braced on the roof of the car, and head swiveled toward Casey. Through it all, Casey just stood there, his shoulders heaving a little with each breath.

As if the man's very poise cracked Hammer's patience, Hammer slammed the car door. He still had the key in hand, fidgeting with it as he stalked closer. Then he let the key tip poke between his knuckles, a short claw of metal. He smashed his fist into Casey's stomach, drawing back a splash of blood as Casey flinched. "Where's the phone?"

Casey hunched around the wound. Did Adam mistake himself, or did the man finally look a little rattled? Casey wet his lips and said, "Far away."

Casey twisted downward and the second blow landed at his ribs, scraping rather than stabbing.

"He's not going to give it up," Adam said.

Hammer drew back his fist then punched again, blood dripping from the key like a prop in a horror film. He held it ready for a third, but he didn't let the blow fall.

"It's this simple, Mr. Casey. I know that you know more than you're saying. That you have something we do not." He pulled the gun away and pointed toward the knife that still lay on the floor some distance off. "Mr. Smith, if you please."

"Sir." Smith emerged from the shadows by the entrance. He retrieved the knife left-handed, not replacing his sidearm, and brought the knife over to Adam's side, waiting until Adam slipped away his own gun and drew the blade, a broad Bowie-style weapon that would make an admirable hunting aid.

His hand sweat against the old man's neck, and man swallowed. "Honestly," Adam said, "I have wondered if you even care whether this man lives or dies, given your attitude. Perhaps an experiment is in order?" He brushed his thumb over the edge of the blade and found it sharp. He shifted his left hand to pinch the old man's earlobe, then he carved into it, slicing it in half from the base of the ear. The old man jerked against his grip. Adam squeezed harder and blood dribbled down onto the man's shoulder. By holding carefully, Adam even managed to stay clean himself. A perfect blow. He moved his hand again, pinching the ear higher up, raising the knife. A beautiful thing, even, or perhaps even more so, with its cutting edge gleaming red. "This looks like a native blade. Surprisingly fine work. Or is it the white man's steel that gives it strength?"

He dug the tip in again, but before he cut, Casey said, "The petroglyphs. Up on the butte. Did you ruin them all?"

"Now is hardly the time for cultural concerns."

At the elevation of Adam's eyebrow, Hammer's fist aimed low and upward even as Casey tried to evade it. Casey's shirt tore and blood streaked his side.

"The fish. The one that looks like a fish," Casey said, gasping half like a fish himself. "It's not, it's a submarine."

Adam pulled back the knife, loath to do anything unnecessary. "A submarine? Really. And what does it mean?"

"I don't know—I haven't figured that out yet." Casey dropped and twisted away from Hammer.

Hammer's off-hand shot out, grabbing a fistful of hair before Casey dropped out of reach. The key-fist punched hard into Casey's shoulder, a little more manly than the usual way-to-go punch.

"I haven't worked it out," Casey managed, back on his knees again, his neck drawn taut by Hammer's grip in his hair.

"You have a code. You needed numbers." Adam nicked the old man's ear, keeping the knife ready to slice downward.

"It's a fucking submarine code! I told you, I don't know what it means!"

Either the submarine image held the clue Adam needed, the one that got the Warden so excited, or Casey was lying—in which case, no amount of pain they inflicted seemed likely to get at the truth.

"In that case, I'll go see for myself." Adam replaced the knife in its sheath, still held in Smith's ready hands. He yanked open the van door and helped the old man inside, as tenderly as if it were his own grandfather. A row of seats occupied the near wall, with the rest of the space left open for storage and hauling. He buckled the old man into the nearest seat. "Don't worry, Mr. Manuel. We'll meet again soon. I'm a little curious to know what else you might be hiding." He even pulled out a smile, but the old man looked away, his chin dropping so he looked like the Indian on that dreary "Trail's End" artwork.

"Hammer? I'll let you handle this evening. I think you've earned it."

Hammer brightened, squaring his broad shoulders. "Thank you, sir." To Casey, he said, "On your feet," adding a tug on the man's hair.

Bracing against the van, Casey heaved himself up, swaying a little. Before he got his balance, Hammer caught his elbow and peeled him away from the supportive vehicle, then flung him through the open door.

Casey sprawled on the floor inside with a muffled cry, and Hammer slid the door shut behind him, then turned to Adam. "You don't think we can use him as leverage against the old man?"

"You just perforated him with a car key, and the old man didn't even flinch. I don't think it'll matter. Casey has enough honor to care. It probably comes from the Mexican blood. For the old man?" He glanced back at the windowless van, with flecks of Casey's blood along the side. "We'll have to locate a different inflection point. Maybe after the ceremony, the old man will loosen up."

Hammer nodded. "Right. I'll take care of tonight. You track down the code."

Pity that Remington was handling other business. Adam would have to drive himself, at least to where he could reach his own vehicle. At least Casey had brought them an option.

"Key?"

Hammer paused to wipe off his impromptu weapon before handing it over. Adam approached the battered vehicle, wrinkling his nose. How Casey could even stomach driving this piece of trash... No matter. Adam just needed to return to his own vehicle. As he pulled out of the barn, he flashed the lights, and waved his other men out of hiding, pointing them back toward the barn. They offered him an arm raised in salute, and Adam settled back into the repugnant upholstery, feeling, in spite of his borrowed ride, like the master of a parade or, better yet, the vanguard of an army.

CHAPTER THIRTY-FIVE

Grant opened his eyes into the dim light of the van. His head throbbed—slammed from the back against the van, and from the front against its unyielding floor. Blood seeped from his temple and oozed along his cheek, scraped against the metal grate that served as a subfloor. "Sit rep?" He spoke into the darkness.

"What?" First word from the old man since Grant arrived on the scene, and likely for hours before that.

"Sit rep!" Grant barked at him. "Are you hurt? What do you know about the situation?"

"Report. Right. Not much. My ear's bleeding."

Grant closed his eyes against the pain and mastered his breathing. It hurt almost as much as they thought it did. "How many men?"

"Three in the van. Three more when we got here. Are...are you hurt?"

Not relevant. "All with sidearms, one rifle—anything else you noticed?"

Frank made a little sound that might have been amusement or disbelief. "It's not your first time like this, is it."

Also not relevant. "We don't have time for that. Two minutes, tops, we get a driver and they're in charge. Have they said anything? Did you hear anything that might help us get out of this?"

"They're already in charge, far's I can tell." He blew out a breath and shifted in his seat, and Grant could picture him doing the same thing at the kitchen table, cup of coffee by his hand, the pose of contemplation. Minutes or hours later, he'd suddenly come out with what he wanted to say. Something else they had no time for.

Grant flexed his fingers. They felt a little chubby already, the cable ties biting in. Head injuries: painful and dizzying, but not disaster. Minor puncture wounds hurt like hell, but not deep enough to hit anything vital.

"Something about an initiation, the ceremony he mentioned. He's upset about somebody you talked to, he thinks he won't get the money she promised. He's also mad that it's a woman. He killed someone this morning. Pretty proud of that, but he didn't speak of it in so many words."

So many words indeed. For Frank, that was a speech. "That's good intel. Names?"

"Fake," Frank replied instantly. "Face names that don't mean anything. The boss gave each of them a name, that's the one they use. Hammer, Smith, Wesson."

And Remington. Gun brands or parts. "Accents? All local?"

"Hammer and Wesson are local. Smith and the boss, no. The others didn't speak. Talked to somebody on the phone from New England."

"Van: the wall between us, is it mesh or solid?"

"Solid. The door has mesh."

"Locked?"

A front door opened and somebody climbed in, rocking the van a little, then another from the other. "Check out this knife—it's like trade goods or something. I've never seen beadwork like that." Hammer.

Opening the doors brought the overhead light on. Grant pushed himself onto his side, reluctant to roll onto his aching hands, though he would if he had to. Mesh in the door, just as Frank said. A horizontal turn handle. No lock in evidence. One piece of good news. Aside from knowing his grandfather was a damn good scout.

"That's a nice piece alright." New voice, unknown, but the accent was out of town. Smith or one of the others. Something briefly occluded the light. "Should we secure the prisoner?"

"More than we already have? No need. Let's go."

Secure the prisoner. That's what he should've been doing. Grant pulled himself to sitting, drawing a sharp pain from those minor punctures.

Frank occupied one of four bare-bones seats bolted to the side wall. Metal struts underneath, little storage nets. The van rumbled to life, then jolted into reverse. Grant pitched across the floor and slammed sideways into the dividing wall with a grunt.

From the cab a few chuckles. "Buckle up for safety!" Hammer called.

The van swung around to the left, hurtling Grant against the featureless sidewall. His head and shoulders crumpled, and his mouth filled with blood. He coughed sharply. They accelerated straight and he slid to the back, the flooring now lubricated with his own blood. He got his feet in position to cushion the impact, but it still jolted through his joints. Abducted before. Check. But usually by people who cared if he got there whole.

When the van braked again, Grant swung his feet out toward the side. His toes snagged the net under one of the chairs and he humped himself in that direction, sticking his foot further under the seat, trying to hook the strut against his ankle.

This time, when the van turned, he scraped against the floor, but he didn't hit the walls. Another turn, the opposite direction. The net tore free and his foot started to slide, the metal strut peeling off his sock and grinding against tendons.

A lean, strong hand grabbed his calf, pinning him, silver cuff around a deep-tan wrist. Grant lay on his back, his hands under him, right foot twisted awkwardly to stay close to the seats. In the feeble light from the door grate, he caught the gleam of the old man's eyes staring down at him. Frank's hand tightened as they bumped over a series of ruts. Each one rocked Grant off the floor and let him thud back again, turning the van into a drum, using his head to keep the beat. His vision transformed into sharp strokes of color and darkness.

As if he appreciated the rhythm, Frank started to sing. Loud, harsh syllables that resembled a pow wow chant, but with no sense of flow or continuity. Grant's eyes squeezed shut and he wished he could shut his ears as well. Every bump struck pain through his head and down his spine, and now his grandfather's howling grated against his ears.

"Knock it off back there!" Smith hollered from the front seat.

Frank paused only to take a deeper breath, then sang even louder, a racket that would carry Grant off to unconsciousness as his skull cracked with the next turn-off. He had never so desperately longed for silence.

"Keep it down, old man. Don't make me come back there and shut you up." Hammer.

Frank cleared his throat. "It's the death chant of my people." He started up again.

Death chant? Like nothing Grant had ever heard. Is this what Frank would've sung at the funeral, if he'd bothered to come? Songs carried great power for the Tohono O'odham people. This one carried the power to make him ill.

The van shuddered to a halt and the grate went dark as someone popped the door open, their bulk filling the narrow doorway. "Is he dead already? Aw, hell."

"Will be soon with these roads." Frank maintained his iron grip on Grant's leg. "You heard of Freddy Gray? Died in police custody, over in Baltimore. They just drove him around in a van until his back broke." He took another deep breath and resumed his song.

Hammer groaned. He pushed his way into the back and hauled Grant up by the armpit, forced to use both hands to peel him off the floor and shove him sideways into a seat down the row from Frank. Hammer tugged the seatbelt down from the ceiling and clipped it in. He confronted Frank and spread his hands, a few drops of blood scattering. "Happy now? No more fucking death chant?"

"No, sir." Frank leaned back into his seat, tucking his hand under the sling on the opposite elbow.

"Jesus." Hammer crouched his way back into the driver's seat, yanking the door shut, and the van lurched again into motion.

This time, Grant swayed in his seat, his left shoulder pressed against the back, his forehead resting on the backrest between him and Frank. His head pounded, his teeth tasted like blood. And his grandfather's "death chant" had just saved his life.

CHAPTER THIRTY-SIX

J amie yanked a handful of things from the first aid kit. She'd already applied the gauze. She grabbed a maxi pad and tore the package open with her teeth, then pressed that over the wound as well. "Fucking Casey is the reason I'm here. He's the one who sent me. Expressly so you wouldn't die."

"Why they gotta shoot me?"

She wanted to smack him, instead, she told Poirier, "Get our bidder after that second car, the black one—that's our gambling ring. If we keep this guy alive, he's our witness."

"Yes, ma'am." Poirier stepped away with his radio.

"These people are not collectors, Randy. They're mixed up with something a lot bigger, something Casey is trying to stop."

Randy's fevered glance rolled away from her face, searching the heavens. "'S for real, then. Real. Shit."

The whine of copter blades grew, and Poirier jogged out to the street to guide it in.

"The helicopter's almost here, Randy. We'll get you taken care of."

"He sent you? To save me?" Randy coughed and winced as the coughing fit tugged at his wound.

"Yessir, he did. I don't know what the hell there is between you all, but I don't think he is what you think he is."

Tears slipped from Randy's eyes and he sobbed, then seemed to master himself. "I'm what he thinks. I know. I am." He gasped a breath.

"Grammie did it. Cece and the stars. Him and the history. Should've been me. Planned for me, but I—shit."

He coughed again, hard, then added a few words in the local tongue. Words she heard often enough around the courthouse or the streets, usually applied to her, or her deputies.

"Don't talk. It's okay. You're gonna see them again, and you can tell them all about it." Wind whipped up around them, and Jamie shifted position, lifting the side of the blanket to block the scattering dust of the copter's arrival.

"No! Nope. The sub. His sub. His thirteenth birthday—she—" He broke off, gasping.

"This is Rosemary, now?" Jamie leaned closer, sheltering them both and drawing her ear closer to his cracked voice.

Randy nodded, making his cheeks shiver. "Fucked it up for him. Asshole. In the shoebox."

He was losing it, no doubt. The roar of the rotors drowned out any sound for a long moment, then feet thundered toward her. "You're gonna be okay, Randy. They're here for you."

She pulled back as two EMTs ran up carrying their kit. "Gunshot. Lower right side, just below the ribcage, no sign of an exit wound. He's awake, lucid—a-and-o times three." Alert and oriented. For now.

"Name?"

"Randolph Manuel, called Randy."

Jamie edged back and let the pros take over. She set her back to the porch and peeled off the rubber gloves, one into the other, Randy's blood captured inside. The EMTs got Randy on a board and hustled him into the copter, face in an oxygen mask, body still swaddled by his family's blanket. A civilian vehicle fishtailed into the lot as the helicopter took off and Poirier leaned to the window to talk with the driver. "Sheriff, you want—"

"Go with him, get moving!" She pushed to her feet and waved him away. Poirier leapt into the car and directed their fake buyer off toward the narcos. Dust devils spiraled in the wake of both copter and cops. Her hat tumbled off her head, and she retrieved it, then called in to dispatch giving details of her location, the two victims—one in a helicopter, the other trying to outrun her deputies—the need for photography and evidence collection—and a ride. The car that had delivered her to the dunes had just taken off after the bad guys. Jamie stood in the street, looking at the twin blood trails about ten paces apart, Randy's on one side, Remington's on the other. Had she honestly just had a gunfight in a ghost town? She laughed out loud, and thought about calling her dad. Was being sheriff all she had thought it would be? Oh, yeah, Dad, just like in the movies! The ones that had helped her mother learn English. Her laughter died away.

She waited on the porch as the sun sank lower and the crime scene team arrived. Jamie directed them on a little tour of the ruined buildings: the artifacts still on the porch, the places where the two cars had parked, the stains of blood in the street.

One of the police officers trotted up to her. "Rizzo! Remington's car hung up on the edge of a wash. Your deputies gave the warning, but the driver's already dead, bled out from where you shot him, so we've got another crime scene. Johannsen blew out a tire on the black one—they're making the arrests."

"What a night! Thanks for the update."

The officer nodded. "Also, you got a message from dispatch. They want you to answer your phone."

Her phone? "Aw, hell." She pulled it out. Sure enough, the sound was off. Three missed calls, all from Casey's number, no message. Oh, that was bad—he wasn't the kind of guy to double up on the comms unless he needed it. She tapped the sound back on and hit the callback. Standing up, her back aching, Rizzo walked away from the bustling team with their giant lights and busy cameras.

"Sheriff!" A panicked voice that clearly wasn't Casey. "I've been trying to call you—I didn't know what to do."

One of the techs glanced up as Jamie passed by. "Hey, sorry I was out of touch!" Jamie answered with forced good cheer. Another tech aimed her way, but she pointed at the phone and rolled her eyes, then hurried away up the road past the line of sheriff's and forensic vehicles. "Did you really call dispatch, Chris? That could get you killed, you know that."

"Sheriff, he's the one who's gonna get killed. They got his grandfather

—"

"Jesus and Mary!" Jamie smacked the crown of her hat. Two Randy's one of them bleeding half to death on the ground in front of her, the other one supposedly picking up his grandfather. "We had a situation here, shots fired. Hang on, Chris." She pulled an earpiece out of one of the pouches on her duty belt and stuffed it in her ear, switching the call over as she ran down the line of cars. At the edge, another officer stared into the darkness, rocking on her heels, guarding the perimeter. "I need keys—I have an urgent call back in town."

The officer stared at her. "Sheriff Rizzo, I can't just—"

"Keys! Lives are at stake!"

"Right." The officer fumbled them out and pointed to her vehicle.

Jamie jumped in and squealed the tires in a circle too tight as she flew out of the area. "I'm on the way, Chris—tell me everything."

She'd gotten to the outskirts of town, still on the far side from the Motel 6 before he'd finished. "Casey wants me to find the bodies? Shit on a shingle—why am I always two steps behind?" Find the bodies. She hit the siren and swung hard, punching the squad car to the max as she swerved around other cars and rocketed to a stop in front of a darkened building. She jumped out, leaving the lights flashing and ran to the side door for after-hours pick-up. "Open up! It's Rizzo. I need my dog."

CHAPTER THIRTY-SEVEN

The utilitarian seat felt like heaven. It took way too long to regulate his breathing and heartrate. The battering had been worse than he thought. Grant rolled his head back in spite of the pain, letting the blood ooze toward his hair rather than into his eyes. His stomach roiled. Not bad enough for traumatic brain injury. Probably.

Frank hummed softly, the same tuneless tune he used to fill time decades past. After a moment he said, "Always were a mess of bruises."

From the rodeo. From the bullies before he learned to outrun, outfight, outfox them. Grant coughed and spat out a mouthful of blood. Thankfully not teeth. He dredged through his memory, and found the words in a language he hadn't spoken for fifteen years, the language of his grandfather's people, who prized their songs above almost anything. "Thank you for your song, Grandfather." *Grandfather*, a term of honor, not of blood.

Another sound, sharper this time, and Frank shifted in his seat. "You speak the language." He used English, the words of the conquerors.

Grant opened his eyes, staring at the darkness until he could make out the ribs of the metal roof above. "I have a facility with languages. It's part of what makes me good at what I do."

"Kill people in the army."

Why did he always come back to that? "Special operations intelligence unit. Killing is the least of it. If I have to kill, it's already gone south."

"Special operations, like Seal Team Six?"

Grant would have shaken his head if it didn't hurt so goddamn much. "Intelligence. We go in without being spotted. Interact with and identify local sources. Identify targets and key locations. Get everything we need to call down a strike, or to exfiltrate a source. Sometimes a perpetrator, sometimes a defector. Get out again without them ever knowing we were there. Guys like me tell Seal Team Six where to go." He switched back to Tohono O'odham. "Tell me what you know about—" How to refer to the treasure hunt without using English words that would tip off their captors? —"the basket maze."

"Is this one of your interrogations?" Before Grant could rise to that bait, Frank took the hint and answered in the same tongue. "That was Rosemary's work, her and the sailor. I don't know anything."

Bullshit underlay the old man's voice. "Don't lie to me. I don't have time."

The old man grunted again. He was only making noise at all because he couldn't be sure Grant could see him. Otherwise, he'd be silent. The grunt made sure Grant knew he had been heard, and that Frank declined to answer.

"When we stop, they'll kill me. That's how this goes down. As long as they think you know something, they'll keep you alive. When they ask you, stay silent, or make something up. Whatever it takes." Every word, every breath, made something hurt.

Frank shifted, sitting taller. "They won't kill you. You know more than you told him."

"I hurt them, I scared them. They can't risk it." Blood slicked his tongue and he coughed again. Any cuts in the mouth bled too much. "When we stop. I'll make it count, I'll make them work for it." Maybe even get a dozen yards away. There were only two of them. His head and hands were a mess, his abdomen stung, but his legs worked fine. What else did he need to convey? Again, words failed him. It wasn't a language he learned for tactical reasons, and he'd never had reason to build the vocabulary. "If we get the keys, you go through the door and drive north. If not, get out and hide. The —"sheriff?—"law chief will be looking for you."

For a time, they bounced in silence, then the old man said, "You could have escaped, couldn't you, before they got you in here. Unless you lost the skill since leaving here, you could've made that shot. Why didn't you?"

Why didn't he? Why not discount the life of a man he hated? "Because this is what I do: defend other people's cultural artifacts." In which category, his grandfather certainly qualified. The van made a turn, sharply downslope and the lowest puncture wound pressed against his bound arm. "Because that's not who I am."

"Special Operations intelligence," the old man mused, as if trying out the term, or rolling over a discovery. "So you have to learn the language of your enemy." Then, with a little curve of his lips. "I never taught you."

A mass of bruises, the old man said; on the road to becoming a hundred and ninety pounds of vulture meat. His stomach roiled with every turn of the van. He hurt in places he'd forgotten he had.

"Why not? Because I'm a half-breed?" There, he'd said it to his grandfather's face, for the first time ever, the word, in whatever language, stinging his lips. "The fact that I could pass for somebody else, anyone else. That's another thing that makes me good."

"You're not—" Frank began, then his lips pressed together, his eyes cutting away, resolutely forward.

Not good? Even Frank just acknowledged he could've made the shot, made his escape. Not a half-breed? His father had been New Mexican Spanish. Then Grant seized upon the truth, what he'd maybe already known. "Not a half-breed, a quarter. My mother wasn't your daughter, was she."

Frank's Adam's apple bobbed, but he made no reply.

One half Spanish. One quarter Tohono O'odham. And one quarter Nazi.

CHAPTER THIRTY-EIGHT

Adam drove through the night, fuming all the way from Phoenix. He had photos of the pictogram, at the cost of a scraped knee and palms as he came down in the darkness. Search as he would, he didn't find anything else there that looked important, nothing like a code. What else did Casey have? Whatever it was, he wasn't telling, and Adam wished he hadn't been drawn off on this chase while Hammer had the pleasure of presiding over Casey's liquidation. He found himself hoping for poor aim, for Casey to be paralyzed, spewing blood, feeling his death approach and himself helpless to stop it.

Adam performed a brief calming ritual. It never paid to get involved. Casey was an obstacle, nothing more. Or, no, perhaps something more: a pointer in the direction of the next clues, the diagram of the submarine, the existence of, if not the location of, the code. What else did Casey have? He'd grown up here, and Adam had not. He had been related to the weaver and to the old man Adam had beaten and now abducted. Related to that fool Randy who would now also be dying in the desert. Adam frowned, flicking his watch so it showed the time. Long past when he should have heard from Remington.

Adam pulled up his police band app.

"—out in Ruby. We're gonna need a tow truck. We have a car that's also a crime scene. Do you copy?"

"We'll get it out there. I hope you don't need much else. Half the damn force is already there."

The first officer chuckled.

Tension drew Adam's shoulders toward his ears and he forced them back again. If all had gone well, nobody would even know where to look for Manuel's body. This entire day had been a clusterfuck. This entire operation, in fact, aside from a few rays of light like his new recruit. The Sons needed the money for a strong new kingdom but the Warden, too, was fucking with him. He set aside his destructive thinking. In fact, most of the troubles, from the entire situation with Manuel, to the Warden's perfidy, arose from a single source: Casey. He rather wished he had asked for Casey's scalp

The chatter on the police band hinted that something large and dangerous had gone down in Ruby, including an officer-involved shooting, and a Lifeflight helicopter that may or may not have destroyed evidence.

"Dispatch to Rizzo."

Adam cocked his head. No reply.

"Dispatch to Rizzo? Anybody out there seen Rizzo?"

"Dispatch, it's 229 at Ruby, she left here an hour ago. Nothing since."

She must've gotten the call and gone out there herself—but why? And why had she left again? Adam's neck prickled and he rubbed his palms over the steering wheel. All of his work to insinuate himself with law enforcement, only to have the sheriff go rogue. At least she wasn't his only connection.

A reservation border sign flashed by in his mirror. This time, he went without subterfuge. He didn't even slow down: the cops were spread thin tonight. Everyone who lived on the property was accounted for, even that wetback gardener of theirs, a minor complication he'd not even known about. He pulled up between the houses and killed his engine, out of the door before it even stopped ticking. This far from the anus of anywhere, there was nobody to see as he used the elder Manuel's keyring to let himself in. He flicked on the lights and headed straight for the back bedroom, the one that still looked like a boy's room. There it was, pretty-as-you-please on the bookshelf: a perfect scale model of a

Nazi U-boat, complete with call numbers carefully hand-painted on the side. But he didn't think the Nazis ever used Roman numerals to number their boats. At the eleventh hour, his day was suddenly turning rosy indeed.

CHAPTER THIRTY-NINE

One quarter Nazi. That was gonna take some working through. The van slewed sideways, skidding in the sand. Grant brought his focus back to the present. The old man lurched against his seat, the edges of his eyes and mouth pinching with pain of his own. He'd just gotten out of the hospital, after an attack most folks his age wouldn't survive. Strong, determined. Grant traced his features, the grandfather who wasn't his. He felt strangely light and vindicated: as the CIA quoted, the truth shall set you free. "Does this mean I shouldn't hate you anymore?"

"You didn't have to be here. Arizona, this whole mess." Frank stared toward the cab, the faint illumination of the dashboard lights and nothing more—not even headlights. "Cece called your office, but she didn't think you'd come."

It sounded like an accusation, the reverse of a child telling his parents he didn't ask to be born. "You didn't want me here. Got it."

His clipped answer sparked something in the old man, some fire long banked. "That's not what I meant. You came anyway, and not just to see me beaten. You knew it was me in that hospital bed, and you came."

Maybe it wasn't an accusation, not at all. What else could it be? Grant breathed carefully, shifting his mindset from injured party to intelligence officer. The pounding in his skull made it hard to focus. "When I got here, you told me to take a run. You wanted me to check on the cache, and you didn't want to worry Cece anymore."

Frank gave a slow nod. "I knew I could count on you. You didn't have to like me to honor what you thought I was." He cradled his injured arm. "You'd honor me. The way I never honored you." The blood from his ear left a track of darkness along the side of his face.

The old man's faith settled awkward over Grant's shoulders, a mantle he had never known he carried.

"How's the cache?" Frank asked.

No point in softening the truth. "Randy overheard Lones ask about baskets. He broke into the cache, hoping for something to sell. Teo showed him the way. Randy attacked him to hide what he was doing."

Frank sagged. "Guess I knew I could count on him, too, just not the right way. Family's more than blood, at least, it should be. I raised your mother like my own. When they died, when you came out here..." He blinked a few times, but never turned. "You were like one of those damn cactus, sharp and solitary. I let Rosemary do the loving. I gave you space... For a lot of reasons." A few breaths, then he said, "They put the phone to my mouth, so I'd get you to come. I kept quiet, thinking you'd go all cactus again." He swallowed and darted a glance. "Was there anything I could've said to make you stay away?"

The rough cloth of the seat rubbed against the side of his face, adding to the abrasions already there. He thought it over, then answered in the old man's tongue. "No."

Another nauseating turn, and Frank's brow furrowed. "They're driving in circles."

"That's how I know they want you alive." No point in confusing a dead man.

"Maybe it's you they want."

"I'm too dangerous." He caught echoes of other vehicle sounds, almost as if they were being followed, but even a blunt instrument like Hammer would've picked up on that. So: Hammer had a posse. Grant didn't.

"How many men have you killed?" the old man whispered.

Wasn't remotely what he meant. Why did they keep coming back to this? "Direct kills? Forty-seven that I can be sure of. I'm not a sniper."

"There's a ritual, when a young warrior kills for the first time before he rejoins his people. So that the dead don't haunt him. Somebody should've done that for you." Frank wet his lips. "I should have."

Grant's chest constricted and he had no words.

"You've got a plan, right? Some kind of back-up?"

His only cavalry was an untrained kid fresh from recovery, and an overburdened sheriff at least a hundred miles away. "The ceremony they're planning, you don't know anything else about it?"

"Hammer was the most recent candidate." The old man shook his head. The fingers of his good hand rubbed and pinched at the bridge of his nose as if he were trying to squeeze something out of his head. "Before they called you, they asked about Rosemary, her baskets, her sailor. Same things you want to know." He let go of his head, staring at Grant. "I'll tell you. Everything. Anything. I—" he broke off. "But now, I don't even know how to start."

The van slowed, then rocked to a halt.

"I'll do what I can to get you an escape route. You get out of here. Get with D.A. and the sheriff, they know everything." His throat felt tight. "Whatever I say next, whatever I do, it's part of the plan, you got that?"

The passenger door opened and Smith climbed out on his side, slamming the door again after.

"I'm gonna need my own plan." The old man ghosted a smile. He raised his hand and his knuckles brushed over Grant's cheek. "I want you to come home, Grant. You hear me?"

He couldn't remember hearing Frank use his given name. Maybe ever.

The old man turned away, shoved his fingers in his throat and vomited on his feet and on the floor in front of him, slumping in his seat, his hand and head dangling. Foul-smelling drool oozed from the bloodied corner of his mouth. Damn, but he was good.

The back doors popped open.

"Come on, Frank, open your eyes!" Grant leaned toward him, shouting. "Come on!" Someone entered the back of the van, and he turned as best he could. "You fuckers—you killed him. Your boss won't be too happy about that."

"What the hell?" Hammer stood at the back of the van. Smith stomped toward Grant, scowling in the light of the stars and the narrow moon. Smith unbuckled the seatbelt and hauled Grant up, though he let his knees buckle, flopping like a drunk as Smith hauled him toward the back of the van and chucked him to the ground. Grant tumbled, absorbing the impact, letting the streak of agony show in his wince and his body. He scrambled as if trying to get to his feet, using this apparent lack of balance to scan his surroundings. Dark mounds of stone to the right, more even ground to the left, a sense of movement in the darkness; his injuries cramping his vision.

"Fuckers," he repeated, gulping for breath.

Hammer stared down the van, jiggling the keys.

"You gonna call the boss?" Smith asked in a low voice.

"I'll handle it."

"Does this change the ceremony?"

"I said, I'll handle it." Hammer thumbed the keys between his fingers, fist clenching.

On his knees, Grant glared up at his captors. Two men. Where were the others—or had the other vehicles been artifacts of his injuries? His bound arms ached, his hands felt numb, and his core burned from Hammer's last few blows. Two men. He could take it. "Oh, that's right," Grant said. "You think you're fucking Wolverine. Cause your fists alone aren't enough."

Hammer glared back at him, then tossed the keys into the van where they cut a metallic scythe through the trail of blood that marked the journey. He grabbed a fistful of Grant's shirt, tearing it as he pulled him to his feet and lined him up for the blow.

Grant dropped his weight and ripped free, pulling Hammer off-balance so that he fell against the van's open door. He ran, his bare feet digging into the desert soil and stone, launching him forward with every step. Two men. He'd run marathons. He could do this.

Howls of rage from behind, then pounding feet and huffs of breath, men who weren't used to this level of effort, much less in this terrain—the ground seemed to give him power, the very earth rising for his freedom.

Light flared in front of him—then swung out into his path. Grant twisted to the side trying to dodge before he'd even absorbed what he was seeing. The tiki torch smacked across his arm, a hard steel handle, the sting of hot metal, the sizzle of flame that briefly scorched his chest.

His feet slid out from under him. He finished on his back again, gasping, the desert night wheeling overhead.

"You lose something, Hammer?" The torch swung up, illuminating a broad-brimmed white Stetson, the face invisible below.

"Thanks, Miller. Nice catch." Hammer's voice, breathing a little heavy, then his boot slammed into Grant's kidneys and ribs. A thunder of blows rolled him on the rough ground that had been his friend only heartbeats before.

"Mongrels." Smith came up alongside as Hammer kicked. "Used his own grandfather's death to make his getaway."

"Fucked that up, didn't he," Hammer said.

An engine started behind them, roaring to life.

They swung about, the man with the torch raised it vertical, planting the sharpened tip at the junction of Grant's collar bones, pinning him down, but not stabbing—not yet.

"You didn't check?" Hammer shouted.

"I just—the vomit—" Smith protested. "Oh, come on, you saw him."

Two other faces closed in. "What's going on? Who's in the van?"

"Another mudman." Hammer leaned down and caught Grant's throat, hauling him up, flinging him against a looming shadow that shuddered when he hit and tore into his back and arms with dozens of spines. Another torch, and another, the flames lighting Hammer's eyes like the devil he was. He grinned, his fingers digging in, stifling Grant's effort to breathe. "Joke's on him. It's running on empty. We'll get the old man, but we've got business to do first." Another torch whooshed to life—or did Grant's dazed vision manufacture the lights?

Hammer pulled Grant off the cactus and threw him aside into a boulder heap, knocking out what breath remained. Two men, maybe he could outrun, outfight, outfox. Three, five—how many were there? Pain pulsed, threatening to drown out thought entirely. A weight on his back, his head pulled up by the hair as if they set him up to slit his throat. Grant bucked against the pressure. The hand slammed his face down and pulled him with the liquid sound of blood spilled. A gag carved into his mouth, then a sack covered his head.

A hand screwed into the sack at his throat, using it as a handle to pull him to his feet and propel him into the aching darkness. "Are you prepared to meet your maker?" Hammer's voice murmured. "Do you people go to the Happy Hunting Ground? Nope, not you. You're gonna bleed out in the desert while the coyotes rip open your stinking guts like a fucking wetback lost in the dirt."

Helluva home-coming. For most of his career in special ops, he had assumed he would die in the desert, he just never imagined it would be this one.

CHAPTER FORTY

J amie had never driven a Prius before and it took her a bit to figure out which button to push. The car's dashboard lights came on, and she flicked on the headlights, waving to the confused, and somewhat sleepy impound man on her way out. The car wasn't really evidence anyway. She retrieved Buster from the squad car along with anything she thought might be useful from flashlight to first aid to blankets and teddy bears meant comfort the scared. She missed the siren and lights as she sped toward the Motel 6, waiting impatiently for the lights to turn green instead of triggering them to do what she wanted. Nobody was even coming from the other direction, for God's sake!

The curtains at the room window twitched as she mounted the walkway and Chris pulled open the door. "How are you driving my car?"

"It was impounded to search for drugs. It's clean."

His bewildered expression followed her as she brushed past and he shut the door behind her. "Gimme a break, I'm improvising! I knew you had a Prius and we need something quiet: It's pretty clear Casey's not supposed to have back-up."

"Come alone, all that." Chris trembled, his hands stuffed under his armpits.

"Are you okay?"

He bobbed his head. "I just—queasy. It comes and goes. They said it would."

"Are you up to driving?"

"For him? Yeah, I would."

She snorted. "I don't think he's your type."

"Hey—a man can dream, can't he?" He shot back. "You don't suppose he's married?"

"I don't think he's the marrying type either." She scanned the room, squatted, looking under the bed and around the corners. "You got the coordinates, right?"

"In the phone. Somebody's called a few times, but they keep hanging up when I answer." He gripped Casey's phone like a talisman. "What are you looking for?"

"His socks. Something he wore, something personal." She rooted through the carry-on bag on the dresser.

"What, you think he's your type?" Chris walked past her, to the corner by the trashcan, and picked up a bag.

Ha. Given how Nathan dumped her ass years ago, she wasn't sure she even knew her type. "Even if he were the marrying type, I'm not the type he would marry. We need something with his scent on it."

From the bag, Chris produced a balled-up sock. "Dusky, sweaty, a hint of spice."

She raised her eyebrows at him. "You're a nut."

He gave a tiny shrug and handed over the sock.

"What was he wearing?"

Chris shut his eyes, brow furrowing. "Long-sleeve outdoor shirt, khaki pants, light hiking shoes. No watch. He cleaned out his pockets before he left. The only thing he took was a knife."

"You ever want a job with the county, you let me know. Come on. Bring a jacket—it gets cold in the desert." She was halfway out the door already.

"Right." He emerged a moment later wearing a thick denim jacket of his own, a polar fleece draped over his arm. At her expression, Chris said, "He'll be cold, too, right?"

She handed over the key and got in back with Buster. "Sorry about the dog. I hope you don't mind."

"Sheriff, somebody's trying to kill me—I don't even know what to

mind anymore."

"Great. I have to pick something up at my place, then you get us to those coordinates. Fast as we can without killing anybody. They've been gone almost four hours already." Shit. She wanted to find people, not corpses, and with every moment, the chances dimmed.

CHAPTER FORTY-ONE

Grant stumbled through the desert, in the hands of his captors, listening, trying to work out how many of them there were. As if it would do any good. They had him blind, gagged, beaten so badly he couldn't think straight, who knew how many miles from safety or help. He'd reached the end game, the final op. The hand shoved him to his knees on stones. Other people rustled in around him, not too close, a circle of maybe fifteen feet. Far enough that they might not be spattered by the blood about to be spilled.

A man spoke from his nine o'clock. "Welcome, Lieutenant, to the ring of the faithful."

"Thank you, Friend." Hammer's voice, dead ahead. "Let our candidate step forward."

The man who held Grant's head straightened, drawing Grant up a little, as if they were getting ready for a portrait. The kind where the next frame showed Grant's body on the ground, his head still in the grip of another.

Another man strode closer, on his three. "Here, sir."

That voice. Grant stilled his own breathing, fought for clarity through the beat of his skull.

"Do you believe in the cause of liberty for the American people?"

"Yes, sir."

Holy shit. The purpose of an op was to stack the deck in your own favor—this had been a crapshoot, and Grant's number just came up.

"Will you fight for a homeland where true Americans can be free?"

"Yes, sir."

Grant's eyes burned and he pressed them shut. Cliché said there were no atheists in foxholes, but Grant had never been so close to praying, right there, on his knees, hearing the voice of his deliverance. But what could he do about it?

"Are you prepared to prove your faith with these friends of our cause?"

"Yes, sir."

Unless the disorientation had affected his hearing, and he was hearing an angel when all he had were more devils.

The men moved a little, then Hammer's voice. "A single shot. That's all it should take."

"Damn straight."

Grant's eyes flared open in the smothering darkness. The man beside him moved a little closer and the cold muzzle of a gun traced a line across his shoulder, bared by the torn shirt. The gun nudged at his collar, intimate and awful, then a familiar derisive snort. "Prison ink and gang signs."

A few men in the circle chuckled, and Hammer replied, "He's covered with 'em. I'll bet this one's got a rap sheet as long as your arm back in whatever shithole country he came from."

"Oh, yeah, he's reprobate from way back."

Grant had been recognized.

More laughter, hard-edged and excited. "I thought the boss would be here."

"Something came up. Is that a problem, candidate?"

"No, sir." A gravelly, smoker's chuckle. "It's like something out of high noon. Me and my posse, taking out the trash." Another derisive snort. "This guy reeks—what do you suppose he ate?"

Grant seized on the words: *Out. High noon.* Straight ahead to his best escape route. The next number: eight. The number of assailants. And the man at his side had only one bullet. How many men could Grant take down, messed up and bound as he was? How many men could his savior take down with only one bullet? Grant shifted a little, getting his toes down, sensing the slope gently toward his noon. He tensed. Perfectly natural for a man about to die.

"I like you," said the man holding the hood: Smith. "You'll fit right in."

"Straight up," said the candidate. "I'm the man for you." And with that, Grant knew the plan. "Does that mask come off? I prefer the vermin to know who's holding the gun."

"And we need to know you can look these things in the face and still do what needs doing." Hammer directed, "Pull it."

The hood yanked up, flapping over Grant's face. Hammer, standing about six feet ahead of him, wore a crisp cream-colored western jacket over blue jeans. His white Stetson glowed faintly orange in the light from a half-dozen torches planted in the ring of men. At Hammer's back, a few crags of stone, mesquite brush, a narrow avenue between. The gun snaked from his shoulder to his ear, to his temple. Grant resisted the urge to pull away.

"Damn, but I like this view." A touch of humor that curled in Grant's stomach.

"You men sure know how to give a guy a thrill. This is one vacation I'll never forget." Gooney's voice, booming, getting louder to cover his nerves. Eight men. One bullet. Grant with his hands tied and his head bashed in. Well—they'd faced worse odds.

No, actually, they hadn't.

"Whenever you're ready," Hammer prompted.

"Yes, sir." Gooney squared off, the gun resting at Grant's temple. "Hope you're ready for this." His foot shifted. Gooney turned hard, smoothly drawing up the gun, squeezing the trigger in the same moment. Powder stung Grant's skin and the deadly breeze of the bullet rushed past. Smith flew backward, spraying blood and bits across Grant's shoulders. Grant launched himself forward, slamming his shoulder into Hammer's gut, barreling him straight into the crag behind. He stopped himself and spun as Hammer hit the ground hard.

Gooney kicked Smith's corpse over and snatched the gun from its waist. Both hands outstretched, forward stance. Shoot, turn, shoot, turn, shoot—before the men even had the chance to react. Then, chaos. The three still standing fumbled for their own guns, focused on Gooney. Grant scrambled up a rock and leapt, kicking one of them in the head, dropping on top of him and letting himself roll back off again, letting his lack of balance be an asset. He hooked a torch with his foot and yanked it down, killing the light. Knocked down the next torch.

One of the wounded pulled his own gun and squeezed off a shot that went wild. White Stetsons tumbled between the torches. Men screamed and cursed. One of them was sobbing.

"Go, Chief, go!" Gooney shouted. Two more shots. One man took cover behind a slab, firing over the top of it. Gooney dodged and got off a shot of his own. How many in the mag? Had to be low.

The man Grant had landed hauled himself up again, gun drawn, aiming for Gooney. Grant kicked the weapon away, and the guy lunged for him, drawing a second gun from his boot.

Two steps, a bend of the knees, a controlled slide down the narrow exit, then he lit out running. Gooney had the gun and two good hands. Gotta have faith in his people.

His bare sole stung already, and the remaining sock shredded as he ran. The sliver of moon and a thousand stars glittered over a field of boulder mounds and brush. Had to go to ground soon—no way he'd make it far, not in his condition. A few hundred yards more, teeth clenched on the gag, breath in sharp gasps and the taste of blood that hadn't left him. High noon. More gunshots behind him, but only two—and the cursing didn't end. The survivors wouldn't be mounting a search any time soon. He cut left and scrambled up the cleft between a pair of slabs, leaning against stone, finding his breath, stilling his racing heart.

Running steps, not nearly as fleet, and Grant froze, his moment's rest cut short all too soon. Then a muttered curse.

He couldn't even whistle to get Gooney's attention. Grant sank down to his haunches and prodded a flake of stone back toward the path. A quiet ping, and the footsteps slowed, approaching. A white Stetson came into view, and a hand with a gun, rock-steady. The nose of the gun tipped the hat back, and Gooney looked up at him. "Howdy, partner."

He tucked the gun into his belt and hauled himself up alongside Grant, scooting a little further back. He spoke at a whisper. "Can you turn away from me a little? I need some light."

Grant obliged, every injury returning now that he was, miraculously—
and temporarily—safe. His throat closed as Gooney picked at the gag and
finally peeled it away, letting him breathe freely. The Arizona night tasted
cool and sweet.

Gooney's hands ran around Grant's wrists, assessing the binding.
"Cable ties? Jesus H. Christ, Chief, I got nothing for you. I don't even have a
knife. They made me strip—all the way to the tighty-whities, and gave me
this monkey suit. I thought it was just gonna be an oath and a ceremony, that
kind of shit. Patrolling the border, maybe. Then they got me out of the car,
and I saw what was up." Gooney caught his breath. His fingers worked
carefully around the cable ties, to no avail. "I figured whoever the poor
schmuck under the hood was, he and I were gonna go out together in a blaze
of glory—then I spotted your ink, and I thought maybe we'd do some blazing
for ourselves. Jesus, Chief, I'm sorry. I'm babbling. I just—all the training in
the world, they tell you to be ready for anything, but no fucking way I
would've been ready for that."

Grant found his voice, rough and hot, burning over his lips. "Swear to
God, Gooney, you with that gun to my head was the most beautiful thing I
ever saw in my life."

Gooney's hand shifted upward, rested lightly on Grant's shoulder,
gave a squeeze so gentle Grant wouldn't have guessed him capable of it.
"Don't worry, Chief. I'll never tell anybody you said that."

"Go ahead," Grant murmured. "They'll never believe you."

CHAPTER FORTY-TWO

Adam's phone shrilled as he was searching the rest of the room, tumbling books, taking photos off the walls—none of Rosemary, as if she'd never even lived there. He pulled it out. "Yes?"

"Boss! Fuck." Hammer's voice, strained and weak as a drowning man, with another voice wailing in the background.

Adam grew still. "Hammer. I think we've spoken about your language."

"That guy, the candidate, he was with Casey! Shot Smith between the eyes and got his gun. I've never seen anybody move that fast. We've got three men down, dead. Wesson's working—" then he apparently turned away from the phone. "Don't stop! You can't stop compressions, for God's sake!"

The empty house closed in around him like something from a horror film, the walls pulsing as he listened with utter amazement. "Chest compressions?"

"Miller went down, but he's not dead yet." The last two words on a rising fury. "How do we get an ambulance? We need, there's only two of us uninjured."

"You may tell them to load the wounded into the van. While you drive, you may develop a narrative to explain what happened. I suggest you begin with downing, and spilling, all of the alcohol purchased for the initiation party."

Hammer made a strangled sound, then said, "The old man. Manuel. He stole the van. We thought he was dead! I—"

Adam drew breath, sucking in the fury. "Hammer, enough of your justifications." He waited while Hammer took a few ragged breaths. "Tell them to load the wounded into the cars. Please walk away from the scene. Let me know when you can't see them anymore."

"Boss, I—yes, sir." The phone went distant as Hammer relayed the orders, including the alcohol, then Hammer's footfalls, unsteady, scratching through gravel. After a moment, he came back on the line. "Here, sir." His voice was nasal and wrong. "They're gonna have trouble carrying Miller without me."

"Then we'll be quick. In addition to the candidate, you had nine men —"

"Eight. Remington never showed."

He gripped the model sub in his hand, the conning tower burrowing into his palm. "Tell me what happened."

Even knowing the facts, at least, the facts as Hammer was able or willing to relay them, hardly revealed anything. "Nothing you say makes any sense. Fine, so he was a mole—that's why we only give one bullet. It wouldn't be the first time a candidate backed down. We have a number of insurance policies for that eventuality. But Casey was secured—how could they even coordinate their actions?"

"He was joking, talking like someone from a Western film. The guys— Smith—they loved it. We were laughing. I was thinking about the barbecue afterward. The guy was one of us."

"Until he wasn't. Get the living to the hospital. Half or more of local law enforcement is out dealing with Ruby—" Dealing with Remington's death, obviously— "so I hope you are able to handle this. Are you? You sound about ready to get drunk in any case. Can I trust you to even keep shut about everything we can't say?"

"Yes, sir." A few more breaths, a little more even, then Hammer said, "They'll want names, at the hospital."

"Pretend you're the fucking Masons." Adam clenched his jaw and the submarine cracked in his hand. At least Hammer was thinking a little more clearly now.

"Yes, sir. And sir—about Casey. Next time I see him. I'm gonna blow his face off. Just like his buddy did to Smith."

Adam clicked off and opened his palm. The submarine model lay there in two pieces, not cracked after all, but popped open, the conning tower sliding free, releasing a catch that revealed a hollow interior. Empty. Had this compartment been the source of the code? But then Casey would already know the Roman numerals. Unless that was another accursed double-cross, luring the Warden into trusting him without giving anything away. Hammer wanted to blow the man's face off. Adam, on the other hand, began to picture his tattooed hide transformed into a lampshade. Preferably while the former occupant was still living.

He strode back to the kitchen table and sat down, placing the sub to one side as he brought up the app and made a call. It rang and rang. He let it. At last, the Warden's ambiguous voice came on the line. "I believe it is rather late in Arizona, is it not? It is rather late here, as well."

"I know about Casey. You tried to hire him over me. He's not intending to play your game. You need to deal with me, and you need to deal straight."

"Casey..." She rolled the name around as if she didn't know what it meant. "I take it you've been listening in."

A chill swept over him. In his fury, he'd shown his hand.

The Warden laughed, a few dry, short sounds. "Oh, be not dismayed. I wasn't surprised by your Trojan Horse, Mr. Lones, only by how long it took you to think of it. I gather that something has happened to rattle you."

"My people are getting hurt, Warden. When the cost goes up, the price goes up. By at least thirty percent. And I need that diary. If you want this treasure of yours found, you help me find it."

"Mmm. I could be there by ten am. Would that suit you?"

"I'll clear my calendar. Where do we meet?"

"The Marana Regional Airport. My companions and I will be waiting. And let's just say, in the event you're feeling dangerous, that private jets don't have the same carry-on restrictions as commercial flights."

"Understood. It'll be a pleasure to finally meet you. I plan on checking my bank balance on the way over. If I don't like what I see, then—"

"Then perhaps your Mr. Casey will be available after all."

"No. He won't." Adam closed the call before he could say anything else. He hated the unsettled feeling that coursed through him. Feeling dangerous? Oh, yes. Setting down the model sub, Adam took photos of it, and put it back together. Fortunately, he had a little time. How long would it take Casey and his decrepit companion to get this far? He had time, at least a few hours.

Adam headed back to his car and drove toward a storage shed on the outskirts of town, a shed that echoed half-empty without the van inside. From boxes labeled, "Law Records, 1992-3" he removed a few bricks of C4. From a file cabinet labeled, "IRS documentation and Schedule C's," he pulled a timer, a trigger, a few other necessities. As he closed up, he considered the missing van. From Hammer's description, they were well shut of it, assuming the evidence would wear away before it was picked up by law enforcement. Better to take care of it now. Had his brothers followed protocol, shedding all personal identifiers? Hammer clearly had his phone on him, but he was new to the work, too new, perhaps—but while Adam anticipated a balky candidate, the idea that the candidate was Casey's man hadn't occurred even to him. Hammer did not bear the full blame for that debacle.

Placing his supplies in a triple-layer wrap to block any trace evidence, he pulled out his phone, and placed a call.

CHAPTER FORTY-THREE

The shivering helped Grant to stay conscious, even after Gooney draped his shoulders with his oversize suitcoat—"Like my frickin' girlfriend in a skimpy dress—" In the distance, the screaming stopped and cars drove away. They waited long moments more, in case someone was conscious and furious enough for pursuit. When they heard nothing, Gooney climbed heavily down from the cleft and steadied Grant's own descent. What would have been an easy scramble sent shocks of pain. His body betrayed him. He wobbled and nearly fell, his vision sliding toward darkness and flicking back again. Stay alert. Stay alive for the next hour. Then the hour after that.

Gooney's hand remained at his lower back. "Are you up to this?"

"Tell me the options." He needed shoes, rest, a gallon of water and about a hundred Aspirin. And a knife to cut the cable ties off his hands before he started to lose his fingers.

"Yeah. Got nothing. Where do we go?"

Grant tipped his head back, grateful for that arm as he swayed on his feet. "You see the North Star? Up there? In the dipper?"

"The what in the fucking what?"

"Just...walk." He indicated direction with his chin. They moved together, painfully slow—painfully, in any case. Thirst grew at the back of his throat, and he wondered idly if he was bleeding internally. He didn't think so, but he was down a fair amount of blood in any case. The desert hid streams and seeps, but he had lost any immediate sense of where they were;

still miles from any territory he'd recognize. Water-dense cacti loomed up from the dark, blocking out the stars, and he considered how to get at the water inside without a knife, without either of them getting spiked. Again. *Like a cactus, sharp and solitary.* Smaller varieties would cling to the outcrops and hills around them, but they'd be hard pressed to find one unless they fell on it. They stopped now and again so Casey could glance at the sky, with its blurry points of light. He blinked a few times and brought them back into focus.

"Shit, Chief, that's the Milky Way," Gooney breathed. He kept his arm at Grant's waist, a third point of balance he hated to need.

Grant had stopped answering. He leaned a little harder on Gooney, lifting up first one foot, then the other.

"You're pretty wiped."

Another remark that needed nothing from him. Good. He didn't have much left to give. Coyote voices rose in the distance, barks into howls, choppy and inelegant. Gooney stiffened. *While the coyotes rip open your stinking guts like a fucking wetback lost in the dirt.* Grant indicated their path, and they started walking again.

"Why does it always come down to you and me in the desert? Why can't we kick some ass in the tropics for once?"

Grant huffed a laugh. "Almost had you pegged for Employee of the Month. You just blew it."

"Fuck you," Gooney growled. "Your breathing rate's falling, y'know. And you wouldn't be shaking so damn much if you'd put on a few pounds. Look at me? Do I look cold?"

Grant closed his eyes and focused on breathing.

"It might be faster if I carry you. Have to be over the shoulder, though, and I've seen what's left of your scalp. I'm guessing your head hanging down's not such a great idea."

"And he stabbed me in the gut with a key. Three, four times."

"Oh, shit."

Another sound, closer. They both froze. Gooney's hand shifted to the gun at his belt. From a low rise at their two o'clock came another whistle, almost birdsong—to someone who didn't know the sounds of the desert.

Gooney pulled the gun. Empty, but nobody had to know that except the two of them. The whistle became a hum, low, tuneless, familiar.

"That's Frank," he breathed.

"Frank—is that you?" Gooney hollered, his voice echoing and dying in the darkness. He aimed the gun at the rise, shifting his weight toward a shooting stance.

A quiet rustling. Grant twisted aside, ducked low. A knife flashed in the starlight, held back-hand and pointed at Gooney's throat. "I don't know you."

"The fuck you say." Gooney pivoted, but Frank had slipped back a step, knees bent like a dancer, out of the big man's path.

The old man still had it. Grant might've laughed, but without Gooney's bulk at his side, he sank to his knees in the dirt, nearly pitched onto his face.

"Chief!"

Both men dropped beside him. "There's a stream over here—you need water."

"He needs a helluvalot more than that."

Frank's voice, sounding older. "I know, but this is where we begin."

The knife and the gun slipped away to their respective places, then Gooney caught Grant's head and shoulders against his chest while Frank gathered his feet under his good arm and they toted him in the direction the old man indicated, a small pool in the shade of the stones where the old man had apparently been waiting. They lay him on his side next to the pool, but Gooney kept his head cradled. He stripped the loaner coat back from Grant's shoulders and wadded it up for a pillow. Yeah. Employee of the Month for sure.

"Gimme the knife," Gooney ordered. "Do you have a light?"

"Both, yes. Only one hand." Frank handed over the knife—its blade, broad, its hilt wrapped and beaded. He fumbled into his sling and came out with a cellphone. He prodded it to life and Gooney triggered the flashlight function. They positioned themselves at Grant's back.

"You're his grandfather, right?"

"Yes." No hesitation.

"The only man the chief hates more than me! Pleased to meet you." Gooney got to work on the cable ties, ratcheting the knife into plastic. One, two, the last one finally popped free and Gooney unwound the ties, peeling them from the flesh. "Yowch, that's ugly. Your back's a mess, too." Gooney rolled Grant carefully to lean against him, cupping Grant's hands one at a time to rest them on his blood-streaked shirt. Starved of blood and oxygen, his fingers throbbed with every beat of his heart. Grant hissed a breath.

"Face it, Chief, you're a mess from head to toe."

Frank snagged the Stetson off Gooney's head. He scooped it into the pool and brought it to Grant's lips. Grant managed to swallow some over the bent brim. He let more of it wash over his face, tipping his head back so it could streak down through his hair, cold fingers of water stroking the blood from his temples. Water was a beautiful thing, even if the bed and the aspirin had to wait. No, not aspirin. The last thing he needed in his condition was a blood thinner. After a few more swallows, he let himself lie back. So tempting to shut his eyes, even against the crystalline perfection of the night sky. Cece must be having some great viewing tonight. If she hadn't been called down from the mountain for her brother's stupidity. "Frank Manuel, this is Tony Gonsalves, Detective Lieutenant, Boston PD."

"Chief calls me Gooney," he said, putting out his hand. "He's just trying to be extra polite because I saved his ass back there."

The cellphone's light pointed at the sky while they shook hands. "Chief?" the old man echoed.

"Funny story—I got pissed off at Casey, so I went digging and I found this picture—" Gooney broke off abruptly. "Doesn't matter. He's in charge."

His rodeo Indian get-up had been one of the things that riled his grandfather the most. Time for a new subject. "What are you still doing out here, Frank?"

The old man gazed down at him, dark and distant as ever he had been, his silhouette carved out of the stars. "Praying."

Gooney snorted. "Maybe next time, the prayers should come first."

A jangly melody cut the night and all three of them jerked, then stared at the phone.

"Where'd you get it?" Grant pushed himself up on one hand—a very serious mistake.

"In the van. Thought it would come in handy."

The phone rang again. Grant lunged for it and flung it away, a small light tumbling in the darkness. It clattered on stone.

"What the hell, Chief? We could use that."

It rang a third time, with a warped sound, then went dead.

"Do you want me to—"

Grant caught his grandfather's arm before he could rise. With a flash of light and a whiff of sulphur, the phone exploded into crackling flames. The old man drew back and Grant let go, easing against Gooney's side, that much exertion punishing him all over again.

"Jesus."

"Boss made you leave everything. He doesn't take chances. Gotta go." Grant curled forward and Gooney helped him pull the jacket on, then slung Grant's arm over his shoulder as they stood up.

"We can't move him, not in this condition." Frank rose as well.

"There's no fucking cavalry on the way, Pops. The boss put a bomb in his own guy's phone, you wanna bet there wasn't a tracer too? Let's go."

Frank took a place on the other side, taking some of Grant's weight. "And this man is your friend?"

Their arms burned across his back and Grant focused on keeping alert.

"Hardly." Gooney snatched the hat from the ground and slapped it on Grant's head, damp and cool against the pounding.

"Best kind," Grant murmured. "Mean, fast, and relentless when you wish he'd give up."

"You must be hallucinating, Chief. Too many blows to the head— you're talking like a nutjob. You know your way out here, Pops? Gotta be miles from the Rez. Or is it some kind of ancestral wisdom?"

"I know it for miles, both sides of the border. It's not a native thing." Frank leaned and brought them around, moving North and East. "I'm a coyote. Teo and me. We don't charge more than we need, sometimes nothing at all, just to get people through safe."

"Holy shit, Pops! And your boy here's been covering for you?"

Grant managed a shake of his head, reeling in more ways than one. "News to me."

"This is my secret. Was. I missed my daughter's funeral because I had a run, a family. One of the reasons he hated me all these years. Somebody else's family needed me more."

"Honor the dead," Grant whispered, and his grandfather finished, "Work for the living." He gripped just above Grant's wrist, mindful and strong.

"Teo's house, the rest isn't just storage, it's a bunkhouse, hidden entrance and exit, the whole thing. I'm getting too old for that now."

"Coulda fooled me, Pops!"

"Rosemary knew. She started the cloak and dagger with that sailor, laying a maze though she wouldn't say what she was hiding. But he gave her a secret she couldn't hide for very long." They took a few more steps, and Frank continued, "She was my heart. I don't know if you know that. Even back then, after her sailor. I don't know the clues—she never revealed his secrets, same way she kept mine—even from you."

Grant remembered his fury, the anniversary of his parents' deaths, finally being there long enough to lash out, demanding answers, Rosemary trying to reassure him that his grandfather's absence at the funeral, his frequent absences ever since, were nothing to do with the extra grandson he never wanted. His whole youth had been haunted by mysteries nobody ever explained. Maybe intelligence work was the obvious answer.

"I knew about the basket," Frank said. "The real one. She confided more in Teo, toward the end. I took too many runs while she was dying. It was too hard to watch her go."

Grant never forgave that, either. They came to the top of a rise, a long sweep of desert before them, and a sky full of stars. "Teo—he was painting."

Frank nodded. "Restoring the frescoes at San Xavier."

"No—on your roof. We need Cece."

"One of the things I prayed for was to keep her out of this."

"Hammer threatened to go after her. What's his disposition?"

"Living, you mean?" Gooney said. "Fraid so."

"After tonight, nobody related to us is safe."

Frank's shoulders sank.

"And we need an astronomer. That painting on your roof? It's a map of the stars."

CHAPTER FORTY-FOUR

Mounted on Princess, Jamie trotted through the desert night. The horse's ears flicked, nervous at the darkness. Up ahead, illuminated by a flickering light on his collar, Buster led the way. They started at the coordinates, where he went still for a smear of blood that made Chris look like he wanted to vomit. She agreed on that one. Another crime scene, and one that she didn't think their boy walked away from. At first, they followed tracks into the desert, but the tracks crossed and wove, more cars came and went, like somebody ran a damn rally in the desert that evening. With every passing moment, her hopes grew more faint. Then Buster stopped dead, sniffing the air, and gave a pivot into the wind. Fresh scent, fresher than the blood spattered vehicle he'd been tracking.

"Find it," she ordered, and he bounded in that direction. She nudged Princess to speed up, waving her arm in a broad gesture and pointing.

The Prius made for a crappy off-road vehicle in terms of undercarriage, but at least it was nimble. She didn't know if Chris were the swearing kind—if he were, he'd be doing it now, trying to keep up with her on their strange path through the desert. At least anyplace the getaway vehicle had gone, the Prius could go, too. Now they were winging it, and she wouldn't even let him use headlights. They followed Buster, but he slowed his pace, weary, even, of the thrill of the chase. Jamie circled back toward Chris and leaned down toward his open window. "You mind if the dog rides shotgun? You gotta watch him for signs, though. As long as the breeze keeps steady, I think we've got our course."

"Right." Chris leaned across the seat and popped open the door. At Jamie's whistle, Buster picked up a little energy and jumped into the car, hanging his head over the passenger side window. "You think we're on a live scent?"

"God, I hope so. Let's pick up the pace." She rode alongside the car, half an eye on Buster, using her superior height to direct Chris toward better tracks. Then, ahead in the darkness, a flash like lightning, but far from a storm.

"Oh, hell!" At the change in her body, Princess bolted forward, Jamie lying low along the horse's neck, reins in one hand, revolver in the other. "Hiya, go, go," she muttered. "That's my beauty."

They galloped into the night, the horse's mane flicking against her face, the flash already gone. Ahead, to the right, she caught movement, a large shape, bigger than a man. Then the glint of a muzzle. Shit on a shingle. Her palm sweat against her own gun. Declare or run?

Behind her, a soft woof, and the gravelly purr of the Prius sneaking up. That woof meant victory, but what kind?

"It's the sheriff! Drop your weapon and freeze where you are! Chris," she bawled over her shoulder. "Hit the lights!"

Hi-beams lit the night, casting tall shadows from the saguaros, their arms up as if they were complying with her orders. Caught by the light, squinting, three men stood. One in a shooter's stance, weapon drawn with a bead on her in spite of the darkness or the sudden light. One with his arm in a sling, supporting the third, a guy whose head looked as if they used it for a battering ram.

Frank Manuel gave a nod. "Guess we had a cavalry after all."

Casey raised his free hand in the slightest wave at the horror that must've been all over her face. "You should see the other guys." He aimed a finger at his bodyguard. "Don't mind him—it's empty."

The guy with the gun stared at her hard, unwavering. "No need to spill my secrets, Chief." Deep voice, almost a growl at the moment: committed to his man, all business, whoever he was. Another special operator?

"Don't worry—she's cool."

Chris pulled up within a few feet of them, Buster popping out the window on his side and trotting over to sit by Casey's feet. Chris emerged on his side, clutching the door as if he were using it for cover. "We need to get you to a hospital."

"Lazarus. Nice work."

"Lazarus, yourself."

Casey's lips quirked. "Founded the club."

The big guy finally stood down, but he didn't drop the gun. Instead, he tucked it at his waist, and a hint of relaxation flowed over him, eyes crinkling at the corners as he swept his gaze over her. He wore a crisp white shirt, stained with other people's blood, strained by his broad shoulders. Blood and dirt smeared his jeans, and the suitcoat that sagged off Casey's lean form. Frank Manuel looked worn-out, dried blood marking the side of his head, but otherwise not too bad.

Jamie sat back on her mount and scanned the area. "Any chance of pursuit?"

"Negative," said the big guy. "Four men down, two injured. Chief wasn't joking about the other guys." He snorted, and flashed a grin, a touch of humor that illuminated handsome features. "Helluva crime scene for you. Back there a lot further than I ever wanna walk for the rest of my life. Tony Gonsalves, Boston PD. Temporary assignment with the Bone Guard."

A fellow officer, maybe somebody a little more orthodox than Casey, somebody she could work with instead of falling behind. She twirled her gun around her finger and stuck it back into its holster. "Jamie Li Rizzo, Pima County Sheriff. How come, when I'm being a hero, there's never any voters around?"

Gonsalves snorted with laughter, then he stepped away to the edge of the light, guarding the perimeter, empty gun or no. Four men down, plus two injured, and it was pretty clear Casey hadn't had much part in that. Gonsalves had some serious skills. Thank God he was on their side. She swung down to join them, dropping Princess's reins. "First aid."

"Right." Chris dove back into the car and emerged again with the kit and the pile of blankets which he dumped to the ground. Frank eased his grandson into the headlights' glare and Jamie gave him an inspection as best she could, wrapping his head when she realized a couple of Band-Aids wouldn't do the job, patching a series of punctures across his abdomen and chest, winding gauze around his wrists. "Have to agree with Chris on this one: you need a doctor. At least one of those scalp wounds needs stitches— it's a flapper."

"I'll start with a shower." He mumbled against the cuts at the corners of his mouth.

"Let's go."

Chris went back into the car, cranking back the passenger seat to recline and laying a blanket over it; defending the upholstery. Smart move. Frank eased Casey to his feet and Jamie helped him over to the car.

Casey met her eye. "Sitrep?"

"Randy's deal went bust, he's in the hospital. I took out a guy called Remington. From what you say, Adam's on the defensive after tonight—he's lost at least five men."

"Negative. Don't believe that for a minute. We don't know all his assets, and we don't know how far he'll go." Casey's voice trailed off and Chris handed him a water bottle which he hung onto for a long time before he mustered the strength to drink from it.

"This guy's leading an army of fucking white power freaks." Gonsalves spoke without stopping his vigilance. "He's gonna hit back, and hard."

"I need to reach my granddaughter," Frank said, his face gone eerily pale since Jamie's report.

"Use my phone," Chris volunteered. They stepped a little apart from the others.

"We need to pick up my truck and trailer at the barn. Randy told me something before he went down. He was babbling about your thirteenth birthday, how he's an asshole. Something about a sub and a shoebox?"

Casey's eyes opened. She hadn't noticed when they closed. "I should go over there. Find the sub."

"Bullshit, Chief," Gonsalves interjected. "You rejecting the hospital, that's on you, we let you run into danger, that's on us. At least get something to eat and give yourself a goddamn break for an hour."

A faint smile. "My boss won't like it."

"Your boss is a fucking asshole. Mine, too."

Jamie suppressed her smile. Gonsalves insulting his boss to his face. They could joke at a time like this? Then again, they were alive, after whatever had gone down. Reason enough for some levity. "Chris can get you guys back to the hotel. I'll head out to Frank's place and see what I find."

A weary nod from Casey. "He needs a rest, too. Both of them."

"I hear you," Jamie said. "I'm pretty impressed with how well they're holding up."

"Civilians," Gonsalves muttered.

"So, I'll head over—"

"Nobody goes anywhere alone. Nobody." Casey took another swallow.

"Guess that's me, then." Gonsalves glanced back. "But I'm gonna want some ammo. No way am I down to a single shot with these guys."

CHAPTER FORTY-FIVE

Frank sat in the back seat, leaning forward, Chris's phone still in his hand in the hopes of Cece's callback. Nothing untoward at the observatory, not yet, and they were right: Grant was already gunning on empty. He asked for a stop at the twenty-four-hour superstore and sent Chris in with a list: dark sheets, dark towels, more bandages, bottle of Ibuprofen, mouthwash to maybe get the taste of blood off his tongue and the biggest pack of Twinkies Chris could carry. Stocked up, they headed back to the motel, driving streets emptied of traffic, still and peaceful after all that went before. Setting Frank up in the room he'd been using for an office, Grant limped next door and cranked up the shower. He devoured enough calories to properly raise the dead, with an Ibuprofen chaser. Stripped off Rizzo's bandages. Took forever to peel off the tattered ruin of his shirt, the pants that would never be the same. Braced his palms on the wall inside the shower and let Heaven pour down over him, searing every scrape, soothing every bruise. His scalp felt loose over his left temple. Another man's brains circled the drain. It was meant to be his skull cracked open, his brain spattered across the desert. His head still ached as if it had been.

Grant stepped out of the shower, the last of the dirty, red water spiraling away. Steam enveloped him, warm, damp, delicious. He went to the door, and called, "Towels?"

"On the floor, just outside."

He snaked a hand through and snagged one of them. Super-plush, burgundy in color. Somebody cared. He unfurled it and slung it over his shoulder, then winced as the towel snagged across his back. Cautiously, he felt around and found a fine, stiff spine piercing his skin, sending a sliver of pain when he touched its end. Perfect. He hadn't even noticed until now. He dried the rest of his body, pretty stiff himself, then pulled on his running shorts, easing the waistband low so it didn't press on his injuries. He opened the door a crack, letting out some of the steam. "Hey, Lazarus."

"Yeah, Chief?"

Smiling, even the slightest, made his mouth hurt. "You don't have to call me that." A pause, then, "It is not my intention to torment or harass you, but I need an extra set of hands. And a pair of tweezers."

Hesitation, then, "Okay."

He opened the door the rest of the way and stepped onto the tile of the anteroom that contained the sink. Chris returned from the adjoining door, and Grant turned away so Chris wouldn't have to meet his eye. He propped one arm against the door frame, resting his head against his forearm, letting the bright light over the sink wash across his back. "Cactus spines. No idea how many."

"Oh, man—ouch." Chris approached, lining up for the best light, then the tweezers brushed Grant's skin, drawing a shiver. "Sorry. I have to—"

"Yeah, I know."

Chris set his off-hand carefully against Grant's back, framing a needle of pain. He fished around with the tweezers, plucking the first one. He retreated a moment and dragged the trash can closer, then got back to work, his touch growing more deft with each spine he pulled. Drips of blood struck the floor around Grant's feet and sometimes splashed on his bare skin. The wound on his left temple and two of the punctures seeped blood. Can't stitch a puncture. "Remind me to leave a big tip when we check out."

"Definitely." His fingers rested lightly over one Grant's scars on the way to the next spine. "Can I ask you something?"

"Shoot."

Chris flinched, and Grant said, "Sorry—spec ops humor."

A nervous chuckle. "Right." His hand shifted. "This one's a little deeper. Sorry." A tug of the tweezers. "What you went through today—like, it's not the first time you've been through something like that. Kidnapping, death threats, the usual—that's what you said, right?"

"Affirmative."

"You survived, but it was a pretty close thing—Lazarus club, and all that. I just... How can you live this way? I don't understand how you're not bat-shit crazy."

"Who's saying I'm not?" Grant's smile tweaked the gouges carved at the corners of his lips. "This is the job. I've put my life on the line daily for years. Mostly, I'm on the other side of the gun."

"What happened to me this morning—God, not even twenty-four hours ago—and I'm, you're planning your next moves, coordinating a team, and I can't even imagine going back to my apartment."

Fear echoed in the other man's words and his hands trembled. He must be a wreck after the day he'd had. Adrenaline was the only thing keeping him vertical. Well, that and being invited to touch Grant's near-naked form. He didn't figure he was in any condition to make somebody blush. He'd been wrong.

Grant turned his head, leaning his temple, meeting Chris's gaze. "Lazarus. You've got no reason for shame. I walked into this, eyes wide open. Every time I step into a minefield, I know there's a chance I don't get out the other side. That's the risk, every time." The odds had been worse this time, much worse, given he couldn't be sure he'd even stacked the right deck, but Chris didn't need to hear that. "You didn't ask to get mixed up in any of this. All you wanted was to go home."

For a long moment, Chris worked on gently prying out a cactus spine. "Couldn't the same be said for you?"

Grant blinked at him. "Fair enough."

On the central nightstand, Grant's phone rang. Once, twice. Chris walked over to retrieve it, and the ringing stopped. "It's been doing that, but nobody answers."

"That's—" he started to explain.

Somebody knocked on the door. Grant straightened, scanned the room for a weapon, thought about the scout's knife his grandfather carried.

Chris took two steps toward the door. It burst open and he stumbled back, an out-thrust gun in his face. "Who the hell're you and what are you doing with that phone?"

CHAPTER FORTY-SIX

Roman numerals, two sets of three letters or maybe a six-letter word the Germans would've known," Jamie muttered. They'd traded the truck for the borrowed squad car, and she called in on a private line with an update—and strict orders that dispatch shouldn't call her. The radio in the car stayed on low, with a mutter of ambulance activity and routine calls-for-service now that the big excitement at Ruby was over with. And given that nobody knew about the other crime scene. Those three or four bodies weighed on her mind. "We check out the house, then you come down and give me an official statement, on the record. I need a paper trail on this train wreck, okay?"

"Yes, ma'am." Gonsalves shifted in his seat. "Damn. I'm not used to riding shotgun anymore. Drive by the house, windows down. I do not want to walk into another ambush."

"Weren't you on the inside of the last one?" She flicked off the radio and poked the widow buttons as they approached the turn, then drove on by. He leaned toward his window, his hand restless on the gun that had remained in his lap ever since they'd swung by the house. She was placing a lot of trust in this guy. Why? Because he saved Casey's bacon? Or just because she liked the feel of him. Casey was...slippery, somehow, a born chameleon, rock-solid, but kinda scary. This one, on the other hand, felt every inch a cop.

"Nothing. Park past the compound. Facing back."

"I'm not a rookie," she said mildly, used to the strapping cops and deputies around her acting like they were in charge.

"Right. Sorry. Working with Casey again, I drop right into the mindset. If you're not ops, you're a civilian—no matter your rank."

She swung the car around at the next wide spot and came back, pulling off to the side at a distance from the house. No lights, no movement, no sound. They opened their doors simultaneously, the dome light already turned off. No sense making a target of your head. She kept her own gun easy in the holster, and he dropped in behind her, gun held at his chest, small flashlight in his left, still off. "I'm taking your lead, Sheriff," but he hesitated a step. "Can't get over those stars." A soft breath of appreciation, then he came back to business. "What're we facing?"

"Three structures. We know the model's in Frank's place. I've got probable cause for Randy's, and permission from the property owner on the pueblo."

"So: Bag the model, move on from there. Sorry. I'm goddamn big-mouth, ask anyone."

She suppressed her grin. Maybe it wasn't just the cop-ness of him she liked. He sounded like her, deliberate, committed, irreverent.

At the door, she flicked on her own light, waited a moment, and tried the door. Unlocked. She stepped into the kitchen and flicked on the lights. No reason to expect anyone to be there, and they'd be better prepared if they chased any ambushers with light. She swept her gaze over the kitchen, for some reason, thinking of Chris, maybe because of entering his place, finding him down. Coming back later with Buster to get a scent on the bastard behind the attack.

"Clear," she said, indicating the right. Gonsalves stepped past her, moving in that direction.

Something about Chris. She frowned.

"How many rooms?" Gonsalves asked.

"Four and a bathroom. You take point." She swept her gaze more carefully around the kitchen, trying to figure what was bothering her.

He stalked by, turning on every light he reached, scanning the entire house in a matter of moments. "This's gotta be the room," he hollered from the back bedroom.

She spotted it, her eyes catching. "The sub's right here." Sitting on the counter next to the stove. Probably Casey, carrying the thing around, not understanding then what it stood for.

"Well, then." He emerged from the hall and held the gun down, reaching for the sub.

"Wait." The connection clicked. At her word, he froze. She drew a deeper breath. "That smell—gas?"

He cast her a look and shrugged. "Hell if I know, I just quit smoking. Mostly. Days like this, I want to start up again." He edged by the fridge, studying the sub from a different angle. "Just a toy, right? There's some letters on the back, but I can't see from here." Reaching out.

"Don't touch it!" Jamie lunged at him, grabbing his arm. Her urgency caught him and he backpedaled.

They bumped the table in their retreat and the opposite chair, jostled backwards, tumbled against the counter where the toy sub waited. Something clicked. Like a lighter.

Gonsalves wrapped an arm around her, launching them both toward the door as the room exploded around them.

CHAPTER FORTY-SEVEN

Chris collapsed to the floor, the phone tumbling from his nerveless hand. Any other day, Grant's lunge would've caught him. Not today. Still, he ended on his knees, at least cushioning his fall. D.A. stared down the barrel of a Glock at the both of them. "Sorry, Chief. If I'm interrupting, just say the word, and I'll—"

"Shut up and get in here."

D.A. grinned, her curls bouncing as she slid the gun back under her arm and stepped through the door, shutting it behind her. The bent lock wouldn't close, so she pulled the chain lock on, and used the deadlock as well. "But seriously, that's hardly the scene I expected to walk in on. What do you expect me to think?"

"Obviously, I'm his sex slave." Grant started to lift Chris toward the bed, but his fingers still felt like sausages. "Gimme a hand, better yet, two of them. He hasn't had the best day."

"He hasn't?" Her gesture took in Grant's bleeding scalp, the bruises purpling his stomach, the slender seeping wounds. "I see you got the red sheets and towels going." She knelt beside him, taking the bulk of Chris's weight to lift him onto the nearer bed. "Poor kid. What did you do to him?"

"He was murdered and resurrected yesterday morning—neither one by me. Other than that—" Grant leaned back on his heels and spread his arms, the better to show off his battered, naked torso. "He's gay."

D.A. burst out laughing. "Chief, you are a wicked SOB." She retrieved his phone and slid it onto the nightstand. "You're in a mood tonight—I don't think I've ever seen you like this."

"Twinkies for dinner. Six of them. I'm down a pint or so, and I'm being fueled by cortisol and high fructose corn syrup." And both were beginning to wear off. "What brought you here?"

"You've been out of touch for eight hours, and it was clear somebody else had your phone—I checked the records, and tracked down the last call."

"Never try to hide out from sigint. I've learned my lesson." He pressed the heel of his hand to the scalp wound. "Meantime, I need stitches, and you just gave my nurse a heart attack. Frank's in the adjoining room, getting some sleep I hope, but he's down by one arm."

She hooked the only chair over with her foot and dragged it toward the bathroom lights. "Sit."

Using the corner of the bed to push himself to his feet, and the edge of the second bed to find his place, Grant complied. She paused her search through the first aid supplies to watch his progress. "How bad is it?"

"You should see the other guys."

"Yeah, right." Then, sharply, "Where's Gooney?"

"Blew his cover, big time; I wouldn't be here if he hadn't. As punishment, he's following a lead with the sheriff." Grant tipped his head up. She probed a little, working her fingers through his hair and he winced. "He got off unscathed. Two guns, sixteen rounds, four caps, and he could've gone to a wedding in the same suit."

"When he's on, the dude's magic." She parted the hair with her finger, every stitch tugging at his scalp, the skin that had been unsettlingly loose coming back together. "So. Enigma code. Three Roman numerals, two sets of three letters. The two most likely six-letter combinations are 'Hitler' and 'Berlin,' which is one stupid reason the allies broke the code. I attacked it six ways from Sunday and got bupkus. Without the keys, we're SOL."

"Tell Gooney what to look for." He ran his fingers along a fine line of stitches from his forehead on back. "Not a big fan of keys right now."

"You get attacked by a porcupine or what?" She took his elbow and helped him up, applying new bandages to the wounds across his torso. "Get some sleep. Where's the third room?"

"Room two-one-two. Key under the stand-up plastic cigarette butt holder at the back of the parking lot. Second floor, line of sight."

"Sniper's nest."

"If need be." He faced her, some of the giddiness wearing away. "But I can't let you sleep just yet. I need someone they won't recognize."

She came instantly alert. "What do you need? Tell me it's not another white guy."

"For this one, you're perfect. Somebody's got to drive up to Kitt Peak observatory and get my cousin down. Frank can't reach her, and she hasn't responded to the next-of-kin call on Randy. Cellphones and tablets have to be shut down on the peak so they don't interfere with the radio telescope." He sank onto the bed, staring up at D.A. "They know about her, but the troops are gonna need a re-group. Lones is the one to watch out for."

"I hear you, Chief."

"She's not speaking to me right now, so using my name might not help. Frank's would—she'd come down for him. Use force if you have to. Whatever it takes, you bring her in. She's at the ARO-twelve meter scope: the Arizona Radio Observatory." He looked down at his hands, the bandages that wrapped his wrists. "Cece is the person who made my life bearable. I should be the one going."

"No way, Casey, even if I have to tie you down myself, and I can do it." She touched his shoulder. "It takes just as much strength to admit you need help."

He shook his head, hating that she was right. He was in no condition for another run-in, not tonight.

"I'm on it, Chief." She flicked him a little salute and let herself out the door. "Barricade this. The lock's busted, and I don't trust Loverboy to have your back."

Grant mustered the strength to do as she said. He hit the bed, sinking through darkness like a sub hitting bottom.

CHAPTER FORTY-EIGHT

Heat rushed over Jamie. Gasping for air, she pushed herself up, scrambling out from under the slabs of wood and shattered stucco. Flames billowed at her back, raining bits of the Manuel house down on her head—her hat whirled across the ground, whipped along by the roaring wind of the explosion. She spun around. "Gonsalves! Where are you?"

Firelight stunned her eyes, making it hard to see anything else.

"Gonsalves! Goddammit, officer—speak up!"

A groan from nearby. Jamie pounced in that direction. Smaller flames danced along fragmented roof beams and devoured the edges of the door, blown clear off its hinges but miraculously whole, and bobbing slightly. Jamie kicked it over, seized his arm and dragged him up. They stumbled together out of range of the swirling ash. That same easterly wind that had carried Casey's scent to Buster's nostrils now scattered cinders across the paddocks.

"Gonsalves, are you okay?" She kept her grip on him, as much to steady her own nerves as his.

"Jay-sus," he breathed. "Jay-sus H. fucking Christ." He smeared his hands over his face, for a moment peering at the fire between his fingers, head shaking slowly.

"I'll take that as a yes."

"You totally got my biscuit out of the oven." He took another breath and seemed to draw down courage. "Sheriff, if that's the kind of work I can expect from you, I'll move out here and vote for you myself." His teeth flashed in a wide grin. "Hell, I know some forgers, I can get enough ID's to vote in every district in the goddamn county."

"Shit on a shingle, Gonsalves, don't make me write you up for the voting commission." She pushed him away, but he didn't budge.

"The sub was rigged, tug the wire, light the spark. Boom." He turned his hands into a little explosion, an oddly specific gesture, then noticed the dirt and ash, and wiped them off on his pants. "Fucking boss, out for vengeance. Where's water?"

They broke away, then Jamie remembered, pointed toward the well head with its old-fashioned pump

They started forward, just as the sidewall of the house blew out and smashed down on top of the pump. She jumped back, finding him once more at her side. Fire roared in her ears. Gonsalves' hands moved. She shook her head, and he merely pointed, drawing her back.

"Sign language?" she asked when her hearing had cleared.

"Pretty handy when you can't be heard. It's also great for picking up chicks." His hands moved as he spoke, translating his own words in a series of graceful gestures, right down to the curvy motion of a female figure. Her skin tingled as if his hands had stroked over her. Picking up chicks, indeed.

The sand and gravel of the yard made for an excellent firebreak, thank God. Not in vain that time; her mother would be so proud. If she ever saw her again, her mother wouldn't believe a word of this. As for Frank's house, total loss. Fucking boss: Adam Lones. Her gut hollowed out.

Through the crackle and roar, a thin, sharp sound trilled. "Fuck me. Is that your phone?" They parted, scanning the ground.

Gonsalves turned a circle, then snatched up the phone. Two rings. Jamie reached for it, but it went dead. Then it rang again. "Team code," he said. "That's for me. It's Gooney, what you got?" He listened, laughed. "Called it right, D.A. You bringing the marshmallows? Chief's old home went up in flames." Then the humor fled. "Right. No fucking way. Lones, he must've heard what we did to his boys, and he's trying to do the same. Any hint you're one of us, any wrong move, and you're screwed." Listening, then, "Shit." He held the phone away from his face. "Sheriff, how far to Kitt

Peak from here?"

"Your cover's blown, Gooney! You can't come," said the voice on the other end.

"Hell if I'm letting you go alone!"

"I'm calling in the fire," Jamie said. "Take half an hour or more to get the trucks out here."

"Where the hell are we?"

"South of Cowlic," Jamie supplied.

Gonsalves—Gooney?—hooted with laughter. "You're fucking with me. Cowlic?"

"Besides," the woman on the other end said, "I'm already driving and you've got work to do."

He pulled the phone up to his ear and stalked away from the fire. Jamie reached for her radio to call in the fire, but the holster was empty. Gun still there, utility pouch open and spilled half its guts out somewhere. Damn. As she searched, she found Gooney's weapon where it had flown out of his hand as he fell.

"The sub had the Roman numerals, and it's the first U-boat ever to go airborne," he was saying. She walked over and handed him the weapon, butt first. He accepted, bringing it up to his forehead, and sweeping it down in a formal salute, like a Marine with his sword. Oh, yeah, not just for the cop.

"Gotcha, D.A." Then, with exaggerated patience, "Yes, Mom, I'll eat my fucking vegetables, then we are hitting the peak road. Nobody goes out alone, Chief's orders." He tapped the phone off, and pivoted to face her. "Did I actually thank you yet? I don't think so."

"My radio's melted and half my kit's turned to slag. I need to call in the fire from the panda car."

"That's a negative. We need to finish the search and get the hell out of here. Call the brigade on the way." He shoved the phone into his pocket.

"If the fire spreads—"

"Look around you! What's to burn except what we care about? If we lose the whole compound, we're fucked and they win." He stepped up close to her, his face grim and fierce by the dancing orange light. "You saw what those bastards did to the chief, Sheriff. You know what they expected me to do. No fucking way am I letting them win."

She met his gaze. "Randy called him an asshole, then called himself one, he mentioned Casey's thirteenth birthday, and something about a shoebox. You call it in and get the car. I go after the box." Jamie unclipped the keys and tossed them. He made the catch one-handed.

"On it. Then we go to Kitt Peak. I got a buddy out there who needs back up."

What she said next chilled her through, despite the flames. "Yep. But I'm the one who has to give it. Lones doesn't know I changed sides."

His eyes gleamed in the firelight. "In that case, Sheriff, I hope you're a damn fine actress."

She turned on her heel, setting off at a run for the trailer while the world roared around her.

CHAPTER FORTY-NINE

From a pull-out on the mountain road, Adam watched the dark spread of the reservation at his feet. There, in the distance, a burst of red and gold, as if the sun had suddenly appeared, making its own horizon. He dared hope it was Casey himself, but he had no illusions. Hammer's account left Casey a wreck, and yet fully capable of taking down and disarming two men with his hands literally tied behind his back. Adam included this understanding in his new decision model: even when he believed he was not underestimating his opponent, he must take steps to ensure it. One of which lay up this road. His motor purred to life and he continued his drive. A gate blocked the road up, with some signs about after-hours admission, but the other side was wide open. He blew past it.

As the elevation increased, the slopes around him filled in with brush and low tree cover. A fox darted across the road in front of him, pausing on the other side, its eyes aglow, and it made him think of Casey, too quick, too sly for its own good. Adam stamped the accelerator and the beast vanished into the woods.

He needed to practice control. In spite of the evening's set-backs, he was winning this battle, just as he and the Sons would win their war. On the road between the Manuel place and this one, he'd gotten an automatic notice from his bank for a very nice deposit, and he had an appointment in the morning with the Warden herself, in person for the first time.

Route 386 wound higher and higher, through acres of nothing, and he fought the urge to race. Control. A few buildings appeared to either side, the distinctive short, round silos of telescope installations, designated by letters as if they were radio stations: ARO, WIYN. A handy way to blow taxpayer funds on pretty pictures when the nation had much more serious issues to face. The trouble was, he had no idea where to find the Jessup woman, or even where to find someone to ask. Impulsive to come here without laying the proper groundwork. He headed for the heart of the grounds, where the visitors' center and other facilities clustered close to the summit. More silos emerged against the starry sky, like a farm that mulched pointless data. He pulled up in front of one of the square buildings and killed the engine, though his lights remained on a moment longer as he debated where to go.

"Hey! Hey, what're you doing?" Someone appeared outside the window, rapping on the glass. "There's no public programs tonight."

Adam slipped away his irritation, and played concern instead. "Excuse me? Sorry." He pulled up his uncertain smile and stepped from the car, forcing the woman back. "I'm sorry—I'm looking for someone."

"You can't just come up here and drive around, especially with your headlights on."

He managed a chuckle. "It hardly seemed safe, with that road—"

She jabbed at his chest. "These are the best viewing conditions we've had for days. I don't want some idiot to light-blind all of us and ruin the footage. Do you have any idea how hard it is to calibrate the cameras on these things? We're talking about stuff thousands of light-years away and super-faint."

Nothing she said made the least bit of sense, but Adam tried to look impressed. He blew out a breath. "Oh, I am sorry. I really wasn't thinking. I'm just—no, let me start over. It's very important I find Cecile Jessup. I know she works here. Her brother's been injured, he's in the hospital."

"Oh." His accuser retreated a step. "You still can't just roam around." She folded her arms. "Is she staff or visiting? Do you know which observatory she's with?"

"Staff. She's a member of the Tohono O'odham Nation."

"It's really unorthodox to interrupt anybody's research. If she's staff, the visiting astronomers are counting on her." She tapped her teeth with a fingernail. "Her brother's been hurt?"

Adam nodded gravely. "Very badly, I'm afraid. There's a chance...well, we're closer to God up here, right? I'd hate to say anything prematurely. Her grandfather was attacked last week, beaten by an addict. I just... I didn't want her to get this news over the phone."

"Oh, jeez. Come on. I can find the directory, that'll at least get you to the right installation." She walked confidently into the darkness. Adam, so recently emerging from the cocoon of his vehicle, peered into the darkness then set off after her. His heartbeat pounded in his ears and his breath felt short thanks to his rapid rise in elevation. "She might still want to wait until dawn, though. People pay a lot of money for observation time on these scopes. If their work gets disrupted, it can set them back years, even, on the research."

"I hope they'll consider a man's life in the balance."

"Sure, yes," she said, but she sounded unconvinced. She led the way through a locked door down a corridor with dim red floor lighting, then into an office where she hesitated, and flicked on a red light. "I don't want to blow my vision for the night." Among the dozens of papers tacked between whiteboards on the walls, she plucked one sheaf of papers down. "Jessup, you said?" She shuffled the pages. "She's the telescope operator at ARO on the Southwest Ridge. Do you know where that is?"

"I drove past it on the way in." Wasting precious time.

"Do you want me to call down to her, let her know to expect you?" The woman pulled out a walkie-talkie.

And require him to give a name, which she had so far not asked for. "That's alright. As I said, I think it's really best for me to tell her in person. Thank you very much. I am so sorry I disrupted your night. Happy viewing!" He gave a cheery wave as he hurried back to his car, remembering to turn on only the parking lights as he maneuvered back in the right direction. On the road that snaked into the mountains, he spotted headlights coming up. He estimated better than even odds that it was someone from Casey's rabble, doing the same thing. It would be nice to avoid tipping his hand to this Jessup woman too soon.

He edged up his speed, leaning in to watch the road, and nearly missed the ARO sign. Throw the car in reverse, swing the turn and down the gravel road. It curved around a huge concrete base topped by the familiar ridged metal silo. An old pick-up parked nose-in along the edge of the building. Beyond that, a rectangular concrete structure jutted out. The gravel road continued, and a few other structures loomed among the trees. He turned his car around and backed in, in case he needed to save a few minutes on his departure. Nice and easy. Adam took a moment to put on his charm before he walked over to the building. Pause again, listening. Two voices, low. Hopefully a television. He knocked on the door, and the voices broke off. Not the television then. Unfortunate.

"Coming!" A woman's voice, then the metal door swung open and she peered into the darkness, round-faced, a few shades darker than her grandfather. Mexican blood, perhaps. She wore jeans and a pull-over with a tribal logo. "Hello?"

"Cecile Jessup? May I come in? I have some news."

Frowning, she backed up, swinging the door wider along with her toward his left. He stood on the threshold of a utilitarian space crammed with rolling chairs, computer monitors and banks of wired devices he couldn't identify. Another door led out from the wall not far away. Opposite this, an area with an old couch and a few other chairs clustered around a table with a few supplies for living. Another door into a blocky area suggested a bathroom. One of the rolling chairs still rocked a little, and another woman, short and curly-haired, bent toward one of the monitors.

"News?" Jessup inquired. She glanced toward the other woman. "I'm not used to having so many visitors."

"Well, I certainly don't want to interrupt, but I—"

"This is about my brother?" She shared a glance between the two strangers. "Both of you?"

Compact and distinctly Semitic, the other woman looked comfortable in her spinning chair, her face open. "I didn't want to spring anything on you, Cecile, but yes. He's been mixed up in a bad business."

Jessup folded her arms. "Really. That's what everyone wants me to think these days. Let me guess, one of you is law enforcement, here to get information, and the other one's from the mafia—is that even what we get these days? I think I've seen this show—maybe we can cut to the credits?"

Adam reached for the gun at his back. "In that case, let's clarify. I'm with the law, but I'd rather not say which office." Before he'd even got his hand on the butt, the Jew sprang from her seat into a shooter's stance, weapon forward. Perfect.

Jessup shrieked and jumped back.

"Sorry, ma'am, that's just what I wanted to avoid," the Jew said, but she didn't stand down. "You're Adam Lones."

Jessup showed no recognition of his name; she remained focused on the gun. Good.

He drew his own weapon almost casually, displaying it to the women, moving at a calculated speed, not drawing a bead on the Jew. He was an officer now, maybe FBI, trying to defuse a situation that was already spiraling out of control, exactly as he planned. "I don't know who you think I am, but I've been working closely with Sheriff Rizzo on the break-in at the cultural center, where your grandfather got hurt. She'd like to avoid any more bloodshed, but you should know your brother's in the hospital. His condition is critical."

"Randy? Oh, no." She clasped a hand over her mouth. "But if he's the law—"

"No, he's not," the Jew said. "Everything he said is true—and he hasn't claimed a badge. Maybe it's time you showed us? Where's your ID?"

"Where's yours?" Jessup demanded. She took another step back, getting out from between these two armed strangers, aiming equally suspicious looks in one, then the other direction.

Adam still blocked the exit, the half-open door providing him some cover from the Jew's direction. He'd already done the calculations, and he liked his odds. "The minute I reach for a badge, Ms. Jessup, she takes me down. You saw how fast she drew on me." He raised his own weapon in a don't-shoot gesture. "This woman's not wrapped up in her brother's mess. Just let me walk her out of here. You and me, we can do this another time."

Jessup started edging toward him, and he gave her an encouraging half-smile, his brave face, covering her own escape from the dangerous person before them. Casey's Jew, no doubt. Whoever these people were, they were fast and deadly. The minute Jessup was clear, he'd take down the Jew. It would be a pleasure in more ways than one.

CHAPTER FIFTY

Grant's eyes snapped open to the darkness, the soft blue glow of the clock on the hotel microwave, the low mutter of another man's breathing. Sometime in the last hour, Chris had gotten himself properly tucked in and now lay on his side, curled up. A habitual posture, or one adopted by fear? Shadows shifted near the adjoining door. He'd forgotten to check that Frank secured the room. Shit. His feet hit the ground and his hand was on the knob before his grandfather's voice said, "I didn't want to wake you."

Frank stepped back from his side of the door, opening it wider. "Think I woke you just by looking."

His room showed the brighter shade of pale of an open laptop. The rumpled bedclothes suggested he'd gotten at least a little sleep. He wore a white undershirt and his pants, his cast bare of the sling. "It's this thing." He gestured toward the computer. "Some kind of alert? I wasn't sure, given what you do, if I should turn it off."

Grant gave a nod and stepped through. "I'll take care of it. How are you doing?" He pulled back a chair and sat in front of the glowing screen.

"It's hard to sleep. Too heavy."

He didn't think the old man meant the cast on his arm.

"How about you?" Frank watched him approach, his eyes making a pattern of the scars that lay behind the fresh injuries.

"I got some rest," he replied. An alert chimed softly, a winking icon in the corner of the screen from a VoIP app, but this was in text, from the

Warden. He pulled the computer closer and tapped it open.

02:17 twenty minutes ago—*Are you still in the game? I have heard otherwise.*

He stared at the message a long time.

"Trouble?" Frank pulled out a chair as well, supporting his arm on the surface of the table.

Grant shot him a look. "You know me, Frank. There's always trouble." The old man's face reflected his own near-smile. Not possible to find a family resemblance in somebody he wasn't even related to. *Family's more than blood, at least, it should be.* Finally, he set his fingers on the keyboard. Tapping the keys brought twinges across his scraped wrists

02:40 *All in.*

She might have already gone to bed, but something had gotten her up —or kept her up—at that hour.

02:41 *Pleased to hear it.*

And there it was, the fresh shot of cortisol he needed. 02:41 *Roman Numerals?*

02:42 *Text divided into four parts, as follows: Gamma IV-I-VII*

"Gamma? That's not a Roman numeral," he muttered.

"Didn't you have a codebreaker?"

"I sent her after Cece." Their eyes met. "We can't wait for her to come down on her own."

"It's an M4 machine." Anderson's voice from the doorway, then he walked through, barefoot but otherwise fully clothed. "Might as well turn the lights on."

"Sorry to wake you. I get the feeling you need the sleep."

"More spec ops humor?" He walked over and joined them at the table as the thread lit up again. "You wanted me to read up on submarines, right? U-boats?"

02:43 *Do you have keys?*

Grant's hand rubbed over one of the puncture wounds, and the old man's frown deepened. 02:43 *In progress. Will advise.* "Lazarus. What do you know?"

Chris opened up the other laptop and prodded it into life, then read from his screen. "The sub that those POWs escaped from was the U-162, a class IX-C one of the biggest of the U-boats. Every boat of that class was equipped with an M4 Enigma machine, not M3. That means four dials instead of three."

"Oh, hell." Grant's aching head sank into his hands. "Rizzo and Gooney are looking for six letters, they need eight."

"You want the phone?" Anderson asked, but he was already retrieving it.

Gooney's phone had been abandoned in a hotel room across town, something a lot more upscale than this one. Rizzo it was then. No answer. Silent running, just like the sub they were tracking.

Grant held the phone a little too tightly, trying not to read anything into that silence. Rizzo was the next best thing to a civilian, an unengaged party. And Gooney—

02:46 *If you send the code, I can apply my resources.*

"Where is the code?" Anderson asked.

He dropped the phone and snagged a folder off the nightstand, laying out a series of copies, print-outs of the photos he'd taken over the last couple days. "This is what we've got. A bunch of letters on a pillar, taking the form of an Enigma code. Also, a series of paint drops on the roof that I think is a star map. Another reason we need Cece. Diagram of the sub, disguised as a petroglyph. Vintage photo of the prize: the original skull of Peking Man."

Resuming his seat—gratefully, his head already throbbing—Grant finally replied. 02:47 *Sorry, no. Still not that friendly.*

Frank tilted his head, then sifted among the papers. "That sailor, he was clever." He flicked a glance up at Grant.

02:48 *May I send you a file?*

Grant looked at the screen. Hell, no. What else would come along with it? 02:48 *Use file transfer site* he filled in the link.

02:50 *Of course. I am inbound to your location. Perhaps a meeting?*

Switch to a different screen where he'd kept the details of the cover story he spun her on their first call. 02:50 *Palo Alto conference center?*

02:51 *Very funny, Mr. Casey.*

He slapped off the wi-fi and shoved the computer away.

"They know who you are? Who is that?" Anderson put down the code images he'd been squinting at.

"They shouldn't. She calls herself the Warden, and she's the origin of all of this. She put Lones on the scent of what she called a great treasure. He may not even know what it is, only that she's willing to pay a bundle to get it, and he needs the cash for his Nazi nation. There's only one way she could've found out who I am: Lones told her."

"Maybe it's time to stop." Frank lay his hand on the table near Grant's knotted fingers. "Give up the chase. Let Lones find what he's looking for and move out. And nobody else gets hurt."

"Never thought I'd hear you, of all people, counsel me to give up. After what we did to his men, there's no way he's giving up. Not until Gooney and I, and anyone else who knows what happened, is dead. That means both of you. It means Randy. It means Rizzo if he finds out she's working with us. It means Cece because he can't be certain what she knows, and he's not gonna take our word for it." He leaned back from the table, tracing the tattoos on his inner left arm with his eyes, every inch of his skin a record of his tickets to the Lazarus Club. His hand closed into a fist and he hardly noticed the pain. "We have two choices. One, we follow the map. We get his prize before he does, and he's gotta come to us to get it. Two. We take the fight to him. We push hard and we don't give up."

"Until he's dead," Anderson supplied. "Or we are."

Grant pulled the laptop back toward him and turned on the wi-fi. 02:57 *Mission San Xavier, 8 am. Light a candle for the dead and I'll be waiting.*

CHAPTER FIFTY-ONE

K illing her lights, Jamie pulled up alongside the trail. The firetruck that passed them on their way out of Cowlic must've been confused to see a first responder apparently going the wrong direction. She pulled a radio from the deck in the car, and flicked it on, holding down the button as she passed it over. "You sure about this?"

Gooney clipped the radio at his back, the gun already in his lap, ready to go. Flak vest from the trunk strapped over his chest. "You'll hear everything. Don't blow your cover if you don't have to—" he looked up at her. "And it takes a helluva lot before I need back-up, you got me?"

"I gotcha. The observatory's a half-mile up, not the first one, the second one. After I drop you, I'll go past the drive and swing it around, engine running. Don't do anything stupid."

He flashed his grin. "It's like you've known me for years." He opened the door, and shut it without a sound, leaning toward the window. "We get lucky, D.A.'s already got her and got the hell out." He stood away, his hand raised in a gesture of farewell, then he jogged into the darkness. From the radio, volume set way down, she heard his footfalls. She pulled onto the deserted road and drove the final mile, passing the turn for the installation, swinging about in the next wide spot and creeping back down, lying in wait. Gooney's breath came in controlled bursts, then he muttered, "Gettin' out of shape for this shit." Jamie smiled. Should've warned him about the altitude. Seemed like the attitude might be a whole other problem.

From the floor on the passenger's side, she picked up the old shoe box she'd found at Randy's place. Stuffed on the shelf in a narrow closet, the shoebox bulged with the memorabilia of a childhood long passed: photos of friends, a comic book, clippings of motorcycles and engines from Popular Mechanics, bits and pieces of school records and letters. She found a photo of Randy and Cece, arms about each other's shoulders, Randy holding up a medal that he wore around his neck. At the edge of the frame stood a skinny kid in running shorts, a trophy dangling from his hand, half-hidden behind his legs. Grant Casey, aged about fourteen. The only photo of him in the box so far, and clearly an afterthought. She imagined their grandmother, so proud of their achievements, trying to get them to squeeze together so she could have them all in the shot. Must've sucked for Randy, big time, having somebody like that show up: smarter, faster, better-looking. She shuffled the photo back in and kept looking. So far, nothing related to the case at hand. She pulled out a handful of ephemera and spotted what might be the actual medal from the photo: All-State Track and Field, third place. A few other medals and trinkets occupied the bottom layer, sifting down through the papers. Among them, a distinctive swastika and eagle. No claiming that one was a native symbol.

Then she heard the first gunshot.

CHAPTER FIFTY-TWO

With the Jessup woman halfway across the room, the Jew glared. "Don't go anywhere with him, Cecile. Your grandfather sent me."

"She's lying. If anyone, it was Grant Casey."

The name flared her eyes. "What?"

Adam spoke fast. "We think he's behind all of this, setting up your brother—we don't know what he wants, but—"

"Cece. Listen to me. Lones's people kidnapped your grandfather from the hospital and Casey intervened—"

"So he's not lying, Grant really did send you." Jessup's hands balled into fists. "What is wrong with him?"

Adam suppressed his grin, keeping cool, professional, focused. "Sociopathic tendencies. Probably from his father's side. Have you noticed any anti-social tendencies? Trouble forming relationships? That kind of thing?"

Jessup lurched toward him, keeping close to the wall. Good—she was beginning to trust him.

Between one breath and the next, the Jew fired.

Adam yanked the door in front of him and the bullet ricocheted off the back of it. Even better, the bitch was playing right into his hands. "Cecile, hurry!"

Jessup screamed again and ran—not toward him, in the direction of the gunfire, but out the other door, slamming it behind her. Through the door she shouted, "Who are you people?" Idiot mongrel.

"Tell Casey to leave her alone," Adam shouted. He fired three times, using the door as cover, and the Jew dove behind a computer bank. He launched himself across the space, yanking open the other door and slamming it behind him. She stood there, clearly dazed and out of her depth. Looking for guidance Adam was pleased to provide. "We need to block the door. Is there another way out?"

Pale in the starlight, the Jessup woman shook her head. "Just up."

"Go, go, go! My car's waiting."

She ran from his side, clearly all-in with his plan at this point. Adam grabbed a cart of equipment nearby and crashed it down across the doorway, hooking the inside knob with the wire rack. It jerked hard, almost immediately. He spun about. He stood in a round cement chamber with a metal rim towering overhead and the vast bulk of the telescope in between: the mother of all satellite dishes aimed out a broad gap in the roof. Across the room, Jessup ran for a scaffold that stood partway up the far wall, and Adam ran after. How soon before the Jew made her way out of the control room?

Jessup reached the platform and wavered for a moment. A narrow ladder bolted to the wall gave access to the track around the inside of the building that allowed it to turn or move the giant framework between them. She swallowed hard and glanced back at him as he reached the bottom of the stairs. "So Grant's a criminal?"

"Mastermind," Adam confirmed. "He's probably getting into border drugs now that the wall's making it more profitable."

He started up the ladder, and she moved toward the ladder, but she glanced back at him again, doubt gleaming in her eyes. "If this were a movie, that's what the villain would say, to get the heroine to believe him."

He was losing her trust now that she'd had time to think. Keep her going, keep her scared. He reached the platform. "We need to move, before that woman finds another way to get to you." With his gun, he gestured toward the ladder, then a man appeared at the top of it, a towering silhouette.

"Hey, boss. Bad news in the desert tonight." The false candidate grinned down at him. "You gave me a bullet for Casey. I gave it to Smith. Bam. Right between the eyes." He held a gun in his hand, using it to illustrate his story.

Adam's entire body went tense and his trigger finger twitched. He was losing control. Of his target, of the situation—of his desire for the traitor's blood.

Between them, Jessup backed against the wall, hands to her face, sobbing. "Oh, God, what's going on?"

The traitor aimed and Adam jumped for the wall. He slapped a fat green button, and the silo started to turn.

"Shit!" the guy yelped and stumbled a few steps along the rim from where he stood.

"Gooney, that you?" The Jew's voice, outside.

Adam caught Jessup's arm, pulling her close as if to defend her, using her as his shield. "Stay close, Ms. Jessup. This one's trouble." Staring up at the man who had betrayed him, who had killed so many of his own, Adam felt his grip too tight and he eased off. Jew out one door, traitor at the other. Jessup flung out her other hand and slapped the red button. The silo ground to a halt.

"You said a bullet for Casey," she called out. "What do you mean?"

Off-balance, but still strong, the traitor said, "I was meant to kill him. He exchanged himself for your grandfather and almost died for it. I'm still wearing the blood he lost."

"Grant wouldn't do that; they hate each other."

"Hate's never as far from love as you think," the traitor said. "Ask me how I know."

"Cecilia, go! Down, back down!" Adam flung her in that direction, clearing the way, and fired.

The traitor flew backwards and crashed heavily in the darkness. Jessup caught herself at the top of the stairs. For a moment, he saw her face, then she lashed out hard. Her booted foot caught his knee and Adam tumbled from the scaffold ten feet to the ground. He came up roaring. Any mask torn away, any illusion of control stripped by the sight of the traitor's face and now by this woman's own betrayal. He needed her alive. He needed the surety she provided—but he didn't need her whole. He whipped the gun around, the first shots wild, chipping concrete as Jessup flew up the ladder faster than he'd believed possible.

"Cece!" The Jew from the outside. "Come on, come on!"

"What about—"

"Just come!"

Adam ran to the door. Ripped free the spilled cart and ran through the main exit. A car started up—a car he hadn't even noticed. He leaped into his own car and gunned it into motion. A premium piece of German engineering, he could take down the Jew's Jap rental in moments. His engine roared in imitation of his own fury.

He raced down the gravel road, fifty yards from the other vehicle and gaining. It squealed into the turn onto 386. He slowed so he wouldn't lose control more than he already had. Lights flared into motion and a siren. A squad car zoomed down from above.

Tires screeching, he barely managed to avoid hitting the police car. It stopped as well, but a little too late, front tire hanging into the wash between the driveway and the road.

Sheriff Rizzo stepped out of the squad car weapon drawn, then she stopped. "Adam, is that you? Shit on a shingle, I wasn't expecting that."

Adam dropped his gun onto the floor, tempted as he was to simply shoot her. He backed up the car a little. "Sorry. It's been such a difficult time lately, I thought some star-gazing might do me some good. This place is an Arizona treasure. We don't pay enough attention to it."

She looked up as if she hadn't noticed the sky. "Nice night for it. And a lot of other shit—sorry. I need to watch my language, I know." She holstered her weapon, shaking her head. "You would not believe what I've been through tonight. Shoot-out at the Okay Corral time, I kid you not. Did you go up to the top?" She pointed.

Adam mustered a smile, the hardest he had ever manufactured. "I hadn't realized there's no public program tonight. Why do you ask?"

"We had a call about suspicious persons out here. Seems like the whole county's gone nuts in the last few hours, so we're short-staffed, otherwise I'd be in bed where I belong." She took a few steps back. "Sorry about this. You probably want to get to bed, too."

She climbed back into the car and threw it into reverse, lurching out of his path and waving to him as he drove off down the road. Idiot. The Jessup woman and the Jew had gotten away. Another setback. He needed to call in the Sons. The ones who remained would be staunch in their righteous anger. Traitors, Jews, mud people. Ashes to ashes, dust to dust. But his first call was to Hammer.

"Miller died?"

"Yes, sir." Hammer sounded defeated and nasal. "I let the others take on the role you advised. They're sleeping it off. We got the injured to the emergency room."

"Broke your nose?"

"Yes, sir," a little angry. Good.

"Hammer, we will take them down. We will disassemble them this rabble. But I will need your help."

"Understood, sir. If I get another crack at Casey, I won't screw it up. Tell me what you need."

"I need Miller's body, and a machete."

CHAPTER FIFTY-THREE

Steadying her breathing, Jamie watched Adam's taillights wind down and vanish from sight. She pulled into the driveway a little too fast. The last she heard from the radio was a gunshot, a crash of branches, a man's grunt of pain as he absorbed the impact, then nothing. Where was he? Fuck the astronomers. She turned the lights on full and added the spotlight as she pulled in next to the observatory. The door hung open, lights on inside.

Jamie climbed out. "Detective! Gonsalves, where are you?"

From somewhere in the darkness on the far side of the observatory. "Fuck," a wheeze. Then, louder, "Marco!"

She laughed, half tension, half relief. "Polo!" She moved toward the sound of his voice.

"Marco." He lay on his back partway down a scree slope at the base of the silo, his feet pointing upwards and a long tumble of disturbed stones showing his trajectory. She shone a flashlight down at him, and he flung his arm over his eyes. "Fuck. Not dead. Still hurts like an SOB." His other hand rubbed at his chest, then he tapped the body armor. "Good idea. Thanks." He gave her a thumbs up.

"Still too soon to offer back-up?" She looked around and spotted an aluminum ladder lying across the ground, the connection to the bottom of the fixed ladder up the side of the silo. Setting down the flashlight, she dragged the ladder over and lay it along the slope near where he'd fallen, bracing the top end with her butt on the ground.

After a moment, and a few more stuttering breaths, he rolled and grabbed the lowest rung, clambering up the ladder as she leaned back against his weight. He flopped down beside her, then tugged at the Velcro so he could breathe a little easier. "They got out?"

"Yep. And my cover's intact—I think."

"Nice work," he mumbled. "Sorry. Need to catch my breath."

"Double impact: shot to the chest, fall to the ground. That's pretty serious."

"Yeah." His eyes remained shut, but he showed his teeth. "What can I say? Fell hard for you."

As if. Lady cops were hardly guy magnets, even for other cops. But he made her smile. Had Nathan ever made her smile like that—cut through the tension with a joke? "I thought Casey was the one with the headwound."

"Right." He pushed himself to sitting and peeled off the vest. "He's a good shot, straight to the heart." He unbuttoned the top of the shirt and inspected his chest, then finally rose to his feet. "Guess we're done here." He offered a hand, and she accepted the solid heat of his hand around hers until she was on her feet. Fell hard for her. For a minute she wished it had been more than a joke.

Brushing off the grass and taking the flashlight, she led the way around the silo. She stopped in the control room to find the number for the observatory office. "Yeah, this is Sheriff Jamie Rizzo. Just letting you know that Cecile Jessup had to take off. Her brother's in critical condition. You might need to get someone down here to—ah—ARO? To take care of things." That done, she paused at the door, fingering the divot close to its edge. Maybe the astronomers wouldn't know it was a gunshot. She shut the door behind her.

Back at the car, Gooney tossed the Kevlar vest into the trunk. They both climbed inside, with him back on shotgun. "I could use a drink."

"I hear you, but somebody's gotta be alert in the morning, and it's not that far off." She replaced the flashlight and loosened her duty belt. Maybe she was finally done with tonight. "I'll drop you at the motel."

"I dunno, Sheriff. You pulled off that encounter, but I'm not sure you should be alone tonight." He buckled in, not looking at her.

Jamie pulled away from the trees, drumming her fingers on the wheel, thinking it over. "I do have a spare room. And it's not a bad idea to have some back-up handy if he pulls a reverse-course. I mean, if you don't mind."

He scrounged a water bottle from the side storage and took a long swallow. "I'm on board with that."

"You'll need to be careful, though. From what I heard on the radio, you're the second-to-last person I can afford to be seen with."

"It's a risk, no doubt." He nodded. He aimed the mouth of the water bottle at her. "But you know, I think we should take Casey's Law to heart. Nobody goes anywhere alone, and I mean, anywhere." He drew out the last word.

They emerged onto the main road, the landscape opening up around them, and she thought over what he'd said, twice now, feeling like she'd been missing something. Jamie stomped on the brakes, thrusting her hand to the side to reduce the impact on his bruised chest. His heart thundered beneath her hand. "Jesus, Rizzo—What's the trouble?"

She jerked her hand back, the heat of him overpowering, but it was too late, as if his heartbeat struck a match that exploded within her. She turned, leaning her arm on the wheel, to stare at him. "Detective Gonsalves, are you flirting with me?"

Gonsalves' hand went still and lowered the water bottle, finally stuffing it into a cupholder. He tipped his head, and she caught the flash of that irrepressible grin. "Dumbass move, I know. Frickin' awful timing. It's been a helluva long night, and I'd blame the lack of sleep, but—full disclosure here—I'm no damn good at subtle."

Got that right, even though it had taken her way too long to get the message.

"You're smart, fast, sassy, curvy. That whole riding to the rescue thing makes for a kickass first impression."

She was riding to the rescue sure, but he was the one who carried it off. She flipped on the dome light and studied his face, streaked with dirt and scratches, still marked with other men's' blood. Buzz cut, green eyes, full lips, strong chin: a powerful, dedicated, and sometimes ridiculous man.

"Jesus, don't look at me like that. I'm a flippin' disaster." He leaned to get a view of himself in the side mirror, and scrubbed a hand over his stubble. "Yikes. Why'd you even let me in the car?" He reached up and flicked the light back off.

Surely she didn't look any better. "You are flirting with me."

The grin turned to a gale of laughter. "Hey, sorry! You've got a husband or a boyfriend or whatever, and I didn't even ask. I gotta keep my big mouth shut." He put up his hands. "Take me to the motel—'s better for both of us. We can send D.A. over to your place."

She slapped the steering wheel. "Shit on a shingle, but I get sick of men telling me what's best."

He opened his mouth as if to apologize again, then slumped back in his seat, with a palms-up gesture of surrender.

"I cannot believe you're trying to flirt with me at a time like this." He was right, frickin' awful timing. Both of them pumped full of adrenaline, not thinking straight. Maybe just drawn together by the wild ride of this whole night. Maybe...

"I'm an idiot. Ask anybody. Ask Casey, he'll give you an earful. If he hasn't already," he added darkly, his eyes tracing something outside the vehicle.

She wanted him looking at her, his eyes meeting hers, his eyes closing when they—aw, Hell. "Casey's law," she muttered, leaning back in her own seat, sitting a little taller. "Well, y'know, as law enforcement professionals, it's our duty to obey."

His head cocked, then he glanced at her sidelong and the grin crept back. "You're shittin' me."

"I'd hate to be found in violation of the law." Jamie looked at the road ahead. With the flip of a switch, she hit the flashers and punched the accelerator all the way home.

CHAPTER FIFTY-FOUR

Grant studied the aerial photos he'd found of the church, and the hand-drawn floorplan his grandfather dictated to Anderson, resisting the urge to check his phone. They'd call in. Or they'd come in. Frank lay on the bed nearest the windows, his back to Grant, not sleeping, but doing a good imitation.

A soft rap on the door, and Grant was on his feet, suppressing the pain. He'd pulled on a shirt earlier, one of the Bone Guard khaki's Nick was so fond of. As he passed the bed, Frank stirred, watching him go by.

D.A. stood outside. "I brought her to the room, but she wants to see you." Her gaze flicked toward Frank who was already rising.

"Him." Grant tipped his head.

"Both of you. Gooney came through at the observatory. He called in on the drive back: he's going to Rizzo's—they're worried about Lones figuring out she's in on it. She got us out of there, but she may have exposed herself."

"Good call."

D.A. moved a little forward, and Cece stepped up from the shadows. She looked haggard, her eyes red-rimmed, her arms crossed too tight. Grant stepped back, giving ground, and she walked inside. "Grampie!" She caught the old man in a fierce embrace, and he gathered her close, one-armed. D.A. closed the door, taking a stance like a guardian. Grant walked back toward the table with its hanging light and laptops. His team was safe. Must be time for a few more hours' rest before staging at the church.

"Grant."

He stopped, his fingertips resting on the table's surface.

"Look at me, Grant. Let me see you."

He squared his shoulders and took a deep breath before he turned. Cece's lips compressed, then she said, "That man, the one who showed up at the scope—he told me that Grampie was kidnapped, that you offered yourself instead. Is that true? I wasn't sure I could believe it."

"Close enough."

"It is true," Frank said. "Every word. He got me out of there. I—" His voice cracked and Grant avoided looking at him. "I didn't think I'd see him again."

Her brow furrowed, her gaze flicking from the stitches at his forehead to the bandages at his wrists, down to his feet, still bare, his right ankle scraped by the attempt to keep still, back up, to the corners of his mouth, torn by the gag. The old man stood at her back, his hand still lingering on her shoulder, then she broke forward. Her fingers traced over his face and he flinched in spite of himself. She wrapped him in both arms, her face pressed against his chest. "I'm sorry, Grant, I am so, so sorry. You told me, and I didn't listen, and I pushed you away—oh my god, you look like you traveled to the underworld."

"Close enough," Frank echoed.

The harder she squeezed, the more his breath eased, tension seeping away though his throat still burned. Grant slid his arms around her and let his cheek rest on the top of her head. The warmth of her tears seeped through his shirt. Or was it blood? He should check the dressings. He'd been moving around too much. It felt good, for the moment, to be utterly still.

Cece pulled back from him a little. "What do we do? I'm scared."

He found his voice, slipped into an easier role. "When daylight comes, you and Frank, and another guy—a friend—you get out of town. I don't care where, but it's gotta be out of range. I can't—" He abandoned that line of thought. Across the room, D.A. gave a nod. She'd make sure it happened. "We call Rizzo, ask for a safe-house, or an introduction to the next county. Anderson can't go out of state."

"What about you? Shouldn't you be in the hospital?"

D.A. smirked and rolled her eyes.

"Not while I've got work to do." He took a step apart from her. "Are you willing to help?"

"What can I do? I don't have any skills, not like you and your friends."

Thank God for that. "Remember back at the house, I said I had to show you something?" He waved her over to the table and sorted through the photos until he found the one he wanted: a seemingly random pattern of white dots. "Teo made these. From what I can guess, he got up on the roof sometimes to maintain them."

Frank muttered, "Wondered what he was doing up there."

"I think it's a star map. It's probably based on a photograph of the night sky, a view from one of the guys on that submarine."

Frowning at the image, Cece took a seat. "It could be, but there's nothing to go on, no information. Not even relative intensities to help me identify the stars. We need the date, at least, an approximate location—Northern or Southern hemisphere. All that."

"Lazarus," Grant called.

From the other room, a muffled reply, "September second, 1942. How do you live on so little sleep?"

"Location?"

"Somewhere near Trinidad. Best they could tell."

Cece mouthed, "Lazarus?"

He focused on his cousin. "Is that enough to go on?"

"It's a good start, but I'll need some computational power, and I don't think it's a good idea to go back to Kitt Peak."

"Yeah, sorry."

She reached up and took his hand. He froze, the shock almost electric. "You don't have to apologize, Grant. Not for sending the people who saved my life."

"You heard the plan, Lazarus?"

"Get out of town. I heard."

"I've got some contacts at ASU, Tempe," she began.

"Not far enough. Can you do Flagstaff?"

"Sure. Dr. Summers is one of my distance observers. The boys are with my in-laws. I can tell them I have a research project."

"That's good," said Frank. "You get safe."

"You're coming, too." She swiveled in her seat. She hadn't let go of Grant, as if she could take him with her. As if she wanted to.

The old man shook his head. "Nope. I let him alone for far too long. Rosemary gave you all the tools for this—astronomy, history, even Randy's mechanical interest, not that he's used it. She set the man outside the maze. I'm gonna stay and help him find the center."

CHAPTER FIFTY-FIVE

From the nightstand, Rizzo's radio buzzed high alert. She jolted awake. "The hell." She felt surprisingly rested, in spite of the early hour, and how long it had taken her to get to bed last night. Or rather, to get to sleep... Tony lay on his side facing her, eyes closed, but eyelids flickering. Sitting up, she snatched up the radio as if not to disturb him.

"Don't worry about it," he mumbled. "Hazards of the job." He grabbed her pillow and crammed it over his head.

5:30 am. Ugh. Jamie pulled a nightshirt over her head. Walking toward the en suite bathroom, she dialed down the volume and clicked to the automated bulletin system. After a night of gunfights and fire, what could it be? Flood? Plague? Anything. "... Suites hotel. Suspect is considered armed and extremely dangerous. Message repeats. The Tucson Police Department has issued an all-points bulletin for a man traveling under the name Derek Montgomery, impersonating a police officer from Storrs, Connecticut. Suspect is approximately six feet three inches tall, two hundred ten pounds, short, dark hair, green eyes, clean-shaven. Last seen wearing denim jeans, western-style jacket and formal shirt. Suspect is wanted in connection with capital murder—"

Denim jeans. Formal shirt. Six-three, green eyes. She turned on her heel, back toward the bed.

Tony had rolled onto his back, holding the extra pillow in place with both hands, his powerful arms tense. From underneath the pillow, his voice, very soft. "Holy fucking shit." He pushed it back and looked at her, direct. "I have not been impersonating an officer. I am a goddamn officer."

"Capital murder."

He threw off the pillow and sat up. "I killed four men last night, a hundred miles from Tucson, at least. Self-defense, and in the act of trying to prevent further crimes."

Jamie walked away into the kitchen, to her office nook, and prodded her computer awake. Inside his crate, Buster whined up at her, then pushed himself up, stretching from his stubby tail to the curl of his tongue. Seventeen goddamn messages. She dropped heavily into the chair as Tony walked up to her side, shorts on. She pulled up the advisory. Not a county case, but they were looking for full cooperation from all law enforcement. She scrolled down the images: A driver's license with Tony's picture and somebody else's name. A business card from the Storrs, Connecticut police department in that same name. Another file labeled "Eyes Only." She opened it.

Fancy hotel room, king-size bed, big windows on one side, curtains drawn, flat screen television on the bureau and a floor-to-ceiling mirror by the closet door. Blood-spatter radiating out from the bed. On top of the covers, a man's dismembered corpse, his head—

Jamie lurched away from the chair and ran to the sink, bracing herself with her arms, her stomach heaving. Buster whined again, louder, his claws clicking on the floor of the crate.

"Holy fucking shit," Tony said again, just as low, then he dropped heavily into the chair she had just abandoned. She didn't look. "Everything I did was in the desert. Lones's men picked me up at the hotel, told me to leave everything, any form of ID, told me where to hide the keycard." Keys clicked as he worked the computer. "The video surveillance image shows somebody about my size, in one of those damn hats—can't see his face, propping up the other guy in the elevator—he's already dead. Probably passed him off as drunk. They must've gone back to the desert and brought up one of the bodies."

The low, factual litany washed over her, the sound of a man doing his job: analytically looking for clues, but it sucked at her like a riptide. "'That's an armed-and-dangerous APB, Tony. Every cop, deputy and security guard in the state is looking for you, guns drawn." She turned, setting her hips against the edge of the sink, that horrible image still captured in her eyes no matter where she turned.

"Look, the timestamp on the elevator video is four AM. I've got an alibi—Oh, shit!" Explosive that time. He flung himself away from the computer, knocking over the chair in his retreat. "I'm sorry. Jesus Christ, Rizzo, I am so sorry." His hands knotted into his hair, dragging his forehead upward.

"Cut it out! That—" Her hand trembled a little as she pointed toward the screen—"that is on them. They're trying to fuck you over for betraying the cause. This." She pointed to the floor between them, to her bare feet on her kitchen tile. "I chose, Tony. I was in the driver's seat all the way. Yeah, okay, it was a fucking stupid idea. My political career's about to be dead in the water, even if I survive this damn thing. My campaign manager is sending his friends out to kill people in the desert." She sucked in a breath. "You got no idea how it felt to have—to find something good in the middle of all this crap."

He almost smiled, with a little snort of laughter. "I haven't been good for anybody for a fucking long time." Then the spark died and his hands fell. "Casey's gonna kill me." Eyes closed, head tipped back as if he were waiting for a noose. "Jesus H. Christ, I'm a dead man. Your people are gunning for me, Lones wants my ass, and Casey—he's gonna blow a gasket, aside from the fact he fucking needs me. He can't do this alone."

She crossed the room and let the dog out before he had a total breakdown, rubbing his back and sides. "Okay, look," she said, looking into Buster's warm, dark gaze. "There's a boatload of evidence out in the desert, right? I just have to find it. Your cover was already blown. Yes, you were Casey's back-up, but you've already done that, above and beyond the call of duty. It's not like you can just stick by his side and play bodyguard, right?"

"So I run? What are you gonna do, smuggle me out in the trunk?"

She straightened up and walked back over to face him, toe to toe. "Tony. We've been working this thing like ops, right? Casey's way. We need to start thinking like cops. We find the evidence, we've already got the witnesses, and you're one of them. Chris, Cece, Frank, Randy—assuming he made it through the night—Casey himself."

"Only one problem—okay, a million fucking problems—but here's a big one: Lones wasn't there. He didn't come for me, he didn't go out to the desert. He was around for a few minutes at the warehouse, but he can disavow that shit. How did he know what his buddies were up to in the desert? Drinking beer and shooting at bottles, right? All he did was make the introductions. Maybe you and I know he's behind it, but we've got nothing on him."

"Right. So, Detective Gonsalves, we run a sting. Send in a plant, wire someone he trusts and back him into a corner."

He tapped a finger on the angry bruise over his heart. "This is not a guy to back into a corner. Besides, he doesn't trust me anymore."

She shook her head. "Not you. You're about to turn yourself in."

"The hell I am! They've already sprung Lazarus out of jail to force an OD, am I right? You might not be there to save my ass."

"Save your own ass. Spill everything, on the record. I bring in the resources I've got. Good news, bad news is, there's no way they can spring you out of lock-up for this. You're gonna be maximum security, every minute."

He tipped his head, considering, then said, "What can I do for Casey from prison?"

"Lay the trail he can follow back out of this mess. Someday, God willing, we all have lives to get back to. Those guys—Adam and Casey both —they're like chess players, and we're the pieces on the board. Adam's trying to take down Casey by forcing him to sacrifice you or fight to save you. We can't stop him doing it, the damage is partially done." She pointed toward the screen. "He thinks you'll run, or stick by Casey and get yourself killed: murder by cop, and he gets his vengeance. We don't let that happen. I'm gonna make it very, very clear that you are my collar, and call in every damn favor anybody owes me to make sure nobody gets ahold of you who doesn't go through me."

He rocked back on his heels. "That's a helluva limb you're going out on, given the position I've put you in." A little wince as they both, however briefly, imagined the positions they'd been in not that long ago.

"You feel guilty for compromising me, I get that."

Tony cracked his neck, one way, then the other. "I can leave you out of it. I tell them everything else: the set-up, the desert and what I did there. I let Frank, Casey and me walk home? Leave them at Frank's place, but the place blows. Maybe I start walking to find help? It could work."

"Long enough for me to get the evidence together, but I need to get out there. They've already reclaimed one corpse, but from what you say, there's plenty of evidence to go around. Lones knows that you and I were both at Kitt Peak last night—God, I hope he's not already suspicious from that. So, we claim you flagged me down on the road after that. You told me this wild story, so I was prepping to bring you in under security—then we found out about the APB."

"I'll draw you a diagram, what to look for." He was nodding at last, then he swallowed hard. "It's a plan. Could work. I just have to do the most dangerous part: I have to call Casey."

CHAPTER FIFTY-SIX

G rant was halfway through his first real food in hours—a fast food breakfast platter D.A. had acquired once the take-out window opened—when Gooney called in.

"Two things you gotta know, Casey. One: the model sub at Frank's place was rigged to blow the gas. Sub had something written on it, but I couldn't read it before the explosion."

The relief of hearing Gooney's voice fled in an instant. "The house?" He glanced over at his grandfather, who sat picking at a meal of his own, one-handed.

"Total Loss. Rizzo got me out before I blew with it."

"Glad to hear that part, anyway."

"You might not be, Chief. Thing two: there's an APB out for my head. I don't have much time." He explained in rapid-fire, while Grant listened, carefully setting down his plastic fork.

D.A., noting the change in his demeanor, directed her full attention. He gestured her closer so they could listen together.

After a moment of silence from the other end, the implications swirling through his head, Grant sighed. "Good call on the arrest. I can't think of a better way to handle it. This thing's getting out of hand, big time."

"That's a fucking understatement."

In the background from the other end of the phone, Rizzo's voice. "Tony—tell him not to empty the trash in his hotel room. We're gonna need his shirt, pants, those cactus spines—everything."

"She's good," D.A. muttered, but Grant said, "Did she just call you 'Tony?'"

"No, I don't—maybe?"

Grant pushed back in his seat, holding the phone on his palm between them as D.A. frowned. "You spent the night at her place, right?"

"Yeah—for security. Nobody goes anywhere alone, you said, right? We don't want Lones to—"

"Gooney, nobody calls you by your first name. Even your ex didn't call you that."

A hesitation, then "I—" then Gooney shut up.

"D.A., that death and dismemberment policy—does it pay out if I dismember him myself?"

She hooted with laughter, curls shaking.

"Aw, Jesus, Chief, don't say that. You didn't see what they did to this guy, what I'm being accused of. I'm not gonna be able to touch raw meat for a month."

Grant brought the phone back to his ear. "Gooney. What you did for me last night, that's a heavy debt. But you do not screw up this operation. Do you hear me?"

"For fuck's sake, Casey, that's just like you! I get the tiniest bit of happiness you wanna choke it back out of me!"

"Gooney." He took a very careful breath, mastering himself. "It's not just an op—it's my family."

Again, Gooney fell silent, then he said, very softly. "Jesus, Man."

No apology given, but the words echoed with regret or understanding. "Be careful."

"Yeah, Chief. You, too." In the background, Rizzo's voice again.

"Put the sheriff on the line."

"Casey," she said, brusque as ever. "I'm gonna need some documentation on your injuries."

"D.A. can take pictures."

"Also, I'll need statements from all of you: Cecilia, Frank. Story is you and Frank are heading back to Frank's place. When you get home, the house blows. Gonsalves figures it's to get back at him, so he splits. You guys are afraid for your lives, so you get a ride to the hotel before law enforcement arrives. Maybe Frank's got a friend on the rez who's willing to vouch for that."

"I'll ask him."

"When I head to the desert for the evidence, what else do I look for?"

"There's the van. Also near where we met up with Frank, an exploded cellphone, some kind of remotely triggered device he'd given to one of his underlings. Don't accept anything he gives you. If he's capable of that, we don't know what else he's got."

"Right. I'll do what I can. I assume you're not available for immediate questioning?"

"Affirmative. I'll come in as soon as possible. Cece could do a remote interview from Flagstaff when they get there. If this guy has as many inroads to law enforcement as we think, I don't want her exposed locally."

"Good call."

The longer they spoke, the more impressed he became, which only made Gooney's interest the more sympathetic—and the more dangerous. He had to know what was on the line here, for every one of them. "Sheriff." He waited a beat. "When this is over, I'm gonna kick his ass halfway around the world. I don't want to have to go to the morgue to do it."

A sharp intake of breath, then she said, "We're on the same page, Casey. That's why I need all the evidence. We need him free and clear ASAP. Then you kick his ass wherever you want."

In the background, Gooney's booming laugh. He sounded perversely happy for a cop about to get thrown in prison.

"I've got a shoe box over here that belongs to your cousin Randy. Mostly photos, that kind of thing, but there's a few other items as well. At least one of them Nazi. Haven't had a chance to go through it all, but your location's on the way. I'll deliver in about twenty minutes."

"I'll send D.A. out to receive. Thanks." Grant clicked off and let the phone drop. Across the table, he met D.A.'s eyes. "We've got no backup, and we need to get somebody in place in the next half hour. We can't pull this off with just the two of us. No coverage for entrances and exits, no extra eyes."

"We need a posse," she said. "And it sounds like the sheriff's not able to supply."

Frank set his cast on the table with a quiet thump. "You've got a posse, you just haven't met them. This is why I can't leave."

The old man had almost ceased to surprise him. "You're gonna rally the nation for me?"

He shook his head. "I told you what I used to do." He cut a glance to D.A. "Half the janitors, landscapers and day laborers in this town owe their lives or their freedom to Teo and me. One of them told me what you did at the hospital, how you defended Teo. They can't take up arms, they can't come too far from the shadows, but they will if I ask it. They're always around, and nobody—no white man—even notices."

"You have people at the church—other than Teo, I mean?"

Frank said, "Let me make some calls."

Grant slid him the phone. "We're looking for an older woman, guessing middle-sixties. She won't be alone, but she might have a professional team—they might not be obviously together. She dropped a picture in my transfer account of the book where she's finding her intel. Small, beige, leather-bound. Looks like a missal, but I'm guessing it's a diary."

"So, we're rallying illegal immigrants to mug an old lady for her holy text?" D.A. asked. "Gooney's gonna be awfully sorry he missed out on this one."

CHAPTER FIFTY-SEVEN

After she made a few phone calls—"and don't look at the pictures—you can't know what happened in that room!" she shouted over her shoulder—Jamie and Tony dressed quickly, in last night's clothes, coaching each other over the parts of the story that deviated from reality. "Almost sorry I showered," he said. "Would've made a better story."

"I'm not," she said. "Tell em you showered at Frank's place, that they probably blew it up to get at you, after you guys left." She collected her gear into her duty belt, the loop of a handcuff digging into her palm. Her heart raced and her eyes stung. Damn but last night had been good—better than good—fucking precious. How long had it been since she cared about someone? Not since Nathan left, four years ago. How long since anyone cared about her, enough to hate himself for trouble he never meant to cause? Nathan had stopped caring years before he left. She turned the loop in her hand.

"Do what you gotta do, Sheriff," he said, offering his wrists, the grubby shirt already strained by his broad shoulders, already a little short. His hands were in fists, his arms strained as if he wanted to break free. "I fucking hate this part."

"Jesus, I hear you. But if I don't do it now, they'll get you at the station." With a sigh that hitched in her throat, she snapped on the cuffs. She slid her fingers through his, squeezed gently, and let him go. "The minute we leave here, we're all business. Two cops, getting a job done." Reminding the both of them.

He lifted his hands together for a mock salute, the edge of his grin returning. "And I gotta hope my big mouth doesn't ruin everything."

She rested her hand over his bruised chest. "I kinda like your big mouth."

A breath of laughter. "Said nobody, ever." He stared down at her, then caught her face in his cuffed hands, his thumb stroking over her lips, and kissed her, long and fierce and finally let her go.

Jamie led him outside to the squad car, still too early for the neighbors to be up. She helped him fold himself into the back seat, then climbed into the driver's seat once more meeting his grim expression in the rear view mirror—and he hadn't even liked riding shotgun. They reached the downtown police department and she drove into the secure entrance. The officer on duty behind his bullet-proof glass gawked at her. "That's the perp from the APB?"

"You got it, Officer Demarco. Except his story is pretty different from what you might've heard. We need isolation on this one, full security, the works. If what he says is true, somebody's gonna be gunning for him."

Demarco looked skeptical. "Name?"

Tony squared his shoulders, managing to look like the cuffs were just a fashion accessory. "Detective Lieutenant Anthony Gonsalves, Boston PD. You'll find my ID and wallet in a PO Box at the Box Shop on Seventh. The key to the box is in my hotel room, taped to the drain."

"Fuck," the officer blurted. By then, some of the brass, alerted by Jamie's phone calls were also present.

"Nice work, Sheriff." Captain Bryce put out his hand—a first—and she shook it. His paunch jiggled, and his mustache quirked up. Something like a smile?

"The work's just beginning, Captain. I need a copter and a photographer. There's a crime scene in the desert we need to get documented, and fast." From the corner of her eye, she saw Demarco bring Tony over to the fingerprint scanner, then line him up for a mug shot. Her stomach knotted and her shoulders would not relax. "He's cooperated fully, told me a story you would not believe, but my damn voice recorder screwed up. Then I got the APB." She leaned closer. "There's a good chance he was actually in my car, spilling the beans, when the lobby video was captured."

Bryce sputtered a laugh. "Really. I hope he's not angling for leniency because he claims to be an officer."

"Boston PD's got him on the rolls, sent a photo and all." She displayed the record she'd requested earlier, Tony's face, a few years younger. Looking fucking hot in his uniform. "Is Special Agent Kornitzky here yet?"

The captain, already on the chubby side, puffed up even further. "You called in the feds, Rizzo? And not even local—where's Mike?"

Demarco turned Tony around, removed Jamie's cuffs, and replaced them with a jailhouse model, Tony's wrists at his back for better control. "We're gonna need you to change into a jumpsuit, so we can take your clothes into evidence."

"Understood."

Another officer brought the empty cuffs over to Jamie, still warm.

Gripping the cuffs, she lifted her chin. "Captain, I have enough witnesses and evidence to suggest he's telling the truth. His story makes a lot of things fall into place. I've been working on two cases, and this is where they come together. The fire on the rez last night, the shoot-out at Ruby—it's part of the same case. It points to an active white nationalist organization, a border vigilante group performing what we'd have to call hate crimes under federal statute."

Bryce said, "The people you've mentioned so far are all American citizens, and mostly white."

"Or Native. Yes. They're the ones who lived." She let the words sink in for a moment. "We need federal oversight on this one, and our local office hasn't been on board so far."

"Let's take this upstairs." He indicated the secure passage to the civilized part of the station, leaving Tony in the dungeon, chained up like a monster.

Before she left, she turned back to Demarco and his partner, pointing her finger. "He's my collar, you hear me? This is the biggest damn case in Pima County history, and if anything goes wrong, I'm coming for your badges. He's one of us, and you know what'll happen to him in general lock-up. Protective custody, you hear me? Innocent until proven guilty."

"I know you're up for re-election, but don't make this political, Rizzo," the captain snarled. "It's murder. The remains are such a mess we haven't even ID'd the body yet."

Through it all, Tony never looked at her, playing his part, expecting her to play hers. Counting on her to get him out of there again. She followed Bryce upstairs, where they settled into his office for the long haul, complete with a carafe of Tucson's best coffee. She started by getting the official version on-record, turning over her video of Anderson's recovery and the name of the judge who'd okay'd his custody arrangement, talking herself dry a few times over once SAC Kornitzky showed up from Phoenix.

As she spoke, the men's skepticism, their repeated references to that whole "armed and dangerous" thing kept rolling through her head, then she put down her coffee cup. "Hang on a sec." She pulled out her phone and dialed, while Bryce rolled his eyes, and Kornitzky gestured toward the recorder. She shook her head, not letting him turn it off. "Dr. Lindsey? Sheriff Rizzo. You remember you were talking about the number of migrants shot in the desert the last few months? Can you get me a count on them, full forensic reports, along with whatever ballistic information you have." She met Kornitzky's quizzical look. "It's not coyotes offing their clients, it's a serial killer. A vigilante gang trying to clean up the desert."

"Really," said Bryce after she rang off. "This is...a lot to take in."

"You're telling me."

"Mike Allen should be in on this." Kornitzky frowned, his black widow's peak, together with the expression, making him into a Disney villain. Not a bad look for a federal agent, all things considered.

"Agent Allen's been AWOL on the whole case, never even returned my call on the break-in."

Kornitzky's cell buzzed and he said, "We've got that copter. Let's go see if the story checks out."

"Great. Just let me get my dog."

"Are you turning this into some kind of dog and pony show, Sheriff?" Bryce smirked at Kornitzky.

She already had at least one horse's ass along for the trip. "Just the dog," she replied sweetly. "The pony's afraid of heights."

CHAPTER FIFTY-EIGHT

A dam—I don't have much time, but I'm glad I caught you."

Rizzo's voice. Adam plastered on his smile. "I'm on the way out myself. What can I do for you?"

"I made a collar—big damn deal. Have you seen the news? Anyway, there was a murder at the Papago Suites early this morning. I caught the perpetrator."

He set down the bag and schooled himself to the right attitude. One of his contacts had already informed him of the arrest, of course. He had expected the traitor to go down fighting rather than submit, but he had little time just now to formulate a response. The traitor had slaughtered four men: the last thing he could claim was innocence. However, Rizzo's call gave him a little more confidence in her loyalty. "Congratulations—that is exciting."

"I've already been warned not to make this political, but that doesn't mean you can't, 'm I right? We can polish the Hell out of this thing."

"Absolutely." His voice swelled with warmth. "A high-profile case like this can do great things for your reputation."

"Great! Let's strategize later." She paused, then said, more quietly. "At some point, I need to talk with you about Casey. I feel like he's running some sort of extra-legal operation, maybe out of the reservation. I've got no idea what he wants. That's the real reason why I was out at Kitt Peak. I wanted to catch his cousin and see if she knew anything, but I guess she'd just taken off around the time we met. No idea where she is now."

Adam matched her tone. "I was afraid of something like that. He's clearly a dangerous person. Let me know how I can help."

"Thanks—it's good to have you on my side. I need to get back on the job—and maybe take a nap! That was a helluva long night."

"For me, as well. Take care of yourself." He rang off, and turned as Hammer entered the room. Darkness ringed his eyes, highlighting their furious energy. The events of the night before galvanized his men: an assault against them, staged from within. By now, the entire organization knew about it. They were already mobilizing on his behalf against the traitor and his mongrel dog, Grant Casey. But truly, which was the dog, and which the master? Adam lay his money on the mongrel, slippery creature that he was. Too many liabilities. At least he had significant assets on the way.

"Sir."

"Last night was a setback, a serious one, but you've recovered well so far. With the recent issues, there will need to be some changes in our organizational chart. I'd like to advance you and Wesson, and perhaps the other survivors when they've recovered from their injuries. Do you have any objection?"

Hammer's brows rose. "After what happened with the candidate, I—sir, I'm honored. I was afraid the organization would be done with me."

"As I said, no one could have anticipated what happened." He rested his hand on the other man's shoulder. "You have done your best to carry out orders, and I feel that our plans are soon to come to fruition." Besides, Adam's decision tree had begun to look rather slim of branches. Hammer was a badly compromised tool, exactly what he might need to craft his own exit strategy. With every order he followed, he became more committed to the cause, to the Sons, to Adam himself. If one of them broke, the whole thing began to crumble. Adam hated the idea of that happening, but he was prudent enough to seek a way to avoid being trapped in the rubble. He reached into his desk and took out a cellphone, keeping it lightly on his palm. "This is preloaded with the contacts of five other members. You understand what an enormous responsibility I'm giving you."

"Yes, sir." He took the phone with appropriate gravity, and no idea what else it contained.

"Call Browning and ask him to take all the guns over the border. We have a buyer over there who'll be able to disperse them among the invaders. In case there are ballistic considerations, that will cast doubt on anything the traitor claims. We'll need to retool our ceremony and our look. We'll add our suits to the incinerator on the way out." He gestured toward the bag at his feet, containing his official uniform, and padded with some other old things. Hammer's suit—stained as it was from the night before, including the coverall he'd pulled on for the work at the Papago Suites—he stored separately. In case he needed to fulfill his own exit strategy. To that end, and in the absence of Remington's financial oversight, he had initiated certain protocols for the bank accounts that should leave him nicely prepared in the event of an evacuation. "You've already taken care of the vehicles?"

"Yes, sir." Hammer slid the phone into his pocket. "What about the traitor?"

"If we act too quickly, it builds his credibility—but don't worry, we're keeping an eye on him. I have some ideas of how to handle him. It's mostly a matter of how long I want him to survive after I've done it." He folded his hands together. "Tongues and testicles are a common price for such betrayals. Given the opportunity, I think an excellent start would be watching him choke to death on his own balls."

CHAPTER FIFTY-NINE

After bidding farewell to Cece and Chris, Grant's small party moved out into the dawn. D.A. drove—the only one of the three in good shape to do so, a fact that clearly concerned her. He watched her knead the steering wheel of the rental car, until they stopped off at Walmart—the only place open 24-hours—and sent her in for a few necessaries before heading to the church.

While Frank dozed in the back, getting what little rest remained, Grant went through the shoe box on his lap. Rizzo had delivered it through an open window, pausing barely long enough for D.A. to wave to Gooney in the back of the squad car. She described him as slumped in his seat, his eyes fixed on his driver. His lover, apparently. That was a mess Grant hadn't seen coming. Soldiers went over the top sometimes in the heat of battle, did things they otherwise wouldn't, like take a tumble with someone they couldn't afford to compromise. Gooney had done everything Grant asked of him, and more. He deserved all the joy in the world—when the op was over.

Grant leafed through photos and ephemera, and found the medal Rizzo had described: the Nazi insignia cast in... He held it up to the light, frowning, rubbing at the black background. Cast in lead? The irregularities of the surface looked unlike any Nazi-era items he had examined in the past.

The door popped open and D.A. climbed back in, laden with a couple of bags. "What's that? Some kind of military decoration? Or part of a uniform?"

"It's a fake." He indicated the poor quality of the edges, the way the black areas turned gray. The pin on the back wasn't even military, it was a safety pin embedded in the cheap metal. "He probably bought it at the swap meet."

Still...with his maybe-dying breath, Randy wanted Rizzo to know something about this shoe box, about the thirteenth birthday when Rosemary gave Grant the model submarine she had treasured, because it reminded her of his biological grandfather. The sub had been another gift that nurtured his love of history, another gift Randy resented. One of the photos near the top showed Randy, Cece and Grant after a track-and-field competition, Grant as ever on the margins of their lives.

Birthdays with his parents meant parties, vacations, the lavish spending his Casey relatives were capable of. Never quite as lavish as what they did for their fully Spanish grandchildren, but it still made for a harsh transition to a quiet birthday greeting, and a handful of gifts, one of which had clearly already been opened. As he revealed the sub, his grandmother beaming, Randy glaring at him, as usual whenever Rosemary showed him any favor. But that day, under Randy's sullen expression, something else. The kind of face his cousin made when he'd swapped out the sugar for salt before Grant had his cereal. When he'd pulled the pin on the corral and it was Grant's job to trudge across the desert and find the horses. The sub and the insignia went together, yet Rosemary never said a word about the missing part of her gift.

Frank shifted in the back seat. "The sailors made that stuff. Sold it to raise money for their escape. Clever, I thought. Melted down toothpaste tubes and the eyelets from their shoes and poured molds they made from their own medals. Genuine Nazi fakes."

Grant squinted at the bent metal and made out a series of markings below the sub: a Greek character, three Roman numerals. Old news at this point. He slipped it into a pocket. "You guys didn't talk much about that time."

"Nope. She..." He pause, then tipped his head toward D.A.

Grant said, "I've got no secrets from my team, Frank. It's okay." The moment he said it, he wondered if this, maybe was the one secret he should have kept. The one person he should have kept it from.

"Rosemary had so much compassion," Frank went on, and Grant nodded. How else had she kept him from falling apart? "She'd been working the cotton fields alongside some of the prisoners, and this one befriended her. She thought he liked her. Maybe that was true. Maybe he just wanted help on the outside when they escaped. That knife, the one you're carrying, it belonged to my father. He carried it when he joined the scouts looking to get back the Nazis after they went through their tunnel."

As Frank spoke, D.A. and Grant prepared themselves, changing clothes in the front seat of the car with the un-self-conscious efficiency of those who've seen it all before—and then some.

"But Rosemary. She thought he'd come to her. He got captured on the way, like they all did. Maybe he was just heading for the border to get back to fighting his war. She'd made some things for him, helping him keep this secret. I guess she knew what it was, and that's how the bone ended up in the cache.

"Wasn't long after the escape and all that she knew...she had a problem." Frank stared out the window, his profile chiseled and familiar. "We knew each other. Some thought we'd be a good match. Sure I thought so, even if the circumstances..." He rubbed his shoulder above the sling. Those things got heavy after a while, even the most comfortable strap digging in and making itself a groove.

D.A. pulled a pair of sunglasses on a string over her head, then paused and mouthed an obscenity. She gave him a sharp look.

Grant turned his palms up. He'd only just found out himself, setting aside the truth until they were out of the battle. If they ever would be.

"We had two more kids after that. It's not like I didn't love her." Then, quietly, "Who wouldn't have loved her?"

"She sounds like an amazing woman," D.A. offered, starting the car.

"She did her best to make me a home." Grant flipped down the sun visor, eyeing himself in the mirror. The bruises didn't help, but at least his natural skin tone was dark enough to make them non-obvious, and the hat would give some additional shade over the worst areas. He affixed a fake mustache that trailed down at the corners of his mouth. A little exaggerated, but it covered the marks of the gag. "She was the light after my parents died."

"She insisted we take you in—she wouldn't hear otherwise, and we had that Indian Child Welfare Act to make sure it happened."

"A year older, and I would've been able to object."

Frank tipped his head to acknowledge what they both knew: Grant would've objected with all his heart, refusing to be shipped off to family he barely knew.

Whatever showed on his face, D.A. stepped in, maybe thinking she could defuse the tension. "Your life would've been pretty different with your father's people, I'm betting. Came from money, right? New Mexico?"

Grant slapped the visor back up again. "They never asked."

"Well, now," Frank said mildly, looking out the window, "with the Indian Child Welfare Act, they wouldn't—"

"They never asked." Grant turned in his seat—drawing a twinge of pain from those puncture wounds. "You've been telling me the same story for decades, Frank, that you had to use the law to get custody, making it sound like a battle, just like Rosemary said. Randy's the one who told me the truth. The reason I never heard from the Casey family after that." He traced his grandfather's face with his eyes. "I used to hope that I'd turn out to be one of those lost orphans you always read about—whose been kidnapped away from where he really belongs, and someday, the Caseys would find me and take me to live with them. The fact of the matter is, they didn't want me either." Half breed, the product of their golden-child son taking up with a professor ten years his elder.

"Randy told you that?" D.A. said. "He's a real piece of work." She drove past the mission, situated on a corner of the road, with a backdrop of cornfields, and sighed. "Crappy location for a getaway." Pulling up by a cafe, she said, "You sure he wasn't just jerking your chain?"

"I called them." In tears, begging them to take him away from his silent grandfather, his bullying cousin. "They made it clear it was better for me to be with my own kind." Yep, still hurt, a burn through the ages. "It's a good thing Randy never found out I'm a Nazi, though—one of us would've left that farm in a box."

"Randy's always been more impulsive than you."

"Is that what you call it? He had two years and thirty pounds on me.

He used to get impulsive on me with his fists—and one time with a horse whip. You taught him what I was worth by how you treated me."

His grandfather shrank in the back seat. "I took care of you as best I could, even though—" He stopped again.

"I'm a Nazi?" Grant should let it go, let it drop—move on to the work of the day. "Is that why you're always asking who I've killed or how many?"

"Shooting is something else you're good at. I made assumptions."

"I was fifteen when you made me shoot my own horse." The last time he had cried.

He shrank a little further, directing his answer to D.A. "The horse had broken two legs. It was suffering."

Grant said, "So was I."

Frank's mouth opened, then closed, and he bowed his head. "What I was praying for, out there. Not just for your life. For your forgiveness."

D.A.'s profile never changed, as if she hadn't heard a thing, a mark of how closely she was listening.

Time to move on, regardless. "Frank, this is where you get out. Your people know what to do?"

"Grant." His grandfather's voice, older, but just as stern: the voice of an elder owed respect regardless of whether he ever gave any. That was another thing: Thanks to Ulysses S. Grant's disastrous "peace policy," nobody with any respect for native heritage names their son "Grant."

Their eyes met. "Your Casey relatives should be ashamed of themselves. As I am. You lost everything that day, and I didn't bother to give any of it back. Rosemary was already sick, and we didn't know how bad. Somebody should've been teaching you the language, giving you our culture. It should have been me, and I refused. Yes, I was watching you, waiting to see how the blood would reveal." He shrugged a little. "Every year, you got stronger, smarter, more capable. Angrier, too, maybe, but you never made that anyone's problem but mine. Even then, I know you didn't act out half the time you wanted to. Halfway through high school you could've taken Randy down, but she asked you boys not to fight, and you—you heard her. Integrity? Self-control? I don't even have a name big enough for it. You made yourself the man you are today. She was so proud of you, then and always.

She'd be even more proud today."

He paused for a moment, as if he were really looking at Grant for the first time, or maybe looking at himself. "It shouldn't have hurt for all those years, the fact that nothing of who you are came from me."

"Is that what you think?" Grant absorbed the impact with a little puff of breath. His grandfather—his not-grandfather, as the case was—ashamed of how he had treated a child? "I wouldn't be what I am, who I am, without you. Shooting, riding, running, keeping secrets: all of that, I learned from you." His entire life path from the moment his parents died snapped suddenly into focus. "Even when I thought I was running from you, it only ever brought me closer."

In the backseat, his hand on the door handle, Frank softened into a half-smile. The only thing Grant had ever wanted from him.

Grant straightened his collar. "How do I look?" He spread his hands, and Frank laughed out loud.

"That's your grandmother, that is—no blood of mine would wear that get-up."

"Well, it sure isn't the Nazi part. Go on, we've got work to do."

Frank reached forward and, for a moment, gripped Grant's hand, then he stepped out the door, the strength of his grasp and the power of his words lingering as he walked away.

CHAPTER SIXTY

Y ou have to admit, the story's pretty fantastic!" Kornitzky said, talking loudly over the noise of the rotors in spite of the headphones.

"I know it—I wouldn't believe it myself if I hadn't spoken with the victims and seen the effects," Jamie hollered back. She sat just behind the photographer, in the front seat, a drawing fluttering in her hand: Tony's sketch of the stone outcrops where the battle took place, marked with the positions of everyone involved—where they started when he was brought into the arena, where they ended up, like a football strategy or a battle plan. "There's a lot of details that just don't make sense otherwise. Why would an off-duty Boston detective come out here and murder some total stranger in his hotel room?"

"You think he should've done it back home?"

"Maybe he has," said Bryce, hunkered in the back, giving Buster the side-eye. "I've asked my team to look for any cases with a similar m.o."

Great—now they thought Tony was a psycho serial killer. "I think he's not that dumb. Also, whoever axed the guy in the bed would've been covered with blood. A lot more than Gonsalves had on him." Jamie stayed on target, scanning the horizon. A blackened area of the desert caught her attention. "What's that?"

The sixth man in the copter, an agent from border patrol leaned closer with his binoculars. "Burned-out van. Looks like an explosion, actually. Probably narcos used it as a transport but now it's hot for some reason."

Hot, as in, law enforcement had become aware of it. Looked cold enough now. "Could be the one that brought Casey out here. We'll check it out later."

They came a little lower and the photographer snapped a number of shots of the ruined van and the ground around it. They had to be careful not to get so close the rotors kicked up dust and wrecked the scene. Damn. Given what a mess it made of Casey, that van had been a crime scene in its own right. No wonder Adam's crew had to destroy it. In the middle distance, she spotted a series of crags like the ones that sheltered the Bone Guard after their escape. "There!"

"Could be anywhere," Bryce grumbled.

She held the picture between the seats for him to glare at. "It's pretty accurate for someone who's never been to the desert before." Score one for the detective's eye. He'd be a fucking star witness if they could keep him alive long enough to reach the stand.

The pilot came on. "I'll set down on those slabs, less debris to kick up, and it should be far enough away."

They did a fly over and Jamie's heart sank. The bowl of desert where Tony killed four men and saved his chief's life showed little sign of occupation: certainly no other bodies. The gang had come all the way out here to grab the guy they butchered, it was to be expected they would deal with the others somehow. But you don't have four men bleed out without some evidence. The copter set down with a quiet thump and the rotors circled around to nothing as they piled out. Buster hopped down next to her, looking up expectantly. From an evidence bag she carried, Jamie offered a scrap of blood-soaked fabric from a Western shirt identical to the one Tony had been wearing—only this scrap had been peeled from a chunk of the body that was found in his room. The dog sniffed it all over. "Get it," she said, and he took off, nose to the ground, tail wagging. They trotted after him, Jamie and the photographer—a woman fresh out of college—in the lead, then Kornitzky and the border guy, Bryce bringing up the rear, clearly skeptical of the whole concern while Kornitzky was willing to keep an open mind. Buster circled around a large area above and behind the arena, showing some interest in a towering cactus and an outcrop of rocks nearby. Jamie indicated for the photographer to take some shots, and they scanned the ground as they approached. The cactus showed some recent trauma, seeping liquid from a bruised trunk. A number of spines had broken off, and a larger indent showed just about at the level of a man's head. She winced. "Make sure you get this." Dark flecks stained both the cactus and the rocks. "We've got trace. Looks like blood, maybe hair."

Bryce glared down at them, then pulled out his phone and made the call. "We need a crime scene team out here."

Buster kept moving, and Jamie moved with him. At least she'd get some more steps on her fitness tracker. *"You gonna wear that thing all night?"* his voice in her ear. *"Don't you want me to win my fitness challenge?"* *"Let me know if you need to do intervals."* Casey should be kicking her ass halfway around the world, too.

They crossed between stones into the more sheltered area beyond. The desert sand and soil showed streaks of color, which, in any other location, would be rust from oxidizing iron in the stones. Buster signaled, and received his treat, then he hurried on. Standing there, in the shadow of the stones, she pictured the scene by starlight. A man forced to kneel in the sand, another man standing over him with a gun and only one bullet. No way out except by the speed of his hand and the skill of his aim. She would've been terrified in either of their positions. *"That's your mom?"* *"She's a missionary in China—last time she went over, she wasn't allowed to come home. We're still trying to get her out."* *"Aw, shit,"* a profane man's expression of sympathy, then, *"I can do missionary—but I'll leave that up to you."*

Buster brought them around another outcrop. The sand around here looked raked or scattered, someone's attempt to cover their tracks. And tucked into the crevice of the stones, the wink of brass.

"I've got casings!" she shouted. Every step through the crime scene corroborated Tony's story. This gap would have made an entrance for him and his escort, an egress for men carrying bodies—and a refuge from Tony's hail of bullets for one of the assailants. The map he had drawn showed where each of the men had been positioned and where they had fallen.

"The story looks solid," Bryce grumbled. "But I don't like what that means. We've got, what, white supremacist vigilantes working our territory, and we never noticed? We're gonna look like idiots."

"The main thing is, we're on it now—and we stop it now." She glanced behind him as the photographer shot the spent casings. "Where's Kornitzky?"

"Took a call."

They proceeded through the gap out to a flat track with scrub to either side, and a hint of tire tracks in the lee of the stones. Someone had brought a car up here, close. Buster trotted around a little, then returned to her side. The trail was gone. She rubbed his ears and forehead. He had been a very, very good dog.

"Crime scene's on the way. The border patrol guy's gonna wait it out and meet with them. Sounds like you've got some witnesses to bring in, get their statements, any kind of trace from their personal effects. The Papago Suites is my jurisdiction, this is—" Bryce looked around—"practically no-man's land. You've been working the case already, before the rest of us even knew there was one, and I don't mean to get in your way. We just need to get a task force together on this and get 'er done."

Jamie kept the smile from her face. "Yes, sir. If you can loan me a couple of detectives, I can delegate the testimony. I'd like—"

Kornitzky stormed toward them, marching fast, sat phone gripped in his hand like a weapon. "Rizzo. I'm taking the case."

The words slapped the excitement right out of her. "We were just talking through the logistics, Agent, and I definitely—"

"No, I'm taking over. This guy's ass is mine." He shoved the phone in her face, the image of the mutilated corpse filling his screen, now grotesquely reassembled on a morgue table. "They ID'd the body from fingerprints on the federal registry. That's my agent, Sheriff—that is Mike Allen."

CHAPTER SIXTY-ONE

A number of people, many from the local part of the rez, flowed into the church, and Grant joined the crowd, passing the adobe outer wall. To his right, a gate led into a walled garden overhung with drooping green branches. A pair of groundskeepers worked under the trees, raking and prodding at the roots. Ahead, the mission church towered up, its elaborate sculpted arch guiding the eye toward God. Imposing white towers flanked the entrance. Sandstone statues of saints guarded the doors, along with a sandwich board stating the rules: no food or drink, no photography during services. A sign on the left pointed toward restrooms, a chapel, a gift shop, of course.

"Padre," said someone near him, giving a little bob—an abbreviated curtsey. Grant acknowledged the gesture with a touch of his hat. His long black gown covered his tattoos from neck to wrists, hid anything he might have in his pockets, and, curiously, made him an utterly familiar sight at a pilgrimage destination like this. In fact, he spotted three other priests— presumably genuine—in the crowd entering for Mass. A few nuns as well, though the suggestion that D.A. could be one of them had earned him a deadpan stare that he might have expected to see on the far side of a loaded weapon. Indians, a number of brown folk, and an equal or greater number of tourists, people either too pale, or too red, depending on their adoption of sunscreen. As he entered the shade of the building, Grant had to remove the hat, drawing it over his face as he bowed his head, genuflecting, slipping off to one side and taking up behind a small group of nuns who spoke in quiet

Spanish whispers. He kept the hat in front of him, held to his chest and partially obscuring his face. A black wig a bit longer than his own hair itched over his stitches. He looked a little unkempt for a priest, but the wig also concealed an ear piece. He kept his hands still, in spite of the growing aggravation of his torn and battered scalp.

Richly painted scenes enveloped the crowd: the lives of saints intermingled with native imagery including a tapestry of the man-in-the-maze that hung over the altar. Grant scanned the crowd as he presumably took in the artwork. A priest in white took to the altar and began the mass, the crowd coming to order. Grant's protective nuns ended up opposite the chapel of Saint Francis, where a wooden effigy of the saint reclined and received prayers.

From his left, a soft whistle, his grandfather's tuneless tune, performed by another. In the chapel across the church, a figure in a pale dress placed a candle next to one already lit. Shoulder-length gold-tinged hair the color of old parchment. Thin, but with strength in her movements. She carried a purse over her elbow, the sort of thing that advertised wealth in a whisper. Every stitch that she wore whispered the same until she was a shouting litany. She didn't belong here, and she didn't care. The first of her henchmen was the same, a tall, blond presence lingering nearby, very Aryan, and awfully stiff, as if the dome high above were oppressing him. The second took a place at the back, where the entire crowd could be scanned, and Grant made him by his high-class shoes when he knelt during part of the service.

Not everyone followed along, but he and his nuns did, reciting the prayers with Mexican-edged Spanish. He thought of the car ride over, the references to his Casey relatives, so proud to be Spanish in New Mexico—old blood—rather than Mexican, in spite of the fact that ninety-nine percent of Americans didn't know there was a difference. A bent old woman approached the Warden, shuffling and murmuring prayers. When they came to the end, turning to one another with gestures of peace, the old woman took the Warden's hand, and the Warden's lips pressed together, then parted. The note slipped into her hand.

Grant moved his hand by his ear, as if trying to hear the priest better, tapping twice, then a third time as he spotted another.

The third member of the Warden's entourage mingled more successfully with the tourists, moving forward as the crowd began to depart. This guy snapped photos, with exclamations of delight—except he was shooting the crowd, not the art, and Grant turned toward one of the nuns, wishing her "Paz," when the camera moved their direction. She returned the wish and they parted, Grant joining the surge of departing congregants. The Warden walked swiftly at first, then became mired in the crowd, somewhere behind him. He stepped out into the sunlight, sliding the hat back onto his head.

"Two in a car outside," D.A. muttered in his ear. "Burgundy rental."

"Out of towners," he replied. "Six. I'm guessing East coast. Took off last night to get here, hence the time stamp on the messages. They didn't come out here to see me."

Across the way, a woman worked over the trash cans in the courtyard, tidying up the mess the tourists left. Grant crossed toward her and moved as if to drop something into the trash can. She glanced up at him, eyes widening, then gave a quick nod as he followed the restroom sign. A moment later, the trashcan rattled twice, and again, followed by a mild oath in a Guatemalan dialect.

Grant turned back, cut across the yard where a fresh batch of tourists trundled about, taking selfies. The groundskeepers hauled a wheelbarrow loaded with dirt and tools, and he hurried his step, slipping past as the awkward load tumbled and the two began shouting at each other, trading accusations of incompetence. Blocking the gate as Blondie came out of the church. In the yard ahead of him, Shoes strolled at the far side, while the Warden lingered in the middle, under a tree. Two pairs of tourists bent their heads together, and a fat woman lounged on a bench, fanning herself already. Sunglasses aimed skyward.

The Warden scanned irritably, purse over her arm, note crumpled in her hand. Three strides, and Grant had caught her elbow, steering her toward a colonnade. "Madam, I think you'll enjoy the plantings."

"I beg your—Mr. Casey?" She twitched in his grasp, glancing back, but not resisting very hard.

They passed beneath a shaded arch as the fat woman groaned to her feet, then swayed and collapsed against a passing gentleman who just couldn't seem to fend her off as she floundered. Nice work, D.A.

"What are you doing?" Her glance flicked from his feet to his head, to the clerical collar at his throat.

"Buying us a little privacy." He walked her swiftly down the side of the building under a colonnade. Benches stood between the columns, with an open yard beyond, a fountain at its center. Brick pathways formed a cross and plantings of Sonoran native species occupied the corners. Saguaro cactus loomed up from several directions, and his back itched. A work crew in nondescript coveralls and broad sun hats worked the paths, plucking weeds and setting bricks. "Did you bring the book?"

"Do you have the code?"

From beneath his robe, he brought out a folded paper, while she set down her purse on a bench and withdrew a small leather-bound volume. "I am unused to so much cloak and dagger, and I dislike being separated from my people."

He tensed a little as she reached into her purse, but her words rang true. This wasn't a person used to doing her own dirty work. Or any work at all. "At least nobody's shooting at them." He held out the paper, and they made the exchange. She stepped toward the sun, lifting her glasses to her forehead to peer at the page while Grant hovered near the column, book in hand.

From an archway to the inside, a family spilled through into the shaded colonnade, a half-dozen giggling, running children and two harried-looking Indian women hollering as they scattered. The Warden drew herself up and Grant took another step, letting the children stream past him. A half-step, a pivot, he stood with the thick column between them. He stripped his garb, and vanished, cutting quickly through the nearest planting.

"Children," the Warden growled as the family spiraled toward the fountain, swirled again at their minders' direction, toward the front of the complex. "Mr. Casey, this isn't even—Mr. Casey?"

She spun on her heel, glaring at the landscaping, the gardeners, the retreating backs of the children.

"Mr. Casey! I do not appreciate this!" She snatched her purse off the bench and marched into the center, forcing one of the workers to grab his trash barrel and pull it out of the way. Her gaze swept over Grant, and did not see him. Again, she lifted the paper in her hand, and Grant pictured the simple cypher, the key alongside making it easy for her to decode: *I'll be in touch.*

Her face turned livid. Her blond minder rushed through the outer arch. "Madam, please forgive me. There was a woman—"

"One of his associates no doubt." She cast another glance among the workers. Grant troweled another patch of mortar. Two of the others stared openly back at her.

"Where did he go? What does he look like?" The guy tapped something in his pocket, and Shoes appeared shortly after, taking his direction to scan the inner yard where the family had come from.

"He was dressed as a priest. Long black robe, black hat. I didn't get a good look at his face." As she spoke, her voice shifted from indignation to something warmer.

"Hey—did you guys see a priest around here?" Blondie shouted at the two staring landscapers.

One of them started laughing, smothering her giggles with her hand, while the other said, "Pardone, señor. It is a church, yes? If you need the priest, you go—"

"Knock it off." Blondie turned away from them, looking twitchy, his hand rising in that too-familiar way. Grant shifted from his knees to one foot under him, in case he needed to defend his impromptu posse. Blondie stalked back to the Warden. "Trash," he muttered, in the way a man whispers when he wants to be overheard. He checked his watch. "We need to go."

She held her purse close to her, and regarded the courtyard. "If you do know Mr. Casey, please assure him, I will not be so careless next time. And I do expect the return of my property."

CHAPTER SIXTY-TWO

Hammer drove, parked, stepped out to open Adam's door, every inch the model brother, aside from the bandage across his nose to support the break. The new level of responsibility made him that much more rigid. He would do. Adam stepped from his vehicle, a silvery merc owned by the firm. He wore a slim-cut suit a grade better than his usual attire, complete with cufflinks. He out-classed the dinky regional airport with its handful of buildings, two rows of hangars and acres of uninspiring wasteland. A handful of old planes that belonged at the graveyard occupied one section, close by a series of tiny planes and a few larger tourist craft for people who wanted to stare down at the desert rather than confront its reality. And one shiny contemporary jet of the corporate rental variety for someone who didn't travel in coach.

Near the entrance to the Skyrider cafe a man lounged, his head lifting as he saw them approach. He stood up, a stocky fellow that screamed "bodyguard." "Good morning. Mr. Lones, I presume?" The bodyguard held out his hand, and Adam accepted, offering the appropriate level of grip strength.

"Good morning. I take it you're part of the meeting we're here to attend?"

The man swept his glance over Hammer, then gave a nod. "This way. The Warden has secured a private meeting room."

"I'm glad to hear it. I could have found us a more...congenial atmosphere, of course."

"The Warden prefers to minimize her local exposure," he said, but his shoes—stylish and very New York—had red dirt in their freshly scuffed toes. He, at least, had already been off the airport grounds. He led the way toward the airport's small cafe, then took a turn and brought them into a conference room with half-a-dozen cushy if aged office chairs around an oval table. A woman sat at the head of the table already, a tea pot and all of its accoutrements on the table in front of her, an expensive handbag set to one side, and two men flanking her. Powerplay. Very well, should Adam then choose the seat at the other end of the table? He rejected this option, strolling closer, and Hammer held a chair for him to the Warden's right-hand side. "Coffee, if you please. Espresso, if they can."

"Roger?" The Warden flicked her fingers and one of her underlings gave a nod and headed back to the cafe.

"No need for your staff to be diminished even further." She smiled faintly, but her tone, lingering on the word "diminished" grated.

He studied her face. Likely an attractive one forty or so years ago. "I appreciate your consideration, and your taking the time to meet with me."

"Almost as much as you appreciate that bank balance you seemed so concerned over." A soft chime sounded, and she poured her cup of tea. "I feel that we are very close to finding what we seek."

Another chime, and this time, frown lines notched between her well-plucked brows. "Adolph, do you mind?"

The hulking blonde to her left slipped a phone out of the purse and peered at it. Adolph. Or did she, too, employ an emergency naming protocol with her people?

"I'd like to see that diary if you don't mind."

She measured a precise half-teaspoon of sugar, stirring it in and setting down her spoon with such deliberate care that Adam's neck prickled. "Not just yet, Mr. Lones. Do you, by any chance, have any information about the code?"

His jaw twitched. He had returned to the petroglyphs and found nothing but the diagram Casey pointed out. "What do you know so far?"

"That the code was found but not the key. There is, alas, little sign of it in the diary either, but more careful examination may yet result in—" She broke off as Roger re-entered, balancing a small tray with a coffee cup. "Thank you."

Adolph leaned down and whispered in her ear. She blinked a few times, then gave a nod, and he straightened, tapping at the phone in his hands. Her cheeks looked warmer, her lips faintly curved, in a way that rather made Adam want to reach for his gun.

"Maybe you're at least prepared to finally tell me what we're looking for? The greatest treasure the Nazis ever lost, you said."

"Perhaps that was a little disingenuous of me, Mr. Lones. What I seek is no less that the bones of Peking Man." She took a sip of tea, while he registered that tidbit.

Not gold or paintings or other valuables accumulated by the Nazi's during their fight, but—what, the achievement of some graverobbers after the good stuff is already gone? "I see." He shifted a little in his seat and caught Hammer's bewildered expression darkly reflected in the flat screen mounted on the wall. "Well, that's certainly an item of special value, especially if you're Chinese." He found his smile, then reached for his own cup, swallowing a bitter splash.

"I'm not sure you do understand, Mr. Lones. My father worked with the governing body of the team that discovered the remains. He knew right away they had found something of international interest, and that the Chinese would use it as evidence of their own claims to the birthplace of man. He had... other considerations. Considerations of lineage that I think you may share, and he had associates back in Europe who would be keen to have their hands on any human remains of the period. Even comparisons with the casts of the skulls demonstrate the refinement and more advanced capacity of the European strains of humanity. When the Japanese drew close to the university where the discoveries were held, my father arranged for their transport to, he hoped, an area of safety and further study. Given the upheaval in Europe, the shipment had to be diverted toward a safer destination, smuggled away. As far as anyone knew, the bones had been lost, never to be seen again."

Through this explanation, Adam kept his face attentive, and seethed. He imagined five ways to slay them all, from electrocution to strangulation.

He imagined drawing his gun and taking them down one by one, but he wouldn't be fast enough to get her and her flankers, before the bodyguard who stood by the door. The traitor came to mind, the man who, given one bullet, had slain four men and wounded two others. It was superhuman. It was not to be suffered without reprisal. What would the slaughter gain him except some measure of pride? Besides, the money remained good. Better still if they could get the money and the bones, then auction them to the highest bidder. Not gold, but not without value. Then he and the Sons could rise again and pay back the Warden for her lack of trust. "But the diary says otherwise."

She inclined her head. "Thank you for your magnanimity, Mr. Lones. I harbored some concerns that you would be less interested in the mission if you knew its true object."

"Money is money, Warden. As long as you're paying, we're hunting."

"I am glad to hear it."

A knock at the door. Another of her henchmen, no doubt.

"Enter," she called out.

The door opened and shut, and a man walked up on the opposite side of the table. He tossed the diary with a precise movement so that it slid toward the Warden and came to rest alongside her teacup. "Interesting reading. Thanks for loaning it to me." Silver on his wrists, silk sleeves rolled up to expose the tattoos on his coppery skin like some barbarian prince, Grant fucking Casey took a seat opposite. "Adam Lones. I had a very long night—how's the coffee?"

CHAPTER SIXTY-THREE

For a moment, seeing the flash of shock, then fury that crossed Lones's face, Grant wished the bug had video capability as well as audio. D.A. would've liked that moment. Rodeo riding had given him a sense for how to make an entrance, but he rarely nailed it quite as well as this one, at least for its effect on his audience. D. A. had even chosen the costume for the occasion: a midnight blue silk shirt, sleeves rolled back to show his ink, crisp black slacks, the scout's blade hanging openly at his belt, advertising that he carried no gun, that he didn't think he needed one. Wide silver bands at each wrist covered the bandages, making him look that much more capable, and exotic. His grandfather's silver, pressed onto him before they said good-bye. A more formal get-up than he'd worn for a long time. It reeked of James Bond, and he planned to take every advantage.

"Did you wish to order something, Mr. Casey? Roger will be pleased to bring it."

Martini, shaken, not stirred? "No, thanks. I don't think this will be a long meeting, now that we've got all the principals in one place, as it were."

Hammer, stationed at Lones's back, had yet to recover his stony demeanor. His jaw worked as if he were chewing on Grant's head. Which would explain the grinding throb that built in his temples. He needed another dose of the meds, but he hadn't wanted to delay the moment once the bug in the Warden's purse had led them here. He had sent a message to let her know he planned to deliver the diary, without specifying how or when.

Before she could reach for the diary, Lones slapped his hand on top of it, drawing it toward his side of the table. He started leafing through it, glaring at the German text. Grant kept his focus on the Warden, but watched for any sign that Lones recognized what was missing.

"I was just telling Mr. Lones how I became involved, but I don't believe I need to recap that."

Recap how her family history with Nazi eugenics and the intention of supplying proof of European superiority now that there was a brown guy in the room? Yeah, no need for that. "I was curious how the diary came to be in your possession."

"A few of the men in the transportation crew—"

"The U-162," he prompted, and she acknowledged.

"A few of them knew of my father's involvement, mostly through his work with...a certain German doctor of great renown. In any case, the sailor who kept this diary asked that it be sent after his death to my family estate. After his imprisonment and subsequent release, he seemed ill-inclined to undertake any mission on his own. I gather there may have been some mitigating factors in his views during his time in Arizona." She leveled her gaze at Grant.

Like falling for a native girl, one of the mud people he was meant to despise? "Dr. Mengele."

Her gaze flickered as if he'd made a faux pas by mentioning the name.

Across the table, Lones's page flipping ceased abruptly. He fingered one of the pages, tracing the cut edge, then leaned back in his chair, suddenly much more in command of himself. Grant had been tempted to remove the page entirely once he made the connection, but the Warden would have noticed. Other pages were damaged, crimped and yellowed by time, but only one was missing a piece, neatly cut along the lines.

"So." Lones set the book back onto the table, pinning it under his fingers. "You have a code, and I have the key," he sharpened the word as if to thrust it home.

Would that word would ever again be neutral to Grant's ears, or would every repetition draw a sting in his gut?

"And I have an airplane in need of a destination." The Warden sat back with her teacup. "When shall we depart?"

Grant eyed Lones. "We need to translate the code before we can confirm a destination."

Lones shook his head. "Take off first. You know the general whereabouts, right?"

"Presumably," said the Warden, "close to where the sub last had contact with the British navy, where it sank. The diary indicates that their 'passenger' as he calls the cargo, went down with the ship. Trinidad it is then. Adolph?"

"We need to refuel, and we can be ready to fly in another hour."

Lones set down his demitasse cup. "If all we need from him is the code, then perhaps we can find another way to get it."

"Do you think so." Grant remained seated, in a relaxed posture. The windows behind him, a long strip at about chest level, gave out onto the parking lot. Push back, swing the chair around into the nearest man: he could be out of there in half a minute, but he felt no need to run.

"Now Mr. Lones. I know that you are given to a certain rather coarse brand of action, but I really don't think threats are either necessary or helpful. So long as we each have something the other desires, I see no reason we shouldn't cooperate. Besides—" She raised her cup in Grant's direction— "I am developing some admiration for Mr. Casey's more nuanced approach." She toasted him from a distance, and drained her cup.

Grant couldn't imagine anything she might have said that would be more calculated to inflame Lones's fury. Hammer loomed closer, a vein standing out in his neck, his battered nose thrust forward. "With all due respect, madam," Lones said carefully, "he's not even..." He gave a slight shrug.

"On the contrary, I believe at least one quarter of him is."

Hammer smirked, showing a glint of teeth, and Lones swept his glance over Grant once more. "There are a few things I need to wrap up here before we can be ready for departure, Madam."

"Take your time, Lones." Grant folded his hands together, lounging in the chair, legs stretched out in front of him. "I wouldn't mind the Warden and I getting better acquainted."

Lones pressed his hands against the arms of the chair, about to launch, or perhaps holding himself back from doing so.

"Oh, really, Mr. Casey. You are a charmer." She rested an elbow on the table, propping her chin, a smile lolling about her face, suddenly a cougar.

With a nudge, Grant sent his chair a little closer. "I've been meaning to ask you—"

"The two of you are playing me," Lones said. "I've had just about enough. Either he goes when I do, or the key will never be found. I don't need this. The Sons of a New America can get bankrolled some other way." He waved a finger at them.

"Ah. Pity. Just as I was beginning to enjoy myself."

"These boys're a little obsessive about keys," Grant said. "But we need this one, so I'll say farewell." He rose and held out his hand. She placed hers atop: papery pale and softly wrinkled, a sharp contrast for the blunt bronze of his skin. He slipped his fingers lightly around hers, bent forward and kissed her knuckles. She laughed and fluttered her off hand near her face like a school-girl.

"How do you know he's not playing you, too? Look at him. You don't know what he's like. You don't even know what he wants. If he's not in this for the money, then what is he up to?"

Grant released her fingers and she steepled them together at her chest. "Of course he is playing me, Mr. Lones, or at least, he intends to. The difference is, he's good at it. As for what he wants?" She swept a speculative glance over Grant, then said, "I suspect he wants to be the man who solves the greatest missing person case in the history of the world."

Lones thought she didn't know him, and Grant found himself a little surprised by how well she did.

"Now, then, if you've business to close, you'd best go about it. I shall see you both at, say, two o'clock? I don't have room for many passengers, perhaps two each of you, and anything—" She opened her hands to take in both sides of the table—"anything *else*—dangerous will need to be in the checked baggage, understood? There will be no bloodshed in my airplane."

Tipping her an imaginary hat, Grant saw himself to the door. Lones fumbled a farewell of his own as the door shut between them. Grant put on a burst of speed, lengthening his stride to put enough distance between them, that, if Lones or his proxy decided to take a shot, Grant would at least have a chance of evasion. By the time Lones and Hammer had reached the exit, Grant had slipped behind a dumpster, cursing the sparse desert vegetation that left him with few places to hide.

The two men emerged and stopped short, each looking a different direction, watching each other's backs, each with a hand ready to snatch his gun. They scanned the area, then relaxed.

"The fucking nerve," Hammer muttered.

"Which one of them? I've been doing the work. I've lost soldiers to this —and him—I thought you said he was barely standing? His head split open?"

"We messed him up good, then he spent the night in the desert. He's gotta be on drugs. Uppers." Hammer took a few faster steps, popping open the door for Lones to climb into the back seat of another high-end European car. "I don't know how else to explain it. When do we take him?"

Lones made some reply from within, something Grant was too far away to make out, and Hammer said, "Yes, sir." Slamming the door, then climbing into his own seat. What was he, really? Why had he slid so easily into being Lones's flunky?

Once their car vanished from sight, Grant stood up and walked briskly toward the feed store on the opposite corner where a couple of pick-ups hulked as their owners loaded up grain and hay.

"Chief, you're not seriously getting into a plane with those people— any of them." D.A. popped one earbud out as Grant pulled himself into the cab of the old blue truck. The seat squeaked as he settled, cracked vinyl and all; the truck welcomed him like an old friend.

"Unless you've managed to read the key, we both are."

"No dice. The sailor wrote with pen and ink, a light touch, so there's no imprint on the page below, and the ink dried fast, so no reverse image on the page above. There's all kinds of crazy technology to bring back stuff like that, but not in Tucson on a Sunday afternoon. I tried enhancing your photos, but the image is too small and grainy. The damn thing's gone." She sighed. "Which means we get a tropical vacation with a plane load of lunatics."

"The Warden won't let anything happen until she decides. She likes being in charge, watching us fight for her favor. No way she lets him win that easily."

"So you're counting on the real Nazis to protect us from the fake ones. Great plan, love it already." She fired up the engine. "She and her crew are still in there, enjoying their coffee."

"Confident. She's letting me play along, thinks she can ditch me any time."

"Can she?"

"I'm not that easy to lose."

"On a private plane over the gulf? Yeah, right. You're talking about a very long flight, crossing international boundaries, with people who, need I mention this—don't like our kind."

"We need to get Lones and his lieutenants out of town—I'm willing to bet he's calling the troops right now and arranging for them to get to Trinidad before us. If we drain this town of hostiles, we give Rizzo time to make her case and take the heat off Gooney, not to mention my family."

"So, we're a decoy mission, you and I?" She met his gaze. "Except you'd really like to find those bones. You've been itching for this kind of thing since you were a kid."

"You're not wrong. If you want to bow out, I won't blame you. There's no money in this, nothing but risk—and it's not your people on the line."

Her face grew still and cool, as if his words had uncovered a side of her he'd never seen before. "These people're Nazis, Casey. If they win, it will be my people on the line. It's always been my people." She started toward the road. "Where to?"

"We need to clear out of the motel. Pack for the trip, off-load anything we don't need, and see if we can line up an exit from the islands. Any word from Frank?"

"Teo's looking better; Randy's in a recovery room, sounds like he made it through the surgery, but it'll be a while before he's allowed visitors. One of this morning's crew has a place for Frank to stay in the meantime if he stays low-profile, but I still think he needs to get out of town."

"Affirmative. Not that he'd listen to me." Grant propped his elbow on the window frame, fingers braced at the top, his grandfather's silver shining on his wrist. The drugs were starting to seem like a very good idea. Anything to kill the pain. At least he was apparently hiding it well.

"Chief." She kept her eyes on the road ahead. "I know you're always saying that you're not the subject."

He went still as a sniper.

"But all that stuff between you and Frank? That was one messed-up childhood."

He returned his gaze to the flat desert architecture as they came into town. "Copy that." Beyond rose the mountains and the clear desert sky. "Served me well, though. I was in training for a whole messed-up life."

CHAPTER SIXTY-FOUR

By the time the copter touched down on the roof of the federal building, Kornitzky was out of his seat, issuing commands. Bryce heaved himself up. "Well, guess you and I are in the backseat. Can't say I'm disappointed. This is a big damn mess and I don't want to be the one to step in it."

Jamie jumped down from the copter and reached up to lift Buster down alongside. To the photographer she said, "We need those photos, ASAP. Everything you've got." She charged after Kornitzky. "Sir! I'm already in this—it's not about the politics, swear to God." Truer words were never spoken. "Like Bryce said, if this has been going on under our noses for months or years, we're all gonna take the flack for it. It's gotta stop."

"Show me your witnesses, Rizzo. I don't buy this, that they're not coming in because they're afraid. We're the goddamn Federal government. I have resources."

"No offense, sir, but some of them are Tohono O'odham. I don't think natives put a lot of trust in federal resources to be on their side."

His widow's peak looked even sharper. "I'm hearing excuses, Rizzo. My agent is dead."

Because his agent was a fucking white supremacist. "Look at what we have. Four men in identical suits: one of them's dead, two of them hospitalized with gunshot wounds, claiming some kind of drunken escapade, and the fourth one turned himself in. Nine bodies found in the desert over a period of sixteen months with execution-style gunshots, all the same kind of gun, but not the identical weapon. Now we have a crime scene that corresponds in every detail with what our witness claims."

"And our witness, as you call him, is a corrupt out of town cop with blood on his hands trying to cover his own ass for getting involved in whatever the hell is going on." He shoved a finger in her face. "I am not saying nothing's going on. I just don't think it takes some mad conspiracy of killers to explain it. Maybe it was a drunken escapade, grown men acting like frat boys until somebody got killed. Could be your Boston vigilante's been vacationing here for the last sixteen months, using immigrants for target practice, and it was my guy's death that forced him to grow a conscience. And please take care of your animal."

The elevator stopped, and Kornitzky stepped out. Jamie started to follow, Buster at her heel. Her phone rang. Two rings, stop. Oh, shit. She did an about-face and rode back to the lobby as the phone rang again. Buster came along as she answered. "Chief! Jesus, what do you have?"

"Not much time—as usual. We've got a flight out at two o'clock from Marana Regional. Lones and Hammer should be on it. They're gonna send the rest of their boys out separately. Here's the thing: Lones is seriously pissed. He's starting to break down, and that makes him dangerous."

"Can I pick him up before that?"

"Do you have the evidence?"

Not if Grant wouldn't come in to give his account. "Oh, Hell, Chief. And it's fucking Sunday—even if I put together enough to convince the attorneys, it's gonna be hard to find everyone who needs to sign off on the warrant." She paced down the front of the building, letting Buster check out the sparse landscaping. "Two o'clock doesn't give me much time to make a case." But at least she'd know exactly when and where to nail him.

"If you get the warrant, you'll need to be careful. Get plainclothes people in, now if you can. Set it up, if you even think you'll get the warrant. If anybody tips this off early, if they see the place suddenly crawling with cops, they'll run." He sighed. "Do it if you can. The sooner this guy's off the street, the better."

"I hear you. We found the arena, the rocks, the cactus—Jesus, man— plenty of trace. The forensic lab's gonna be busy for days. I'd like to send a crew to the hotel—"

"Do it—we're already out, but not checked out and I hang the do-not-disturb sign so they won't clean the room for a while. I'll ask Cece to get in touch when she's safe."

"Thanks." The phone was already dead in her hand. Great. Now what —an ancient station wagon pulled into the parking lot—were there any other kind?

A man stepped out of the passenger seat wearing a battered hat, a sling on his arm. Jamie walked toward him as he stepped up to the sidewalk. The station wagon put on a burst of speed and shuddered out of the parking lot a little faster than it should. "Mr. Manuel?"

He turned at her voice. "Sheriff Rizzo. Your receptionist told me to look for you here." He offered his hand to shake, his customary silver bracelet missing. "Grant, on the other hand, told me to get out of town."

"Your grandson's a pretty bright guy."

Something kindled behind his eyes at that remark. "My family is being hunted. He told me, all of us, that we're more obvious targets if they know where we are, even if that's in a police station."

"He's not wrong, but he's trying to get the heat off right now, maybe give us some room to work."

"He's got a friend in prison already, the kind of friend we all wish we had, or maybe, the kind we wish we'd turn out to be." The old man knelt and put out his hand to Buster, who sniffed graciously, then submitted to an ear scratching. "I'm an old man. I've done...a lot of things. I'd rather not die for this, but if somebody's got to, let it be me." He straightened. "I need to report a crime, bunch of them, actually. Assault and battery, abduction, attempted murder. I want a sketch artist. I want to name names."

Jamie's heart soared. If he were the type, or if she were, she'd hug him right there in the parking lot. "This way, sir. There's a federal agent who's eager to talk with you." Casey was gonna kill them for this.

Kornitzky gave her a flat stare as she brought Frank up to the office the SAC had occupied. "Please ask my receptionist to hold all calls, and send in Agent Jackson," he told Jamie, dismissing and demeaning her in a single sentence.

"Yes, sir," she said to his now-closed door. Goddamn it. This was meant to be her case: somebody had to play guardian angel for Tony Gonsalves, and she damn sure couldn't count on Kornitzky to do that, not once they had ID'd the victim. Buster gazed up at her from his warm, dark eyes as if he were commiserating. "Yeah, buddy. You're not wrong."

She relayed the messages, waiting until Jackson—a black officer with a good rep—arrived and was admitted before she stalked out of the office. Lord knew she still had plenty of work to do, even if Kornitzky was shutting her out. Her phone rang again, and she waited for the third ring. Not the Bone Guard guys, then. She took the phone in hand, noticing the number. Her fingers refused to grip and she almost dropped it. Adam Lones. Blood seemed to drain from her body, as if he could suck her dry through the telephone.

Matthew, the receptionist, watched her curiously. "Is there a problem, Sheriff?"

"Nope. All good." Her voice squeaked in her own ears. She clicked the app that recorded her calls. Strictly speaking, illegal without a warrant. Fuck it. "Adam. Hi. It's been—Jesus, sorry." She pressed the heel of her hand against her forehead as if she could ease the mounting tension.

"You don't sound well, Jamie—are you alright?" The warmth of concern filling his voice.

"This case, everything. I'm not sure I can handle the stress."

"Speaking of. I have something that might ease some of your stress. Are you able to meet with me? Just for a little while?"

"*Casey's Law. Nobody goes anywhere alone. And I mean, anywhere.*" Tony's voice rang in her memory, teasing at the time, and now in deadly earnest. Reel the fucker in. Get him the hell off the streets. "Yeah, but I'm spending way too long in the office. How about El Barrio? I could use lunch, and the fish tacos down there are to die for." Shit—like she needed to plant that seed in either of their minds.

"The Farmer's Market?" His voice slipped a little. "Right, okay. Twenty minutes?"

"Yep." She tapped off, her palms so sweaty now she nearly dropped the phone again. Public, open, crowded. What could he do? She might not be going with back-up, but at least she wouldn't be alone. Not really. She thought of what Frank had said, that Tony was the kind of friend everybody wished they had. If she couldn't have that kind of friend, then she was sure as hell going to be one. "Matthew? I need a wire—and I need it now. I need an emergency writ for probable cause, based on the testimony of the witness Frank Manuel." She pointed back toward the office. "Kornitzky's busy. Who can set me up?"

CHAPTER SIXTY-FIVE

Walking the market, surrounded by Mexicans, and worse, Adam worked his pleasant smile. He'd abandoned his suitcoat in the car, hoping to look a little more casual, and even rolled up his sleeves—but it only made him feel like some cut-rate imitation of fucking Casey. And what were those bracelets? Some kind of Native pride garbage? Like a pawn shop reject. Adam counted breaths and forced himself to slow down, smile, take in the sights and smells of the market. Even shaded as they were heaps of vegetables wilted in the afternoon heat. Jars of honey, bottles of craft brewed beer and loaves of local bread: it all blended into that same gold-to-orange-to-brown range, like his parent's living room, left over from ancient times. Times like this, he allowed himself to dream of the New Republic. Not only would its streets and markets be full of beautiful, proud people, but the entire place would be more vivid, more beautiful in a range of soft greens and cool trees. Rugged mountains, yes, perfect for hunting, camping without worrying about some foreigner in the next site blasting their dreadful music. In spite of himself, the Warden had intrigued him with her talk of anthropological research, Dr. Mengele and the scientific truth behind the differences in the races. The Sons didn't have a research division —they focused, as noted, on action, but there was no reason not to sponsor the right kind of studies. A private university, for the right kind of people, bringing together bright minds and abundant resources to discover and spread the truth.

A number of whites moved through the crowd, of course. Well-meaning people who thought the path to harmony lay through unity rather than separation. They, too, would be relieved to have a place to go where they could simply be themselves, allowed their own space to breathe and flourish. The flat-brimmed brown hat of the sheriff bobbed through the crowd, working toward the food vendors, and Adam strolled over to intercept, once she'd gotten her meal in hand.

"Mr. Lones, thanks for meeting me here. I'm famished." She took a big bite, chewing with a show of delight. A show. The sheriff was worried. "And I still need to get Buster back to his kennel, so I don't have much time."

"I understand completely—I'm glad you were able to give me a few minutes." He inhaled deeply. "That does smell good. Maybe I'll pick one up on the way out." From his pocket, he produced an array of pens, three of them, red, white and blue. "Here's something to cheer you up! That new logo—looks great, I think."

She nodded, smiled, with a little sauce dribbling down her chin. She reached to wipe it off.

"Here." She flinched as he reached for her, but then stood as Adam arranged the pens in her pocket, their re-election campaign logo peeking over the flap.

Glancing down at the pens, she swallowed her bite. "Those are nice—thanks. I've been completely neglecting the campaign the last few days."

"Mmm. We haven't seen you around the campaign office for a while."

"Sorry. I'm glad one of us is still on it."

"Everybody misses you downtown, that's for sure, but it's your dedication to the job that makes you such a great candidate. It's not just politics for you, not a stepping stone to something bigger." He stepped in a little closer. "Besides, I know you've got this big case you're working."

A hint of white edged her eyes, wary. "That's right. I'm not at liberty to say much."

"Understood, definitely." He took her elbow lightly, steering her out of the crowd toward a patch beyond the market. "You asked me to look into the Casey matter, to figure out what he's up to." He took a dramatic breath. "I think I've got it—but it's going to sound a little crazy." He flashed a nervous grin, one he'd learned from a movie.

"Oh, yeah? After everything that's been going on, I don't even know what crazy is any more. What have you got?"

"He's here looking for Peking Man."

She blinked and frowned. "Peking Man. Like the missing missing link from a million years ago?"

"That's the one—crazy, right? I can't go into detail, it's very complicated, and I'm not sure I understand it all. Here's the thing." He took a half step back, placing himself squarely in front of her. "Peking Man. The Chinese are very serious about this. They've spent millions on their own searches. If this is true, if it pans out, well." He tucked his hands under his armpits, working to look excited and dubious at the same time. "That could be the thing that gets your mother back, couldn't it? If you were the one—or, y'know, one of them, who brought home this national treasure they've been looking for. You'd be a hero to them. I'm sure they would negotiate. They would do just about anything."

Her eyes—usually more Asian in shape—widened, looking more American by the moment as he spoke. "You really think you can find it? Before Casey does?" The fish taco hung half-eaten in her hand.

"I have a very good chance. Good connections. Some solid people willing to help me out." He swallowed and glanced around again, acting cagey. "But if we're going to pull this off...it won't be easy. That guy you arrested, the machete-killer—" He added a little cringe—"He's a crony of Casey's. One of my associates saw them together. He thinks the killer might have some information about where to find the bones."

"You're shitting me. Sorry." She pulled a napkin from a pants pocket and wiped her mouth as if she could wipe away the words. "That guy's under maximum security. Nobody's allowed to talk to him. Even Casey wouldn't be able to get to him."

Adam brought his head close to hers. "But you're the sheriff. You could arrange a meeting, something private. My guy just wants to ask a few questions. Even if he lies to us, what he leaves out could point the way. This could be your mother's ticket home." He placed a gentle hand on her shoulder. "I know you don't want to politicize her capture, but she could be home on the eve of the election—that soon. After two years, it must be crushing, not to have seen her." He moved his hand in a slow circle. "I know I'd give everything for a few minutes more with my own parents." He looked away, calculating whether to try for tears, and blinked a few times, letting his breathing go a little ragged with "emotion."

Jamie felt rigid beneath his touch, her face hidden as her hat tipped forward. "Damn," she whispered. "You're right, though. It's pretty awful, knowing she's in there. Worrying that I might never see her again."

"Think it over," he whispered. He gave her a shoulder hug, side to side, not unprofessional, not intrusive, the kind of hug that they might be expected to share after how long they'd been working together, at an emotional moment. "But we'll need to move fast. Give me a call. I can send him over in a matter of moments, okay? He's a lawyer, he'll have a card and everything, all above board—nothing that would raise any eyebrows. Just a few minutes with this guy, and maybe we can bring your mother home."

She raised her head at last as he stepped back. "Thanks, Adam," she said hoarsely. "You have no idea what this means to me."

Hoarse, and practically trembling. Unless all of his study on emotion had gone sorely wrong, his words had moved her, even more than he had a right to imagine. "Back to work, right?" He offered a wry smile. "You take care, Jamie. And don't be a stranger." He walked swiftly back along the street, carrying himself above the mud people, already thinking of the next elements to get in place.

CHAPTER SIXTY-SIX

J amie practically fled the Barrio once Adam was out of sight. She trashed her taco—almost vomited the rest of it into the trashcan—and jerked the pens out of her pocket, but stopped herself before trashing them, too. If she met him again, he'd expect to see them, at least one of them. Besides, they might be evidence. They might be bombs or bugs or—oh, fucking Hell. She wasn't undercover, never wanted that, couldn't understand how Tony or Casey could ever do what they did without freaking out every goddamn time. She wanted to snatch up the phone and insist on calling the prisoner—Adam was right, she was the sheriff, the arresting officer, they'd let her ask "just a few more questions." But one of the things in her in-box was the schedule of his interrogations. They'd gotten him out of his cell every thirty minutes to two hours, trying to keep him disoriented, just short of fucking cruel-and-unusual. The guy would be a wreck. Would hearing her voice make it better, or worse? It's not like she could say a damn thing to him that might be personal, no aid-and-comfort to a man who was meant to be, if not the enemy, at least a Person of Interest.

Back at the car, she gripped the wheel, leaned her forehead on her hands and took a few minutes to master her breathing before trying to drive anywhere. Buster whimpered a little from the backseat. He could always tell when she was worked up. Needed to drop him at the kennel—too far to bring him all the way home. But first, they had another stop to make. The whole way, those three pens rolled on her seat, red, white, blue, like a little fucking white supremacist flag waving in the passenger seat. Is that what her campaign had stood for? Her campaign...

Jamie drove to the campaign headquarters a little faster than legally permissible, took the nearest spot. Sunday afternoon, nobody there. Buster trotted happily along at her heel, sniffing the air, the ground, the trashcan on the corner. She jingled out the key she needed and let herself inside, firing up the computer while Buster moseyed around and finally curled up behind her chair. She didn't have full banking privileges—a security measure intended to prevent her from lining her pockets with donor funds. But she could view the accounts, and what she saw almost brought the fish taco back up again. In the last few hours, a series of transactions through the campaign account: some of the names looked familiar—a local firearms market, a travel agency, a charter aircraft company—others meant nothing to her, but showed up in a search, going back for a few months, people she didn't have on payroll. No doubt, Adam would have a good explanation for all of it. Almost two hundred thousand dollars' worth in the last few hours. With shaky hands. She dialed the number.

"Thunderbird Charters."

"Hello, this is Sheriff Jamie Li Rizzo, I—"

"Oh, gosh, is anything wrong with the flight, Ms. Rizzo? You guys should be in the air by now."

Her eyes burned and she hung up. She tried Casey's number, then D.A.'s. Nothing, not even when the second set of rings went on and on. Adam Lones chartered an airplane and took off with a bellyful of guns and God knew how many soldiers. Trying to be that kind of friend. He was bringing her down, using her campaign as a shield to launder money and make purchases he didn't want to have tracked. Jesus. She grabbed a campaign branded thumb-drive and popped it into the computer to start downloading all of it. The screen flickered for a moment, then the machine went black and no amount of cursing or poking would bring it back to life. The whole network had gone down. She stared at the thumb drive like a middle finger poking out at her. Adam again, some kind of virus. She started going through the drawers, looking for any evidence of Lones's malfeasance, then slammed it and called her volunteer coordinator. "Janice! Whoever does the files, I need them down here. We've got a situation—all the computers are down." She gave a quick summary without fingering Adam, then called Bryce.

"Who do you have on cyber security? Someone who can do forensic computing?"

"On a Sunday? Look, Rizzo, I know this is a big case, but the world can't come to a halt because you get a bee in your bonnet."

"The detective, Gonsalves, you've gotta know who he's fingered. I came down here to check into my campaign finances, and found a fucking disaster."

"Well, it's not going anywhere until Monday, is it? We're all a little busy here, and I can't just have my people drop everything."

"Okay, I'll come to you." Sometimes, she missed the visceral pleasure of slamming down a landline. Buster whimpered behind her, his tail thumping the floor. "Sorry, Buddy." She patted his head, then picked up the last machine she'd tried to work with—a laptop—and tucked it under her arm, thumb drive in her pocket. A few more campaign pens littered the desk and she grabbed a trio to replace the ones she didn't trust. "Come on." She and Buster headed out, locking the door behind her and making for the car.

Buster came alert outside, ears up, tail straight, and Jamie stopped short. He scented the air, then trotted forward, tail wagging, and sat at the door to the car. He gave a single bark, and waited for his treat. Like he'd been a good dog. Her mouth felt too dry. Who was he tracking? Only four people he'd been asked to track the last few days: the dismembered corpse that turned out to be FBI; Teo, who remained in the hospital; Casey, who was miles away and getting further by the moment; and the creep who tried to kill Chris Anderson. She retreated a few steps from the car and dialed up Janice. "Don't come in—I'll call you when it's a good time, okay?" Hang up. Call Bryce.

"Rizzo," he said.

"Captain, I have reason to believe someone's messed with my car. I'm requesting the bomb squad. Thought you should know."

"The Hell you are, lady! Fine—I'm coming, is that what you want?"

"It's a start." She hung up on him, too and dialed her own dispatch. "If deputies Johannsen or Poirier is on duty, can you have them meet me at my campaign HQ with a bomb detection kit."

Her hand trembling, she hung up and called Buster over to her, stroking and praising him as she sat down on a concrete planter. In moments, a squad car pulled up and Bryce stepped out, slamming the door and strolling toward her, crotch forward. "You did fine this morning, you and that dog, and maybe you're just getting a little tired, and ought to go home and get some rest."

She pushed to her feet. "It's about the dog, actually. He just alerted to my own car. We were inside maybe forty minutes. He didn't alert when we got in the last time."

Bryce cocked a skeptical eyebrow. "So you're calling out the bomb squad because your dog's tired, too?"

She squared off against him. "He's trained, he's got a better nose than you or I." And she trusted him more than she trusted most people, come to that.

"Open the doors."

"Captain, I really don't think—"

"Just open the doors."

She brought out the key chain and poked the fob. He strolled over and opened the door, swinging it wide, and spreading his hands. "You want all of us to believe this guy's some kind of mastermind, ripping off your funds, orchestrating some kind of, what, vigilante death squads? Then he goes and plants a bomb in your car outside your office? What is he, a genius, or a dope?"

"What he is, captain, is pissed. We're closing the noose and he knows it."

Bryce sank into the driver's seat and Jamie flinched. "Seems like, if he were that smart, he'd go after the men at the top."

As if she weren't one of them. "He's disintegrating, lashing out. He'll go after the people he believes have betrayed him."

"And you think he knows you have." He regarded her flatly.

"He's got people at all levels of law enforcement—he had Mike Allen, for God's sake." She broke off abruptly, aware that she was becoming desperate, sounding like the hysterical woman he thought her to be.

Her deputy's car swerved into view, but parked a block away, the two men hurrying toward her. "What's going on, Boss?" Johannsen called out.

"Give me the keys." Bryce wiggled his fingers at her.

"Are you one of them?" Jamie whispered. "One of Adam's vigilantes?"

His scowl deepened but she swore she'd seen him flinch. "Oh, for— just give me the keys."

She tossed them over, and he caught them, his foot still on the sidewalk as he reached. She put up her hand, palm out to stop the deputies in their tracks as Bryce turned the key. The engine started. Bryce let out a very, very long sigh, as if he were deflating somebody's balloon. "You want me to take her for a spin? Check the wheel alignment?"

The deputies chuckled, starting forward again, but more slowly.

Bryce pulled his leg in and slammed the door shut.

The explosion blew out the side and front windows and flung Jamie to the ground, sliding as if she were making the scoring run for a pennant, bases loaded. Buster howled and tumbled along with her. They halted together twenty feet away, her shoulder throbbing as she gathered the dog against her, both of them trembling and panting. Her sleeve had shredded, but protected her arm from the worst of the impact. Still ached like an SOB, but it worked just fine for clinging to the dog who saved her life. She managed to push up to sitting, looking for her men.

At the far end of the block, Johannsen and Poirier peeled themselves off the sidewalk, wiping dirt and flecks of glass from their faces. Poirier got on the radio as Johansson ran toward her in a crouch. His mouth was wide, as if he were shouting, but his voice came through in a whisper. "Sheriff, are you hurt?"

Jamie rubbed her ears, rubbed Buster's ears, still keeping one arm around him as he shivered against her.

Her car sat at the curb, the driver's side blown all to hell, and Bryce's smoldering figure still inside, right where she should've been. So much for her fish taco.

CHAPTER SIXTY-SEVEN

On the tarmac outside the plane, from behind a pair of aviator shades, Grant watched his small duffel bag being loaded into the belly of the plane, containing the gun retrieved from Randy's car and almost anything else the Warden perceived as dangerous. Well. It had been a while since he'd killed anyone with his bare hands. Improvised weapons were another fine choice, of course, anything from a pen to a cigarette lighter could do a fair amount of damage. And the scout's knife strapped to his calf with surgical gauze could handle the rest.

He made at least ten minions for the Warden: the crew servicing the jet were clearly not the usual union guys, whom, he suspected, got a nice bonus to get scarce for a while. Across the field, an enthusiast regaled two men with some line about the antique aircraft under restoration. They took turns climbing in and out of the cockpits, never both gone at the same time. Local law: Rizzo's people, but they were doing alright. It took one to know one.

"Are you traveling alone, Mr. Casey?" The Warden stood at the top of the boarding stairs, for all the world like some obscure member of British royalty.

"No, Ma'am. She'll be along."

"She? Well, now I am intrigued."

"This would be easier if you had a name."

"Wouldn't it just. But I do appreciate your punctuality."

He noticed the building door opening an instant before she did, and two men walked through, dressing in upscale outdoor gear, packs on their shoulders. Neither of them Lones. That quickened his interest. Hammer took the lead, the other man half a step behind. Wesson, the bacon-colored body-builder from the arena. Last night, Wesson managed to take cover behind a crag while Gooney shot the hell out of his buddies.

Most of the time, Grant felt pretty comfortable in his own skin, but as the flight accumulated Aryans, he got a little itchy. This wasn't just the usual room full of Caucasians with a handful of everybody else, it was a white supremacist expedition to dig up evidence of eugenics once intended for Josef Mengele. Maybe D.A.'s skepticism was fully justified. Not that they could actually dump him from an airplane into the Atlantic.

"Mr. Hammer, is it? Where is Mr. Lones?"

"He had another commitment, I'm afraid, but we've got what you need." He patted the bag at his side.

"Weapons below, Mr. Hammer. And when next you communicate with your employer, please convey my disappointment."

He hesitated, looked Grant over, then pulled the basket out of his bag and handed the rest to one of the baggage handlers. The man waved a wand over him, getting a shrill beep at his ankle, and pulling the small gun from that holster as well. "Can't blame a man for trying, right?"

She sniffed. "We should like to get underway, if—"

Hammer looked directly at Grant, and flung an arm in the air. "Hiel, Chief! Isn't that what they call you?"

Grant had undergone the wand treatment earlier, then asked permission to replace the bandage on his scraped leg—a patch of cloth doctored with a enough dye to suggest a much worse injury than it was. When the Warden wrinkled her nose and turned away, he bandaged the knife onto his leg and tugged his sock and pants back into place. Now with Hammer pasting on his grin, casting his Nazi salute, Grant restrained a powerful urge to rip free the blade and gut him where he stood.

Instead, he tipped back his panama hat, sending a signal. D.A. detached herself from the building's shadow and the Warden tracked her progress across the strip. Ignored, Hammer let his arm fall. D.A. joined them slipping out her laptop before she handed over the bag.

"I'd prefer if your electronics were stowed as well, Miss? Or is it Mrs.?"

"Silverberg. Ms. Thanks for asking." Curly hair pulled back with a bandana, she looked especially perky, and Jewish. "We've got a code to break. We're gonna need this. Does your bird have wi-fi?"

Grant stood at parade rest, concealing his amusement as the Warden stared at him. Then back at his companion. "I should hope we can offer a few more amenities than Southwest Airlines, though perhaps that's what you're used to. If you're ready?"

He turned his shaded gaze on the two men. "After you. I insist."

Hammer tipped his hat and swaggered up the stairs, basket tucked under his arm. Wesson followed, taking along a folded magazine from his own things, maybe so he could swat pests. Grant entered last, a little apprehensive about how air travel would affect his injuries. Plush carpet and leather captain's chairs lined the jet, with a separate conference-style table toward the back, all in tasteful shades of grey. D.A. whistled as she gazed at the opulence on display. Adolph and the Warden occupied a pair of seats just in front of the wing and two others sat at the back. Another man stepped inside—Roger—pulling up the stairs, shutting and securing the door. He poked his head into the cockpit. "All clear." Took a rear-facing seat against the bulkhead wall. His suitcoat hung casually open, revealing a holstered taser at his side. Prepared to keep order, without jeopardizing the integrity of the plane itself.

A series of thuds and rumbles indicated the plane getting ready. Grant scanned outside the windows. As he expected, the baggage handlers had vanished—and not by walking away. So. Warden plus four inside the cabin, two in the cockpit. Four more elsewhere in the plane, some kind of crew compartment. He'd lay odds they had already cleaned the weapons out of the luggage.

"What d'you say, Chief? Maybe we can get one of these with our next big score?"

"I dunno. Nick would be doing barrel rolls to see if anybody noticed."

"Please take your seats for lift-off," said a voice over the intercom.

Grant chose the spot opposite Hammer who cozied into his seat like cat and fanned himself with the basket. D.A. sat across a little table from

Grant on his side of the plane. After a moment, acceleration pushed him gently against the warm leather.

"Don't suppose they have any of those sexy stewardesses?" Hammer inquired. His companion, Wesson, flicked open his magazine. Forbes. His address label still on the cover. Very smooth.

"Not today, Mr. Hammer," said the Warden.

Outside the windows, the mountains and desert fell away below them, dwindling quickly into a golden haze of distance. D.A. propped the laptop open. "Key?"

"Do you ever relax?" Hammer asked.

"Nope, sorry. I'd like to get this underway."

"Carry on then," The Warden prompted.

Hammer passed the basket across the aisle and Grant took it from his hands, turning it over, that slip of paper still attached to the back. An archival tag, he'd thought when he first saw it, recognizing the old style of the writing, and its somewhat cryptic nature. Two sets of four letters, on a rectangle of paper with one rounded, gilt-edged corner to show where it had been cut from the diary page. He lay it down on the table and D.A. leaned in and started typing.

The Warden's hands rested on the arms of her chair. "So many vulgar people in the world these days."

"Not everyone has the leisure to be civilized," Grant said. He slid into his casual, flirtatious manner, taking off the shades and tucking one arm of the frame through the collar of his shirt.

"But you do."

"I take it when I need it."

"Roger will take your drink orders. We have a well-stocked bar, but it's not recommended to over-indulge while at altitude—the alcohol can have unexpected effects."

D.A. tapped the table once, a question, and Grant answered with a gesture that he turned into a stretch. "Just a club soda for me," she said, "but can you give me an olive so I look like a grown-up? Thanks."

"Martini," said Grant.

"Shaken, not stirred?" Roger sauntered down the aisle. "And for you gentlemen?"

"What do you have on tap?" Hammer lolled in his chair, trying for the air of a businessman on a junket. Not too bright, especially not compared with his boss, but he was big, fast and strong—and feeling way too secure for Grant's pleasure.

Wesson looked up from his magazine. "Scotch, neat."

"That's more like it," the Warden said. "Glenlivet?"

Roger moved on toward the back and returned a moment later balancing a tray. He first delivered a cognac to the Warden, then set out the rest of the drinks, placing their near-identical flared glassed on the little table. D.A. moved closer, and Grant ducked in with her. He took his drink in hand as she turned the laptop to face him. "Gamma four one seven?"

"You may want this." The Warden offered the diary. When D.A. got up to take it, Grant set his drink down alongside hers and picked up the soda. He raised it in a toast and took a sip.

On screen, an Enigma device emulator waited for input: the dials set across the top, the key letters input, then the code down below. D.A. returned and got back to tapping, taking a sip from her drink every now and then. Across the aisle, Hammer watched avidly while Wesson and the Warden chatted about the problems of balancing a portfolio in uncertain times.

A few more taps, and D.A. pulled out a folded piece of paper, copying the letters from her screen. "Right. Who reads German?"

The Warden set down her glass, the liquid shivering a little with her excitement. Roger retrieved the paper and handed it over, along with a pair of reading glasses.

"The first and last sets of letters are junk—they're kind of like quotation marks showing the message is inside. Some of those letters might be abbreviations. Kriegsmarine had a special book for abbreviations and codes, to make it that much harder on the allies," D. A. explained. "And it's always sets of four letters, which can make it hard to parse into words." She handed over her pencil.

"You're very knowledgeable." The Warden offered an expression as if she'd like to nip D.A.'s clever fingers right off her hands.

"I have a few years in intel," D.A. told her, not mentioning the Israeli service that had given her her start. "Most of the thanks go to a Polish mathematician, and a queer British genius."

The Warden's lips moved as she murmured, a soft stream of German syllables. She paused, made a line on the page, then another—then erased one of them. "Wretched abbreviations." She took another sip of her cognac, frowned, and worked a little longer. D.A. brought the laptop over, kneeling at the Warden's side, the two of them puzzling out the abbreviations, the names. They worked from a crew manifest and everything D.A. could bring up about the codes. Hammer rolled his beer bottle in his fingers. He kept glancing at Grant as if waiting for a chance to jump him. What were the odds Hammer, too, had concealed weapons? Better assume that he did. The Sons were in home territory, with big-money backing, they probably had an arsenal to choose from. Knife in his belt buckle. Plastic or ceramic blade. Key chain in his pocket.

D.A. settled onto her heels. "I think that's it. Does that make sense?"

The Warden's eyebrows rose and she glanced over the rim of her glasses. "Well, well. Boat is hit. Orders to scuttle. The engineer and another crewman remain on board to take their passenger to safety. Details to follow." She leaned back. "Of course, they didn't follow, did they. The message was never sent, and the survivors dare not share their secret. It ends with a few letters and numbers: EE7277"

"Chances are, most of them didn't even know what they were carrying," Grant observed. The two men who went down with the ship— they didn't sink, they scuttled, steering their boat in a deliberate direction for their own reasons. And the passenger was still on board.

CHAPTER SIXTY-EIGHT

Clasping an ice pack to her shoulder, her ruined sleeve cut off at the emergency room, Jamie marched into the penitentiary holding room. "Gonsalves, Anthony. I need to see him."

The desk officer blinked at her. "Weren't you just—? Seems like maybe you should see a doctor."

"I just did. Now, I need to see a suspect." Her ears still rang and she tasted cement dust and barbecued captain with every inhale.

"Right. Wait over there, I'll have him brought up."

She paced near the chair on her side of a thick Plexiglas window, a narrow chamber on the other side. If Adam was so far gone that he tried to blow her up, that he had assembled the plan, the bomb and its deployment in the bare span of time since they spoke on the phone—what the Hell else might he do? And there was his offer, lingering in her mind. Do exactly what she was doing, ask for time with the prisoner, but with Adam's henchman, or hitman, in attendance. Shit fucking hell.

The door opened on the other side, and Tony entered on a stumble, his shackled wrists hanging down, linked to a belt at his waist, the orange jumpsuit doing nothing for his off-color complexion. He looked sick. But not dead. For now, that had to be enough. Across the short space, he spotted her and stopped, lips parted—stricken, if only for an instant. Jesus, she hadn't thought of the effect her appearance would have on him. She hooked out the chair on her side and sat down. A guard prodded him closer on the other side of the window: Denise, a woman Jamie recognized from the interagency softball league. Jamie gave her a smile and a nod, a reassurance that, despite all appearances, she was fine. A reassurance for Tony.

She picked up the phone on her side, putting down the ice pack. Not much comfort left there anyhow.

Tony sank into the chair on his side. He reached for the phone with a chained hand, and the receiver clattered to the counter next to him, then he got hold of it again, bending awkwardly. Could they make this any harder on the poor guy? Jamie waved to the guard and pointed. Denise took the phone out of Tony's hand. His utter lack of expression said more than anything else. She'd just seen a man go up in flames in a seat that should've been hers. He watched her like he could see the moment replaying in her eyes.

"Hey, Denise—how's it going?"

"Doing all right, Jamie. You're a bit of a mess. What happened?"

"Car bomb went off near my office. I'll be okay. My dog is still at the vet though." Those green eyes, a pale jade, looked jaundiced in the prison lights. He was watching her lips. Lip-reading. Of course.

"I hope Buster's okay," Denise said. "You should be taking the rest of the day off—maybe get in the hot tub or something."

Jamie couldn't address the car bomb directly with Tony, but he'd given her another way to reassure him, or to warn him. "I'll be heading home after this, with a couple of my deputies outside, just in case. I won't go anywhere alone just now." Casey's Law. A smile edged his lips and vanished. Message received. "Look, I just wanted to ask a follow-up of the suspect, but would you mind holding the phone for him—he looks miserable enough as it is with those chains on without tying himself in a knot just to talk to me."

The guard hesitated, then lowered her arm and held the phone by Tony's head. He straightened, letting his hands stay loose on the counter in front of him.

"Good afternoon, Detective."

He swallowed, his voice rough when he spoke. "You had some questions, Sheriff?"

Full disclosure: she just needed to see him, alive, unharmed, to hear his voice. "This is all going on the record." She placed her phone on the counter between them, and he gave a nod. "Detective Gonsalves, in your experience with Mr. Lones, or with other members of the organization, did the topic of explosives ever come up?"

Was that a trace of a smile? "There's two answers to that question, Sheriff: what we talked about, and what I saw. I met with Lones only once, then followed up with some phone conversations. After that, his associate, a man he called Hammer, took over. During that time, nothing was said about explosives." He took a breath as if he were about to finish, then his eyes met hers, and he slowed down, taking his time, his voice regaining the timbre that seemed to reach into her chest. Talking because he could, because they were together, because she needed him. And maybe he needed her, too. She let herself imagine, as the tension of the last few hours began to seep away.

"Hammer is probably not his real name. My take on the organization is this. They start with mutual antipathies, things they mutually hate—in this case, immigrants. Their initiation involves the commission of a witnessed atrocity. They all become complicit, whether it's the guy with the gun in his hand, or the others who are just watching. The atmosphere of ritual gives the impression that their crime is... Almost sacred."

He wet his lips. "Each man is given a new name—Hammer, Smith, Wesson—the fake names not only ensures they can't rat each other out, it's also like a brotherhood thing, another aspect of being initiated into their society. The more of these crimes, these initiations, you participate in, the deeper you get. The harder it'll be to step away from the organization—and the more," he paused, finding the word, "the more *normal* they seem. They're gonna make any excuse for believing that what they do is right. Shared atrocities. That's one of the elements that makes a death squad work."

Jamie leaned back in her chair, letting his voice wash through her, missing his smart mouth, and totally understanding why he turned it off— fascinated by the idea that he could turn it off. At his shoulder, Denise shifted her weight, frowning as she listened. He sounded every inch a cop today. His hands moved as if he were trying to articulate a thought, a series of small, precise gestures. Repeated. Sign language. She lifted the phone in her right hand, as if to get a better angle for recording his voice, but aiming toward his hands. When he'd repeated the phrase again, his hands rested, cupped together, just a few inches away on the wrong side of the glass. His hands twitched a little. He needed rest, and probably food, and here she was dragging him out again.

"So. You want to know, am I aware of whether or not they use explosives? When I was in the desert with Frank Manuel and Grant Casey, Frank had a cell phone he had taken from the organization's van. After someone rang the phone, it exploded. Some kind of remotely triggered device. The explosion at Frank's place wasn't a bomb, though. They set up a striker to make the spark, and all they had to do was leave the gas running. In both case, I believe they weren't trying to destroy evidence, they were trying to kill people."

His glance fell to the ugly scrapes on her arm, the ice pack lying nearby, rose again to her face. "In my opinion, they'd do it again. They are led by a sociopath who will deliberately manipulate everyone around him. Without regard for consequences. He's gotta be on a short fuse after what happened. Sheriff, he is the fucking explosive."

She absorbed that, so much like what she'd been saying to Bryce. Had Bryce been one of the Sons? If so, if she'd been wrong about the bomb, he would have made her look like an idiot and maybe added some doubt to the case she was building. And if she were right, he never had to face the consequences of his involvement in shared atrocities.

The longer Tony spoke, the more his voice returned, down to the profanity in the final line, as if, in talking to her, he'd remembered who he was. "Thank you, Detective."

Denise lifted the phone back to her ear. "We done here?"

"Yes, thanks. Keep a sharp eye, okay? If they came after me, they're coming for him."

"Will do, Jamie. Hope that's not gonna affect your pitching?" She nodded toward the injured arm.

"Me, too." Jamie hung up the phone on her side, and Denise did likewise, then cupped Tony's elbow and drew him toward the door, maybe a little more gently than she had on the way in. Good. As the door closed behind them, the rattle of his chains delivered her back to the ugly reality: in spite of everything, it could be the last time she saw him. She picked up the ice bag, pressing it between her palms to see if it still had any power. Head bowed, Jamie did something she hadn't done for a couple of decades: she prayed.

CHAPTER SIXTY-NINE

G rant woke to the sound of landing gear lowering. D.A. gave an exaggerated sigh. "I don't get how you can do that. We're in the lion's den, you're out like a light."

"Cat naps," he replied. "Didn't you get some rest?"

"Some, but not that easy."

"You didn't spend enough time in war zones. Take it where you can get it, even when the bombs are dropping. Airplanes put me right out." High-quality pain killers helped.

Across the aisle, Hammer snored like a saw. The Warden had retired to somewhere in the back while at least two of her men stayed awake all night, from what Grant could tell: making sure the passengers didn't kill each other. Given Lones' desire for the prize and the money it represented, Grant figured his own neck was safe until they found it. After that, the gloves came off.

The plane taxied down a runway marked by red and white lights, at the edge of a city glowing with a modest number of towers and houses, and beyond that, the blackness of an empty sea. Hammer stretched and sat up. The Warden emerged from the back of the plane. "Well, gentlemen, and Ms. Silverberg, there is little purpose to continuing our journey now. I have taken the liberty of hiring transportation and accommodation for the remainder of the night, and in the morning, I presume we proceed to the coordinates of the last sighting. I had hoped the matter could be resolved without a lengthy oceanic expedition, but it seems we may be in for a longer sojourn."

Hammer scowled at that, and Wesson murmured in his ear before they rose. As before, Grant took up the rearguard position. After days in the dry desert heat, they stepped out into a muggy Caribbean night, tinged with salt and seaweed. A handful of other planes lurked in the darkness, tied down near hangars, including a mid-sized jet with a Thunderbird logo on the tail. Conspicuous. How many could it hold? How many could Lones have gathered on such short notice? A soft whistle and a gesture, and D.A. noted the plane as well.

The Warden's ever-helpful men loaded their bags into a group of waiting SUV's, including a number of hard-sided cases that, to Grant's eye revealed the x-ray outlines of a dozen or more guns, probably big ones. Nonetheless, he kept it casual as they loaded up, asking the Warden if she'd brought her swimsuit, which earned him an expression of mingled amusement and disapproval—but a hint more of the former than the latter. The vehicles whisked them away to a hotel at least a few grades above even the one where Gooney was meant to have butchered someone. Towering columns in the portico, dazzling chandeliers in the lobby, and a legion of black and brown staff members ready to make sure madam and her guests were comfortable. "I took the liberty of presuming you would comfortably share a room, if not a bed," she remarked as they waited for an elevator. "Shall we meet again in the lobby at eight?"

"Eight it is, ma'am." Grant bowed over her hand as she swept off to the penthouse while he and D.A. landed on the second floor, with two of the Warden's men trailing them to the room next door.

"How can you flirt with that woman?" D.A. muttered.

"She's a mark and she knows it, but she thinks of me as her pool boy, angling for a better tip." He slid the card over the door lock and let them in.

D. A. went first. "I'm glad I don't have the face for that kind of work. I remember everything Jessica went through with the Unit—oy! You remember—yeah, you would. Sorry."

Jessica. In intel parlance, she'd been the 'looker', stuck with every damned cliché femme fatale role in the entire history of the espionage game. It sucked, but it worked. He'd been the pimp to her prostitute, the jilted boyfriend, the eyes on the other side of the binoculars as they sent her into one hellhole after another. Jessica taught him to dance. Oh, yes, he remembered. The room contained two beds with thick coverlets and golden palace drapes at the head, a marble-topped table, mirrors with sleek, dark steel frames and a separate seating area with a view of the dark ocean beyond. She whistled. "That is one gorgeous room."

Grant deposited his bag on the floor in front of the door, blocking the crack, making another obstacle for anyone trying to enter. "It's a pity we're not sleeping in it." He found his phone, found that his gun was missing. Big surprise.

"Yeah, Chief, I know. Please tell me we're at least gonna sleep?"

"They pulled the weapons—do you still have your make-up?"

She pulled a few things out of her own bag, dumping a pouch of beauty supplies on the foot of the bed: hair gels, tubes of lipstick, three different kinds of brushes and a set of curlers which, oddly, nobody ever questioned. She started disassembling them into their component tubes and rods, accumulating the parts before re-assembling them into a compact handgun. Grant almost wished he affected sufficient vanity to get away with his own version.

"Do you have much ammo?" Tossing his hat and sunglasses on the first bed, he crossed the room to the French doors and pulled them open, the drapes billowing.

"Hey, one shot was enough to get Gooney off and running." She pulled the mag from the base of her brush, popped the bullets, popped them back in again. Eight.

"Against a ring of armed opponents looking straight at you? No offense, D.A.—I mean you're very good, but there's maybe five people I've ever met who could've pulled that off. Note to HR—he needs a plaque for Employee of the Month." Grant scanned the road between the hotel and the waterfront, leaned, looking down.

"Hope I never have to earn it that way. So, what's the plan?" She slipped on a sweater that concealed the weapon.

Grant waved her out onto the balcony and shut the doors behind them. "Hanging out in bars." He climbed the rail, wincing a little as the movement tugged at the punctures across his arms and back. He hung down, then dropped the last few feet, landing silent in a crouch. In a moment, D.A. landed beside him. They moved fast from the shadow of the hotel, then more deliberately back into the tourist area beneath the lights of rival lodgings, restaurants and bars.

"You planning to get rip-roaring drunk? Might help with the pain."

"Not tonight. We have three objectives: get the intel from Cece and Lazarus, scope out where Lones's army is hiding and how many, and hire a dive boat."

"Pretty sure the Warden'll have that last one covered."

He pointed back at their hotel. "She's rich as an unrobbed grave. She'll hire something plush and safe and pointless. What we're looking for, if it were plush and easy, it wouldn't be lost." He moved efficiently past the first rank of establishments, looking for something local, the kind of place where the men didn't brag about where they'd go and what they'd fish, because they didn't have to.

"You ever been drunk?"

"Negative. Too dangerous. You?"

"Not since Panama City."

"When you hooked up with Gooney."

She stopped short, then ran a few steps to catch up. "Why am I surprised that you know. That's your job, after all." Her eyes gleamed in the streetlights.

"I keep an eye on things. You came back to me and the Unit, he went on to the PD. Aside from a certain attentiveness toward each other, it never affected your job." He studied her. "You don't mind about him and Rizzo."

"We had a good time. We both woke up with headaches. We let it lie and hoped you'd never find out." She gave a shrug that bounced her curls. "It was the anniversary of Avram's death. I needed...something. I chose him."

"Gooney is something alright."

"His ex ripped him good when she left—he's been nothing but casual ever since. I hope the sheriff's not getting too attached."

He paused at a small parkland. "You mind locating Lones and company?""

"I'm on it." She gave a salute and slipped off into the night. He pulled out his phone and dialed. Two rings. Hang up, dial again after a slightly longer pause—presumably, they were sound asleep. He gave them a minute to get to the phone.

"That you, Chief?" Anderson sounded groggy.

"You don't have to call me that."

"So you can call me 'Lazarus', but I can't call you 'chief?'"

"Sorry, Chris. Do you want me to stop?"

"God, no."

Grant shook his head. "It's not a pet-name, y'know? Besides, I already have a gay best friend."

"Oh? Is he anything like you?"

"Only in the ways that make us trouble. What've you got?"

"Hang on—Cecile's next door. One of her professor friends gave us a rental apartment." Cloth rustled and Anderson took a walk. "You guys doing alright? No more of the usual?"

"Kidnappings, assaults and murder attempts? Not yet."

"Somebody bombed the sheriff's car, but she's okay," he rushed to add. "They've given her a protection detail. They want us to come in for interviews. I said no. Not until Lones is behind bars."

"Good man, Lazarus."

On the other end of the phone, Anderson knocked on a door. "It's Grant. He needs the coordinates." He came back on the line. "She'll pick up in a minute."

"Tell me about the sub. I need a map I can follow by touch if I have to."

"Right. I did an overlay of the pictograph with the diagram of a class nine-C U-boat. Give me a minute. By touch..." he muttered, and Grant could hear the clicking of keys. "Okay, so the markings correspond with the mechanical room behind the battery compartment. From the back, that's just one room away. From the middle, the tower, I guess you call it, it's two. The ship sank from the back, so there's probably a big hole you can swim through. Otherwise there's a hatch in the middle. There's also this thing they call an escape trunk? It's like a tube they could use to get out if they started to sink. That's in the galley, which comes after the command room." He paused. "Are you really diving this thing?"

Grant parsed Anderson's description—he didn't even know bow from stern—assembling the order of the rooms in his mind. "Still gotta find it."

"People are still dying in U-boats. Even people who didn't just get beaten half to death the night before." In the background Cece's voice murmured.

"I warned you I might be crazy. One last thing. Does the designation EE7277 mean anything to you?"

"Um, yeah. The Germans had a special system for mapping the ocean. Hang on, I found a website about it... EE7277? It's off the coast of where you are now. Uh..." a pause, and Anderson mumbling to himself. "The guy who made the site I'm looking at says they used an offset, they picked a city to start the grid, and they changed it up sometimes."

"Thanks for the intel. Funny: Rizzo brought you to me because she thought I could protect you. Seems like it's worked out a little different."

"Yeah. I kinda like it, though. Let me know if you're hiring."

"What do you actually do for a living?"

Pause. "Graphics and web marketing. Anyway, here she is."

"Grant," Cece said his name gently. "Are you about to do something dangerous?"

"That's kind of my thing. Did you find it?"

"Took a lot of number crunching, trying to match the intensity of the stars. Teo painted really carefully, making some of them bigger and some smaller. I think I have a match, but it's nowhere near you—it's in France. You want me to text you the numbers?"

"Negative. I don't want anything these people can take off of me."

She was silent for a moment. "Off of you. If you die."

"I am doing my level best to stay alive."

For a moment, her breathing filled his ear, then she said, "You come home when you do."

CHAPTER SEVENTY

Jamie took a pause in the parking lot—Deputy Poirier telling her to take her time, by which he meant she should be going home. Instead, she was googling on sign language to work out Tony's message, taking way too long to figure out what excrement had to do with roofing, then recognizing the shorthand he made of her name. The last part was easy. He looked her in the eye, talking dead-serious, as if their relationship were strictly professional. Meanwhile, his hands revealed a different truth. *Shit on a shingle, J-li, stay safe.*

Stronger by the minute, getting hungry, even, she marched through the foyer. Everyone in the federal building gave ground. As the elevator doors opened, Kornitzky emerged from his office, his frown of irritation turning solicitous when he saw her condition. "I heard what happened. I'm sorry to hear about Captain Bryce. I'm sure the community will be feeling his loss a long time." When she didn't respond, he said, "Are you sure you should be here?"

"I need to file charges against Adam Lones, my campaign manager. We need to get this guy, sir. I just found out he's been embezzling campaign funds. I'm afraid he might have already left the country."

"We'll add that to the charges. So far, I've got a federal hate crimes case, every assault on the reservation is also federal, along with the abduction charges. Assault and battery, criminal threatening. I'm not sure we've got enough yet for Attempted Murder, but we've made a good start. I will need to officially excuse you from the case, Sheriff."

"I know," she said, but hearing it sapped her power. She sagged into one of the chairs for waiting supplicants where Frank Manuel sat as well, a clipboard in his lap, probably reading through his statement. "I could really use a cup of coffee about now."

Matthew got to it, pressing a hot cup into her hands. The steam smelled wonderful, but the idea of drinking it turned her stomach even further. Removed from the case. Campaign funds down the toilet. It took a moment for what he was saying to sink through. "So you're issuing the warrant."

He nodded. "Mr. Manuel's case, on top of the other evidence, is extremely compelling."

"Grant Casey tipped me off that Lones is planning to leave the country." She tipped her wrist. Her fitness watch displayed an exclamation point, warning of elevated heart rate. No shit. "Half an hour ago. I sent two plainclothes deputies over—"

"They called in when the plane took off," Matthew supplied. "Lones was not on board."

"He got a charter. With my donors' money."

Without a word, Frank shifted a seat closer to her, his hand resting on the seat between, as if he could direct his strength into her. For an old guy, and a civilian, he was holding up surprisingly well, maybe no surprise that Grant was related.

She looked for someplace to put down the coffee cup and Frank lifted it out of her hand. She started to unbutton her uniform shirt, wincing as it tugged against the scrapes. She pulled out the wire she'd been wearing. "Met him for lunch. He offered me an unconventional bribe to give an associate access to Gonsalves. I told him I'd think about it. He also planted some ideas about the campaign—that sent me to the office, and my guess is, he followed me there to plant the bomb. Even with Lones out of town, Gonsalves is in danger."

Kornitzky's brow rose even as his mouth pulled down, making his face almost comically long. "It's not the first time you've said that, but I can see why your level of concern might be elevated. Gonsalves is maximum security. Not a chance anybody gets to him."

She buttoned back up again, Agent Jackson taking the wire from her. "How soon can we get him released?"

"I and my team need to integrate these revelations with the rest of the information we've received."

"He's a cop, in a prison, accused of killing another cop. There's literally nobody on his side in there."

"Noted. Jackson can take a statement from you, if that's alright."

"Yes, sir." She lifted the cup from Frank's hand, giving him a nod as she rose. "You saw the preliminary report on Allen's body, Sir?" Hours dead before the cutting began, traces of desert plants and dirt ground into his injuries and his hair, bruising consistent with attempted resuscitation. In the fucking desert, just where Tony shot him.

"I saw. Thank you for your work on this." He extended his hand, and she shook it with a solid grip. "I hope for your sake, and the county's, that the investigation doesn't take your campaign along with it."

"Thank you, sir."

Hours later, and a few sandwiches when she finally felt ready to eat, she emerged from Jackson's interview room. Justice finally ground forward, even if the perp had fled the country. They'd find him, eventually. If Casey were right, Lones fled intentionally, taking the money, not caring any more about covering his tracks as he got the hell out of the house of cards even while it collapsed around him. Retrieving Buster from the veterinarian, Jamie returned to the office hung up her belt. She stripped out of the ruined shirt, grateful for the cool breeze over the t-shirt she changed into. The blue pen poked from her pocket. *With Justice for All.* Nothing—no trace of anything sinister. Just a pen he designed with her slogans on it. A crazy little parting gift. She transferred it to a replacement shirt and hung it there to wait for morning.

Back at home, she waited for the okay to enter from the team that was sweeping her place for explosives. One of her deputies would be parked outside all night, with additional sweeps by the Tucson PD, and maybe a surveillance boost from the feds as well. Jesus—how was she ever going to sleep? She got a Corona from the fridge and walked outside, trying and failing, to unpack everything that had happened that day. A tricky task, given that the "day" had started in the middle of the night. She desperately needed rest.

Instead, she sat in the fenced backyard, reclining on a lounge chair, seeing a few stars peek out overhead, thinking how Tony had seen the Milky Way as he walked his friend to safety. Not that safety ever lasted, not where men like him and Casey were concerned. Her throat ached in spite of the beer. She finally forced herself back into the house, and stripped out of her clothes. Then she had to face the bed. Shit on a shingle. J-li. When she'd gotten out of that bed this morning, Tony had still been lying there. The rumpled bedsheets outlined his absence. Had she walked him out of the wilderness, or into it?

She snatched her phone off the nightstand and dialed. It took a few rings, then her dad's muffled voice. "Hello? Jamie? Do you know what time it is?"

"Yeah, Dad, I know. I'm really sorry to wake you."

"That's okay, Jamie. What's up?" Her father's voice echoed through the distance between them. The distance between her and her mom had been there for so long, she sometimes forgot it, as if her mother was just back in San Francisco, not halfway across the world, not knowing when she'd ever come home. Next to that, what was her new-found hollowness? Nothing at all.

"Are you alright?" he said after a minute.

Got bombed, watched a man incinerated, left Buster at a friend's so he wouldn't get killed for her, stared into Tony's eyes through bullet-proof glass, trying to give each other courage. "I was thinking about mom, in prison."

"I think about her all the time." He sounded a little more alert, pillows shifting, and she pictured him sitting up in the bed, the other side empty for far too long.

She ran her hand over the pillow on the other side of her own bed. "I have a friend. He's been imprisoned, wrongly, like Mom, but—he's in danger. They want to shut him up, like Mom, but permanently. I'm—I don't think I really got it before, Dad. What it meant for you that she's not there."

"Wait, wait, wait. A friend?" He emphasized the word, then his voice turned teasing. "A special friend?"

"Yes, alright! Jesus, Dad. Sorry." She covered her face with her hand, as if her father could see her cheeks flush, anticipating the next question: how, exactly, had his daughter the sheriff gotten involved with a criminal?

Her father chuckled, a warmer, lighter sound than she'd heard from him in a long time. "Tell me about him."

Self-sacrificing, too damn trusting? "Tall, smart, green-eyed, infectious grin that half the time shouldn't be there. He's in law enforcement—super-dedicated." She felt a hint of that grin coming on. "And he's a profane wise-ass."

"He sounds about perfect."

"Mom will hate him." If they ever had a chance to meet.

"She wasn't a big fan of Nathan either."

"Well, she wasn't wrong about Nathan, but it's way too early to be talking like that." Tony had an ex of his own, a throwaway line, like his ex hadn't stomped his heart the way Nathan had stomped Jamie's. Or like it hurt so bad, the best he could do was joke about it.

"Mmm," her dad said. "I've also heard a lot of warnings during my interviews and such about dating within the profession."

Chances of either of them still having a job after this were pretty slim—one of the reasons why it hurt so bad. "I know. This thing is a minefield on so many levels."

"Except the one where you call your dad in the middle of the night because you finally care about somebody enough to worry. I know it hurts a lot where you are now. Lord, how I know it. But, Jamie, you can't spend your life afraid of hurting. If this guy's all you say, if he's worthy of you, it might be worth negotiating some minefields. My relationship with your mother has hardly been an easy road."

"Yeah, Dad, that's the truth." Then there was the fact that Lones offered her something that could win her mother free—and all she had to do was give up Tony. She was the sheriff, one of the lead officers on the case, no matter what Kornitzky said. He'd blown in from Phoenix. He was brass, sure, but he wasn't local. She'd been working with these guys for years, assisting investigations, facilitating transfers, all that crap. She could go to the pen right now and request exactly the access Lones wanted. Call him, he said, he'd make it happen. Lones was a very dangerous man. If she appeased him, maybe her whole life could go back to normal, and with her mother in her rightful place. The picture of her parents' wedding day smiled down at her, her mother dressed in a traditional Chinese gown, her father glowing with joy. What would her mother ask of her—Honor thy mother and thy father?

Not if she had to deal with the devil to make it so.

They could find a way to win her mother's freedom: a way that didn't involve Tony's death. Thank God Lones was a thousand miles away by now.

CHAPTER SEVENTY-ONE

Slipping back into the hotel as dawn was almost breaking, Grant unbuttoned a few buttons on the silk shirt and ran his fingers through his hair. He found a housekeeper preparing her cart. "There's a woman who checked in last night, very elegant, older. She and I hit it off, and I'd really like to surprise her this morning. Can you help?" He offered a few folded bills.

The woman looked him up and down, smiled a little, and slipped the money into a uniform pocket. "Just a minute." She vanished in the direction of registration, and returned a little later, giving him a tip of the head and leading him into the service elevator.

"Thanks—this means a lot." They rode up together in silence, her gaze beneath her lashes still fixed on him, and he thought about D.A.'s relief at not being the sexy one. Part of the job was leveraging all of your assets to achieve the objective, sliding into whatever role the scene required. Grant could be invisible when he needed to be, and he could be the center of attention.

The maid pushed her cart down the hall and he followed along as if he were just heading to his own room, when she casually swished her access card over the lock, and he happened to catch the handle as she kept moving. Sliding a tool through the narrow gap, he popped off the inside chain and stepped through.

On the other side, Roger bolted up from a chair, ratcheting the gun in his hand.

"Stand down, soldier. I need to see the Warden." The door shut softly behind him.

A door opened in the side wall and the Warden entered, knotting her robe firmly. "Mr. Casey. I am not surprised you slipped out in the night, but I am a little surprised that you returned. What brings you to me?" She crossed the sitting room to open the doors onto the balcony—about three times as broad as the one from Grant's room, and set with a cafe table and two chairs.

"Lones brought in a dozen men last night. They're staying at the Hilton down the street. They've already got a charter for today, a speedboat, not a dive boat, and they are the crew. They're counting on us to lead the way, and they don't want any witnesses. Their boat's already loading." He pointed in the direction of the harbor. "My guess is, they'll wait off-shore in the right direction—they'll have the message from Hammer, and it contains a set of coordinates, so they think they already know where to go."

She blinked at him, then settled into one of the chairs, and offered him the other. "Well, Mr. Casey. Much as I enjoy our flirtation, I think your competence may be even more attractive in the long run. Roger? The coffee, if you please."

Roger shouldered his semi-automatic and headed into the kitchenette. There was a guy who had some varied roles to fill.

"Our boat is lined up for nine o'clock," the Warden continued. "I despise the fact that this may be a protracted hunt, but I see no way around that, unfortunately. I don't know that Mr. Lones and his crew are prepared for a long search."

In the sky above, the stars faded as blue shifted toward pink. "It doesn't have to be." Grant rested his hand on the table, the silver cuff giving a quiet clink.

"You say they *think* they know where to go—what is it you haven't said?"

"The location they have, the one in the message, is a fake. We have another clue, a star map, but the stars are over a different city. I think it's the offset the crew used to obscure their true location. It puts us about a hundred nautical miles to the southwest of the given grid marker." He and

Cece had gone over the numbers until he had the new position memorized.

"You are proposing that I abandon my allies, and go off on a wild goose-chase with you?"

He leaned in. "You and I want to find this thing. They just want the money. Pay them off if you want to." He rolled his hand up, palm open in a gesture of release. Her gaze dropped, noted the bandage under the silver cuff, and rose again to his face.

"I don't believe that is all that they want, Mr. Casey. Mr. Hammer watches you with a gaze at least as predatory as my own, but with rather different intent. Even if I were to send them off with a bundle of money, these men are not done with you." Her own hand, pale and papery, rested on the table not far from his. "Or did you hope I wouldn't notice? The only reason you came back to me, my dear Mr. Casey, is that, in lieu of your own people, you believe that I can protect you."

"I've hired a second boat, a serious dive boat. She's not pretty, but she's fast enough, big enough, comes with an experienced crew." The local equivalent of the Millennium Falcon. "Lones is gonna be looking for you to travel in style. I'm sure the boat you hired is top of the line and looks it. We send it out as a decoy, take the other boat and beeline it for the location. If it's a multi-day expedition, the captain doesn't bring us back here—he brings us over to Tobago, or even Grenada. Lones gets pissed. He either wastes time in searching, or you tell him to call off the dogs." With Rizzo working the investigation against him, Lones couldn't go home, but the rest of his team had jobs, families, other lives that weren't so dependent on vengeance. His army would drift away. Then it was just the Nazis for Grant to deal with.

Roger arrived with the coffee, setting a small cup down for each of them before retreating again. The Warden took a sip from hers. "This captain of yours. You trust him?"

"I beat him at arm-wrestling. We're good." And showed him the fake Kriegsmarine insignia in his pocket to prove what they were looking for. He raised his own cup. "Cheers."

The Warden chuckled, a warm, throaty sound, a little too intimate for a grandmother. "There may be more of your grandfather in you than you believe."

She meant the Nazi, but he pictured Frank, risking his life in the desert to bring frightened people to a new home.

"What shall we do about Mr. Hammer and his associate?"

"At the very least, lose their cellphones. They'll have tracking devices installed, at least, and probably explosives. As for them, well, I have some ideas, most of which would get me arrested for illegal dumping or shark-baiting." The coffee was strong, rich, and complex, clearly not hotel brand even for a hotel like this one.

"Would you really." The Warden leaned toward him. Thirty or forty years ago, she would've been the 'looker.' Or at least, she knew how to play as if she were. Her words unfurled with the deliberate pace of a rattlesnake stretching out into the sun. "I don't mean to sound flippant, Mr. Casey, but who do you think you are?"

Her blue eyes sparkled in the growing light of dawn. "Have you ever killed anyone in cold blood? Just taken up your weapon and murdered them, your bare hands, perhaps? Not in self-defense, not for your comrades or for your country. A preemptive strike."

Grant took another sip, choosing his moment to break eye contact, the silver at his wrist, his grandfather's gift, suddenly very heavy indeed. Who did he think he was? A man without a home. A man who took on a new role every day—sometimes more than one, who slipped his skin and made himself what his mission needed. A lover, a scholar, a priest. A killer. A Swiss-army knife of a man, ever-changing, revealing something new, and likely dangerous. A man his family never knew except to ask him how many he killed. Sometimes, he'd been who they thought he was.

"You're thinking of how to say yes, of course, that you kill people all the time. And yet...you think of yourself as the hero, don't you, and that's not the sort of thing that heroes do." Her fingers traced the pattern of the tabletop. "I think it very likely that you'll die a hero's death, in spite of anything that I or mine might do."

He let his lips curve up again, gave her a nod. What was he now? Her pool boy again? The last fifteen years, his relatives assumed they knew exactly who and what he was, and it took a Nazi to see the truth. Grant's scalp tingled beneath the careful stitches that patched his head back together after his last encounter with Hammer. The man was far from innocent. Could Grant kill him in his bed, or pitch him off a boat? Physically, functionally, Grant was more than capable. But would he?

He set down his cup and found her still watching, a prim little smile playing over her lips, thinking she had him. And maybe she did. "I'll do what I have to, with whatever I have."

"Indeed." She set her elbow, curled her fingers to cup her chin, leaning into his space, her other hand still resting there, her coffee cup forgotten. "You'd like to be James Bond, but you didn't even drink the martini."

He spread his fingers on the table, his hand so close to hers that he could feel the heat, like that game that Randy always played, who'd slap first and who would flinch. Who was a target, who was a coward, and who won because he hurt someone. Grant had played every role. "Here's the thing, Warden. No matter who you think you are or who you've ever been: heroism is not about how you die—it's about how you choose to live."

CHAPTER SEVENTY-TWO

S trutting into the dining room, Hammer swept the room with his gaze. He almost offered his mock-salute, but stopped his arm in time. Too many witnesses. He walked toward Grant and the Warden at the head of a table. "Where's your little friend?"

"She didn't like the company I keep. I can't imagine why. She's done her part anyway. Probably halfway to the mainland by now." He speared a bite of sausage and devoured it. "Do you dive, Mr. Hammer?"

"Wesson does." He hooked his thumb toward his companion.

"Certified dive instructor. You?" The other man plopped down with his filled plate.

Interesting. "I've got some experience." Last time he dove a wreck, it was an airplane and there were survivors still inside. Very different sense of urgency.

The meal passed in light conversation about dive conditions, world politics, Caribbean holidays everyone had been on except him. Made him think of Gooney. *"Why does it always come down to you and me in the desert? Why can't we kick some ass in the tropics for once?"* He raised his glass of orange juice in silent tribute. Monday morning in Trinidad—and in a few hours, it would be in Arizona as well. Rizzo could get the tide of justice turned in the right direction with Lones otherwise distracted. He had to trust her with that mission. Restless, he forced himself to be still, to flirt with the Warden, to lock eyes with Hammer like they were fifth graders fixing to brawl, to size up Wesson as a dive partner. Nothing better than having your back-up be somebody who wanted you dead. Finally, they disembarked at the blue-collar end of the Port of Spain docklands while a classy white powerboat took off from another dock, promptly at nine am, empty. The skipper waved to Adolph as he left. Opening the car door, Hammer stepped out and swung his head around. "What's going on?"

"A bit of subterfuge, Mr. Hammer." The Warden accepted Grant's hand to step down from her car, Roger following, and a few of her other thugs unloading gear at the back.

The *African Dream* stood alongside, Captain Avinda Tuore hopping down to the dock, in a white hat set off by his very dark skin and bright smile. He extended his hand to the Warden. "Madam, welcome aboard. Captain Tuore, at your service."

She cast Grant a reproachful look as she accepted the grasp. "Thank you, Captain. We should like to load and launch as quickly as possible, if you don't mind."

"Of course." He turned to Grant, seized him by both shoulders, and air-kissed to either side of his head. "My friend! We need a re-match. After the dive?"

Grant returned the greeting. "Sure, Avinda—any time. You got my gear?"

"Anything for you. Oh—madam. If you'll pardon my asking. Ulysses here says you'll pay half up front? I asked him for the whole thing, but he says you'd not forgive that." He named an outrageous sum—covering more than just taking some visitors for a fishing expedition. Even so, his real payment was quite different.

"Yes, well, it's good of—Ulysses—to keep an eye on my purse-strings." She gestured for Adolph who brought out a wad of bills and started counting.

Tuore gestured for his deckhands who started loading the thugs' cases and hand luggage. Hammer started toward the ramp, but Roger stopped him with a hand at his chest. "Your phones. We'll need to put those away for now." He made a grasping gesture.

Hammer's eyes narrowed, but he pulled it out and waved for Wesson to do the same. Wesson glared at the brown people carrying his dive bag—

apparently more concerned about them than about the Warden's demand for their phones. Grant got a little closer to shoving them both overboard.

"Yours, too, Casey."

He turned it over, and watched as another man packed all three phones into one of the big scan-proof cases they'd brought along.

Tuore eyed the cases and tipped his head in their direction. Guns and more guns. So far as the captain knew, this particular charter carried rich Nazis in search of their heritage—and a rival crew was expected any moment. And there was Grant in the middle of it all, a schemer, looking to run his own hustle on the side. Close enough to the truth, after all. Once the Nazis cleared out, Grant offered Tuore a captain's dream: access to an undiscovered U-boat wreck. Assuming they found it. He and his crew would put up with some amount of aggravation for that kind of pay-off. Inside the deck cabin, a spread of fruits and drinks awaited. Grant flashed him a thumbs-up, then the captain headed for his bridge to get them underway.

"Ulysses. It makes sense," the Warden observed, "Not merely for the president, of course, but for the twisty-minded general of old, Odysseus, or perhaps No-man as he claimed to those he would betray."

He leaned his hips against a counter, feeling the thrum of the ship's motors. "You don't like my choice of ship."

"I'm sure this will be adequate. And I shall ask my own vessel to rendezvous with us in the event of success. I see no need to endure such conditions for longer than necessary." She drifted her hand through the air, taking in the serviceable benches and tables. Maybe his time in the military had spoiled him for true luxury. Tuore's ship was well-maintained, clean and orderly, well-appointed. Dive ships live by their crew, not their cream teas. For the occasion, she wore a wide-brimmed hat to shade her fair skin, and custom sun-glasses.

"Yeah, Casey. Nice pick. Personally, ma'am, I think he did it just to piss us off—or maybe," Hammer lowered his voice, "so his own mongrel face doesn't stand out so much. Makes him look almost white by contrast." He popped a grape in his mouth.

"Humble apologies if I've overstepped," Grant said, hand to his heart, offering a slight bow. "There's a chessboard, if a game might appease you—or there's always tic-tac-toe if Hammer's feeling up to it."

The Warden's sly smile returned, and she tucked her hand over his arm. As they walked to the chess board, Hammer strolled a few steps behind —jingling a set of keys inside his pocket.

CHAPTER SEVENTY-THREE

A few hours into the voyage, Grant left the Warden and mounted the steps to the pilot house where he tapped lightly.

"Enter!" Tuore and his pilot stood, gazing out to the unblemished sea. He beckoned Grant over to the charts table. "Ulysses. These numbers you gave me—" He shook his head, taking off and replacing his cap. "No reason to expect anything special, but we're close."

"It's been lost for seventy years—if it were easy to find, somebody would've done it already."

Tuore pursed his lips. "I hope it's not so hard as that. I don't want to subject my people to these people any longer than I have to." He pulled his hand out of his pocket, revealing the Nazi insignia Grant had given him, running a dark finger over it. "This thing. Sure, it can be worth a lot to a man like me, keep my crew in rum and my kids in sneakers for a good, long time. But you ever think maybe it's better left unfound? Who's gonna come and hire out for these trips? Some of them maybe history buffs, yeah. Some of them—more like this lot." He slid the pin back into his pocket.

"You're not wrong." The captain's speculations reminded Grant of the Warden's words, about Odysseus and his betrayal. "That's why I told you what I did. I wanted to make sure we both knew what you were in for. A U-boat is a big deal, no doubt, but it's got a lot of baggage. I'm putting your crew in an awkward place. I hope to god it doesn't get more than awkward."

"From your lips." The captain pointed skyward.

From the narrow deck outside, a crewman with binoculars rapped on the window and pointed. Tuore and Grant hustled over, out the pilothouse door. Waves broke in a curve off the starboard bow, and a narrow shred of darkness could be seen as the boat rose with the swells. "Island?"

Tuore took the binoculars. "More like a glorified coral reef. It's caught enough debris over the years to stay dry. Half-mile long, narrow. High toward one end. Barely any soil, couple of shrubs." He offered the binoculars.

Through that view, Grant made out the shape among the swells, a miniature archipelago with a rise maybe as high as the pilothouse at one end, and something...

"That." He pointed. "At our two o'clock. Somebody's been here. Those stones look stacked, not random."

Tuore nodded. "You have something. And we're almost on the numbers." He turned about and started calling out orders. The crewman on deck scrambled inside, and two others appeared. "The sea floor drops off on the other side, so we can maybe land the Zodiac on the rock if you want, have a little shore excursion, such as it is, and check out the cairn. Meantime, we'll get on the radar, make a circuit to establish a scanning pattern. Maybe drop a few lines in the water and bring up something for later." He flashed a grin. "No twenty-year voyage for you, Ulysses!"

In moments, the pilothouse contained not only captain and pilot, but the Warden herself and Wesson.

Hammer cooled his heels outside rather than get in the way while the rest of the Warden's muscle hung around on the deck below.

"These pings?" Wesson traced the patterns emerging on the screen.

"Probably just a rock pile, or another part of the reef." Grant leaned in at his side, all of them bunched together, barely breathing, as the scan unfolded on the screen in front of them. It tracked the topography under the hull, ranging from a hundred to barely fifty feet down where a ridge rose up and made the water shallow enough for growth. Jagged peaks and sudden valleys, then rising up again—then—

"There! Captain!" Grant's finger on the screen. They had rounded the far end of the islet, keeping at a distance from the higher patches of coral. The jagged pattern of natural growth shifted to gradual, a slope that led off into the distance. The Warden gripped his arm, and he squeezed her hand briefly against his chest. Two seekers. In this one thing, they were united.

"It's her, isn't it." The Warden watched as the shape emerged on-screen.

Tuore slowed the vessel even further turning a bit toward the island to get a better position for scanning. "Oh, she's something alright! No wrecks on the charts in this area. The coral's too high, too easy to avoid if you just go 'round, and we got plenty of nice fishing and dives closer in."

"She's not too deep, but the choppy seas around the coral would make it hard to distinguish the wreck from the rock without top notch equipment." Grant traced the outline with his fingers as if he could pick it up like the model that Rosemary gave him, the one that Lones used to level the home she had lived and died in.

Wesson grinned and slapped Grant on the back, a stinging blow. "Let's go, partner. Suit up and splash."

"You saw the sub diagram at the butte?" Grant asked over his shoulder as he trotted down the stairs, tempted to grab the rails lightly and slide the rest of the way. Anything to hurry the moment.

"Pictures of." Wesson clomped down the steps more slowly, his bulk and his fitness level outweighing his excitement.

"It's a plan of the whole ship: the marks are near the stern, one bulkhead past the breach in the hull, if the battle records are right."

"Unless the so-called passenger got blown with the boat."

"It's possible. We're looking for two chests, about the size of steamer trunks. They'd be hard to wrestle through the hatches, especially in an emergency when they had other priorities. Most of the crew evacuated and the Brits scooped them up, then transferred them to our side." Our side, deliberately claiming the Allies—but he wasn't at all sure Wesson would've rooted for the Americans.

By the time Wesson hit the back deck, Grant had stripped off his shirt and reached for a rash guard. He'd left the silver cuffs in his duffel—no sense in risking them. Changing in the open exposed the cuts and bruises across his shoulders and sides. He had applied some liquid bandage, hoping to reduce the sting of the ocean, but that only made him look more vulnerable.

As quickly as possible, he pulled the swim shirt over his head, and lifted his head to find Hammer perched on the rail nearby, his teeth set in a feral grin, tracing Grant's injuries. Hammer twirled a keyring around his finger and caught it with a jingle. Twirl, catch. Twirl, catch.

Grant envisioned his approach. Two steps. On the third, he would take a half-leap and slam his foot into the other man's chest, knocking him back off the rail. Hammer would land with a splash that reached all the way to the deck, and come up sputtering, his fucking key ring lost on the ocean floor. Three steps to sink him.

Dang, but that was tempting. He tugged the too-long sleeves of the rash guard into place over his scored wrists. Much as he looked forward to the splash, he braced in advance for the sting. He already felt narked, half-high as if he'd been breathing in nitrogen after a too-long drive. Shouldn't let Hammer get to him.

The Warden stood on the half-deck above, with an indulgent smile.

Grant withdrew to the corner by his gear, checking the gauges and regulator. He'd already swapped out his kit twice from the spare equipment Tuore brought along—just in case. One of the crew lingered nearby, a man he recalled meeting in the bar the night before. "Marko, right? Give me a hand?"

"Yessir." The deckhand got to work, helping Grant hoist on his dive rig and fasten a weight belt and straps.

"Thanks, Marko." He selected a dive knife and weighed it in his hand, meeting Hammer's eye. The other man forgot to catch his key ring, and the keys jangled at the bottom of their arc around his finger. Grant grinned, and slipped the knife into a Velcro sheath.

"Don't do anything stupid, Casey." Wesson thrust a meaty finger in his direction. "You got no allies here. You got no help, all you've got is our sufferance, and we've been suffering your kind for far too long."

"Right. Sorry—I forgot you guys were suffering." He gave a little wave of apology to Hammer. "Sorry!" he called across the deck. "That's gotta stink. All that suffering. Are you ready for this or what?"

"Prick," Wesson muttered.

Tuore came down the stairs and took up a position between them, while the Warden followed at a more stately pace. The captain looked more like a wrestling referee than anything else. "Okay. We can't get any closer with that coral. One big trough and we'd be scraping bottom, one big wave and we're on the rocks. Marko's gonna take you guys closer in the Zodiac, and drop a buoy line—you follow that on back, and we send the Zodiac out for you, right? The structure ranges in depth from eighty feet at this end, up to sixty at the other, with another thirty feet to the floor below. That gives you a dive time without decomp of maybe 30 to 50 minutes. But I'm still gonna say you take a stop at fifteen feet and rest for ten. I haven't lost anybody yet, and I don't want this to be the trip." His voice had the tone of a canned speech, then he glanced at his two divers, pulled his cap and put it back on again, then blew out a breath. He glanced toward the sky. "Why did I sign on for this?"

"For the money, I presume." The Warden waved her hand, and Roger brought over a deck chair which she sank into. "Gentlemen. Mr. Casey. Your position has become increasingly tenuous, as I am sure you are aware. Recent attitudes haven't helped, and your alternatives have evaporated. But you have done well so far—we are here, above what we seek, and about to receive the reward for our efforts. I shall be pleased to negotiate a cessation of hostilities if things continue to go well."

Bring back the ball. There's a good boy. He eased a tight cap over his hair, mostly to defend the stitches across his scalp. Before he pulled on thin gloves that would defend against fire coral, Grant reached for her hand. "Thank you, ma'am, from the bottom of my twisty little heart."

Her eyes flickered uncertainly, then she drew out her smile. "Have I made myself clear, Mr. Wesson? Mr. Hammer?"

"Clear," said Wesson. Hammer swept his gaze across the horizon behind them and North, and finally let his gaze settle on her. "Crystal."

Tuore caught Grant's eye, and gave him a salute, which Grant returned. "Don't take crazy risks, Ulysses. These old wrecks can get dangerous."

"You either." To Wesson, and the assembled crowd of Nazis and deckhands, Grant said, "This dive is exploratory. We take pictures, we look for access. If we have an access point, we recon and see if we find what we're looking for. I wouldn't expect to bring back anything but the video—then we plan for what we can bring up." Wesson gave him a nod. An experienced diver, and an asshole. Great combo.

Grant set his dive timer for 40 minutes. A good average. He clipped an underwater slate to his arm so he and Wesson could communicate. If they resorted to gestures, he guessed the guy's communication would be limited to a single digit. Gooney should be there. Dive knife at the other arm, in case he needed to cut loose from something. And another at his ankle. Last was an underwater camera clipped to the top of his mask which would record for the benefit of those left behind. He climbed down to the platform, then onto the Zodiac bobbing alongside. Wesson followed, toting a carry bag. Each man pulled on a pair of narrow, short fins, good for a little extra power, not so big that they'd ruin the visibility.

In a few minutes, they were fifty yards from the *African Dream*, midway between the boat and the islet and Marko dropped the dive buoy, reeling out a long cord with marked intervals for decompression. From this angle on the land, the cairn on the high side revealed a battered pair of sticks forming a makeshift cross.

Wesson leaned and squinted, pulling up his dive mask. "A grave?"

"Yessir," Marko breathed, and crossed himself.

"Damn." Wesson shook his head, and tugged his mask into place. "You ready for this?"

"Never more," Grant told him. He tucked the mouthpiece between his teeth and gave a thumbs up. No choice but to go first on this one: the man with the camera took point. He leaned back into the water and splashed, letting it envelope him.

Water stroked over his exposed skin, stinging his cuts. A moment later, Wesson hit the water as well, and Grant fell downward, following the cable with one hand. He'd need to secure it on the wreck somewhere. As he dropped through the water it shifted from clear-blue to flecked with particles. Waves rushed the coral above, murky shapes glimpsed at his nine o'clock. The blue of the water deepened toward royal and a school of snapper swirled around him, briefly obscuring his vision. Then a shape came into view.

Crusted with corals and waving with sea fans, it loomed up from the gloom down below, a long, slender shape. No pile of rocks or mistake of the reef, she was sleek and deadly, a one-time wolf of the oceans, preying on Allied vessels until they took her down. U-162 lay stern low, cracked and sidelong, but unmistakable. His grandfather's U-boat. The search they began in the desert a thousand miles away, ended here beneath the waves.

CHAPTER SEVENTY-FOUR

The tail of the sub twisted up and to the side, laying open a wide area toward the sand and rock of the bottom. A scatter of debris from the wreck marked the area: broken pipes, loose equipment, a thick round shape that might be a torpedo. Fish darted around them—a spiral of slender silver shapes, then the longer, careful movement of a barracuda, a sleek form pretending it had nothing to fear. At least, until a bigger predator came along.

Rocks accumulated along the inland side of the sub, and Grant thought of that grave, the two men making it this far, taking their ship down and out of enemy hands. Which of them died first, which of them had to bury his friend and live on alone? Had they been Nazis in truth, believers in Hitler's nightmare vision? Or merely sailors, sworn to service as teenagers, performing their duty and scared shitless—same as soldiers the world over, throughout the history of man. Maybe he did have more in common with this grandfather than he'd thought. Grant settled on the sloping ground a short distance away and swam nearer, locating a strut in the cracked tail section where he could secure the line so they could find their way home again. Even in great visibility, with a relatively shallow wreck like this, there were too many things to go wrong, too many ways to panic and die. Wesson landed closer, with a puff of sand and a scattering of fish. For any other partner, this would be the moment of victory, that bonhomie of shared discovery.

Grant panned slowly along the wreck site, recording everything he saw before he moved closer. Every stroke of a fin from here on out could spoil their vision. Patches of pink and white camouflaged the wreck, claiming it on behalf of the sea. Not far ahead, the conning tower jutted sidelong toward the open water, its rails crumbled and thick with new growth. Survivors claimed they had seen the engineer atop the tower, clinging to one of those rails as the ship went down, a bit of embellishment to appease their British and American interrogators. The bulk of the sub aimed away in that direction. Tempting to swim the length of it, the first man to visit for decades, he wanted to embrace the whole thing, the urgency of his mission at odds with his explorer's heart.

Finally, he closed in, swimming toward the wound in the aft section. A thicket of tubeworms sucked back in at his approach and shrimp scuttled away. He set his hand lightly on the wreck, through his gloves feeling the slight give of the old metal. Seventy years drowned, its bow wedged against the rocky base of the islet. He imagined the engineer, triumphing in this, his final act, only to then be trapped without rescue, without fresh water. A desolate and lonely death. He might've improvised a still to get drinking water and lasted a few weeks that way. Maybe it would've been better if the sub went down in deep water, trapping the two men with no choice but to give up and die.

Flicking on his dive lights, Grant swam lower, adjusting his buoyancy, and drifted for a moment in front of the gaping side. A little lower, and he was inside, swallowed into the arching bones of the sunken sub.

The breech pressure hull provided shelter for hundreds of creatures that fled when he entered, feathery things that recoiled at his passing and flickering shapes that dove away into the murk. An eel took advantage, lunging out of the darkness to snap up one of the escaping fish and gulp it down, then slither its way back into the darkness to await another victim. The gap narrowed into the primary hull and Grant swam carefully, keeping his breath even so he didn't burn through his oxygen. And yet—every sight, every moment, took his breath away.

The aft torpedo room opened before him, torn by war and time. The long shape of a torpedo lay partially buried where it had tumbled during the sub's fall. Bunks hung at an angle from the wall-become-ceiling, where men had slept above the weapons they fired. Fish swam along the beds as if they passed through the men's dreams, then scattered as Grant slipped all the way inside. The wall arched over him, narrowing the already small and sloping chamber. The bulkhead buckled under the weight of metal and ocean above, the hatch hanging open, a cluster of pipes broken off from the wall at one end thrust out toward him like a beckoning hand, a siren seeking to pull him down. Beyond the open hatch lay darkness where neither sunlight nor his dive lights could reach.

Something brushed his leg, and he glanced back to find Wesson at the breech, gesturing for him to move along. He held up a hand for patience, and proceeded toward the bulkhead at his own pace. Haste on a wreck dive was a good way to get them both killed. Slow is smooth, and smooth is fast. The light stretched out before him, illuminating a shaft of specks eternally falling through the water, golden flecks of mica, tiny coral polyps and a hundred other things that tumbled in the ceaseless grind.

He reached the opening, regulating his breathing, keeping his excitement in check, holding himself back like a kid on Christmas morning. What surprise would the next chamber hold? Delight or disappointment? The treasure he'd been searching for—or a defeat as crushing as the ones the Germans had suffered? Had those last two men died on their lonely island secure in the knowledge of victory, or mourning the loss of all they had fought for? Head and shoulders through the opening, turning carefully, making sure he didn't snag his gear on the broken pipes or the wires that bobbed in the current of his passage. His lights swept the chamber, the electric motor room. The bank of motor controls tilted off the wall to his left and he edged further away. They'd been off-kilter for seventy years, but largely undisturbed. Would they stay in place, or take the moment of his intrusion to crush the trespasser? More ruptured pipes from the wall above, a broken shaft emerging from the wall next door. Slats of flooring and the ribs that held them reared up alongside, shattered in the impact most likely. Square shapes littered the opposite wall, which now served as the floor. Grant sank down to his knees, settling carefully, scanning for anything the right size or shape, recording everything he saw. A second set of lights joined him, briefly casting his shadow into the emptiness. He reached out, sweeping away the accumulating muck of decades. Spare parts boxes, motor components and crates from provisions spilled across the ground. He finger-walked forward, sweeping again, making little clouds of dust and revealing nothing.

Wesson tapped him again. On his slate, he wrote the word, "Where?"

Grant crept a little further, still scanning, but they could both see it, in spite of the tumult and the increasingly murky water. He took up his own slate and wrote, "Not here."

Wesson pointed toward the next bulkhead door. Grant checked his chronometer: Twenty-three minutes had elapsed. Plenty of time. He gave a thumbs up and moved onward, but without much hope. Had they unloaded their passenger early, or just lost the cases in the devastation of their own wreck? One way and another, the passenger was gone. What next? Scout ahead a little further, just in case the marks on the pictograph had been out of place or misleading. Grant swam to the next door which hung off one hinge, partially blocking the way. He took hold of it, wrenching it aside. The metal groaned, and he winced. At least this particular wreck wasn't also a grave: Everyone but those two men had escaped, and even lived out the war in American custody, returning home again to die as old men in Germany.

He pushed against the damaged door, aiming his lights and camera past the obstruction into the diesel engine room beyond, a larger chamber and almost fully occupied by a jumbled of enormous pistons, pipes and dials. He moved partway inside, illuminating the passageway, scanning the broken floor beneath which something could have been concealed, but the flooring had gone, exposing the inner ribs of the beast that had swallowed him. Claustrophobically narrow, the engine room stretched away before him toward a far end where the beam of his lights faded to nothing. No way the crates could be in there, the engineers and mechanics would've been tripping over them the entire voyage.

Again, Wesson's lights drew up over his shoulder. Then a hand plunged toward him. It snatched the camera off his head, dislodging his mask. Instinctively, Grant pulled back, pulling his feet under him through the narrow opening, swirling to face his attacker.

Wesson's masked and hooded face stared back at him, then with a clang, the broken door shoved into place between them. Metal ground on the other side. Grant lunged and kicked against the door. A hollow thud echoed around him and passed away into silence, leaving him sunk and alone.

CHAPTER SEVENTY-FIVE

Grant stopped his breath rather than give vent to his fury—and his much-needed oxygen. He gave another try at pushing the door open, but Wesson had propped it with something—probably the broken beams he had noticed on the way inside. Grant hung in the narrow span of the engine room, running his options, checking his oxygen. He had time, if he didn't breathe hard. Time for what: to get to the far end of the room and beat himself against another closed door?

Stillness. Breathe carefully. Slow is smooth. Right. He checked his chronometer. Twenty minutes to get out without needing decomp. Nothing like getting the bends to ruin a great day diving. As if this had been a great day. First penetration into an undiscovered wreck: take that off his life list. Hope there wasn't much left on that list—he might not have time for it.

Grant drew a deep, careful breath, then turned from the barricaded door. He swam slowly, keeping his arms in to minimize his form. Still, his tanks clanged off the damaged equipment around him, sending vibrations through the mouthpiece, through his back. Not even a hero's death, running out of oxygen only a hundred feet from the open air. Kick efficiently, not so much concerned about visibility now, but aware of the need to conserve energy. One more bulkhead to the control room beneath the conning tower. Lazarus's voice ran through his head, narrating the journey. That was his next possible escape route. Focus on the next thing. Wreck-diving legend John Chatterton's mantra: solve the next little problem. Keep on doing that until you've solved every goddamn problem the wreck can throw at you.

Next problem: don't die. Funny, that had been the last problem. And likely the problem after that.

At the far end of the engine room, the hatch in the bulkhead stood shut. Grant caught hold of the big wheel at its center—thick with rust and colonies of new life, little things that thrive in the darkness. He hauled back on the wheel. Nothing but a puff of rust and silt that quickly dispersed into the beams of his lights. Didn't help that the door was designed to operate in a vertical fashion, not with the sub pitched to the side.

Hands down, trembling a little. His skin, comfortable enough until now, cooled, his muscles getting a little twitchy. No time for that. He caught hold again, bracing his feet against the door frame, putting his back into it. A dozen tiny punctures stabbed with fresh pain, and the old injury to his left arm throbbed. Part of the handle broke off in his hands. He took a sharper breath, and forced himself to breathe out slow.

Let it go. Can't move on to the next problem without solving this one. He released the handle, shook out his hands, and swept his lights methodically along the bulkhead. The entire wall shifted, leaning inward and making the space even more narrow, but there, above. The force exerted by the sub's fall wrenched the wall away, creating a bulge between the bulkhead and the sidewall near the floor, a gap, maybe wide enough to swim through. Grant pushed upward, climbing along the pipes, twisting a little to get close. The gap was narrow, but gave into the next room, clear for at least as far as he could see. And way too small for his tanks. Unbuckle, wriggle out of the harness, the space around him squeezing from every direction—or was it his own chest that grew too tight? Breathe. Place the freed tanks on the cantilevered back of the engine housing. It groaned under the fresh weight. Rise a little further, fending off the ceiling with one hand. Detach a light and aim it through the gap. Fumble the light and nearly drop it.

The gleam of white beyond. Long and smooth and unmistakable, the shape of bone.

Breathe. Breathe. Slow and easy. Grant moved toward the gap, reaching his arm through, not yet giving up his mouthpiece, though the hose was stretching to the max. Bones: legs, pelvis, ribcage. Definitely not Peking Man: too complete, too modern. One of those two sailors died down here.

Grant hoped he wouldn't have to join him. His extended arm sagged, his temple resting on his arm, his gaze forward and down toward the dead man who might be his last companion. If that guy died in here, then there was no way out.

End of the line, Bone Guard. He closed his eyes, the water freeing strands of his hair to tickle across his brow. Dying alone, unburied. Without knowing if Gooney made it safely out of prison. Without knowing if D.A. pulled off her part of the plan, if he and his grandfather could find a way beyond their past. If Randy made it out of the hospital so Cece could give him a proper what-for. If Teo got back to work on the church. If, if, if, if. His breathing hitched, and he forced it slow, even. He wasn't dead yet. Solve the next problem.

Dying alone, unburied. His head shot up. If one of the men died in here, the other one wouldn't be buried—he couldn't be. There had to be another way out. A way this guy had gotten back in. Grant took a few deep breaths. Switch the tank, take up the whole thing, feeling heavier as he grew weary. Tension drained the strength from his muscles. Don't let it win. Grant heaved up the tanks and pushed them through, turning sideways to follow, arching his back, the tanks scraping, his back scraping, then plunging downward on the inside like an acrobat, uncurling so he lay almost full-length next to the dead man. Dead men.

CHAPTER SEVENTY-SIX

A second skeleton perpendicular to the first, both of them lying on the wall of the control room that now made its floor, the chart table and other gear tossed about by the wreck. Two white skulls. The sub was a gravesite after all, but it wouldn't be his. Pointing out to sea, the ladder from the conning tower showed him the way, another narrow passage, crooked and bent, long and dark, with a patch of glowing blue at the end like the moon on the darkest night. He lugged his tanks in that direction before he acknowledged the truth: No way was his gear fitting through there. The two sailors only made it because they hadn't carried anything. So be it. He brought his gear to the end of the ladder and pulled off his slate. A few deep, lung-filling breaths, then he bound off the hose as close as he could to the tank, giving himself a couple more breaths if he needed them, and cut the tank away. No more breathing, not unless he got desperate, and even then, a little bit longer. What was his free-dive personal best? Fuck it. Just go.

He kicked hard, pushing ahead, twisting, turning, hands forward, to slide or pull himself through, battered by the remains of the pipes and wires, and finally out and free. Now breathe, kick for the surface, but not too fast. The edges of his vision closed in. Tuore recommended a break of ten minutes at fifteen feet. Take your chances. Men had escaped from submarines on a continuous exhale. Right. He drew in the last of his oxygen, pulled out his mouthpiece and let it fall, exhale in a long, controlled stream of bubbles, lungs burning as he reached the surface and broke through into the sky beyond.

Waves lapped around him as he drew breath, leaning his head back, treading water and taking in the sweep of the sky, the sun heading low. He turned, taking in the sea around him. The islet at his back, the near end where the buoy should be. Nothing. And beyond that, where the *African Dream* should be waiting. Nothing but the empty sea. Waves pushed at him, almost playfully shoving him further from land with every swell.

Grant rolled and kicked toward the islet. The ocean pulled against him, urging him out to sea, but he refused it, pulling with his arms in spite of the ache. A handful of people in the world now knew where he was, and maybe half of them cared, and maybe one or two would think he might survive. He tucked his head, turned, tucked, turned, drawing breath with every couple of strokes, pushing hard until his outstretched hand scraped rock and he grabbed hold, both hands then, hauling himself over the shelf, staggering as he got his feet up. As he straightened, breathing hard, he pulled off his mask.

Heard the rattle, and the grind of a ratchet. Grant dove aside as a spray of bullets riddled the water nearby. Shallow dive, scraping stone, then off the edge of the rock, stroking for the far end where knobs of coral thrust up from the ridge.

"Go on, swim for it." Hammer's voice. "Do you know the dog paddle, mongrel?"

Another spray of bullets forced Grant under, turning aside, something stung. He had dropped his mask, but kept his eyes open, burning in the saltwater, looking for safety. He slipped behind an outcrop and reached for his ankle, bringing up one of his knives. To one side, the lower end of the island gave way to coral, in the distance, a big powerboat rose and fell with the waves. A group of men lined the near side rail, each one wearing a Stetson and holding a gun.

"Might be more fun if you let him up, make it last like the boss wanted." Wesson.

Grant risked a glance the other direction. Twenty feet of rough coral and tidepools lay between him and the land. Two men, standing a little apart from each other. The thick gray edge of a Zodiac on the shore not far from the cairn.

"When he's not here, I'm the boss," Hammer answered. "I'm about done with this one."

"Go on," Wesson called toward the boat.

Bullets spat in the water around him and cracked into stone. He pushed off and submerged again. White streaks in the water as the bullets pursued, but could not find him. Grant kicked hard, going deeper then skimming toward the high side of the island. Two knives and a set of swim fins. A lot of rocks. The occasional sea urchin. Great inventory for improvised weapons. He broke the surface in the shadow of the islet, tucked in close.

"The hell is that? A fucking rowboat? Boys—hey, boys! Over there." Wesson's voice, yelling. "Behind you."

"What hole are you hiding in?" Hammer's voice, the crunch of footsteps.

Grant slipped off his fins, dropped one, held the other. He crept out of the water, still as he could be, silent on the rough stone. With careful aim, he flung the fin back the way he'd come. Splat against the surface of the water. Gunfire burst in that direction. Sounded like full auto or maybe a bump stock. No matter. Grant launched himself into a run, pelting in the direction of the shots. A man's shadow in front of him, moving. He shifted direction.

Grant burst from the shadow of the cairn, knife in hand, and slammed into Wesson's back. Blood spurted and they fell together. Grant pulled free the knife at an angle, tumbling as he fell away from his target and coming up in a crouch. Blood streaked his fist and sheeted his arm. Wesson choked.

Grant came to his feet as Hammer spun about, raising the gun.

A concussive sound and the ocean flared bright and gold as the speedboat bucked hard and shattered. Men flew from the deck, some of them burning as well as they tumbled into the sea. Waves rocked the splintered hull. Men screamed and fire lit the side of Grant's face, casting an orange glow on Hammer's wide-open eyes.

Grant launched himself, but Hammer recovered, turning about with a stumble that saved his life. He swung up his gun and knocked Grant off-balance. As he fell, Grant seized the hot barrel of the weapon, wrenching it away. They rolled partly into the water. The gun flew wild and landed with a splash. Grant reached for his second knife. Hammer kicked him and the knife clattered away, sliding into a pool.

Grant got his feet under him, but Hammer hooked his ankle and set him sprawling into the water.

Hammer pounced, slamming his foot into the center of Grant's chest, his face barely below the surface. Hammer pushed hard, shoving Grant further down the slope to where the water grew deeper. Waves washed over his face, fracturing his view of Hammer's fury. "What the hell? How? Mother-fucking mongrel! Those were my friends—my men!" He leaned his weight into Grant's chest. Grant's fingers groped. Two knives, gone. Swim fins. Gone. Rocks. The occasional sea urchin. He yanked it free, the spiky ball prodding at his scrape-proof glove, and smacked it into Hammer's leg as high up as he could reach.

Hammer twisted aside. "Shit!"

Grant struck again, gouging the spines into the back of Hammer's knee, scoring deep. Hammer screamed and staggered off, dragging his leg, slapping to dislodge the creature.

Grant rolled and hauled himself to his knees, coughing hard. His knife winked from the tidepool and he swept his hand through the water, snatching the hilt.

As Hammer pitched off the sea urchin and came at him again, Grant flipped the knife and threw.

It caught Hammer in the gut, sinking deep. His knees buckled as he crumpled around the blade. Blood spilled from his lips. His head sagged. His hands for a moment still reached, still struggled to prop himself up, then to hold his life in. He collapsed, head to the ground, blood pooling around him.

Grant sank back on his heels, taking his first deep breath in far too long. His throat and lungs burned, his eyes stung from the sea, and from a seep of blood escaping his stitches.

A rhythmic sputtering drew his attention to the shore.

"Chief!" D.A. landed her little boat. She jumped out into the water and pulled the boat up alongside the larger Zodiac, then splashed toward him. "Chief. Are you okay? Tell me where it hurts." She draped his shoulders with a thick towel.

Where didn't it hurt. Grant wiped the water from his face, flicking away the swirl of blood that came with it. "We need a phone. We need to call Rizzo—Lones wasn't here—he never left Tucson."

CHAPTER SEVENTY-SEVEN

The transcript on Jamie's screen looked blurry and she rubbed her eyes, then took another swallow of coffee long since cold. There'd been a power blink last night, affecting the office and setting off an alert that woke her up at her home, in spite of the sleeping pill she'd taken. An electrical crew had gotten everything back on line, and Rachel even re-set the blinking clocks after the deputies determined nothing was amiss. Given what happened to Bryce, they weren't taking chances, but there was no sign of anything out of place, no bombs or threats or bugs turned up in the scan. She wanted to bring in Buster for a scan of her own, but that was just paranoia. Still, the incident set her on edge, the whole world conspiring to make sure she couldn't relax, even just to go through her paperwork.

The sooner she got through all of this, the sooner they made the case rock-solid, the sooner she could hold a press briefing and get the truth out about Tony. And Adam. The one was already pilloried by the press as a cop-gone-rogue, and the FBI, for pigheaded reasons of their own, wanted every t-crossed before they'd release the full story. She was already getting pretty cross herself, and she couldn't imagine what Tony was going through. Had they at least kept him in isolation? There were only so many times she could call the prison to check on any given prisoner before people started to wonder.

Jamie's phone rang and she reached for it, then hesitated, checking the number. Unfamiliar extension. It was her own phone: Adam couldn't have replaced it with a bomb. It rang again, then stopped. On high alert, her hand hovered over the phone and snatched it up again the moment it started to ring. "Rizzo."

"It's Casey." His voice sounded distant and crackly.

"I can't hear you very well." She plugged the other ear. "You still in Trinidad?"

"No time: Lones isn't here."

"What?" She punched up her volume, hunching over to protect it from any office noise.

He spoke again, separating the words very clearly. "Adam Lones. Isn't here. Get Gooney out. Now."

Adam didn't go? What the hell? They had people on all the airports, his photo out with every agency, the whole fucking state on the watch. He had the perfect fucking escape route, where else would he—

Too much, too long. "Oh, shit. I'm on it." She broke the connection.

She rocketed her wheelie chair away from her desk and grabbed her duty belt from its hook. It took three tries to buckle as she stumbled out the door. "Rachel! Call Kornitzky! He needs to expedite the release papers on Detective Gonsalves! He needs to send a fucking fax over there, now! Lones is here—he never left!"

Rachel jumped up as well, turning as her boss blew past her out of the building. "Release papers. Got it!"

Where had the bastard been all night? What had he been doing? Maybe he really was behind the power outage, but if so, he hadn't done anything with it. Maybe he's been so upset, he screwed up his own plan. And maybe she was the next Miss Arizona. He had a plan, she just didn't know what the hell it might be.

Jamie flung herself into the car, starting the engine with one hand, the siren with the other. She peeled out of the parking lot, startling a few drivers already on the road. Straight shot down the highway to the prison, a fifteen minute drive and she made it in eight. Slam into the parking lot, barely remembering to turn off the siren or the engine before she ran inside, flashing ID, the metal detector shrieking at her as she passed through.

"Sheriff Rizzo, how can I—" the desk officer began.

"I need access to your surveillance room. The guy behind the murder of Agent Mike Allen—"

"That Boston detective?"

"Hell, no—don't they fucking tell you anything?" She backed off a step and took a breath. "The detective is innocent. Kornitzky is getting his release papers in order right now, as we speak. The perpetrator's got it in for Gonsalves, big time. He's our key witness, and this guy wants him dead."

The desk officer stared at Jamie, deadpan, as he had since her outburst. Hands folded, pushed back from his desk. "Alright, Sheriff. Thanks for cooling your jets for me. What is it that you really want?"

She hooked her thumbs over her belt. "I want those release papers expedited. My assistant has already called Kornitzky on that. In the meantime, I need to make sure that the perpetrator cannot get access to Gonsalves."

The officer pressed his lips into a smile and waved a meaty hand at the apparatus she'd just set off. "That's why we have all of this, Sheriff. You can't get a weapon in here without me knowing."

She wanted to leap over the desk and throttle the man. "Yes, I know. And this guy is a fu—a chameleon. He'll change guises, convince one of you that he's somebody else, and slip in where he's not expected. I'd like to monitor your surveillance cameras to see if we can spot him before something happens."

"Right, well, the—" A tone sounded from his computer and he glanced over, then squinted at the screen. "Those release papers. They just came through. I don't know what your assistant said, but she must've done a good job of it."

"Great," Jamie said, with feeling, some of the terror that clouded her mind starting to ebb away. Thank God. "I assume it'll be a few minutes before Gonsalves works his way through the system. In the meantime, I'd like to check that surveillance if you don't mind."

"Sure thing, Sheriff." He poked a button and the next door buzzed open. "Guard station on the left, it's right by the corridor your perp—I mean, your detective's gonna come down. I'll let the monitor know you're coming."

He raised his voice to follow her as she sprinted for the room. The officer inside, his face lit by a half-dozen screens, barely looked up at her.

Views of the prison came and went from the screens. To one side, a few views were permanent: the entrance and exit gates. "Anybody new or unusual come by on your screens in the last few hours?"

"Hours? We don't have any special visitors if that's what you mean."

"The Boston detective, the one you were holding on suspicion of murder, can you show him to me? He's being released, and I need to make sure he gets there."

With the tap of a few keys, he brought up the interior view of a cell, a small room for anyone, much less a man of Tony's stature. She leaned in. How long had it been? Maybe thirty hours since she'd last seen him. Longest thirty hours of her life, for more reasons than one. He wore the regulation orange jumpsuit—and a set of irons on wrists and ankles, bound to a belt at his waist. He looked gaunt, hunched and haggard. The chains flamed her fury, but she squelched that. As far as the feds had been concerned, he was a rogue cop, deadly with or without a weapon, fast enough to shoot six men, kill four of them. He was alive and on the verge of freedom. Something happened beyond his door and he glanced up, revealing an ugly bruise that spanned from his right eye down to his chin. "What happened to his face?"

"Walked into a door." The guard whuffed a little bit, looking smug. "Which door was it, that's what I want to know. Cops in prison is bad news. Cops who kill other cops?" He gave a shrug. "Coulda been any one of a dozen doors I can think of. Maybe I'll go back through the footage on my lunch break and get a view of the action."

She'd never wanted so badly to walk somebody into a door herself. The cell door opened and Tony stood up awkwardly. A guard took him by the elbow and guided him out.

"There you go, on release." The guard pointed at another screen. "Just as you'd expect." She saw Tony led into an anteroom, the door closing behind him. They moved through a series of images, the officer clicking through to indulge her in following the prisoner's path. Finally, his escort waited with him as another door opened. The waist restraint hung a little low on his hips, like a gun belt, or was it his native swagger that made it so? Almost there, almost free.

"There you go," the officer said, as if it were a done deal.

"Where does that lead?"

"Straight down there." The guard pointed ahead of him toward another anteroom. "They push the buzzer, I open it. It's an airlock entry on both ends: can't have the inner and outer doors open at the same for extra security."

Images circulated over the screens again: prisoners in the mess, others in the yard, guards on patrol, a maintenance man in a utility corridor working on a duct.

"Shouldn't that guy have an escort?"

The guard shrugged. "Maintenance. Routine stuff. All of the contractors pass background checks."

The view with Tony came around again. He talked with the officer, who stepped back, offering him the door. Tony looked back at him. He was going to his freedom, he should look happy, eager, right? "Shouldn't the guard go with him?"

"You sure ask a lot of questions." The guard in front of her switched screens deliberately that time, cutting off her view of Tony. The same series of views. The empty access corridor, at the base of a duct, a patch of open darkness.

Adam waited, cramped, breathless: listening. After a few minutes, a door opened with a metal swish, somewhere to his left.

"Can't we do something about the chains?" the traitor asked, and something rattled.

"They'll take care of it at the other end. Go on—I've got work to do." The voice of a brother, a true believer in service to the cause.

"Thanks for nothing." The traitor sounded weary and exasperated. Good.

With a rattle like a Dickensian ghost, he approached below. Adam shifted position, sliding back the hatch with precise movements. Tempting to make the leap now, to make the traitor see his face—but he'd know soon enough. Five, four, three. The traitor passed his location, and Adam launched. He smashed into the traitor's back, felling him like rotten timber with a crack of bones. The traitor tried to cry out, but managed only a gasp. Shattered ribs shifted under Adam's weight.

"Be silent in the presence of your betters, traitor," Adam hissed. He slipped the loop over the traitor's head in spite of his thrashing and pulled it snug, then a little bit more. "Give Satan my regards."

CHAPTER SEVENTY-EIGHT

Grant rang off and handed the phone back. His hands still felt shaky, but didn't show it. He pulled the towel tighter. Another boat, larger, slower appeared on the horizon, growing steadily, but his mind hadn't left Arizona. The whole thing had been a gamble, betting on Lones' desire to get the money, to get in good with the Warden, and get out of town before the truth broke over him. A gamble with Gooney's life.

"You were right, though, every one of their damn cellphones had a bomb inside. Took a little while to work out the trigger, but I guess it turned out fine." She gripped his shoulder, drawing his gaze back to her. "Honestly, from the minute I stowed away, I wasn't sure I'd ever see you again. The boats rendezvoused like clockwork, the fancy one, the speedboat, the *African Dream* so the Warden and her people could get the hell back to their comfort zone. They watched the video and wrote you off. I think she spotted me swimming over to meet up with Tuore, but she didn't say a word."

"You weren't a threat—not to her, anyway." He met her eye. "Sorry, it's a little hard to concentrate. I keep thinking of him."

She pressed her lips together, nodding weakly, and a fringe of teardrops glistened at the edge of her lashes. "Yeah. Me, too. But I keep trying."

He stripped off his glove and lay his hand over hers. "Nothing else we can do." He murmured, then he rose slowly, releasing her. They walked down the rocky slope toward the boats.

"You didn't find it, though. Any ideas where it is?"

He nodded. "One or two. Nothing I need to pursue, but I know who should."

Together, they shoved the Zodiac back off the shingle to where it was deeper, and tied off the smaller boat. "Tuore didn't want to get too close. Sorry."

"Understandable. I wanted to be pretty far from those guys myself." He smiled. "You came through, D.A. No worries."

"Right. Nick's gonna hit the roof about this whole thing when we get back to the office." They clambered into the boat and she took the rudder, starting up the motor.

"I was thinking we should take a vacation."

"Oh, yeah? Someplace tropical, you think? Or maybe the desert?"

"Paris," he said. "I've never been."

"No joke? You've never been to Paris?"

"Way too nice for the likes of me."

Crossing over the wine-dark sea, they passed in silence through the debris field of the Sons of a New America. On the other side, Marko in the *African Dream* zodiac fished another survivor from the water. Five men, battered and shaken, some of them burned, who stared at Grant with haunted eyes as he sailed by. He waved. One of the men raised a hand in response, then let it fall.

"What do we do with them?" D.A. asked.

"Ship them back to Arizona and turn them over to the sheriff, after a detour to the local hospital. They might be willing to open up given everything that's happened."

"Y'think?" She shook her head, then looked at him sidelong. "Y'know what gets me about you, Chief? Everything you've been through, everything you've done: you're an optimist."

"Don't say that out loud—you'll ruin my rep."

They reached the back deck of the *African Dream* where Tuore himself waited to secure the Zodiac and help them up. "So, Ulysses. That must've been quite a dive." He tipped his head toward the island, its small shore lapped with blood.

"I can't thank you enough." Grant shook the captain's hand.

"I don't know yet if I should be thanking you in turn, but I saw the footage. It's really there—the U-boat."

"Really there. If you want it, it's all yours. I think you should exploit the hell out of it and use the money to punch the Nazis every day."

"You'll pardon me if I don't take that advice too literally. C'mon. Shower, bunk, food, beer—whatever you want. I'll be drinking off this story for years."

Grant climbed up the ladder and mounted the deck. The wreckage of the Sons boat lay between him and the island and the secrets it held. He turned his back and walked away.

CHAPTER SEVENTY-NINE

Jamie stared at the montage on the screen. "Where's the maintenance man? He left that hatch open. Get me a view of the long hall."

The guard fussed over his controls, then found an empty hall. "Should be the right one," he muttered under his breath, and flicked some more switches.

"Fuck it—get me in there! Now, now!" She ran around the guard's desk and jumped over the counter, running for the door even as he hit the buzzer. It slid open too slow and she stopped short, waiting for the outer door to close before the inner one opened. "Come on! Come on, get it open!" Her gun felt wrong in her hand.

"Hold your horses, lady, there's a system."

Beyond the door, a clatter and a the rush of a large weight hitting the ground. Rustling. The door behind her shut, the one in front started to slide open. "Freeze!" she shouted, weapon extended. The gap widened at an agonizing pace. The long corridor stretched out before her, gray linoleum floor, barf-green walls, a man's feet lying down kicking at the ground, another man on his back.

Adam turned, hauling on the belt he held as if Tony were his mount and he'd ride him straight to hell.

"Let him go!" Jamie took aim from twenty paces, staring down the barrel at them both. She lifted the gun, zeroing on Adam's head and pulled the trigger—to the gut-dropping sound of an empty chamber.

Adam's face turned cold. "Mongrel bitch. After what he did to me—

after what you've done to me—you really think I'd leave you even one? Careless, leaving your gun in a darkened office. Not even checking the ammunition in the morning." Adam stumbled to his feet, pulling hard, putting all of his weight into strangling his victim.

Tony's chained hands couldn't reach his throat as the ligature tore into him. His face grew livid. Jamie ran. She hurled the empty gun and it glanced off Adam's shoulder, then she barreled into him, knocking him away, his hands sliding from the belt as he fell. Tony crashed back to the floor.

"Mongrel bitch," Adam wheezed. He feinted, then lunged, shoving her back to the wall, stumbling over the downed man. The dying man. Fuck. She dodged away from Adam, letting the wall guide her, but he followed, grabbing her hair, holding on, wrenching her neck, greedy for her life. Jamie broke loose, dropping to the floor to slip his grasp.

He followed, his arm knotting around her chest from behind. Would he break her neck, right here, right now?

He snatched a screwdriver from a loop on his coverall and drove it toward her.

From the top pocket of her uniform shirt, she pulled a shiny blue campaign pen. As his weapon plunged for her throat, she shoved against his shoulder, rocking him and twisting away to face him. With a sickening thrust, she rammed the pen through his eye. *Justice for all.*

Astonished, he froze. His hands dropped, the screwdriver clattering across the ground. He slumped sideways, but she was already turning from him, scrambling back along the floor.

Tony lay face down, a leather belt wound tight around his neck. She found the buckle, her sweaty fingers fumbling as she tugged it loose. She whipped the belt away from the groove it had carved into his flesh. Her fingers landed by instinct at his pulse—at where his pulse should be. Oh, God, no. Rolling him to his back, his chains rattling. His hands curled, seeping blood from his impact with the floor. Head tilted, clamp his nose with her hand, her lips pressed to his, breathing for him, watching his chest for any sign of movement. Each breath took far too long. Jesus no, compressions first, compressions only. Shit.

"Officer! We need a defibrillator, and oxygen! Get your ass in here!"

One hand locked into the other, the heel of her lower hand pressed against his sternum, willing his heart to beat again. One-and-two-and—don't die—don't be dead—dear God—Jesus Lord—don't—let—him—die. Broken ribs groaned and shifted under the pressure. Was she only causing more damage, hurting him more? Her strength thrown into every compression, trying to force him back to life. Bargaining that she'd go back to church, that she'd tithe from her salary, that she'd ditch politics altogether and become a nun. She wanted to lock her mouth to his again, breathing for him. She swore off that last promise, if he would just wake up. She pumped his chest willing the ferocious beat of her own heart to somehow become his, her eyesight blurry. Don't die—please—Tony—don't—be—

He convulsed under her hands, gasping for breath, coughing desperately. Cradling his head, Jamie rolled him to his side, stroking his back with her other hand. "It's okay, keep breathing. It's okay," she chanted. He choked and gasped, curled into the concrete floor, struggling for air. His eyes remained shut tight, body shuddering.

"Tony, it's okay." Barely whispering his name. Tears streaked her face and she smeared them away, bringing her hand to his shoulder, pinning him to the earth beside her. Thank God, it didn't matter now: her tears could be blamed on the excitement, her touching him on the need to save his life. Thank God, at least for now, she didn't have to let him go.

His manacled hand snaked up and seized hers. He pulled her hand back to his heart and held it there.

She wanted to curl herself around him, to lean down and kiss the corner of his jaw where the angry bruise marred his skin and the buckle had gouged his throat, but she could already hear the thunder of approaching footsteps, the buzz of the outer door opening. She murmured, "Jesus, Tony, don't do that to me."

He held her hand to the beat of his heart and tipped his head back. A hint of his grin returned, the corners of his eyes damp as well. His voice hoarse, he whispered, "Helluva third date, J-li."

She wasn't sure if she wanted to punch him or kiss him. "Jesus, Tony." She swallowed hard, then said, "Next time, just bring flowers."

As the guard finally made it through the damn doors, arms loaded with first aid gear, Jamie reluctantly freed her hand, shifting to grip his wrist —checking his pulse, maybe, but honestly, just holding him. She was shaking so much, her own pulse racing so hard, there was no way she would get an accurate count.

The guard stumbled to a halt, swaying over her. "Holy—you—did you do that? Where'd he come from?"

"Fell from the sky. Did you bring the fucking key?" She rose to her knees and took the gear from him, spreading the array around her knees.

"Sure." He didn't take his eyes from the body behind her, her campaign manager, the psychotic serial killer.

Jamie unwound the tubing for the oxygen bottle and got it assembled, cradling Tony's head while she pulled the oxygen mask over his nose and mouth. The terrible wrong color of his face subsided, his tortured gasps evening out into something like normal breathing, each breath labored and long.

"The key?" Jamie prompted, putting out her hand.

The guard finally jerked out of his paralysis and found it on an attached keychain. She dragged it toward her and started with the locks at Tony's wrists. "How about an ambulance?"

"What? Isn't he—"

"Yes, that one's dead. I killed him. Get the fuck over it and get back on the job. We've got a man down: asphyxiation leading to cardiac arrest, broken ribs, possible internal injuries." Cataloging the damage, acting like a professional.

"Ambulance. Right." The guard retreated again, radio in hand.

She took Tony's wrist again—finally freed of the manacle, even the prison-orange sleeve too short for his arm. She clipped a blood oxygen monitor to his finger. "Just hold still, okay?" Three fingers of his left hand looked bent, drops of blood shivering free from scrapes.

He made a series of small gestures over his chest: pointing to himself, cupping his fist, something that looked like drawing a gun. Sign language. Handy—ha. Sucked that she didn't understand. "You're making a joke, aren't you," she murmured.

His expression beneath the mask approached a smile, retreated to something almost lost, terribly lonely, his eyes searching her face.

"I got your back, Tony. It's okay."

The slightest nod. His eyes closed again, relaxed this time, and she found the steady beat of his heart.

CHAPTER EIGHTY

I n the waiting area of the Port of Spain hospital, where their "friends" underwent various treatments for their injuries and tried to explain how their boat had blown, Grant and D.A. enjoyed a quiet cup of coffee, waiting for the laptop to load all the messages that came through while they were gone. Waiting for the phone to ring. It lay on the table between them, stubbornly silent.

Grant wore his silk again, his silver cuffs in place, warm as the Arizona sunshine, his damp hair, freshly washed, draped his forehead. Then, on the laptop screen, a notification from an instant message app. He withdrew, and D.A. glanced over. "What's that?"

He turned it to face her, then opened the message.

17:28 *We heard the explosion. You certainly drank the martini that time.*

Three hours ago. Around the time the Warden would have made landfall, gathering her men around her, piling into luxury vehicles and taking off in her private jet—it had already gone by the time the *African Dream* returned.

18:06 *Of course, I may be speaking to dead connection, to a ghost lost in a submarine, to a legend lost on an island. Ulysses, indeed.*

18:09 *It is hard to know what to hope for in that regard. I had wished our partnership to bring more fruit.*

18:27 *But I do prefer to work with those who have similar sensibilities. I hope you shall forgive me for that.*

371

19:01 *Or indeed, for anything.*

D.A. blew out a breath. "I think she likes you."

He laughed. "That kind of friendship, I can do without. Let her think I'm dead." Except that the message app showed he was on-line.

A message blossomed on the screen before him.

20:41 *Cheers, Mr. Casey. And salud. To your health.*

"Cheers," he whispered, then shut it down.

The phone rang and D.A. snatched it up, not even waiting for the second ring, she pressed it into his hand. She closed her fist, stopping it from shaking.

Grant wet his lips. "Rizzo: You alright?"

"I will be. Maybe later. I'm not hurt, but Tony—Gooney—" She stopped to catch her breath.

That hitch in her voice was like a gun being cocked. "Tell me." His eyes locked to D.A.'s.

"He died. Lones killed him. But I brought him back. He's gonna be alright, but it might take a little while." Another long breath. "Chief?"

"Yes, ma'am."

"Don't kick his butt just yet, okay? At least give him a day or two—maybe a week?"

Grant let the tension drain away, beaming at D.A. who collapsed into her chair, eyes rolled back in dramatic release. "No promises," he told her. "But thank you. He gets a reprieve anyhow—I've got no idea how we're getting home from here."

"Turns out I have a charter plane on the tarmac down there. Thunderbird Air? My former campaign manager hired it. I'll let them know you're coming."

"We're bringing you home five members of the Sons of a New America, Arizona Chapter. What's left of them, anyway, so get us a solid welcoming committee. I think we softened 'em up for you."

"You got it, Chief." A pause, then, "Any luck?"

"Lucky to be alive, as usual."

She snorted. "That's hardly luck when you're involved."

CHAPTER EIGHTY-ONE

J amie led a small parade of police vehicles toward the Marana Regional
Airport to await the touchdown of the world's craziest charter flight. Her
vehicle carried the weight of all the things she wanted to say and didn't
know how. Tony once more rode shotgun, staring out the window, an angle
of the back of his head that showed the heavy bruising at his throat. His
breathing, contained by a heavy wrap to support the broken ribs, looked
even, but short, his gaze already a thousand miles away.

"It's gonna be a long road home," he said to the window, the first words
he'd spoken in a while. His voice still sounded hoarse, too weak, and she
wasn't sure which injuries were the most raw: those she could see, or those
that she couldn't, the bloodstain on his reputation, the nightmare of his sight
gone dark.

"We'll get it sorted out, Tony. They can't be too upset about you
helping the FBI, right?"

"And about me moonlighting for the Bone Guard? Not to mention me
in chains on national TV, accused of butchering somebody in my fucking
hotel room." His voice faded to a whisper that hurt just to hear. "I've got two
kids. I'm not allowed to see them because she says I have a history of
violence." He swallowed, winced. "I was in the fucking army. I'm a fucking
police officer. Violence is something I do, a tool I can use, it's not what I am.
She makes me sound like one of them—one of those assholes I shot." His
head sank to his hand, thumb and fingers digging in above his eyes.

"Jesus, Tony," her voice sank to match his. "I don't care if it makes me

look like a fucking political whore, I will blanket the world with press
releases proclaiming your innocence."

"How innocent can I be? It's not like I didn't shoot those guys." He
offered a glint of teeth, the turn of his head to slant his gaze back toward her.
"Then there's you, and I dunno how innocent I wanna be."

Back to the jokes. Maybe she'd never see him in more than glimpses.
Maybe that was one of the things that attracted her. Jamie reached toward
him, awkwardly squeezing his hand above his mummified broken fingers.
No sign language for a while.

"Guess this is it," she said, pulling in.

The charter plane taxied down the runway, pulling up close, lending
an ominous rumble to the air, then shut down, and long moments passed
before the stairway was pushed up and the door opened. A legion of cops
awaited the incoming flight, and quickly began escorting prisoners back to
their cars, jackets pulled up over the men's heads to defend them from the
gathering of reporters lurking nearby. The Sons were businessmen from in
town, from out of town, professionals. Vigilantes and murderers. A pair of
deputies corralled the waiting press with some effectiveness.

"Beginning of the end," Tony said. "Can't say it's been my favorite
vacation—but there were some definite highlights." His grin slipped out, but
wistfully.

Jamie exited the vehicle before she could say a hundred things better
left unsaid. He had to go, to face the brass back home and see if he could
make up for the consternation his visit had caused, and distance himself
from the scenes of death. By the time he stood on the sidewalk, Tony had
wiped the emotion from his face, walking tall, all cop. Seeing them arrive,
the knot of reporters who had begun to disperse pulled back together again.
A little apart from each other, Jamie and Tony crossed the tarmac toward
what passed for a terminal, where D.A. and Casey emerged into the
sunshine.

"Holy shit, Gooney, is your head still attached?" D.A. dropped her bag
and flung her arms around him. In spite of the broken fingers, he lifted her
up in his embrace—taking advantage of a height difference close to a foot,
and set her back down again.

"Barely. Some folks might've preferred otherwise." His attention moved toward Casey.

Casey put up his hands. "Don't speak for me, Gooney. I'm glad you made it, if only so I can strangle you myself."

"Jesus, Casey, I cannot believe you had the beach brawl without me. I fucking hate you."

"I fucking hate you, too." Casey shifted the duffel on his shoulder and gripped Tony's hand. "If it makes you feel any better, it wasn't much of a beach. That Employee of the Month thing still stands, though."

Tony burst out laughing and Jamie's heart rose. They didn't have much time left, she might as well enjoy it.

"All I can say to that is, I quit."

"Resignation accepted. You're still on payroll through the end of the month, though, in case things go south when you get home."

"Oh, no! Fool me twice, shame on me!" Tony backed away, hands up. "I'm staying the hell away from you and your fucking job offers."

"Hey—we've got the finest death-and-dismemberment policy ever written," D.A. said. "Not to mention a kick-butt arcade in the basement."

Casey folded his arms. "He's had a rough weekend. He'll come around."

"The hell I will." He spoke hard and fast that time, and Jamie flinched. "You have any idea how hard it was, sitting in that damn prison cell, being hauled off to answer the same fucking questions over and over? No, I didn't know who he was—everybody called him 'Miller'. No, I'd never met any of them before. No, I didn't hesitate—if I fucking hesitated, Casey and I would be dead and you'd all be sitting here with your heads up your ass, not even knowing you had a problem! No offense, Rizzo, but most of your guys took way too long to get up to speed—" He paused for breath and added, "then back to that goddamn cell, chained up, just waiting for someone to shank me, and I couldn't do a damn thing about it, and thinking only one person on the whole goddamn planet gave a damn what happened to me." He blinked rapidly, working back toward control.

Jamie hooked her thumbs through her duty belt, restraining herself from touching him. D.A. stepped in, setting her hand on his back, at his waist, the touch of a friend who'd known him for years. Maybe more? What was Jamie, after all, but a fling—an hour of joy in a harrowing night. It still tightened her throat, hearing him talk that way, seeing another woman step in with the comfort Jamie burned to offer. For a moment, his eyes met hers.

He looked away, the gaze haunted. He ran a hand over his hair, gripping his skull. "Sorry. I'm sorry. It's just—I've been damn close to dying before, but I never actually died until yesterday."

"Welcome to the Lazarus Club," Casey said softly. "No apologies, Gooney. I asked for everything you had, and you gave way more than you got."

D.A. turned her supportive touch into a slap on the back. "And we've got the best damn PTSD counselor in Boston on retainer. Lemme know if you want the number"

"Oh, shut up."

The three of them shared a knowing expression, and Casey tipped his head toward the parking lot where a pair of deputies held back the growing mass of reporters. "You starting a parade, Sheriff?"

"They've been following me around lately, waiting for shit to go down, I guess. I think it's good for my rep, especially with my all my campaign assets frozen pending investigation."

"Oh, ouch."

She managed a shrug. "I'd love to get Tony over there and go on record with a few things. You, too, if you're up for it."

"No cameras—sorry." He donned a pair of aviator shades, hat tucked low, chin down—making himself a smaller target.

"Go on, Gooney," D. A. said. "I'll give you a ride to the real airport afterward. Maybe I can jump the same flight."

"Thanks."

"Are you leaving town, Casey?" Jamie asked.

"I'm around a little longer—not least because you've been waiting for a statement."

"I mean, the principals are dead, but we've been tracking down the rest of these fuckers as best we can, and sharing information with the other states where the organization is active. They've already issued a statement that the Arizona chapter was rogue, but it's bullshit. Any ammunition we can use against them can only help."

"I'll be there." He gave Tony's shoulder a squeeze, then stepped back into the shadows.

"C'mon," she murmured. "Help a girl out. You don't even have to talk."

"He's the fucking boy scout, but I'll do my best."

Tony trailed a few steps behind as Jamie led the way back toward the little crowd. The moment she entered their radius, the shouting began. "Detective Gonsalves, how does it feel to be exonerated? Anything to say about Arizona justice?"

"Sheriff Rizzo, can you tell us anything?"

"Yeah, Rizzo, like, can you tell us what the hell's going on?" Another man hollered from the back of the crowd, and a ripple of nervous laughter crossed the group.

Jamie waved them into silence. "Special Agent Kornitzky will be holding an official press conference this afternoon, and he's going to give you the whole story, at least, as much of it as the feds are willing to share." Another chuckle.

"In the meantime, here's my statement." She squared her shoulders and spoke up. "The Pima County Sheriff's department, the Tucson police department, and the Arizona branch of the Federal Bureau of Investigation would like to acknowledge the contributions made by the Bone Guard, LLC, and especially by Detective Lieutenant Anthony Gonsalves of the Boston Police Department in exposing the activities of the Sons of a New America, a white supremacist organization. Without their investigation, courage, and sacrifice, this organization might still be sowing hatred and committing murder on our southern border.

"Unfortunately, Detective Gonsalves has a flight to catch—and he's still recovering from the assault, so he won't be answering questions at this time. But I would like to offer my thanks, on behalf of the entire law enforcement community." She turned to Tony, extending her hand. He accepted, a solid grip, a big grin as the cameras flashed. "Detective Gonsalves. Thank you. I hope you'll give us another chance to offer you some true southwest hospitality, and show you a better side of our beautiful state."

Her own smile felt fixed, compared to that dazzling grin.

He took a step closer, for the benefit of the photographers, and murmured, "At least we'll always have Cowlic."

She suppressed her laughter, and whispered, "Fucker."

"You wish." His green eyes had that soft crinkle that suggested he wasn't joking.

Gripping his hand in both of hers she said, "You, too." He stared a moment longer, then broke away to where D.A. waited to bring him to the airport. Jamie refused to watch him go. The deputies herded away the reporters and she moseyed back to her own car. The relentless Arizona sunshine beat down at her as if it were pouring rain. By the time she got there, Casey had come alongside.

"You need my statement."

"Yes, sir, I do. But maybe not as much as you need a good night's sleep."

"Occupational hazard."

They climbed in and she started toward the federal building. "Sucks that you didn't find anything. Seems like a lot of trouble to go to."

"About that..." He produced a slip of paper from his pocket and held it up between two fingers, then placed it carefully into the flip-down eyeglass holder above her mirror. Silver glinted at his wrists. "We found a grave on the headlands, dug there a long time ago—maybe not long after the sub went down."

She nodded, keeping her eyes on the road. "For one of the crewmen."

"Only I found two skeletons in the wreck, in the conning tower, with the hatch open. It had to be closed when they submerged."

"What are you saying, they got out? They left the sub, they buried something, then they climbed back inside to die?" Her gaze flashed to the compartment. "No, shit, Casey—you found it? That's the find of a lifetime for a guy like you!"

He shrugged. "Could be. But for you, it could be even more." He pointed toward the hidden paper. "I wrote a name on there, a guy I know in the Chinese government. He can help with arrangements—excavations, exchanges. Tell him I sent you, and he'll know the numbers are good."

The clouds of Tony's departure parted and her day got a whole lot brighter. "You're just—giving it to me?"

"I'm not saying you shouldn't give me a call when you head down there. I'd still like to hold that skull in my hands, but don't connect my name to the discovery or there might be some unpleasant repercussions from the Warden's direction. Let it out that you found the information as part of your investigation." He settled back in the seat. "I was on a hunt for the dead, Sheriff, and you were working for the living. I won't forget that."

"I don't even know what to say. Thank you." She blinked back tears, suddenly a winner—Tony, still alive, and her mother's freedom almost within her grasp. Only the election polls left a dark stain: turns out the public got a little leery of a candidate whose politics turned into blood sport.

"Sheriff. He's one of the finest men I know, for all that we don't get along very well. If he worked for me full time, chances are we'd just kill each other. I'm not saying you need my blessing, but if it helps, then you have it."

"Thanks, Chief. It means a lot, actually. Come to that, if we spent much time together, I'd probably kill him myself."

"Yeah," Casey said, "but at least you'd bring him back to life again."

CHAPTER EIGHTY-TWO

Hours later, Grant finally got out of the office. Agents Kornitzky and Jackson took turns grilling him on every detail, eyeing his cuts and bruises, asking for the stories over and over again. Rizzo looked a little ill, interrupting when their questions pushed too hard or veered off-track, and he thought of Gooney's take, the same damn questions, but at least Grant was free to walk away, acknowledged as a victim and finally released. Rizzo saw him to the door, gripped his hand and gave a nod, but didn't say a word. Something lingered behind her eyes, drawing her gaze behind him to the side, anywhere Gooney might be. A plane glinted silver in the sky as it aimed toward its cruising altitude, and she retreated back inside, deflated. Could that be what love looked like? No idea.

A blue pick-up truck sat in the parking lot, a newer model Subaru next to it. Cece leaned against the grill of the truck, talking to someone in the car. She turned and straightened when he came out, walking toward him. A hint of darkness circled her eyes, but she shaded them with her hand. "Grant, come on. There's some people I want you to meet." She held her other hand out toward him.

Wary, he approached. "You doing alright?"

"Better now that Lones is off the streets."

Four people piled out of the car, two boys around twelve and ten, an older couple, all Tohono O'odham, by the look of them. Cece tucked her hand around his elbow. "My cousin Grant. He served in the army, and now he's a hero on the home front."

He tensed a little, wondering how to extricate himself. Which of his roles did he put on now?

"Grant, I'm Roy, and this here's Joan." The older man reached out and shook his hand. "Cece's our daughter-in-law. I remember you from the track and field days, but it's been a long time. Army, huh? Your mom'd be proud. She was quite a looker, that one."

"Quit it, Roy." The woman nudged her husband. "Thanks for keeping Cecelia safe during all of that. Can't have been easy." She, too, shook his hand.

One of the boys gazed up at him with open admiration. "Do your tattoos go all the way up? That's like a full sleeve, right? What do they mean?"

"Andy, you can't just ask stuff like that." The older boy cuffed him lightly on the back of the head. "Sorry about my bro. He's kinda rude. I'm Jason."

Grant shook his hand as well, gravely. "Jason. Pleased to meet you."

"Mom talks about you all the time, like every time there'd be some army thing in the news, whatever, she's like, I wonder if Grant's involved with that. Maybe your cousin's up there in the fighting."

"Who knows? Maybe I was." He met her gaze over her son's shoulder.

Andy blurted, "She used to say that she was keeping an eye on heaven, and you were keeping an eye on earth."

Grant's smile froze, and Cece nodded, her eyes gone moist. The truck door opened and slammed, and Frank strolled over. A wave of gratitude washed through Grant at the interruption.

"I'm pleased to meet you, too, Andy. Maybe I can tell you about the ink some other time."

"Teo's come around," said Frank. "Know he'd like to see you."

"Great, glad to hear it."

"If you don't mind driving, Grant," Cece said, I'll let you two catch up. My in-laws talked about taking me and the boys to Longhorn, then to a movie."

"Oh, yeah!" Andy immediately leapt back into the car, while Jason rolled his eyes and waved before he followed.

Cece held out the keyring, a few discount cards and club cards, a dozen or so keys dangling, catching the light in jagged reflections.

Frank wrapped the keys in his fist, lifting them out of her hand. "You go on, Cece. Thanks for getting me over here."

"Sure, Grampie." She gave him a swift hug, then turned back, almost shy, and caught Grant in her embrace, warm and brief. She waved her fingers as she scooted into the back with her sons. "Gimme a little space, boys! My goodness."

The car pulled away, everyone waving out the windows. Grant watched them go, still a little dazed. His grandfather stood at his side. "It's not easy, returning from the underworld."

"No, sir, it isn't." He reached into his duffel bag, the only thing he'd brought with him, the only thing he'd carry away, and pulled out the silver cuffs. "You loaned me these. I appreciate it, but—"

Frank was already shaking his head. "All yours now. We got those as payment for helping somebody out of the desert. Teo told me to keep them, he said they could stop a bullet like Wonder Woman's, and pay off a debt if need be. I don't suppose I'll ever make up the debt I owe you for the last few days, or y'know...before."

"Family's more than blood." Grant turned the silver through his fingers. "You're the only grandfather I've ever known, and I'm not sure I ever knew you."

"Better than I tried to know you."

They stood a moment, a dry desert wind warming them, facing the mountains. Didn't matter which way you looked, you were always facing the mountains.

"Let's pay a call on Teo, and then." Frank faced him, their eyes on a level. "I don't have a home for you to come back to, but Teo's place is empty, and he'd be happy for us to stay there, a little while. We've got some business, you and I. Some things to say. Maybe some things to un-say, if we can. If you can stay."

"I'll talk to my boss, but I think I have a few days." Grant slipped the silver cuffs back into place, one around each wrist. "What did you have in mind?"

"Honor the dead, and work for the living." The old man blinked suddenly, then his fisted hand rested against Grant's shoulder. "Thought for sure you'd left the one to join the other."

"Still here," Grant murmured.

"I've been wrong about a lot of things about you—I cannot tell you how glad I am to have been wrong about that." He held out that fist, the keys still inside, and Grant accepted.

He slung his duffel bag into the truck and pulled up into the driver's seat. "You ever thought about getting a new truck?"

"Grant, I am older than dirt, I don't see me changing any time soon."

Grant fired up the engine, resting that silver band on the wheel as he adjusted the mirrors. Mountains, desert, clear blue skies. "I dunno, Frank, I think you might."

EPILOGUE

The whole of Jamie's house filled with laughter, music, joy as she watched her mother circulate the party, her father never more than a few steps behind. Would he ever let her out of his sight again? Unlikely. And yet the overwhelming glow of their joy cast Jamie into shadows. She scooped up an empty bowl, waved at her dad, lurking near the bathroom door, and kept moving.

"Jamie, tell me about this!" He tore himself away for a moment as Jamie passed by, and he caught her shoulder, steering her toward the poster Denise had propped up on her hall table. Everybody had gotten a good laugh about it, and Jamie put up with it, even letting the poster stay where it was—but she'd have to banish it at the end of the night. Denise had made an enlargement of a meme that went viral for a bit before the election, through no fault of Jamie's. Someone had taken one of her publicity shots: full uniform, hands on hips, looking like she meant business—and surrounded her with pictures of the three men whose lives she had saved: Chris Anderson to one side, Randy giving a thumbs up from his hospital bed, and in the background, Tony, also in uniform. His pose nearly matched hers, arms folded, watching her back with that bold, green stare. Over the top was blazoned, "Jamie Li Rizzo, Sheriff, Resurrection County." At the bottom, in big letters, "You're in good hands," then "Not endorsed by any candidate or candidate's committee."

"Is that your friend?" He pointed to a picture of Chris posing on his motorcycle.

"No, Dad, that's my new campaign manager." Who disavowed any knowledge of the image in spite of his design background.

"Oh?" His eyebrows rose, a particular lilt coming into his voice

"Yeah. And he's gay."

Her father's finger shifted, sliding up along a path that joined Jamie's image with Tony's, and his expression softened. "I recognized him from your description. He is all that, isn't he."

"Yeah, Dad." Every time she'd seen the picture, every time somebody forwarded it, printed it, passed it around at the office for a chuckle, posted and re-posted it on the bulletin board no matter how many times she took it down, it gave her a shiver of heat, followed by a pang of loss. Two months since they'd shaken hands and parted ways. Why did it have to be so fucking complicated?

Her mother emerged from the bathroom. Jamie's dad gave her a quick peck on the cheek, then he hustled over to join his wife as another guest came up to greet her.

Jamie moved from the kitchen to the dining room to replenish the buffet, smile at the guests—even that a-hole, Special Agent Kornitzky, who struggled to look pleased by the whole thing. Or maybe was just being deservedly choked by that awful tie—not that anyone deserved what had happened to Tony. More like the fibbie was taunted by Tony's face on the poster. Take that, Korny. Even Buster had a bow of red and gold around his neck. Every time she glimpsed her own reflection in the mirror, she startled a little. When was the last time she'd worn a dress, much less one like this? Damn—the fitness tracker seemed to be working. The column of Chinese silk clung from neck to hips, then had a slit down the side that revealed her leg. It made her feel fidgety and naked. In a sea of red—the color of celebration and luck—she wore pale green, because it reminded her of—aw, hell. Things that didn't bear thinking of.

Buster gave a little woof and trotted to the door, ears perked. He plopped down on the mat, gazing over his shoulder at her.

A shadow shifted outside, a late-arriving party guest on the steps. Putting down the empty guacamole bowl, she pulled open the door, mangling a proper Mandarin welcome. The words died in her throat.

Tony stood on the stoop. Hair a little longer, clean-shaven—clean, for once, unbruised—sport coat hitched up at his shoulders because of the hand stuck in the pocket of his perfectly worn jeans. Damn those shoulders, the tilt of his chin to look down toward her, then away. He rocked a little back on his heels, his gaze flickering over the row of Chinese lanterns hung across the porch. "I should've called first. I didn't know you were having a party. Me and my timing."

Forcing herself to move, to move slowly, Jamie stepped outside. Buster streamed after her, wagging his whole self—kinda like she wanted to do. She shut the door behind her. "Our timing's been shit since we met."

"Are you allowed to cuss like a sailor when you're wearing that dress?" He looked at her, then away again. "Not that I mind the dress—I—aw, fuck, I don't know how to do this. I'm not sure I ever did." He revealed his other hand, bearing a small potted plant with deeply fringed leaves and a thread of dangling heart-shaped flowers. "Bleeding hearts. Seemed about right."

She took the pot from his hand and set it aside. "They're perfect."

"You didn't even look at them." He ran his now empty hand over his hair. "Are you packing under that thing? 'Cause that's some badass concealed carry."

"Derringer in a slimline thigh holster." She started to twitch open the side slit on the dress and display the holster, then used that hand to gesture back toward the house. "It's like a combination victory party for me and welcome home for my mom. What with the aftermath of the case, then the election, I couldn't get out to the coast, so they came here." Six weeks since her little expedition to meet up with the Chinese at Trinidad. Five weeks since her mom's release. Four days since she won the election. Too damn fucking long since she had seen him, outside that ridiculous meme popping up everywhere she looked.

Tony watched Buster nose around the rock garden in front of the house. "I'm glad it worked out."

"Were you responsible for that Resurrection County thing?"

He shook his head. "Those guys. I don't even know where they got the picture—one of those fucking feel-good meet-a-cop events. They won't own up to who made it or who shared it. I'm laying odds it was the chief's idea,

D.A.'s execution, Nick letting it loose on the Internet just to get a rise out of me." He broke off, lips parted. "I'm babbling. I should go."

"You flew all the way out here from Boston?"

"Southwest was having a sale." He retreated a step down from the stoop. "I'll call you tomorrow. I'm here until Monday for the long weekend, maybe we can—"

She followed him, a hair taller than he was from there. She touched his face, stroked her thumb along his collar, lingering at the scar near the corner of his jaw. "Don't go, Tony. Please don't."

Those green eyes looked a little spooked. "Meet the parents, all the friends—half of them, I'm betting, last knew me from a mugshot on the evening news, and the rest of them from that stupid picture. I dunno, J-li. I don't know if I'm ready for—for any of this." Both hands in his pockets now, he stood there slightly hunched, like a teenager afraid of a reprimand. "What the fuck am I even doing here?"

"Answering my goddamn prayers, Tony," barely a whisper.

A quiet snort of disbelief. "Said by nobody, ever."

"Shit on a shingle, when are you gonna stop telling me what to think? You don't have to come inside. You can sit on the porch. I'll bring us a beer. Nobody's ever got to know you're here except me. SAC Kornitzky's inside, and as much as he should be groveling at your feet, that's a little more tension than we need."

"I should've called first." He retreated another step, breaking the touch. "If there's roles in the Bone Guard, then I'm the brawn without the brains—frickin' reckless meathead, that's me."

She raised her hands to her chest, and made a series of gestures—observed, remembered, studied; thank you, Internet. Him, her heart, a beat, a movement like drawing a gun. *You make my heart beat faster.* The same thing he'd told her after she saved his life, when she accused him of joking, and he looked, just for a moment, like he'd never been more serious in his life.

That stopped him. He pressed his lips together, then finally said, "I'm not exactly leading man material. I cuss like a devil—I drink too much. I just gave up smoking a few months ago, and that's only led to even more cussing and drinking."

"Well, at least you don't taste like an ashtray."

Laughter rumbled through him. "Ah, fuck you, Rizzo."

"If that's your plan, I guess you'll have to stay." She stroked his cheek, her thumb tracing the shape of his brow. He leaned into her touch, but his eyes never left her face. She slipped her hand to the back of his head and kissed him. His powerful arms encircled her and swept her off the steps. Full length against him, he gathered her close, their hearts beating together beneath the desert stars.

If you enjoyed this book, please leave a review online—they really do matter, and I appreciate every one!

Have you read *The Mongol's Coffin?*

When Liz Kirschener discovers a musical map to Ghenghis Khan's tomb, her scholarly life explodes into arson and gunfire. Grant Casey brings in his team for a race to the tomb—to prevent Chinese authorities from burying it forever. This novel speeds from Cambridge, Massachusetts to Cambridge, England in search of clues—then flies to Inner Mongolia, bringing together a Mongolian singer, Grant's ex-commanding officer and a Hong Kong billionaire with a secret past. Mongolian traditions clash with modern priorities in a high-stakes adventure to save one of the world's greatest lost treasures.

Learn more at RocinanteBooks.com, and be sure to sign up for the mailing list to hear about new releases, including future Bone Guard adventures.

facebook.com/ECAmbroseauthor
twitter.com/ECAmbrose

Bone Guard Adventures

Novels

The Mongol's Coffin
The Nazi Skull
The Assassins' Throne (August, 2020)

Shorter Works

The Chief's Boss
The Sheriff's Man

About the Author

E. Chris Ambrose also writes dark historical fantasy novels as E. C. Ambrose: the Dark Apostle series about medieval surgery, from DAW Books. Developing that series made the author into a bona fide research junkie. Interests include the history of technology and medicine, Mongolian history and culture, Medieval history, and reproductive biology of lizards. Research has taken her to Germany, England, France, India, Nepal, China and Mongolia as well as many United States destinations. In the process, E. C. learned how to hunt with a falcon, clear a building of possible assailants, pull traction on a broken limb, and fire an AR-15.

Published works have appeared in *Warrior Women*, Fireside magazine, YARN online, Clarkesworld, several volumes of New Hampshire Pulp Fiction, and *Uncle John's Bathroom Reader*. The author is both a graduate of and an instructor for the Odyssey Writing workshop, and a participant in the Codex on-line writers' workshop.

In addition to writing, E. C. works as an adventure guide, teaching rock climbing and leading hiking, kayaking, climbing and mountain biking camps. Past occupations include founding a wholesale sculpture business, selecting stamps for a philatelic company, selling equestrian equipment, and portraying the Easter Bunny on weekends.